The House in the Witches' Wood

Myles Dann

ISBN: 9798472190435

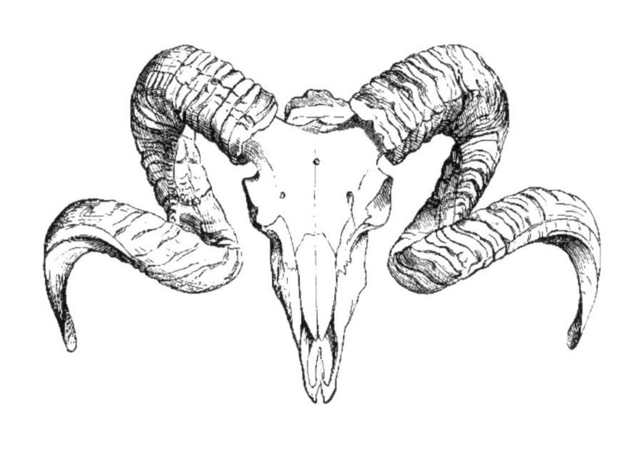

PROLOGUE

During the summer holidays, whenever Isobel stayed at the Manor, she would always wake James early, reminding him, as if he needed reminding, that Will would be waiting for them, hurrying him to get washed and dressed before breakfast, so they wouldn't be late to meet their friend.

No matter what time she went into his bedroom in the morning she would always find him asleep. Usually, he was tired because, even though he'd gone to bed early, he'd stay up late reading. There was always a pile of books stacked on his bedside table. She'd often wondered if she didn't wake him up whether he'd sleep the day away. His was such a lovely room it was not surprising that he was reluctant to get up, whereas she could not wait to leave hers.

'Come on, James,' she said, shaking him awake. 'It's Saturday. We're due to meet Will in an hour.'

Moaning, James rolled over, pulling the covers over his head. He told her he'd meet her downstairs.

'No,' she replied, knowing full well he'd fall straight back to sleep. 'You won't.'

James groaned and rose from his bed.

'I didn't get any sleep last night,' he said. 'It was far too warm.'

The window had been opened but no breeze stirred the curtains.

'It's always cool in my room,' said Isobel, pulling back the curtains. Sunlight streamed in through the stone-mullioned windows. 'You could always sleep up there instead of me, and I could sleep in here.'

James, shielding his dark eyes against the light, told her he did not want to swap rooms, preferring to remain where he was.

Isobel waited for him on the landing, and they went downstairs together, the smell of bacon and sausages sizzling in a pan drawing them to the kitchen. Their parents, having gone to Newmarket for the weekend, had left them in the care of Hodgson. He appeared from the garden; his hands full of fresh eggs he'd just collected from the chickens they kept in the walled kitchen garden. He bid them a good morning and they followed him into the kitchen, took their seats at the table, and helped themselves to some orange juice and slices of buttered toast.

'I take it you'll be meeting Will today,' he said, adding a couple of eggs to the frying pan.

Isobel nodded. 'We're due to meet him at half eight,' she said.

Although he was known by James's parents, Will never came to the manor house, remaining in the garden, hidden from view in the shade of an ancient oak tree that stood at the far end of the orchard. There the garden grew wild and unkempt and became woodland, all that remained of a vast ancient wood that once lay on the outskirts of the village.

Hodgson dished up the eggs, bacon and sausages, placing them on the table in front of them. Fidgeting restlessly in his seat, James glanced up at the clock hanging on the wall and began wolfing down his food.

'Slow down,' said Hodgson, a cup of coffee in hand. 'You'll give yourself indigestion eating that fast.' He pulled out a chair and sat down at the table with them. 'I do wish Will would just come to the house instead of waiting for you in the garden. You wouldn't have to keep hurrying out to meet him.'

Isobel often wondered why Will didn't walk round to the front of the house and knock on the door as any other visitor would, but James didn't seem to think anything of it. He said to her once: 'Why walk through the village when you can just hop over the wall and be here in a fraction of the time?'

Will lived with his parents in a little cottage that overlooked the churchyard. A path ran alongside the cottage following a high stone wall - the manor's boundary wall - out of the village. When he was seven, he'd found a tree stump hidden amongst the wildflowers and weeds that grew up on either side of the path, from which he was able to scale the wall and enter the wood. At first, he'd stayed away from the gardens and didn't dare go anywhere near the manor house for fear of being discovered there. The wood, however, was his. No one else went there. Not even James. He had it to himself, often returning to escape the crowds of tourists that descended on the village in the summer.

'One day,' said Hodgson, 'he'll hurt himself climbing over that wall.'

'He hasn't so far,' replied James through a mouthful of toast.

Just before they left, Hodgson said to them, 'There might be a thunderstorm later, so keep an eye on the weather.'

His words fell on deaf ears, neither of them paying him any attention as they ran out of the house to meet their friend. They found him waiting for them under the oak tree and he led them into the wood, the three friends disappearing from view of the house.

By midday, the heat had become so oppressive they headed down to the river that ran through the wood to cool off. There, the river, little more than a stream until then, deepened just enough for them to be able to swim in. They stayed there all afternoon, playing in the water, and didn't notice the sky above them turning a leaden grey, their laughter and screams drowning out the sound of thunder rumbling in the distance. When the storm arrived it caught them unaware, bursting upon them suddenly, the wind tearing through the trees as lightning flashed across the sky.

When they returned to the wood, Will instinctively sought shelter under the gnarled, twisted boughs of an ancient sweet chestnut tree. He beckoned Isobel to join him, but she stayed put, reminding him he wasn't supposed to stand under a tree in a thunderstorm. They heard James hailing them, but when they looked for him, he was nowhere to be seen, his voice fading until it could no longer be heard, his words lost on the wind.

Isobel realised as the shadows deepened, she was unsure of her way back to the house. In the gathering darkness, the woodland looked unfamiliar, menacing even. Will grabbed her hand and forged his way through the dense undergrowth, the nettles stinging their ankles as they beat back the brambles and ferns. They found James standing on a familiar path lined with wildflowers that led the way to the house and gardens.

When he saw them approach, he hurried them along.

'Come on,' he said, setting off down the path. 'We'd better get back to the house before Hodgson realises where we are.'

With Will at her side, Isobel followed James out of the wood. When the garden came into view she ran ahead, the wind blowing her long hair into her eyes as she overtook James. Seeing her surge ahead, Will sped up, following her as she skirted the orchard and veered towards a stone-flagged path that led the way back to the house. Although quicker than James, no matter how hard she tried she couldn't outrun Will - though that never stopped her from trying. Together they sprinted down a long curving path that followed a lichen-encrusted wall, brushing past the dripping heads of the irises and geraniums in the borders, the rain drenching them before they reached the house.

Ahead of them, in the open doorway, stood Hodgson.

'Get inside this instant!' he cried, ushering them inside. 'Didn't you hear the thunder?'

Overhead a bolt of forked lightning struck somewhere in the village. Will stumbled through the doorway, followed by Isobel, then James. Hodgson closed the door firmly behind them. When he saw their clothes were wet, he told them to go and change. Without pausing for breath, the three friends hurried upstairs, their feet scuffling on the floorboards as they charged up the staircase, only slowing down when they reached the first-floor landing.

James led the way to his bedroom. 'We're in for it now,' he said. 'I wouldn't be surprised if we weren't let out for the rest of the week as a punishment.'

The air was warm and still in the house, the heat oppressive. Outside the rain continued to fall, washing down the bedroom's lattice-paned windows. Will told them he thought it unlikely they'd be going outside again that day. The storm had passed, but the clouds above the Manor remained low and threatening.

Isobel suggested they spend the afternoon playing board games in the games room, but James suggested a game of hide-and-seek instead.

'You go hide,' he told her.

Isobel glared back at him. 'I don't want to play with you anyway,' she snapped.

Turning, she returned to the landing and stomped theatrically up the flight of narrow, uneven stairs, before disappearing into her bedroom, the old, rickety floorboards groaning and creaking underneath her.

She had only just changed out of her wet clothes when she heard Will calling to her from the landing. When she didn't reply she heard James say, 'See, I told you she wouldn't be interested.'

She wondered what it was James thought she wouldn't be interested in and called after them to wait for her. By the time she reached the landing, they were gone. She followed the sound of their voices to a part of the house she'd never been to before, peering inquiringly into each room she passed. Sparsely furnished, they looked like guest bedrooms. There were several guest bedrooms dotted about the house, though she wasn't sure how many.

Hearing floorboards creak overhead, she came to a narrow staircase that led to the attic above. She called up to Will, afraid and unsure whether to join them.

After a pause, she heard James's faint voice. 'Don't come up,' he said. 'There are spiders up here. Big ones.'

The old, warped door at the top of the staircase swung open and Will appeared in the doorway. He assured her there were no spiders and it was safe to join them.

The attic ran the length and breadth of the house. A dim light shining through a dust-covered bulb that hung from the roof joists revealed little but vague silhouettes of boxes, trunks and old pieces of furniture. Outside the wind wailed and howled round the house, the rain beating and battering the roof.

Isobel suppressed a shudder.

'What are you doing up here?' she asked, following Will across the creaking floorboards.

Will showed her a black and white photograph. 'James's grandfather took part in the North African Campaign during World War Two.'

Two army officers in their khaki uniforms stood beside a Bedouin man. A third sat astride a camel. Just visible in the background were the pyramids at Giza.

'My grandfather's the one on the camel,' said James. He was standing in a shadowy corner of the attic where some cardboard boxes had been stacked. 'The photo was taken when he was on leave in Cairo in 1941. He was given a medal - the African Star - after fighting at the Battle of El Alamein under Field Marshal Montgomery.'

Isobel didn't understand what that meant but tried to look impressed.

'We're looking for his medal,' explained Will.

James opened the first box he came to and began sorting through its contents. 'After my grandfather died,' he said, 'my parents gave all his clothes to charity. My mother wanted to throw out the rest of his things, but my father wouldn't let her. Instead, he boxed everything up, telling her he'd sort through them the first chance he got. That was over two years ago now and he hasn't been up here once.' He handed Will a small book. 'It was given to military personnel during the Second World War.'

Isobel read the title: *A Pocket Guide to North Africa.*

Also in the box were some gramophone records, more photographs and a tatty old ration book. It was only after emptying two boxes that he came across the medal. He held the six-pointed star up to the light, its ribbon consisting of red, dark and light blue stripes.

'The number eight on the clasp signifies -' He stopped abruptly, his attention drawn to something lying at the bottom of the box.

Will asked him what he'd found.

Drawing nearer, Isobel and Will saw their friend lift a large bunch of skeleton keys out of the box. About a dozen keys were hanging on a metal key ring, ranging in size from three to five inches. All were black and made from cast iron, except one that was made of brass.

Will thought they were a spare set for the house before the locks were changed.

James disagreed. 'I don't think they belong to *this* house.'

'Then what are they doing up here?' asked Isobel.

James didn't know, but he was sure his father would.

Later that day, when James asked his father about the keys he'd found in the attic, he'd been told, as Will suspected, they were an old set for the Manor. His mother disagreed, suggesting they were for a house in Scotland once owned by James's ancestors. This surprised James. He'd always believed the Manor was his ancestral home. He was keen to learn more but there was very little his father could tell him about the property.

'Your great-uncle Henry Roxburgh and his wife Emily were the last people to live there. Your grandfather never spoke about the house or Henry for that matter. I doubt the house still exists.'

'If I remember rightly,' said his mother, 'the house had a strange name. Something to do with witches or wizards. The Witches' House, wasn't it?'

'Wychwood House.'

'That's it.'

The next day, James told Will and Isobel his father had seemed uncomfortable discussing the house, though tried not to let it show. When he asked if he could keep the keys, he'd been told to put them back where he found them.

'He can keep them if he likes,' said his mother. 'They're not much use to anyone now. Where's the harm in him holding on to them?'

CHAPTER ONE

In the corner of a first-class carriage, Isobel Hamilton-Jones slept peacefully, her head resting against a window. Outside the rain fell heavily, battering the train as it rushed breathlessly on past sodden fields and overflowing rivers, sending autumn leaves swirling and dancing in its wake.

A train travelling in the opposite direction screeched past the carriage waking her from her deep sleep. Through a gap in the seats in front of her, she glimpsed an elderly couple sitting together, both of whom appeared to be asleep. With tired eyes, she looked about her and saw there were only about half a dozen other people in the carriage. The passengers who'd boarded the train with her at King's Cross were gone.

Across the aisle, a man wearing a Savile Row suit and bespoke, handmade Italian designer shoes, sat working at a MacBook. Isobel, noticing his eyes wandering over her, glanced down to see her brown tweed skirt had ridden up slightly. Struck by the awful thought he'd been watching her as she slept, she quickly tugged at the bottom of her skirt, pulling it down over her knees. When the man saw she was awake, a small smile appeared on his lips. He seemed to be about to say something but instead glanced back at the screen of his laptop.

Isobel reached for the styrofoam cup on the table in front of her, took a sip and grimaced. The coffee was cold and stale. How long had she been asleep?

'We'll be in Newcastle soon,' said the man in the Italian shoes, as if reading her thoughts.

Isobel looked surprised. Had she really been asleep for so long? She glanced out of the window and saw that they were passing through Durham. The driving rain pelted against the glass, obscuring her view of the city.

'You haven't missed your stop, have you? I'd have woken you, but you looked so peaceful.'

'That's all right. I'm going to Berwick.'

'I'm heading up to Edinburgh on business. You?'

'I'm visiting an old friend.'

The man's smile turned into a grin. 'You look far too young to have an old friend.'

'I've known him since I was six. We grew up together.'

'He …' His shrewd eyes narrowed. 'Lucky fellow.'

Covering her mouth with her hand, Isobel yawned. 'Oh, it's not like that,' she said, but immediately wished she hadn't. It wasn't any of his business.

'If you don't mind me saying so, you don't seem particularly excited at the prospect of seeing this friend of yours again.'

Isobel's gaze returned to the window. 'I haven't seen or heard from him in years,' she said. 'I don't even know who else is going to be there.'

Raindrops rolled down the window converging with one another as they went, and she began tracing their patterns with her finger. She thought it unlikely James was still in touch with any of his friends from school. He might have invited people he'd met at university or friends he'd made since, though there was only one person she hoped would be there.

She pictured him standing in the parlour, dressed in a dinner suit, his back to her as she descended the staircase. She remembered him holding her close as they danced and the last words they spoke to each other that night.

'You won't forget me, will you?'

'Of course not. We'll be together again before you know it.'

'You promise?'

'I promise.'

With a sigh, she dismissed the memory from her mind. She knew she shouldn't think about him. She didn't want to get her hopes up.

The man sitting across the aisle closed his laptop. 'Well, I'm glad you decided to make the journey after all,' he said, rising from his seat. 'How about a cup of coffee? You look like you could do with another.'

'No, thank you,' she replied. 'One was enough for me.'

The man smiled, and as he passed her, she noticed there was an indent on the ring finger of his well-manicured left hand. When he disappeared into the next carriage, she breathed a sigh of relief and briefly considered changing seats, though thought better of it. She could handle him. London was full of men like him. He'd invariably try to get her number before they reached Berwick.

At Newcastle, passengers in damp coats boarded the train. Two women sat in the seats a few rows down from her and began to talk loudly to one another, waking the elderly couple. The train jerked forward and began to move, the rhythmic clatter of the wheels drowning out their conversation.

Isobel felt her stomach tighten. Newcastle was the last stop before reaching Berwick. There was no turning back now. The train clattered over points and her gaze returned to the window. The heavy blanket of cloud that had covered the sky since Durham was beginning to clear. When the man in the Italian shoes returned, coffee in hand, he proceeded to tell her what he did and why he was going to Edinburgh, but she paid him little attention. Her thoughts were elsewhere.

Had she really known James since she was six? He'd moved to the Manor when he was eight years old, shortly after the death of his grandfather. She was certain she hadn't met him before then, though her memories of that time were understandably a little hazy. She'd been driven to his house by her mother. Her father, Clive, hadn't been with them. She'd known she was going somewhere special because her mother had bought her a pretty dress to wear that day.

Even though it had been over fifteen years ago, she could still remember glimpsing the house through the iron railings for the first time and being struck by how old the building looked. Hodgson had been there to meet them, and after introducing himself, had promptly led them through the house to the South Lawn. There they found James and his mother sitting at a table under a cedar tree, its long branches shading them from the warm midday sun.

James's mother greeted them warmly - she'd probably been

wearing a wide Panama hat and one of those long flowing dresses she liked to wear in the summer - but James didn't smile when he was introduced to her and remained silent all through tea. Once Isobel noticed him watching her. She thought he was about to say something, but he remained silent.

Their mothers were soon deep in conversation, reminiscing about old times. They'd known each other since school and had remained friends throughout university. After a while, Isobel and James were told to go and play together. Reluctantly, Isobel followed James through the garden. When she tried to talk to him her questions were met with silence. Only when they came to the edge of a dark woodland did he turn to her, his eyes meeting hers with a dreadful, piercing gaze.

'I don't want to play with you,' he said abruptly, 'so don't follow me.'

Undaunted, Isobel followed him, but the wood looked too dark and forbidding to enter. She hesitated and watched him pass under the twisting branches of the tall trees, treading gently as he moved deeper into the wood. When he disappeared, tears welled up in her eyes. She stood alone on the edge of the wood, waiting for him to return. She didn't want to go back to her mother, believing she'd be told off if she did.

But he didn't return. For what seemed like hours, she sat in the shade of an oak tree listening to a nightingale sing, watching the shadows lengthen until she heard her mother call for her. On the way home, she asked her if she'd had a nice time. Isobel said she hadn't and told her she didn't want to see James again.

'You'll have to be patient with him,' said her mother. 'He's not been well …' she added hesitantly.

She'd wanted to know what was wrong with him, but her mother wouldn't tell her.

Over the years she'd come to understand James and had even grown to love him like a brother. The last time she saw him, shortly before he left home for university, he was no longer the sullen boy she'd met all those years ago and seemed happier than she'd ever known him before.

A train drew parallel with hers and she glanced into the adjacent carriage. A young girl with beautiful brown ringlets wearing a pretty dress sat chatting away to her mother sitting on the seat next to her. Opposite them sat a man she assumed was the girl's father, his face hidden behind a newspaper. The girl, seeing Isobel, smiled and waved at her. When she waved back, her train gathered speed, pulling forward, leaving the little girl behind.

Moments later they were crossing the Royal Border Bridge and she traced the winding path of the River Tweed upstream. Her destination lay somewhere along the river, hidden away in ancient woodland. Once across the bridge, the train began to slow. She took a deep breath, slid out of her chair, and standing up, pulled her tweed cape round her shoulders. When she reached for her suitcase stowed on the luggage rack, out of the corner of her eye she noticed the man in the Italian shoes run another bold appraising glance over her.

'Here, let me help you with that,' he said, rising to his feet.

'I can manage, thank you,' she said, pulling the suitcase down.

The train drew slowly into the station, coming to a stop next to a long, single island platform.

'You know,' said the man in the Italian shoes, 'I've spent all this time talking about myself, I don't know a thing about you. How about meeting up for coffee when we're both back in London so I can get to know you better?'

Isobel pulled her dark hair behind her ear and looked him cold in the eye. 'I don't think so,' she said.

She followed the other passengers off the train, a blast of cold air hitting her as she stepped down onto the platform. Ahead of her, standing by a footbridge, wearing a heavy wool sweater and thick wax jacket, was Hodgson. He looked older than she remembered. The lines on his face were deeper, his hair greyer.

She waved at him and hurried down the platform, wheeling her suitcase behind her.

'Miss Isobel?' he asked uncertainly.

'Hello, Hodgson.' She embraced him. Drawing away, she noticed he was blushing slightly.

'I hardly recognised you.' Taking her suitcase from her, he led her up the footbridge. 'How long has it been?'

'Five years this December - the last time I was at the Manor.'

'Has it really been that long?'

Isobel nodded. 'How have you been?'

'Well, thank you, miss.'

'I never thought you'd leave the Manor.'

'Since Mr Roxburgh retired there hasn't been much for me to

do. Anyway, James needs me here.'

Stepping off the footbridge, they made their way through the ticket hall.

'How is he?'

'He's …' A crackled announcement came over the tannoy, drowning out his voice. 'He's looking forward to seeing you again.'

Automatic double doors opened at their approach. Once outside they passed a taxi rank and headed towards the car park.

'I was surprised to receive his invitation.'

'He was eager for you and Will to see the house.'

Isobel felt her heart skip a beat. 'Will is joining us?'

Hodgson nodded and led her into the car park, passing rows of parked cars, stopping at a beaten-up old Land Rover Defender, its sides covered in scratches and caked in mud.

'Makes a change from the Daimler,' said Isobel.

Hodgson smiled. 'We're not in Wiltshire anymore.' He opened the passenger door and Isobel slipped inside. As he drove them out of the car park, he said, 'It will be nice to see Will again.'

'Yes, it will,' said Isobel, after a pause.

'I believe he's bringing someone with him …'

'Oh?'

'A young lady.'

Turning, Isobel glanced out of the window. 'Oh …' She hadn't expected that.

'Will anyone else be joining us?' she asked after a pause.

'No one else has been invited.'

They crossed a bridge that spanned the Tweed and headed west, following the river upstream.

*

Will Chamberlain, sat behind the wheel of his Austin Mini Cooper, followed the A7 north as it wound its serpentine way round hills and through heather-clad moorland.

From the backseat of the car, Miriam Crenshaw eyed him in the rear-view mirror.

'How much longer is this journey likely to take?' she asked.

Will's gaze met hers. She was wearing her jet-black hair away from her face, drawing her porcelain white skin tightly over her high cheekbones. He assured her they'd be there within the hour.

Alexander de Villeneuve, thumbing through the car's manual, fidgeted uncomfortably in the passenger seat next to him.

'You know,' he said, 'the last time it took me this long to get somewhere, I was in the Caribbean.'

'We'd have been there by now if we'd travelled by train,' said Will.

'Why didn't we?'

'Because Miriam refuses to travel on public transport. Even in first-class.'

'What nonsense.' Alexander glanced over his shoulder at Miriam. 'When you fly you travel on public transport.'

'First-class on an airline is very different to first-class on a train,' explained Miriam. 'When I travel first-class, I expect more than seats only marginally more comfortable than those in standard. I expect luxury, comfort. Is it really too much to ask for a dining car in this day and age?'

'We're hardly travelling in the height of luxury as a result, Miriam.'

'I thought William was going to hire a car suitable for a long journey. I didn't expect to be crammed in here like sardines in a tin can.'

Alexander replaced the car's manual in the glove compartment. 'We could have flown,' he said. 'In the time it took us to get out of London we could have been there and back.'

'You can only fly economy to Scotland,' said Will. He sighed regretfully, disappointed in himself for looking into it for Miriam.

'It wouldn't be so bad if your car wasn't so bloody small,' said Alexander. He was a tall, broad-shouldered ox of a man. The Mini could not accommodate his large frame.

'Language, Alexander,' said Miriam sharply. She glanced over at the young woman curled up asleep next to her, her head resting on her rose print suitcase. 'There'd be more room if you hadn't invited sleeping beauty. Who is she anyway?'

'Jemima Pearce or Prince. Something beginning with P anyway. What does it matter?'

'I'm sure it matters to her. What does she do?'

'She's a dancer in the West End.'

'What part of the West End?'

'Behave, Miriam.'

Will had never met Jemima before but thought her pleasant

enough. While he knew James wouldn't mind her joining them for the weekend, he was sure Miriam would have a few things to say about her tagging along.

Alexander had been due at his house at eight-thirty but hadn't arrived until nine. From Southwark, they'd headed west to collect Miriam. Traffic jams and road works soon dampened their initial excitement at the weekend that lay before them, and it hadn't been long before Jemima had fallen asleep. They were over an hour late by the time they reached Holland Park where Miriam lived with her father. Miriam, who did not like to be kept waiting, was not in the best of moods when they arrived. Informing her they had an extra passenger did not help matters.

'How long have you known her?' she asked Alexander.

'A couple of weeks.'

'More like a couple of days,' muttered Will.

Alexander grinned. 'Well, I knew it was going to be cold up here, so I brought someone to keep me warm at night.'

'Couldn't you have just packed a hot water bottle?' asked Miriam. 'It would have taken up less room.'

'What are you talking about? She's a tiny little thing.'

The Mini hit a pothole and Jemima's suitcase dug into Miriam's side. 'It's not her - it's her luggage.' She shoved the suitcase away from her.

'It's not her luggage that's taking up all the room,' said Will. 'It's Alexander's. He's packed enough for a two-week holiday.'

'A well-dressed man should be as prepared as possible for any eventuality,' said Alexander.

'Turning up with one unexpected guest is one thing,' said Miriam, 'but turning up with two - especially one none of us has ever met before or will ever see again - is another.'

'You were the one that insisted I tag along.'

Will caught Miriam's eye in the rear-view mirror. 'You were?' Her face, as usual, was expressionless. 'What on earth for?'

After a pause, she said, 'We'll need a fourth for bridge.'

*

Isobel glanced out of her window and saw they were driving over a stone arched bridge. She realised she hadn't paid their journey any attention as though being driven on a familiar route she'd taken many times.

Hodgson asked after her mother, and she told him she was well.

'She was thrilled when she learnt James had invited me to see Wychwood House for myself.'

So thrilled, when she'd told her she didn't want to go, she'd spent the following weeks trying to change her mind. She'd even bought the train tickets for her.

'And how is Clive?'

'The same as ever,' she said ruefully. 'He was surprised to hear James had found the house still standing. He always believed it had been demolished.'

'We all thought it had been.'

Including James's father, she remembered.

She took her BlackBerry out of her bag. 'That reminds me, I'd better let my mother know I've arrived.'

'We struggle for a reception in the valley, but you should be able to get a signal when we're on higher ground.'

She slipped her phone back into her bag. 'Was anyone living at the house when James found it?'

'No. Until about seven years ago, the grounds were cared for by a caretaker, who undertook minor repairs to the exterior of the house when necessary, but no one's lived there for over seventy years. As you can imagine, it was in a state of disrepair. Parts of the roof had to be replaced and some of the chimneys were rebuilt. Walls were straightened and stonework repointed. James worked hard, helping out wherever he could, especially when it came time to redecorate the house.' He paused. 'I'm afraid he worked himself a little too hard.'

Isobel turned to look at Hodgson. 'Has something happened to him?'

'He hasn't been well,' he replied solemnly.

'Nothing serious, I hope.'

'No, he wore himself out, that's all. You see, I was called away when my sister was involved in a car accident.'

'I'm sorry to hear that.'

Hodgson had never mentioned his family to her before. She realised then how little she knew about him. She didn't even know how old he was - he had to be in his early to mid-sixties. The only thing she knew for certain about him was that he'd never married and had no children of his own.

'She remained in a critical condition for months, though she's much better now. When I returned, I found James bedridden with a terrible fever. I called for a doctor who assured me it was due to exhaustion and malnutrition, nothing more.'

'Was he admitted to hospital?'

'No, the doctor didn't think he needed to be. He's lost a lot of weight - though he's much better than he was.'

The road led them up a slight hill with low stone walls on either side. At the top of the hill, a single street of stone-built terraced cottages and houses came into view. Many had fallen into disrepair.

'Until the nineteen-thirties, the village was part of the estate,' said Hodgson as he drove down the street. The terrace of cottages to their right was broken in the middle by a village hall. 'Most of the houses date from the late eighteenth, early nineteenth-century. Many are now empty, I'm afraid.'

When they reached the top of the hill Isobel checked her phone again. Seeing it had a signal, she sent a message to her mother.

'Unfortunately, there are no shops in the village anymore. The pub's still open - it's an old coaching inn - though I haven't been there myself. Although we're only about fifteen minutes' drive from Selkirk, the village is probably too far off the beaten track for many.'

After passing the pub, Hodgson slowed the Land Rover. At the end of the street were two more cottages, their gardens overrun with weeds and brambles. Isobel caught a glimpse of a churchyard hidden in the shade of an immense horse chestnut tree, the sight of the gravestones making her shiver.

'The cottages on either side of the lane used to be gatehouses,' said Hodgson, turning off the street. 'They once marked the entrance to the estate.'

They headed down a narrow, overgrown lane. Isobel glanced at the skeletal remains of the derelict cottages. The walls were roofless and jagged, the doorways empty, the fireplaces exposed. At the end of the lane, a dirt track led them into deep woodland. Once in the wood, they crossed a stone balustraded bridge and followed the track that wound its way up a hill.

'Do you get many walkers through here?'

'No, the locals stay away from the house, and we don't get many tourists passing through the village.'

At the top of the hill, large iron gates blocked their way. Isobel glimpsed a gabled gate lodge behind the gates and saw the drive disappeared round a bend. She estimated the wrought iron gates, supported by large stone posts, stood eight or nine-feet tall. Two stone griffins holding shields in their claws stood perched on top of the posts.

Opening his door, Hodgson stepped out of the Land Rover, taking his car keys with him. After unlocking the gates, he pushed them open. As she watched him return to the vehicle, Isobel felt a sense of foreboding clutch at the pit of her stomach.

Driving past the lodge, Hodgson said, 'I'll leave the gates open for Will.'

They followed the long approach to the house. Banks of azaleas and rhododendrons flanked the drive.

'I'm afraid I've been neglecting the gardens recently. I was hoping to clear some of these shrubs before you arrived, but I haven't had the time.'

The drive straightened and Wychwood House, silhouetted against a blood-red sky, came into view. Craning her neck to look up at the house, Isobel's gaze drifted up the old, weathered walls of the house, past bartizans and thistle-topped turrets, to the steeply pitched slate roof. A dull light shone out from small lancet windows set in the towers and crow-stepped gables.

The drive branched off then forked; the left fork, a rough, rugged track, descended a hill before disappearing into woodland; the right leading them to a courtyard.

'That way,' said Hodgson, gesturing down the hill, 'leads to a dilapidated old building that had, in its time, been a stable block. We're now using it as a garage for the cars.'

When he brought the Land Rover to a stop, Isobel grabbed her suitcase from the backseat. To their left, through a wrought iron gate enclosed by a wall, she glimpsed a terrace at the back of the house.

'You must get very lonely living here so far from your family and friends.'

'There's been so much to do, I haven't had time to notice.'

Taking Isobel's suitcase, Hodgson was about to lead her into the house through the side door when he hesitated.

'This door leads to the servants' quarters,' he said apologetically. 'I should have driven you to the front of the house. If you'd like to follow me, we'll walk round and go in through the main entrance.'

*

From Selkirk, Will continued through the Yarrow valley, driving west against the setting sun, following a river upstream. The road had flooded in places where the river had burst its banks. Raging torrents of water hurled dead branches and debris downstream. Withered red and yellow leaves blown from the trees that lined the road stuck to the windscreen. Flicking on the wipers, brushing them from his view, he saw the terrain was becoming more rugged, the hills steeper and higher. He thought it a beautiful but lonely country, with no sign of life for miles. Since leaving Selkirk they hadn't passed another car going in either direction.

Miriam sought his eyes questioningly in the rear-view mirror. 'Shouldn't we have turned off by now?'

'Not for another mile or so.'

'We're lost, aren't we?'

'We're not lost,' he assured her.

Alexander began whistling "The Bonnie Banks o' Loch Lomond".

'Do be quiet, Alexander,' snapped Miriam. 'You're amusing no one but yourself.'

The sun disappeared behind a far hillside. Through the trees ahead, Will caught a brief glimpse of a house high on a hill, silhouetted against the darkening sky. Rounding a bend, passing the trees, he slowed the Mini and glanced back, his heart sinking when he saw the building was a ruined tower house.

'Maybe we should turn round, old man,' said Alexander.

'Not yet,' he said. 'Just a little further.'

'A little further!' cried Miriam. 'You've less than a quarter of a tank left as it is. If we get stranded out here, I'm not going to be the one walking back to town.'

The thought of having to spend the night in such a remote place sent a shiver down Will's spine. He suddenly felt a long way from home.

Ever since James had told him he'd found Wychwood House and had decided to live there, he'd been eager to see the old place for himself, but no one had been allowed to see the house - Hodgson being the only exception. Over the many months that followed he received regular updates on the progress of the work being carried out on the property. Only when James moved into the house did he stop hearing from him. At first, he wasn't surprised. Although the house was habitable, the rooms still had to be redecorated. But as the months passed, he began to grow concerned for his old friend. He knew he didn't need to worry. James was in good hands. Hodgson would be keeping a close eye on him.

Only Hodgson wasn't at the house.

At the end of August, James's father Robert visited him and told him Hodgson had been called away unexpectedly. The thought of James alone in the house, cut off from the rest of the world, worried them both.

'Is there no way of contacting him?'

'There's no landline,' said Robert, 'but Hodgson gave me his mobile number. I keep trying it, but it keeps going to voicemail. His mother is sick with worry. I don't know what he hopes to achieve by living there. If only someone would talk some sense into him …' After a pause, he turned to face Will. 'Have you been to the house?'

Will told him James had refused to let him see it until the renovations were complete.

'I imagine they're finished by now …'

'If I haven't heard from him in the next couple of weeks, I'll drive up and see how he is. He'll be glad of the company by then.'

'I expect he will.'

But a couple of weeks passed, and Will didn't visit his friend. He kept meaning to, but never found the time. Then, at the end of September, quite unexpectedly, he received a letter from James. Although relieved to hear from him, he found the tone of his letter odd. There was no warmth in his words. Instead, the letter was formal, no more than an apology for not writing sooner, and an invitation to visit the house at the end of October. What struck him most was that his friend's usually neat and somewhat old-fashioned handwriting had become an almost illegible scrawl across the page.

So as not to alarm James's parents, he kept his concerns to himself. All further arrangements were made through Hodgson, who by this time had returned to the house. He did not hear from James again. Over the weeks that followed, a feeling of dread slowly uncurled within him. Now on the day he was due to see his friend again, he wondered if his worst fears had been realised.

He'd know soon enough.

CHAPTER TWO

Hodgson led Isobel under a crenellated gateway, and they made their way across a quadrangular courtyard enclosed by high boundary walls.

'The gateway and its walls were built using stones from the barmkin,' he said, 'the defensive wall that surrounded the peel tower and courtyard buildings that once stood here. The courtyard would have looked quite different back in the sixteenth and seventeenth centuries.'

Turrets had been built into the corners of the walls and yew topiary surrounded a fountain. Through an arched stone screen, Isobel noticed a larger courtyard with a sunken lawn. Set directly across the courtyard stood an archway through which she glimpsed a walled garden. Hodgson hurried up some stone steps and disappeared into a shadowy entrance porch, the darkness swallowing him up. Iron hinges squeaked as the front door swung open and Isobel followed him inside the house.

They passed into the great hall, a gloomy room with wainscoted walls, lit only by flickering candlelight. Isobel stood for a moment, letting her eyes adjust to the darkness. A wide staircase ran up from the hall to a landing where the stairs branched off to the right and left. On the wall beside her, embroidered with rich colours, hung a tapestry depicting a hunting scene. The candlelight danced on figures of mounted horsemen surrounding a stag at bay.

'Shall I take your cape, miss?' asked Hodgson, placing her suitcase at the bottom of the staircase.

A fire blazed away in the hearth but did not seem to be warming the house with any degree of success. Isobel felt colder inside than she had outside.

'I'll keep it on, for now,' she said.

'I left Master James in the library.'

Isobel followed Hodgson across the great hall. A portrait of a boy with two Dandie Dinmont Terriers hung at the entrance to the library.

Before they reached the doorway, Hodgson stopped and turned to face Isobel. 'I wouldn't mention Master James's appearance,' he whispered. 'You know how self-conscious he can be.'

'I'll use my discretion.'

'Thank you.'

Hodgson knocked on the door to the library and slowly pushed it open. 'Miss Isobel is here, sir,' he said, stepping into the room.

There was no reply. Stepping back, Hodgson ushered Isobel through the doorway, pulling the door too behind her.

She found James sitting on a Chesterfield positioned facing a fireplace, his back to her, his body dimly silhouetted against the glow from the smouldering fire. Hearing her approach, he glanced over his shoulder. Despite Hodgson's warning, she found herself shocked by the change in his appearance, though she tried her best not to let it show. His dark hair fell untidily down to his shoulders, his once handsome face was gaunt and covered in a thick beard.

For a brief moment, he didn't seem to know who she was - then a sudden recognition leapt into his eyes.

'What on earth are you doing here?' he asked, rising to his feet.

He looked quite furious - Isobel half expected him to have her thrown out of the house.

'You … you invited me,' she stammered.

His expression cooled. 'Of course I did.' Turning, he glanced towards the crackling fire. 'I am sorry,' he said, staring at the flames, his back still to her. 'It must have slipped my mind.'

She wondered how that was possible. He must have known Hodgson had gone to collect her from the station …

'Well, you certainly know how to make someone feel welcome!' she snapped.

James turned to face her. 'I'm sorry,' he said. 'It's wonderful to have you here. How have you been?'

'Well, thank you.'

'And how was your journey? Not too arduous I hope?'

'Not at all.'

After an awkward pause, he said, 'Well, you must be tired. I'll have Hodgson show you to your room.'

Before she could reply, he called for Hodgson, who appeared almost immediately from the hall.

'This way, miss,' he said, leading her out of the room.

As they left, James said, 'Put Isobel in Emily's room, would you, please?'

'Yes, sir.' Hodgson pulled the library door too. 'Emily was married to James's great-uncle Henry Roxburgh. They lived here during the nineteen-thirties.' He led Isobel back across the great hall. 'You're very fortunate. Hers is by far the most beautiful room in the house.'

'How on earth did James get like this?'

Hodgson shrugged regretfully. 'I don't know. He told me he lost track of time, forgot to eat, and hardly ever slept. Then one day he just collapsed.' After a pause, he continued. 'I'm just glad I returned when I did.'

Isobel couldn't help but feel there was more to it than that.

*

Slowing the Mini, Will crossed the second of two stone arched bridges, passing over the Yarrow. A cottage next to a turning came into view.

'This must be it.'

'How can you be sure?' asked Miriam. 'There's no signpost.'

'No, there isn't one,' he said, turning off the valley road.

Rain from the overcast sky beat down upon the car's roof as they drove into the village. The buildings looked older than other cottages and houses they'd driven past that lay scattered throughout the valley.

Alexander wiped away the condensation building up on his side window. 'He really is living in the back of beyond out here,' he said.

Miriam caught Will's eye in the rear-view mirror. 'Don't you think we should stop and find out where we are?'

'In this godforsaken place!' cried Alexander. 'Who on earth are you going to ask?'

There was not a soul in sight. Although dark, it was still early. It was possible whoever lived there had yet to return from work - though Will thought it unlikely.

'They could be holiday homes,' he said quietly, as though to himself.

'This place doesn't look like somewhere you'd want to spend your holiday,' said Alexander.

Miriam sighed. 'Yet we are here.'

At the end of the street, they came to the inn. Will slowed the car and looked up at the old, faded sign swaying in the wind. Darkness and dirt hid the name of the pub from view.

'We could ask the way in there,' he said.

Alexander peered out of his window. 'The door's shut and the curtains have been pulled too,' he said. 'Probably doesn't open for another hour … if it opens at all.'

They came to a stop beside two derelict cottages on either side of a lane. Was this the way? It didn't look promising.

'You'd think he'd put up a sign or something,' said Miriam. 'How does he expect anyone to find him?'

'Maybe he doesn't,' said Alexander. Dusk was falling and darkness was closing upon them. 'We're going to have to get a move on if we want to find the house before dark.'

'Maybe we should go back to Selkirk and ask for directions,' said Miriam, 'just to be certain.'

Will shook his head. 'It's too late to go back now.' He turned down the lane. 'This has to be the way.'

'It had better be.'

The Mini shook and jolted as they made their way down the rutted potholed lane. The music playing from the radio faded and was lost to static. They crossed the balustraded bridge and Will drove on through the wood, keeping his eyes fixed on the sodden track that unfolded slowly before them.

Alexander gripped the side of his seat. 'Not the easiest place to reach, is it?'

'How long has James been living here?' asked Miriam.

'I believe he moved in about six, seven months ago now,' said Will.

'Why, if he's been living here for that long, has he only just taken it upon himself to invite you now?'

'He wanted the house finished before he let anyone visit him.'

'I heard it was little more than a ruin when he found it,' said Alexander. 'Must have cost him a fortune to renovate. His father was furious with him. Thought it a waste of money. I have to say I agree with him.'

At the top of the hill, they stopped before the iron gates that barred their way. A man appeared from the lodge, his face hidden by the hood of his raincoat, a set of iron keys in his hand. After unlocking the gates, he pulled them open.

As Will wound down his window to thank him he noticed the grotesque statues adorning the gates seemed to be leering down at him.

*

At the top of the staircase, Isobel followed Hodgson across a shadowy gallery. Mounted stags' heads and portraits of men she assumed were James's ancestors hung on the walls. Hodgson flicked on a light switch to reveal a corridor stretching away before them. On each side of the corridor were long carved bookcases with glazed doors. Paintings, mostly portraits, hung on the walls. Framed black and white photographs stood alongside Dresden porcelain figural vases on the bookcases.

Hodgson stopped at the first door they came to, opening it for Isobel. She thanked him and stepped inside the room. The setting sun shone in through a lattice-paned bay window, reflecting off a walnut veneered wardrobe and chest of drawers. Across the room, next to a cheval mirror, stood a dressing table. The furniture had only just been polished; she could still smell the beeswax.

'What a beautiful room,' she said.

She wondered if James had put her in there as an apology for his outburst.

The most striking feature of the room was a seventeenth-century carved oak four-poster bed with flower and leaf decorations. A padded eiderdown lay spread across the mattress, and cushions and soft plump pillows lay at the head of the bed. On the wall facing the bed hung a portrait of an elderly woman. Isobel asked if Emily Roxburgh was the woman in the painting.

'No, that's Lady Roxburgh,' said Hodgson, placing her suitcase down at the foot of the bed. 'She owned the house in the middle of the nineteenth-century.' He gestured to an open doorway. 'The room has a small bathroom en suite.'

There was another door on the opposite wall, but this one was closed.

'Where does that door lead?'

'Before Emily lived here,' explained Hodgson, 'the bedroom had two dressing rooms. One was converted into a bathroom, the other made into a spare bedroom.' He drew Isobel's attention to the bay window. 'The house has beautiful views.'

Isobel glanced out of the window. Terraced lawns sloped down to a stone wall that ran the width of the garden. Just visible beyond the wall was a river.

'Is that the Tweed?'

'No, it's the Yarrow,' said Hodgson, 'a tributary of the Ettrick - itself a tributary of the Tweed. Although not as famous, it is, in my opinion, far more beautiful.' He turned to leave. 'If there is anything you need, just let me know.'

Isobel thanked him and he left the room.

The setting sun disappeared behind dark leaden clouds that hung oppressively low in the sky. As she pulled the curtains too, she thought she heard the faint sound of a car pulling up outside the house.

*

The Mini shuddered as it came to a stop waking Jemima.

Sitting up, she rubbed the sleep from her eyes. 'Where are we?' she said groggily.

'We're here,' said Alexander.

Hodgson appeared at the entrance gate. Opening an umbrella, he approached them.

'Is that James?' asked Jemima.

'No, that's Hodgson,' said Will, unbuckling his seatbelt. 'He's been with James's family for years. Before coming here, he used to manage the Manor for James's parents -'

'He's James's valet,' interrupted Alexander.

Jemima's eyes lit up. 'He has a valet!'

'I think he prefers the term household manager,' said Will, but nobody paid him any attention.

He opened his door and stepped out of the car, stretching out his aching body. Feeling an icy wind on his face, he shivered and zipped up his jacket, drawing up the collar.

'Master William,' said Hodgson. 'It's so good to see you again, sir.'

'It's good to see you too, Hodgson.'

Will noticed a look of sadness on his face he hadn't known before. Remembering his sister had been involved in a car accident, he was about to ask after her when Alexander appeared from the car.

'Help Will with the suitcases, would you?' he said to Hodgson, taking the umbrella from him. He held open a door for Jemima and Miriam and escorted them through the gateway.

Will grabbed two suitcases from the back seat of the car. 'I'm afraid there are more of us than expected,' he said apologetically, passing the suitcases to Hodgson.

'I'm sure I can manage, sir.'

Opening the boot, he pulled out his dinner suit to find his duffle bag and coat had been crushed under the weight of Alexander's large Louis Vuitton suitcase.

'You are only planning on staying for the weekend, aren't you?' asked Hodgson.

Smiling, Will nodded. With his dinner suit slung over his shoulder, Alexander's suitcase in one hand, his duffle bag, coat and holdall in the other, he followed Hodgson through the gateway, the gravel crunching underneath them as they crossed the courtyard.

'Ms Crenshaw and Mr de Villeneuve, I know,' said Hodgson, pausing before the porch, 'but who is the other young lady?'

'Oh, she's Jemima, Alexander's latest girlfriend. He's not sure of her surname. You could try Pearce or Prince. After that, you're on your own.'

'Will you be sharing a room with Ms Crenshaw?'

'Er … yes,' said Will, a little uncertainly. He didn't see why not. Alexander would be sharing with Jemima.

Hodgson continued up the stone steps. 'How was your journey?' he asked, stepping into the porch.

'Awful. Took us all day.'

'You should have come up by train like Miss Isobel.'

'Isobel is here?' said Will with surprise, his voice echoing through the porch.

Nodding, Hodgson led the way into the house. Miriam, Alexander and Jemima stood waiting for them in the great hall.

'There's no electricity in the hall,' said Hodgson. 'Though there is in the rest of the house, you'll be relieved to hear.'

Will, noticing goosebumps on Miriam's arms, set down the suitcase, bags, and dinner suit he was carrying and placed his warm woollen coat round her shoulders. A young woman, wearing a tweed skirt and turtleneck sweater, appeared suddenly on the gallery above as if she had stepped out of one of the paintings hanging there.

'I thought I heard a car,' she said, descending the staircase, her voice warm and friendly. 'Well, welcome to Wychwood House. It's quite something, isn't it?'

Will felt his heart skip a beat. 'Isobel?' he muttered under his breath.

Out of the corner of his eye, he noticed Alexander sweep back his unruly mane of red hair, and suddenly became conscious of how terrible he must have looked after their long journey. As Isobel drew nearer, he saw her small elfin face more clearly. Her large brown eyes, illuminated by the candlelight, caught his and she smiled at him.

'Will, it's so nice to see you again,' she said affectionately.

Will stood dumbstruck, his heart racing. When she kissed him on the cheek, he could feel she was trembling slightly too.

'You too,' he said finally. 'How have you been?'

'Well, thank you.'

Miriam coughed indiscreetly behind them. 'William, aren't you going to introduce us?'

'Oh, of course,' said Will. 'Where are my manners? I'd like you to meet my girlfriend -'

Isobel turned to Jemima. 'It's nice to meet you.'

'I'm with Alexander,' she replied awkwardly.

Isobel blushed. 'Of course you are,' she said. 'I am sorry.'

Miriam stepped forward before Will had a chance to introduce her. 'I believe we've already met.'

'I'm sorry,' said Isobel. 'I seem to be at a loss ...'

'At a party. I believe you went with Alexander ...'

Will glanced at Alexander, unaware he knew Isobel.

'Oh yes, of course,' said Isobel, 'I remember. You were at school with my brother.' She turned to Alexander. 'It's nice to see you again.'

Alexander kissed her on the cheek. 'It's always nice to see you,

Issie.'

Isobel grimaced. She hated being called Issie. Clearly, he didn't know her that well.

'I'm impressed you found the house,' she said, turning back to the others. 'If Hodgson hadn't collected me from the station, I don't think I'd have found it myself.'

Alexander let out a long-drawn-out sigh. 'We drove up from London.'

'Why on earth didn't you come by train?'

'I wish we had. Anything would have been better than his old banger …'

'She's not an old banger,' said Will. 'Considering she's forty-five years old, I'd say she's in great condition.'

'You drove here in your Mini?' said Isobel.

'Yes, we did.' Will glanced at Alexander. 'It got us here, didn't it?'

'I doubt it will get us home,' said Alexander with a sneer.

'You can always walk back to London.'

'I've no doubt we will be.'

'So where is James?' interrupted Miriam. 'It is very rude of him not to be here to greet us.'

Hodgson picked up the suitcases. 'I'll show you up to your rooms.'

'I'll come up with you,' said Isobel. 'I've only just arrived myself. I was just about to unpack when I heard your car.' She picked up the duffle bag and holdall at Will's feet. 'Here, let me help you with those.'

Will thanked her and they followed Hodgson up the staircase.

'Have you seen James yet?'

'Yes, briefly,' said Isobel, lowering her voice. The smile had gone from her face.

'How is he?'

'He's a lot better than he was -'

'He's not been well?'

Isobel glanced up at Will. There was real concern in his eyes. 'You didn't know?' she said.

Will shook his head.

'Neither did I until I arrived.'

'What's happened to him?'

'Apparently, it was nothing serious. He wore himself out, that's all,' said Isobel, repeating Hodgson's words to her. She didn't sound convinced.

When they reached the landing, they took the stairs that branched off to the left and continued up to the gallery. Hodgson continued down the broad carpeted corridor to the bedrooms, the lights flickering as he led the way. He stopped at a door, opened it and led Alexander and Jemima into a bedroom.

Will placed the Louis Vuitton suitcase inside the room and took the holdall and duffle bag from Isobel. There was so much he wanted to say to her but knew then was not the time.

'I'll see you later for dinner,' she said, noticing Miriam glancing back at them as Hodgson led her into a bedroom further down the corridor.

Turning, she made her way back to her room.

*

Miriam cast a critical eye round the bedroom. She thought it a dreary, cheerless room, the wallpaper a drab brown, the furniture old and heavy. Worn rugs that curled at the corners covered the bare floorboards and there was a ghastly painting of a bleak winter scene hanging above the fireplace.

'The room doesn't have an en-suite bathroom?'

Hodgson pulled heavy curtains across a lattice-paned window. 'There's a bathroom down the corridor, on the right,' he said. 'If there is anything you need just let me know.' He held open the door for Will as he hurried into the room. 'Dinner will be at eight,' he added.

He left the room, closing the door behind him.

Will placed Miriam's suitcase down on one bed and his duffle bag on the other. 'This isn't a hotel, Miriam,' he said, hanging his dinner suit in the wardrobe.

Miriam removed his coat and handed it to him. 'I am fully aware of that.' She glanced at a washstand in a dim corner of the room. 'Alexander has decided we should dress for dinner.'

Will hung his coat on the back of the door. 'Well, we might as well make the effort now we're here.'

Miriam shivered. 'It is freezing in here.'

Will felt the radiator under the window and found it warm to the touch.

'The heating is on.'

'It's going to take more than a rusty old radiator to heat this room. Do something with the fire will you?'

Crossing to the fireplace, Will picked up a brass scuttle and tipped lumps of coal onto the dying embers.

Miriam glanced at the two single beds in the room. 'I didn't realise we would be expected to share a room.'

'Is that a problem?'

'Of course it is!' she said, her eyebrows rising in disdain. 'I have my reputation to think about. What will people think when they learn we've shared a room?'

Will placed the scuttle back on the hearth. 'We've been seeing each other for three months now, Miriam,' he said. 'It's hardly scandalous behaviour.'

No, today such a thing wasn't considered shocking. She was sure nobody would bat an eyelid. But that wasn't the point. Just because something had become socially acceptable didn't mean it was right. People should care, they should be appalled … In the past, bachelors and young ladies were kept apart in different parts of the house, without access to one another. It would have been unthinkable for an unmarried man and woman to spend the weekend away together. In her opinion, it was the decline of these old-fashioned values that were to blame for society's current ills.

'Jemima doesn't appear to have any objections to sharing a room with Alexander.'

Miriam straightened an evening gown on a hanger and hung it on the door of the wardrobe. 'I'm sure that's because she already has a reputation.'

Will sighed. He'd walked into that one.

Miriam turned to face him. 'Now, will you please leave while I dress?'

'Where am I going to change?'

'Try the bathroom down the corridor.'

*

Yawning copiously, Alexander began unpacking his suitcase. He was beginning to regret their late night. He had a throbbing headache and felt a little nauseous, though it was nothing a little hair of the dog couldn't cure. The whole evening had been a bit of a blur as Jemima had dragged him from one club in Mayfair to another, hardly pausing for breath. He had no idea when they'd arrived home or what time they'd eventually fallen asleep. He wasn't used to such exuberance, preferring to take things at a slower pace. Where Jemima got her energy from was a mystery to him.

She scampered into the room, a soft, thick towel wrapped tightly round her. Even without her makeup, she looked damned attractive. It wouldn't last of course. He'd stop seeing her as soon as they were back in London. He really couldn't face any more nights out with her, the thought of visiting another club filling him with dread. It was a shame, but the only thing they had in common was that he had money and she enjoyed spending it. He chuckled to himself. He'd have to remember that one for later. It would amuse Miriam.

No, it wouldn't last, but she'd certainly make the weekend one to remember.

Jemima sat herself down on the hearthrug and warmed herself by the fire. 'When you said you were going to spend the weekend in a house in Scotland this wasn't quite what I imagined.'

'Wasn't quite what I envisaged either.'

'When was the house last decorated? The nineteenth-century?'

Alexander thought the Lincrusta dado panels suggested the Edwardian period but wasn't going to argue the point.

Jemima rose to her feet, crossed the room and sat herself down at the dressing table. 'Don't you find old houses creepy?' she asked, running a brush through her hair.

'I'm used to such surroundings. My family's seat is significantly older, not to mention larger than this,' he said, though she didn't seem to be paying him any attention. He placed some large logs on the embers glowing in the grate.

'Have you seen this picture?' she said, drawing his attention to an oil painting on the wall beside her.

'What's wrong with it?' There was not enough light for him to make out what she was looking at. Drawing nearer, he saw the painting showed a nude young woman standing before a skeleton.

'I see what you mean.'

The other paintings in the room depicted similarly macabre scenes.

'Why would anyone hang paintings like that in a guest

bedroom?' asked Jemima.

Alexander shrugged. 'I don't know,' he said. Maybe it was James's idea of a joke, though he thought it unlikely.

Jemima shivered. 'They'll give me nightmares.'

'We wouldn't want that. I'll speak to Hodgson and have them removed.'

Jemima thanked him and began applying make-up to her face. 'What does this friend of yours do for a living?' she asked.

Alexander hung a Harris Tweed jacket in the wardrobe. 'Nothing,' he replied. 'As far as I'm aware, he hasn't had a job in years. After being sent down from Oxford in his first year, he went to work for his father, a senior partner in one of the most respected stockbroking firms in the country, if not the world. This surprised many, not least his father, as until then James had never shown any interest in working in the financial sector. At the time he was living in a two-bedroom set in the Albany -'

'I've no idea what that means,' said Jemima.

Alexander closed the wardrobe doors. 'No, I don't suppose you would,' he said. 'For a time, he seemed to like the life, spending his time dining at the best restaurants, going to dinner parties and generally enjoying all that the city has to offer a young man of means. He'd been with the firm for less than a year when he embarked upon a Grand Tour of Europe for the summer with his girlfriend Victoria. At the end of the summer, she returned without him, which caused a bit of a stink, I don't mind telling you. He'd decided to remain in Naples with a friend of his. Victoria was, understandably, livid. Her father, who until then had been one of James's father's biggest clients, was even less impressed. After that, he took his business elsewhere. James laid low for a while, and no one heard from him for months. Some began to fear the worst. Eventually, he sent his parents a postcard to let them know he was still alive, though he didn't reveal to them where he was living.'

Leaning forward, Jemima applied mascara to her lashes. 'So how did he end up here?'

'Being an old friend of his, I was tasked with tracking him down and hand-delivering a letter to him from his solicitors, the firm I now work for, informing him he was the beneficiary of a trust held on this place.' He sat himself down on the bed and lay back on some cushions piled against the headboard. 'Through a mutual friend of ours, I learnt he was living in Capri and headed straight there to find him. Do you know the island?'

'No, I've never been.'

'Well, this won't mean much to you, but the villa he was staying in stands on the hillside of Anacapri, perched on a ledge at the top of the Phoenician Steps, a beautiful place with views overlooking the Marina and Bay of Naples. On a clear day, you could even glimpse Mount Vesuvius shimmering on the far horizon. James knew my being there had something to do with his grandfather's will but seemed surprised when I told him he'd inherited this house. At the time, he had no plans to leave Capri. The season was just about to start there, and he thought it more than likely it was still snowing in Scotland. I couldn't blame him. The island is incredibly beautiful. You really should go.'

'I'll add it to my list.'

'You do that. I was only booked into my hotel for the weekend, but James convinced me to stay longer, and I remained on the island for a further six nights, moving to the villa when my stay at the hotel ended. The weather stayed fine, and I was able to see the Blue Grotto and even took a chairlift up to the peak of Mount Solaro. On the day I was due to fly home, James took the ferry with me to Naples and showed me some of the main sights of the city. I did not attempt to convince him to return to London. I'd played his part. What James did next was none of my business.'

'So why did he return?'

'I left a copy of Homer's *Odyssey* lying on his bedside table, with a bookmark inside on the page that mentions Odysseus's encounter with the Lotus-eaters. Do you know the passage?'

'I'm afraid I don't.'

'That doesn't surprise me,' he muttered under his breath, before continuing. 'When Odysseus and his men were blown off course by storms, they ended up on an island where the people lived off lotus plants. The plants were so delicious, when his men ate them, they no longer wanted to come home. Eventually, Odysseus forced them onto their ships, and they continued their journey back to Ithaca.'

'I don't get it,' said Jemima. 'Why did that convince James to return home?'

'It's a metaphor,' said Alexander. 'A lotus-eater is a person who idles away his time - oh, never mind. It's not important. The point is it did the trick. A week later James turned up on my doorstep, eager to see the property.'

Jemima rose from the dressing table and made her way towards the bed.

'I haven't seen him since he moved to Scotland,' continued Alexander, 'but then nobody has, not even Will.'

The whole business was decidedly odd.

Jemima opened her suitcase and carefully lifted out an ivory sequin cocktail dress.

'Then why come?' she asked.

'Because James knows his wines and Hodgson's an excellent cook.'

Truth was he didn't have much say in the matter. He didn't know what to expect from the weekend or what was expected of him. Oh well, he told himself, he was here now. Might as well make the most of it. He was sure the weekend would prove far from dull. He hoped for some decent shooting but would settle for fishing in the Tweed. And in the evenings? Well, they could always make their own entertainment …

With that thought in mind, he sat up and pulled an Agent Provocateur gift bag out of his suitcase.

'Something for you to wear tonight,' he said.

Jemima reached across the bed and took the present from him.

'Don't you think I'll be a little underdressed,' she said, examining the contents of the bag.

'I meant later tonight.'

'Oh, I know what you meant.'

'Don't you want to try it on for size?'

'Don't you think you should get ready for dinner?'

Rising to his feet, Alexander moved round the bed. 'Dinner can wait,' he said, prowling towards her, a predatory glint in his eye.

'No, it can't,' replied Jemima, backing away from him, moving towards the door. 'I'm starving.'

'So am I.'

Reaching behind her, Jemima grabbed the handle, pulling open the door.

'Then the sooner we get downstairs the better,' she said, ushering him out of the room.

A smile playing on her lips, she closed the door firmly behind him and turned the key in the lock.

*

Sat at a dressing table, wrapped in a robe she'd found hanging in the bathroom, Isobel applied the finishing touches to her make-up. Her suitcase stood open on a chaise-longue; her black chiffon evening dress lay draped across the four-poster bed. When she'd returned to her room to unpack, she'd found the wardrobe filled with luxurious evening dresses and ball gowns. In a chest of drawers were nightdresses and lingerie. There was nowhere for her to put her clothes.

The house may have stood empty for seventy years, but the bedroom still felt inhabited by Emily Roxburgh, almost as if she'd just stepped out of the room and would be back at any moment. Except perhaps for the picture of Lady Roxburgh, the room was just as she left it. Isobel thought it unlikely Emily, or anyone else for that matter, would have wanted the portrait hanging on the wall, staring down on them as they slept.

Jewellery boxes and perfume bottles lay spread out on the table before her. An elegantly engraved solid silver hairbrush had been placed next to a matching hand mirror and comb. She opened one of the boxes to find it filled with necklaces, bangles and bracelets. She lifted out an ornate necklace, embellished with marcasite and onyx stones she thought would go with her dress. She was sure Emily wouldn't object to her borrowing them for the evening.

From the bedroom next to hers there came a sudden crash that echoed throughout the house. Rising from her seat, she had scarcely taken a step across the room when she heard a loud cry.

'Is there anyone there?' she said, knocking on the adjoining door.

When she didn't receive a reply she knelt down, rotated the brass cover of the escutcheon, and peered through the keyhole.

She couldn't see anything. There was a cover on the other side of the door. All the other guests had been put in rooms on the other side of the house. So, who was in there? It had to be James.

She dressed quickly, eager to find out.

*

Will, dressed in his dinner suit, returned to the bedroom to find Miriam wearing the evening gown with lace elbow-length sleeves he'd seen her hang on the wardrobe door. He was about to compliment her when she pulled out a crew neck cardigan from her suitcase.

'It was my mother's,' she said, noticing his look of disapproval. 'It's cashmere and very expensive.'

'It doesn't even match your dress. Why don't you put on a shawl, instead?'

'Do you want me to catch a cold?'

Will shook his head and decided to let the matter drop.

He realised he'd made a mistake assuming she'd want to share a room with him. Evidently, he'd overstepped the boundaries of their relationship, though that didn't come as too much of a surprise to him. He'd never been entirely sure what to expect from their relationship.

As they descended the staircase, she said, 'I wish you wouldn't refer to me as your girlfriend. It makes us sound like we are teenagers.'

'Would you prefer I called you my partner?'

'We are not in business together.'

'Then what do you want me to call you?'

'Friend will suffice.'

'I'd like to think we are a little more than friends, Miriam.'

'Let's not discuss this now.'

'What's to discuss?'

Miriam was about to say something when Jemima's high-pitched laugh echoed across the great hall. It sounded a little forced as though she was trying to show she was enjoying herself, rather than because she was. Will thought it a shame Miriam didn't share her enthusiasm.

'What on earth is Alexander doing with a girl like that?' said Miriam.

'I can only imagine,' muttered Will.

He'd never understood why Alexander had so much luck with women. He was neither particularly handsome nor charming. They must have seen something in him, other than his money, but Will was at a loss to know what.

'How long has Alexander known Isobel?'

Miriam stopped before they reached the drawing room, turned to Will and straightened his bowtie. 'I don't know,' she replied. 'I saw them together at a couple of parties.'

'When was this?'

'In the summer I think.'

'What parties were these?' he asked, wondering why he hadn't been invited.

Miriam, ignoring his question, stepped into the drawing room. Long satin brocade curtains hung across the French window, and an oak cased gramophone cabinet stood in a corner of the room. There was another door in the far wall that Will assumed led to the servants' quarters.

Jemima, wearing a sleeveless cocktail dress that rose just above her knees, lay on a cream leather sofa laughing at Alexander as he stirred the log fire roaring away vigorously in the white marble fireplace. There were two armchairs in the room that matched the sofa forming a three-piece suite. All were upholstered in cream leather and had walnut veneer back and sides.

Their host was nowhere to be seen.

'Have you seen James yet?' asked Will.

Placing a fluted steel poker back on the hearth, Alexander rose to his feet. 'Not yet,' he said, brushing ash off his Oxford Brogues. 'He's probably waiting to make a grand entrance. He always liked to be noticed when he entered a room.'

And he always was, thought Will.

Seeing Alexander dressed in his Savile Row suit, bespoke shirt and handmade brogues, made him realise how old and worn his dinner jacket and trousers, which were beginning to feel a little tight in place, must have looked by comparison.

Alexander walked over to a demilune cocktail cabinet with a burr walnut veneer. 'I did, however, find the booze.' Opening the lower cabinet, he showed Will the bottles he'd discovered. 'I thought cocktails appropriate in light of our surroundings.' He opened the top cabinet and an interior light flicked on, a pink glass mirror reflecting the glasses stored inside.

Seeing Miriam sit down on an armchair, Will asked her if she'd like a cocktail.

'I'll just have my usual,' she said. 'Alexander knows what it is.'

'One virgin piña colada coming up,' said Alexander, rolling his eyes with disdain. 'Would you like another G and T, Jemima?'

'No thanks,' she replied. 'Could you mix me a dry martini instead?'

'How?'

Jemima shrugged her shoulders.

'Is there any vermouth?' asked Will.

Alexander rummaged through the lower cabinet. 'Yes, there is,' he said, removing a bottle of Noilly Prat.

'Mix three shots of gin and a dash of vermouth in that cocktail shaker.'

Alexander grabbed a cocktail shaker and began filling it with gin. 'You know your cocktails.'

'One of the jobs I held while doing my LPC was as a barman,' said Will. 'So, what do you think of the house?'

Alexander topped the cocktail off with a generous measure of vermouth. 'You'd have thought he would have done the place up a bit,' he said, mixing the drink. 'I imagine it looks exactly like it did seventy years ago when his great-uncle lived here. It's like some god-awful museum … but one only James would want to visit.'

'He had intended to hire an interior designer to remodel the house,' explained Will. He noticed a sterling silver photo frame standing on a side table. The framed photograph showed a young couple on their wedding day standing outside the church they'd passed in the village.

'I wish he had,' said Miriam. 'The bedrooms are in dire need of redecorating. The mattresses are old and the beds uncomfortable, and the less said about the rest of the furniture the better. At the very least he should have installed a decent central heating system to keep the bedrooms warm at night. I don't think those old radiators are going to do that.'

Alexander poured the cocktail into a long-stemmed glass. 'If you want to stay warm overnight just push your beds together.'

'Don't be so vulgar, Alexander,' snapped Miriam.

'She doesn't need to worry,' whispered Will, 'she's packed a hot water bottle.'

'I doubt she'd keep you very warm anyway,' Alexander whispered back. He added a drop of rum to Miriam's cocktail.

'That's not a *virgin* piña colada …'

'Never is. Got to liven the old girl up somehow.' He garnished the drink with a maraschino cherry. 'Whisky for you?'

'Yes, thank you,' said Will.

Alexander lifted out a bottle of Stornoway Scotch and a soda siphon from the lower cabinet. 'This should keep us going for a while.' He broke the seal on the bottle, unscrewed the cap and poured generous amounts of whisky into two crystal glasses, emptying the rest of the bottle into a decanter.

Miriam took her drink from Will. He waited anxiously for her to taste the alcohol, but she took a sip without comment.

'Bad décor,' she said, her attention drawn to the pictures displayed on the walls, 'under certain circumstances, can be excused. Bad art cannot.'

A painting of an Ottoman bashi-bazouk chieftain hung alongside portraits of beautiful dark-eyed women clad in shimmering silk kaftans and tunics. There were two pictures of Bedouins riding camels in the desert, and in another on the wall above the gramophone, merchants selected slave girls in a market. A painting of voluptuous nudes, guarded by eunuchs, lounging round a sultan's harem, hung on the far wall.

'I don't know,' said Alexander, handing Jemima her martini, 'I quite like them.'

'You would,' sniffed Miriam.

'You should see the paintings in our room,' said Jemima. 'They're terrifying. Alexander's going to ask Hodgson to remove them.'

'They can't be any more objectionable than those awful portraits at the top of the stairs,' said Miriam. 'James really ought to consider having them removed.'

Will took a sip from his glass and felt the whisky warming him through as it trickled down his throat. 'He can't get rid of them,' he said. 'They're the Earls of Leithen - his ancestors.'

Jemima's eyes widened. 'James is an earl?'

Will shook his head. 'According to James's father, following the death of the ninth earl in the early nineteenth-century, the title passed to his daughter, Lady Roxburgh. She never married and when she died without issue the title became extinct.'

He cast an anxious glance at a marble mantel clock above the fireplace. It was a quarter to eight and James still hadn't made an appearance.

His concern for his friend was growing by the minute.

CHAPTER THREE

Isobel heard no further sounds coming from the room adjoining hers whilst she dressed for dinner. Before heading downstairs, she replaced the pendant that hung round her neck with Emily's necklace. She'd almost dismissed the incident from her mind when she heard the floorboards creaking outside her room. Listening attentively at her door, her ears straining to pick up every sound, she thought she heard footsteps, faint at first but growing louder. Whoever was out there appeared to be walking very slowly and carefully down the corridor so as not to be heard.

Finding herself reluctant to leave her room, she stepped back away from the door. Realising she was being ridiculous, she pulled on the handle, the hinges groaning as the heavy door swung inward. She peered out cautiously, glancing both ways to see if anybody was there, before stepping out of her room into the empty corridor. Without another moment's hesitation, she made her way down the corridor to the adjacent room, the floorboards creaking underfoot, and knocked on the door.

'James,' she said uncertainly. 'Are you there?'

After a pause, she heard him call to her from within the room.

'Come in,' he said. 'The door's open.'

Tentatively, she pushed open the door and stepped into the dimly lit room. She found James standing by an open wardrobe, dressed in a white dress shirt and black trousers. A bow tie hung loosely round his neck.

Isobel glanced round the room. 'I heard a crash,' she said. 'Is everything all right?'

The bed had been made, and there was a pile of books on a bedside table. A Turkish rug covered the floor, and a similar carpet lay draped over a table, on which stood a hookah.

'I knocked over a vase,' said James, removing a dinner jacket from the wardrobe and hanging it on the door.

'Did you hurt yourself?'

James shook his head. 'No,' he assured her.

'I heard a cry.'

James smiled. 'A cry of despair,' he said awkwardly. 'It was a very expensive vase.'

Isobel drew nearer to her host. 'Was somebody in here with you?'

'Only Hodgson,' he said, avoiding her gaze. 'He cleared away the vase for me. You just missed him.' Turning, he looked at himself in the mirror above the washstand and began tying his bow tie. 'I want to apologise for earlier. You took me by surprise … I hadn't realised the weekend you were due to visit had come around so quickly. I'm sure Hodgson would have said something, but I'm sorry to say I've stopped listening to him. He's become such an old fusspot. Ever since he returned, he's been quite strict with me, making sure I eat regularly and don't stay up too late. He's treating me like I'm eight years old again.' He fumbled with his bow tie. 'Had I realised you were due, I'd have postponed your visit until I was feeling better. I don't like people seeing me when …' he paused, 'when I've not been well.'

Isobel began tying his bow tie for him. 'I know,' she said. He was trembling slightly and there were beads of sweat on his forehead. 'And Hodgson is just worried about you.'

'It's very cruel of me to keep him here, so far from his friends and family, but he refuses to leave - and it seems I just can't manage without him.'

When Isobel finished tying his bow tie, James thanked her and said, 'Well, I'd better not keep my guests waiting any longer. They must be wondering where I am.'

Isobel noticed a painting of two Egyptians playing a game similar to chess on a checkerboard hanging on a wall.

'Did they play chess in Ancient Egypt?' she asked.

'No,' said James, 'they had similar games, but as far as I'm aware none were played on a checkerboard. Many of the nineteenth-century Orientalist paintings you'll find in the house depict imagined worlds. Artists were not granted access to harems - though that didn't stop them from imagining what went on inside them.'

'I'm sure it didn't,' said Isobel. 'Your ancestors were interested in the Middle East?'

James nodded. 'The Orient seemed to have held a particular attraction for Henry.'

'This was Henry's room?'

'He used to sleep in here to avoid disturbing Emily when he'd stayed up late.'

'I imagine the creaking floorboards in the corridor used to wake her up when he crept past her room.'

'He didn't have to. He came up another way.' He gestured to a shadowy corner of the room. 'There's a door concealed in the panelling. Behind the door is a staircase that leads down to the study.'

'Can we go down that way?' asked Isobel.

James removed his dinner jacket from its hanger and slipped it on. 'I'm afraid it's very dusty in there,' he said. 'We'd be covered in cobwebs before we reached the ground floor.'

After flicking off the light switch on the wall, he led Isobel out of the room.

*

'James is certainly living the dream of many,' said Alexander, pouring himself another glass of whisky. 'It's always been an ambition of mine to own an estate where I could fish and shoot to my heart's content, preferably in the Highlands, though I'd happily settle for somewhere in the heart of the Chilterns.' He paused momentarily to top his drink off with soda before continuing. 'It wouldn't be easy of course. Although the industry is worth billions, owning an estate like this is not for the faint-hearted. It's unlikely James will see a return on his initial investment for years - the running costs alone will see to that. But I don't suppose he'll have to worry about that ...'

'Why not?' asked Jemima.

'Because James never sticks at anything for long. He'll soon give up on the whole venture.'

'That's not fair, Alexander,' said Will.

'Isn't it? How long did he spend working for his father? He spent even less time at Oxford before he was sent down –'

'He wasn't sent down from Oxford, Alexander. He left of his own accord.'

'Same difference. You, mark my words, he'll be back home before Christmas.'

Jemima finished her cocktail. 'He must get very lonely living here all by himself,' she said. She set her empty glass down on the walnut coffee table, placing it next to a bronze sculpture of an Arab tribesman sitting astride a camel. 'Does he know anyone in the area?'

'More's the question,' asked Miriam, 'is there anyone in the area worth knowing?'

'Well, the Duke and Duchess of Dalkeith live nearby,' said Alexander.

'You know a Duke and Duchess?' asked Jemima.

'I attended their Hunt Ball last February. Didn't see James there.'

Will heard voices in the great hall and turned to see Isobel, wearing a flowing floor-length black chiffon evening gown, appear in the doorway.

'Look who I've found,' she said, stepping back to allow James to enter the room.

Their host looked unnaturally pale, his lips colourless, his hair lank and lifeless. Although it had only been about a year and a half since he'd last seen him, Will thought his friend looked ten years older.

Alexander crossed the room, extending his hand towards James. 'Ah, Roxburgh, there you are,' he said. 'I was expecting to find you swathed in tartan.'

James smiled weakly as they shook hands. 'How nice to see you again, Alexander,' he said, his voice flat and dull.

'You've grown a beard,' said Alexander, turning to introduce Jemima. 'It doesn't suit you.'

Jemima stepped forward excitedly. 'How nice to meet you,' she said, curtsying.

'Get up, Jemima,' Alexander muttered under his breath. 'He's not royalty.'

Blushing, Jemima straightened herself up.

'Will, it's been far too long,' said James, shaking his friend's hand.

Will felt his hand was limp, his grip weak. 'It certainly has,' he said.

When James turned to greet Miriam, Will exchanged a look of concern with Isobel.

Jemima sat back down on the sofa. 'So how do you all know each other?'

'Will and I played rugby together at Oxford,' said Alexander. 'We weren't in the same college, of course. I was a Balliol man, and Will was a Teddy boy.'

'Ours was the better rugby team,' said Will. 'In my second year we made the final of the Cuppers and were crowned champions the following year.'

Alexander did not comment on this. Instead, he proudly announced that he had been the captain of his rugby team, a position Will knew he'd only held very briefly, though he didn't say anything.

'So, you all went to Oxford together?' asked Jemima.

'We knew each other before then,' continued Alexander. 'We all did a stretch at Marlborough at one time or another. All of us except Will, of course.'

'He went to a … *different* school,' added Miriam quietly.

'Will and James grew up in the same village,' said Isobel.

'We were practically neighbours,' said Will. 'The Manor's boundary wall runs alongside the cottage I grew up in. As a boy, I wanted to see what was on the other side of the wall.'

'And when he was seven,' said James, 'he climbed over the wall and entered the grounds.'

Miriam's eyebrows rose. 'You used to trespass on their land?'

'My mother told me to stay away from the house,' continued Will. 'She said the people who lived there were very private and didn't like visitors.'

James smiled. 'The first time I saw Will he was hiding up a tree.'

'I thought you were going to call the police and have me arrested.'

'If he'd had any sense he would have,' said Alexander.

Will remembered James asking him what he was, but not understanding the question, he hadn't replied.

'Are you a fairy, or a pixie? Maybe you're an elf. You look like an elf to me.'

'I'm a boy, just like you. My name's Will.'

'You may be a boy, but you are not from this world.'

'I'm from the village.'

James had looked strangely disappointed upon hearing this.

'Are you hunting the jabberwocky too?'

Not wanting to disappoint him again, Will had told him he was.

James's eyes lit up. 'I saw him briefly yesterday. He might still be about somewhere.' He started towards the wood, beckoning Will to follow.

Will fell into step beside him, his hands in his pockets.

They hadn't gone far when, suddenly, James fell to the ground. 'Get down!' he whispered urgently, reaching for Will.

Will fell onto the ground next to him, keeping low so as not to be seen.

'Did you see it?' asked James, his eyes wide with terror.

'See what?' asked Will, noticing James was trembling.

'The Jabberwocky!'

Will shook his head, unsure of what to make of this strange boy. Rising to his feet, his back against a tree, he glanced over his shoulder. Something was rustling about in the shrubbery nearby. It was probably just a bird or a squirrel. He was sure it wasn't a Jabberwocky because there was no such thing. He remembered reading about one in a book once, though he couldn't remember its title.

He grabbed a stick off the ground. 'We'll need weapons,' he said, stripping off the leaves, fashioning a sword.

'You're going to attack it?'

Will nodded and James picked up a stick of his own.

'Ready?' asked Will, glancing over his shoulder.

James nodded and they charged at the creature, their swords held high. Together they saw off the Jabberwocky. James was sure it wouldn't return that day.

Later, as James led Will out of the wood, they passed a *Trespasser Will Be Prosecuted* sign, which made Will feel slightly uncomfortable.

'What does *prosecuted* mean?'

'It means if anyone finds you here, you'll go to prison,' James told him, his face expressionless.

Will's eyes widened. 'It does?'

'Don't worry,' said James, smiling. 'I'll come and visit you.'

Will laughed and began to climb a horse chestnut tree. 'Tomorrow, we should set a trap for the Jabberwocky,' he said thoughtfully. 'We could dig a pit and cover it with sticks and leaves.' He stopped climbing when he came to the level of the wall and glanced back at his new friend.

'I'll see you then,' said James. 'Goodbye, Will Trespassers.'

Smiling, Will slipped behind the wall, disappearing from sight.

From that day forward they met whenever possible, Will waiting under the oak tree, James appearing from the manor house, often with Isobel in tow. At first, he thought she was his sister - they certainly acted like siblings - but he soon learnt they weren't related. The first time she appeared, having followed James without his knowing, he'd ordered her back to the house, but Will had invited her to join them, worried if she returned she'd tell James's parents she'd seen him in the garden and they'd prosecute him for trespassing.

Jemima then asked Isobel if she'd attended Marlborough.

'No, I went to St Mary's.'

'Her father's Sir Clive Hamilton-Jones,' said Alexander, 'third, or is it fourth, baronet?'

'Third. My great-grandfather was awarded a baronetcy for services rendered during the First World War.'

'What does that make you?' asked Jemima.

'I'm still a Miss.'

'Still to be reeled in by some lucky devil?' asked Alexander.

Isobel ignored his question. 'James and I practically grew up together.' She smiled fondly at their host. 'Our mothers were best friends, and I spent a lot of time at the Manor. I even had my own room there. As children, the three of us were inseparable.'

'My mother used to make an awful fuss over Isobel,' said James.

'Unfortunately,' added Will, 'Isobel didn't join us at Oxford.'

Alexander finished off his whisky and soda. 'Didn't they want you?'

'I didn't apply,' said Isobel. 'I preferred to study somewhere further away from home.'

'We haven't all been together in a long time now,' said James.

Will placed his empty glass on the coffee table. 'Not since that party your parents threw for you just before we left for university.' He glanced at Isobel and their eyes met fleetingly across the room.

Memories that over the years he'd tried to forget came back to him. He pictured her, dressed in a low-backed satin gown, flinging her heels into a flower bed as she ran barefoot across a lawn towards him, her hand reaching for his before leading him into the moonlit wood …

Out in the great hall, a clock chimed the hour. Moments later, Hodgson entered the room, approached James and announced that dinner was ready. James offered his arm to Isobel and led the way to the dining room.

As they crossed the hall, Jemima turned to Isobel and said, 'I love your necklace, where did you get it?'

'Thank you,' said Isobel. 'I found it in my bedroom.'

'Lucky you,' muttered Miriam. 'All I found in mine was woodworm and damp.'

*

They entered the dining room from the great hall through grand double doors. Six high-back chairs with floral carved backs stood round a long solid oak dining table. Although it had only been set for the six of them, the table could be extended to seat at least twelve. Long candles, set in silver candlesticks, had been lit, the candlelight reflecting off the silverware, china plates and crystal glasses, filling the oak-panelled room with a yellow glow. Two glass cabinets displayed Sevres, Meissen and Dresden porcelains. Above their heads, a chandelier hung down from a high ceiling, its crystal pendants shimmering in the light.

James led Isobel to the head of the table and pulled out a chair for her while the others took their seats.

'The house is fantastic,' she said, sitting down.

'Thank you,' said James. He made his way to the foot of the table. 'I didn't hold out much hope for it at first, but I just had to do what I could to save it - though at the time I didn't appreciate quite how much work that would entail.'

Will unfolded his napkin, spreading it over his lap. 'Well, it's been worth the effort.' He glanced across the table at James's ashen face and sunken eyes. He looked ghostly in the candlelight, a shadow of his former self.

'I'm afraid the house is still not finished. Some of the bedrooms on the third floor were ravaged by damp and rot and have yet to be redecorated … and I haven't even started on the attic rooms.'

When Hodgson began to ladle out large spoonfuls of steaming hot soup from a silver porringer, Alexander took it upon himself to decant the wine. The meal, as expected, was excellent and the wines were a perfect accompaniment to the food. All were quick to praise Hodgson's culinary skills.

'I do think you're rather greedy keeping Hodgson here all to yourself,' said Alexander to his host. He glanced at Hodgson as he refilled his glass. 'If you ever want to get away from this place, you can come and work for me if you like.'

'Thank you, sir,' said Hodgson politely. 'You are very kind.'

Alexander then asked James if he was aware his ex-girlfriend Victoria was now engaged.

'I wasn't,' he said, though he didn't seem surprised by the news.

'Who's she engaged to?' asked Isobel.

'Don't know the chap,' said Alexander. 'Apparently, he's a wealth analyst at Coutts.'

Alexander and Miriam then began running through all the gossip they knew, like two old women nattering over a garden fence. James, his face expressionless, didn't appear to be listening to them. His mind seemed elsewhere, lost in thought. Isobel was equally quiet, contributing little to the conversation. Instead, she spent most of the evening covertly watching James, clearly worried about her old friend.

Only when the meal drew to a close did she address him.

'So, did you ever solve the mystery of Wychwood House?' she asked.

Jemima's eyes widened. 'What mystery?'

James explained that his father had been unable to tell him anything about the house. 'At family gatherings, I approached my relatives hoping to learn more about its history, but no one would tell me anything.'

'Some claimed they'd never even heard of the place,' added Will.

'We became convinced something awful had once happened here,' said Isobel. 'Something James's family wanted to remain a secret.'

'One of your forebears a great one for the ladies, eh?' suggested Alexander. 'Fathered a few illegitimate children, did he?'

James smiled. 'Not that I know of,' he said. 'The house fascinated us when we were children. As we were unable to find any photographs of the house, Will and I began mapping out floor plans, while Isobel drew pictures of the house in incredible detail. We invented names and created lives for the men who lived here. Tragedies were born, love stories created. Wychwood House became our Camelot.'

Alexander gave a low chuckle. 'What exciting childhoods you must have had …'

Isobel cast him a vicious look. 'Don't be cruel, Alexander.' Turning to face James, she leant forward expectantly in her seat. 'But have you discovered why your relatives refused to discuss the house with us?' she asked.

'I genuinely believe they knew nothing about the place. Very few, if any, of my relatives visited Wychwood House. Most had no interest in either it or its history. By the time we were kids the house had been forgotten, becoming a distant memory few cared to remember.'

Will couldn't help but feel a little disappointed by this explanation. By the look on Isobel's face, he could tell she shared his disappointment.

'Will was just telling us your ancestors were the Earls of Leithen,' said Jemima.

'James VI of Scotland,' said James, 'by then James I of England and Ireland, created the earldom in 1612 for my ancestor David Roxburgh. As a boy, he'd been a member of the royal household at Stirling Castle and a close friend of the king's son, Henry Frederick, Prince of Wales.'

'How fascinating,' said Jemima. 'I'd love to know more.'

'I'm sure you will,' muttered Alexander under his breath.

'I wouldn't want to bore you with the details,' said James.

'You wouldn't be boring us in the slightest,' replied Jemima.

'Speak for yourself,' whispered Miriam, though everyone heard.

Alexander gave an amused grunt.

'Wychwood House lies in the heart of the ancient Ettrick Forest,' began James, 'a favourite hunting ground of the Scottish Kings. No one knows when the original foundations were laid. Some say the house rests on a site used by Romans; others say it dates back to even earlier times. Through my research into the lives of my ancestors, I've discovered a peel tower stood on the site from around the middle of the thirteenth-century - one of many fortified castles and tower houses built in the area. During the

Scottish Wars of Independence, life on the borderlands was hard and short; both the English and Scottish armies plundered nearby farms and villages, stealing cattle and burning down houses.

'Before being bequeathed to my family at the beginning of the sixteenth-century, Calidon Tower, the caput of the Barony of Leithen, had changed hands many times. So far, I've only been able to trace my ancestors back as far as the late fifteenth-century to Andrew Roxburgh, who was born around 1473. He was a favourite of King James IV - they would often hunt together in the Ettrick Forest - and was granted the land and barony of Leithen with its peel tower shortly before he fought and died alongside his monarch at the Battle of Flodden in 1513.'

'That doesn't mean much to me, I'm afraid,' said Alexander.

'King James IV was a popular monarch,' explained their host. 'A scholar and patron of the arts, he built castles, fought tournaments, and with his knights alongside him, he united his kingdom. He was seen by many as the Arthurian King of Scotland.'

Isobel's eyes flashed with excitement. 'And your ancestor was one of his knights,' she said. 'This place really is your Camelot. Just as we thought it was.'

Alexander groaned and rolled his eyes.

'Calidon Tower was destroyed by a fire in 1609, but it wasn't until 1616 that the first Earl of Leithen built the house in its place. Having inherited the estates of the barony from his father, he was keen to rebuild his *caput baronium* and approached King James VI, who was well known for throwing money at his courtiers. Through the king's generosity, he was able to tear down what remained of the tower and build the house in its place, moving here a few years later.

'Due to the many alterations made over the years, the great hall is all that remains of the original building. The ninth Earl of Leithen drastically altered the house in the late 1820s. Although the design harks back to fortified buildings of the sixteenth-century, by the nineteenth-century there were no raids or marauding armies to defend against. The battlements and towers are all for show. The time of the Border reivers was over.'

On the wall above the fireplace hung a painting of men wearing steel bonnets, some clad in breastplates, others in padded leather jackets, sitting on horseback brandishing backswords.

'When the earl's only child Lady Roxburgh died without issue, her cousin inherited the estate. William Roxburgh had served with the Scots Greys during the Crimean War and fought at the Battle of Balaclava.'

Alexander waved a knife in the air, "Into the valley of death rode the six hundred!"

James suppressed a smile. 'Wrong brigade, I'm afraid. The Scot's Greys were part of the Heavy Brigade.'

'Of course they were,' said Alexander, embarrassed.

'He was later promoted to Major-General and made a KCB, a post he held until his retirement. During his time here, he spent a great deal of money on the house, which by then had fallen into disrepair. He redesigned many of the rooms, filling them with suits of armour and his hunting trophies, adding the servants' quarters, an office, and a chapel for his wife. After William died, his eldest son continued to live here with his mother, though spent most of his time in Edinburgh experiencing the darker side of Victorian life. He squandered almost his entire inheritance gambling, before overdosing on laudanum that he was taking to ease the pain of the medication he was taking to treat the 'foul disease'.'

'What on earth is the 'foul disease'?' asked Miriam.

'He had the clap,' explained Alexander.

'I didn't realise you were such an expert on the subject,' replied Miriam, 'though I can't say I'm surprised.'

'Following his death,' continued James, suppressing a smile, 'his younger brother George - a much more respectable member of the family - inherited the house. Having made his fortune in the City, he purchased the Manor in Wiltshire, though spent most of the year at his apartment in London. He was one of many absentee lairds all too common in the Victorian era, and only visited his houses when holding hunt balls and shooting parties for his friends and relatives, preferring the Manor for shooting pheasants and Wychwood House for grouse. His first wife died shortly after giving birth to their son Edward. Fifteen years later he remarried. His second wife gave birth to two boys, Henry and then Charles, my grandfather. Edward was particularly fond of this house. Before he was killed at the Battle of the Somme serving with the 2nd Cavalry Division, it was thought he might live here.'

Alexander looked mournfully across the table "'Bent double, like old beggars under sacks, / Knock-kneed, coughing like hags, we cursed through sludge …'"

Miriam frowned. 'You're not going to do that all night, are you?'

'The groom and both footmen were also killed in the war,' said James. 'The butler's face had been badly disfigured by a bomb blast, and as a result, he was unable to resume his duties. The housemaids found better-paid work elsewhere. Only the gamekeeper remained. He continued to rear pheasants and manage the grouse for shooting parties that were no longer held here. It wasn't until the nineteen-thirties, when my great-uncle Henry Roxburgh moved here from London with his young wife Emily, that the house became inhabited again. Following their marriage at the church in the village, they lived here during the remainder of the summer, returning to London in the autumn, though they grew so fond of the place the following spring they returned and made it their permanent place of residence, living here throughout the year. They returned to London a year and a half later, less than a year before the start of the Second World War. The house hasn't been lived in since.'

When Hodgson began clearing away, Will noticed James's plate was still full. He hadn't even picked up his knife and fork. They lay on the table untouched.

Hodgson then brought out the port, placing a heavy cut-glass decanter down on the table in front of James, who offered a glass to Jemima, which she declined with a discreet shake of her head. Alexander, who liked to impress everyone with his palate for port, attempted to identify the name of the port house. To everyone's surprise, he was successful.

'But can you guess the vintage?' asked James.

Alexander set down his wine. 'I'm going to say the mid-sixties - '66 to be precise.'

'1927.'

After filling his glass, Will pushed the decanter into the middle of the table, earning himself an exasperated look from Alexander. 'You found it in the house?' he asked.

James nodded. 'Stored in the cellar.'

'What else have you got hidden away down there?' asked Alexander.

Miriam, bored by the conversation, made no secret of the fact. 'I'm sorry,' she said, rising from her seat, 'but I'm awfully tired. If you'll excuse me …'

'We'll come up with you,' said Jemima.

'*We* will?' replied Alexander.

'I too am eager to get to bed.'

'How on earth can you be tired, you've only just woken up!'

Jemima leant forward and whispered in his ear. 'I never said I was tired.'

Alexander, his cheeks reddening, cleared his throat. 'You always did have the best cellar in London, James,' he said, rising slowly and cumbrously from his chair. 'Glad to see things haven't changed.'

Isobel stood up. 'I'll come up with you.'

'The more the merrier,' said Alexander, departing the room with Jemima on his arm.

Isobel followed on behind leaving Will alone with James. Will briefly considered joining them but knew Miriam would prefer to be alone as she prepared for bed. Hearing their footsteps die away, he poured himself out another glass of port.

'Would you like some?' he asked, offering a glass to his host.

James shook his head. 'No, thank you.' Rising to his feet, he crossed the room to the fireplace. 'I know what you are going to say,' he said, placing a log on the dying embers of the fire, 'but I can assure you I'm all right. It's all very embarrassing really … Hodgson was called away -'

'Yes, I heard.'

'I thought I could manage on my own. It appears I was wrong. There was just so much to do. I'm embarrassed to say I'm just not used to hard work.'

Will thought it a well-rehearsed little speech. 'There's no need for you to explain,' he said. 'Why didn't you let us know how you were?'

'I'm afraid I couldn't. You see, there's no landline connected to the house, and I couldn't get my phone to work. The reception here is patchy at best. There was no way of contacting anyone from the house.' He fell silent when Hodgson entered the room and cleared away the last of the plates. When he'd left, James continued. 'I tried to get to the village but collapsed in the wood. As I said, it was all very embarrassing. Somehow I managed to drag myself back to the house.'

'Are you resting now?'

James nodded. 'Hodgson is keeping a close eye on me. I'll be back to my old self in no time.'

'I would have come up sooner if I could,' said Will, 'but trainees, if they know what's good for them, don't take time off in their first year.' He looked at his old friend and smiled. 'It's nice to finally see the place for myself.'

'Miriam and Alexander hate it, don't they?'

'They wouldn't be happy in the Savoy. I apologise for bringing Alexander with me. I know having to spend the weekend with him is rather more than your liking for him warrants …'

'That's all right. He always did have a habit of turning up uninvited - it didn't come as too much of a surprise. To tell the truth, I was more surprised to see Miriam here.'

'We've been seeing each other for about three months now.'

'You must have settled in all right at Crenshaw, Willoughby, and Stern if Bill is letting you see his daughter.'

'I don't think he gets much say in the matter, though he doesn't appear to have any objections.'

'So, how's the training going?'

'Well, thanks,' said Will. 'It's hard work, but it will all be worth it in the end.' He drank down his wine and set the empty glass on the table in front of him. 'You know,' he said, shifting uncomfortably in his seat, 'you could have let me know how you were getting on. I haven't heard from you since you moved here.'

'You didn't receive my letters?'

'No, I didn't,' said Will with a hint of scepticism in his voice, knowing full well he'd never written to him. 'When was the last time you left this house?'

His friend shrugged. 'I haven't been back to Edinburgh in a while now.'

'In a while,' asked Will, eyeing him suspiciously, 'or since you moved in? You need to get out of this house. Why don't you go and visit your parents for a few weeks until you are well again?'

'I can't …'

'Why not?'

James sighed heavily. 'Because the house isn't finished. Leaving now would be tantamount to admitting defeat. My father said I'd never see this through to the end. And he's not the only one who thinks that, is he? It's easy to be overheard in this house, Will.'

'You can't risk your health just to spite your father … or anyone else for that matter.'

'The last person I want to see right now is my father. He's never understood my fascination with this place. No one has … except you, and Isobel of course.'

*

Upstairs in her room, Miriam fidgeted restlessly in her cold bed listening to the wind howling round the house. No matter how many blankets she piled on top of her she couldn't get warm. The fire had burnt itself out and she hadn't been able to get it going again.

At dinner, she'd been angry at herself for not insisting on separate rooms. She'd wanted to say something, but had decided against it, not wanting to make a fuss, worried Alexander would tease her if she had. But now, having witnessed Will and Isobel's furtive glances at each other across the table at dinner, she was glad she hadn't said anything. Clearly, they'd been more than just friends once. Much more. At least with Will in the room with her, she knew where he was and could keep an eye on him.

She had a feeling she was going to have to keep a close eye on both of them throughout the weekend.

*

With a spring in his step, Alexander made his way down the corridor to his bedroom, his washbag in one hand, his towel in the other. The night may have been over for everyone else, but for him, it was just beginning. He pictured Jemima laid across their double bed wearing the outfit he'd bought her. He felt his heart beat a little faster at the thought.

To his surprise, when he stepped into the room, he found her lying in bed wearing a pair of his monogrammed silk pyjamas, the covers pulled over her.

'I hope you don't mind,' she said. 'I saw you'd packed two pairs, so I borrowed one.'

'Why aren't you wearing the playsuit I gave you?'

'I'll catch my death of cold sleeping in that thing.'

Alexander began unbuttoning his shirt. 'I wasn't anticipating you wearing it for long.'

Outside the wind dropped momentarily and the house fell silent.

'Can you hear that?' asked Jemima, her eyes wide with fright.

Straining his ears, Alexander heard a faint tapping against a windowpane.

'Sounds like someone's knocking at the window,' said Jemima.

'Well, I'd better let them in.' Alexander drew back the curtains. 'Cathy, is that you?'

The long spindly branches of a tree brushed against the window.

'See it's nothing,' he said. A draught from the window sent a shiver down his spine. 'It's cold in here. What happened to the fire I lit earlier?'

'It went out.'

Alexander sighed. 'So it would seem.'

*

On the other side of the house, Isobel lay in her bathtub, the hot steaming water soothing her after her long day. Her surroundings were opulent, lavish, the bathroom's walls and ceilings covered in aluminium leaf. All that was missing was a cocktail perched on the edge of the bath.

She desperately wanted to relax and forget about her day but found she couldn't. Ever since she'd woken to find the man in the Italian shoes watching her as she slept, she'd been on edge. Her unexpected, unnerving encounter with James had only made matters worse.

She knew full well he hadn't simply 'worn himself out'. Something had happened to him. Something awful. And she knew she wouldn't be able to leave until she'd found out what.

*

As their conversation progressed, Will began to feel there was something James wanted to tell him, something weighing heavily on his mind, but whenever he paused to allow him to speak, his friend remained silent.

'Did you ever find out why this house wasn't demolished like everyone thought it was?'

'I'd hoped to uncover a letter or some other correspondence that revealed my grandfather's intentions for the house, but so far

I'm no closer to learning the reason it's still standing than I am to knowing why he left the property to me. I have several theories, all of which might be wrong.'

'Such as?'

'I believe my great-grandfather tried to sell the house following Henry's death. He wouldn't have been able to afford to run two houses, so put this one up for sale. Unfortunately for him, at the time no one was buying stately homes and country houses. The house may have been on the market for many years. Often when no buyer could be found, the furniture and contents were auctioned off and the stone, fireplaces and anything else that could be salvaged was sold and the house was razed to the ground. By the mid-fifties, when my grandfather took control of the Roxburgh estate, one was being torn down every five days.'

'So why didn't Wychwood House suffer the same fate?'

'Henry had spent a lot of money renovating and redecorating the house, running himself into considerable debt in the process. My grandfather probably held out hope for a sale in order to pay off his brother's debts. I also like to think that having spent a lot of time here during his childhood, my grandfather may have felt a sentimental attachment to the place. In thirty years, if I were unable to maintain the Manor, I wouldn't be able to tear it down. I'd try and keep it as best I could, if not for my children, for future generations. My grandfather would have been only too aware my father had little or no interest in the house or the men who lived here. Maybe he hoped I would.'

Will thought it seemed a plausible enough explanation, but for some reason, he wasn't convinced that was the whole story.

James sighed. 'I've come to accept that many of the questions I have about the house are going to remain unanswered.'

Sensing his friend didn't want to discuss the issue further, Will let the matter drop.

It wasn't any of his business anyway. His only real concern was convincing him to leave Wychwood House, if only for a short time. That, it seemed, was going to prove more difficult than he'd originally thought. His friend appeared determined to stay put - at least until the house was finished. How long that would take was anybody's guess.

Outside in the great hall, a grandfather clock struck eleven.

'It's getting late,' said James, rising from his seat. 'You must be tired after your long journey.'

Will stood up and followed his friend out of the room.

As they crossed the great hall, James said, 'Have you seen the cornices in here and in the library? The arms of the Border families are painted on them.'

Will shook his head and glanced up. Dark shadows hid the ceiling from view.

James led him up the staircase. 'I'll have to give you a proper tour of the house tomorrow.'

'I look forward to it.'

When, halfway up the staircase, they came to the landing, James came to a stop. 'My bedroom is in the other wing of the house.' He gestured up the stairs that branched off to the right.

They exchanged goodnights and Will watched his friend climb the stairs. Once on the gallery, he disappeared into the darkness, his footsteps fading away into silence.

CHAPTER FOUR

Nineteen Months Earlier

The church bell struck the hour, the chimes resonating over the village. Only after it had struck for the eleventh and final time did James proceed. Finding the gate open he followed the lavender lined path that led to the front door. Hodgson only ever locked the gate in the summer to keep out the tourists. The Manor wasn't open to the public, though that didn't stop people from asking to have a look round the house and gardens.

The house appeared just as he remembered it, and there didn't appear to have been any alterations made to the gardens. Glancing up, he saw the small window of the room where Isobel always slept in when she stayed at the Manor, his eyes falling on the window of his own bedroom below. As he continued down the path, he wondered who he would find at home. His grandmother was bound to be there - she hardly ever left the house anymore. So was Hodgson. But his parents? He tried to remember what they did on Saturday mornings. He thought it unlikely they'd be away at this time of year.

Although he had a key to the house, he decided to knock before entering, hesitantly at first, then with more force.

The door swung open to reveal Hodgson stood on the threshold.

'Master James?' he asked, as if not believing his own eyes. 'Is it really you?'

'Hello, Hodgson. How are you?'

He told James he was well. 'This is a surprise. You should have rung to let us know you were coming.'

He should have, but he hadn't. There were lots of things he should have done, like contacting his parents to let them know where he was and what he was doing. He realised then he hadn't spoken to his mother in over a year.

'Are my parents at home?'

'Your mother is. Your father won't be back until later this afternoon.'

Thank God for that, he thought. It would give him time to speak to his mother before the inevitable arguments ensued.

'Is that Alexander's car parked in the courtyard?'

James nodded. 'I've been staying with him.'

'Why didn't you go to your apartment in the Albany?'

'I thought it might have been let out in my absence.'

'As far as I'm aware, it hasn't.'

Hodgson looked like he had many questions but didn't know which one to ask first.

'Please, come in,' he said finally, stepping back to let him pass, closing the door behind him.

'How has everyone been?'

'As well as can be expected.'

James detected a note of criticism in his voice.

'Was my father angry with me when I didn't return?'

'More disappointed than angry. We all were.' He spoke in a cold, reproving, almost contemptuous tone. 'I'll go and tell your mother you're here.'

When he'd left James wandered into the low-ceilinged parlour where he found his grandmother dozing in her Cranford armchair before the fire, a book resting in her lap. The house was quiet and tranquil, but the peace did little to calm his nerves. Not wishing to wake his grandmother, he turned and left the room, and passing the staircase, wandered into the room that had once been his nursery.

The room looked smaller than he remembered. The ceiling that had always seemed so far away didn't look so high to him anymore. The tapestries still hung on the walls, but the old worn Wilton carpet had been removed. A table and chairs now stood in the room in place of his toys. He wasn't surprised to find this light, airy room with its windows overlooking the gardens being used as a dining area. His mother had never cared for the previous dining room, finding it too formal.

He looked out of the window, gazing out over the grounds. Beds of flowering tulips flanked the paving stones that led down to the water garden. When he was a young boy, he'd spent many happy hours by the lily pond under the watchful eye of his grandparents. He'd always enjoyed his frequent visits to the house, spending Christmas and Easter and a week or two in the summer there. He particularly enjoyed spending Christmas there when his aunt and uncle and their two daughters would also stay at the house. On Christmas Eve, his grandfather would gather the children round the fire and tell them ghost stories, stories James believed he'd made up himself, though later learnt he hadn't.

His love of the Manor had been one of the reasons his parents had decided to move there, however, following the death of his grandfather the house was no longer the happy place it had once been. When he'd struggled to make friends at his new school, he began to feel increasingly lonely and isolated. Of course, all that changed when a young boy from the village climbed the boundary wall and began exploring the gardens …

James had never believed Will when he told him he lived in the village. He seemed wild, untamed and free to come and go as he pleased, living in the moment, never thinking about the future or the past - very different to the children he'd met at his school. James thought he lived in the wood, playing amongst the trees and wildflowers, and was certain he would remain there forever a child, long after he himself had grown old.

Seeing the garden again made him realise how much he missed both Will and Isobel. He hadn't seen Isobel since he'd left for Oxford, and although Will had joined him there, they'd only seen each other fleetingly. To his great regret, they hadn't parted on the best of terms and hadn't spoken since. He didn't even know where he was or what he was doing. He wondered if his mother was still living in the village. If she was, she would be able to put him in contact with his old friend.

Hearing the floorboards creak behind him, he glanced over his shoulder to see his mother standing in the doorway. She turned pale at the sight of him, as though she'd seen a ghost. For a moment he thought she was going to faint, but she recovered herself and stepped into the room. She spoke quickly, her questions coming thick and fast, hardly pausing for breath. Before he could answer, Hodgson appeared and suggested they take tea in the library.

Over tea, he told his mother how Alexander had visited him in Capri to tell him he'd inherited Wychwood House and asked her if she'd known that he'd inherit the property.

She told him she didn't. 'I wasn't present at the reading of your grandfather's will.'

'Dad never mentioned it to you?'

'No, he didn't.'

'Why not?' asked James. 'Seems like something you should have been told.'

'I don't know why,' replied his mother. 'You'll have to ask your father.'

His father returned home later that afternoon, but it was not until just before dinner that he sought out his son, finding him in his bedroom rummaging through his wardrobe.

'I believe you're looking for these,' he said.

Turning, James saw he was holding up a bunch of keys in his hand. He glanced at the keys first then at his father whose face betrayed no emotion, his steely blue eyes meeting his.

After a pause, he said, 'I take it Bill's been in contact with you.'

'It's disappointing I should learn of your return from him, instead of from you personally. Embarrassing even. But then I don't know why I should be surprised. In recent years, you've caused me no end of embarrassment.'

'I assure you I would have caused you even more if I'd returned and continued working for you.'

'I've no doubt you would. But that's beside the point. If you wanted to leave the firm, you should have told me personally. I can assure you I would have wholeheartedly supported your decision to leave. It had become glaringly obvious to both myself and others you were not cut out to be a stockbroker.'

This reprimand had barely left his mouth when he began listing all the people James needed to apologise to, including Victoria and her father. He then went on to tell him how his mother had been sick with worry the whole time he'd been away, causing undue strain on her already fraught nerves. James didn't want to listen to what he had to say, but while he held the keys to Wychwood House, he had no choice. He was only too aware he'd upset many people and was eager to make amends. And he would - though not before he'd found his ancestral home.

His father remained standing the whole time he spoke, occasionally pacing round the room. Once he'd said his piece, his temper cooled, allowing James to cast his own aspersions.

'Did grandfather tell you he planned to leave Wychwood House to me?'

'No. He never spoke about the house. I only learnt he'd left it to you at the reading of his will.'

'Why didn't you just tell me I'd inherited the house then?'

'Because at the time I was contesting the will. You see shortly before he died, your grandfather wrote a codicil - an amendment to his will - which named you as the beneficiary of a trust held on the house. At the time your grandfather was believed to be of sound mind and the codicil was witnessed and signed as required. I disagreed, believing he'd become confused and didn't realise what he was doing.'

'Who stood to inherit the property before this amendment was made?'

'There was no mention of Wychwood House in the will your grandfather wrote in the 1970s. In the 1930s, to avoid paying death duties in the event of the death of your great-grandfather, a private estate company was set up. All properties and land owned by our family, including Wychwood House and the Manor, became part of the estate company, later known as the Roxburgh Group.'

'Currently managed by you.'

'Amongst others.'

'When I found the keys, grandfather had been dead for about three years, hadn't he? By then your attempts to contest the will must have failed. So why instead of telling me then, did you think it better I learnt the truth on my twenty-first birthday?'

'Because by then you'd be old enough to go looking for the house by yourself. If I'd told you when you were younger, you'd have expected me to help you find the place. I had better things to do with my time than traipse across Scotland in search of a house I didn't, and still don't believe, exists.'

James wasn't convinced that was the real reason.

'Even if the house hasn't been demolished, it would have fallen down by now.'

'When the house was put into trust,' replied James, 'the trustees became responsible for maintaining the property.'

'The trust was set up in 1993, by which point the house, which was built centuries ago, had stood empty for over fifty years. You can't maintain a property that has fallen into ruin.'

'There has to be a reason why grandfather left Wychwood House to me.'

'Why not just forget about the house? What purpose will finding it serve?'

'I have to see it for myself,' said James, resolute in his decision. 'I have to know why he left it to me.'

'That's assuming you can find it of course.'

'Bill's given me the address of the trustees. One of them will be able to provide me with an address for the property.'

'Enid Boyd died years ago, I'm afraid. I'm a friend of her daughter. Fairbrother's non compos mentis and hasn't been for years.'

'And Wrayburn?'

'Last I heard he'd left the UK for tax reasons. He wasn't a young man when I met him in the late seventies. He must be at least a hundred years old by now. Even if, by some miracle, he is still alive, it's unlikely you'll ever find him.'

Moments later James's mother called up to them to tell them dinner was ready. Before leaving the room, James took the keys from his father. He felt glad to have them back in his possession. Still, the question remained, how was he going to find Wychwood House without an address?

Once downstairs, he was welcomed home by his grandmother, and they dined in his old nursery. Wychwood House was not mentioned during dinner. Although he was eager to find out what his grandmother knew about the property, he decided to wait until his parents had gone to bed before asking her any questions. She often stayed up late, so he'd have plenty of time to speak to her before she turned in for the night.

Not long after dinner, when his parents retired for the evening, he found himself alone with her. She asked him about his holiday, and he told her all the places he'd visited. He then promptly asked her what she knew about Wychwood House.

'Nothing, I'm afraid,' she said. 'I never visited the house - but then no one did after Henry died. Henry was your grandfather's brother. I never met him, of course, being only four when he died. I'm afraid your grandfather never spoke about the house, or Henry for that matter - I don't think they were very close, Henry being six years older than your grandfather. He died during the Second World War.'

'He fought in the war like grandfather?'

'No, I don't think so. I don't know what happened to him.'

James was just beginning to think he'd reached another dead end when she continued.

'The only person I ever heard mention Henry, or Wychwood House, was his mother. She lived with us for a time in the early seventies. I'm afraid her memory began to fail her in the last years of her life and she often became confused. She would ask to visit Henry and his wife Emily in Scotland. Of course, I would remind her Henry was dead, but she insisted I take her to see him, assuring me he was still there. She would then proceed to provide me with directions to the house.'

'Wychwood House?'

'Where else?'

'Well,' urged James, 'what did she say?'

'I'm afraid to say I wasn't paying that much attention. For some reason, she always insisted on telling me just as we were sitting down to watch the Forsyte Saga together. Whereas now you can record programmes on those video recorders, back then if you didn't watch the programme live you missed it.'

'Grandma, no one's used a VCR in years.'

'Thank God for that. I never could get the blooming things to work.'

After that she paused, so James gently reminded her she was about to provide him with directions to Wychwood House.

'Oh yes,' she said. 'So I was.' She paused again before continuing. 'Remember, this was a long time ago, and as I said, I wasn't paying as much attention as I should have. However, I still have a vague recollection of her words. She told me I was to drive west out of Selkirk and follow the river -'

'Which river? The Tweed?'

'No, the Ettrick. The house lies about five miles from Selkirk in the Ettrick Valley and can be reached from a village where gatehouses marking the entrance to the estate are to be found.'

'Is there anything else you can tell me?'

'She mentioned something about griffins.'

'Griffins?'

'Horrible, ugly things staring down at her as she drove through the gates. She shuddered every time she saw them.'

It wasn't much, but it was a start. After all, how many villages could there be five miles west of Selkirk? She couldn't tell him anything else about the house, and the subject was soon changed.

He stayed the night at the house, leaving the following morning shortly after breakfast. He didn't see his father again. He was not there to see him off. Before he left, his mother made him promise he'd spend Easter with them, to which he reluctantly agreed. Breathing a sigh of relief as he left the house, he felt a weight lift off his shoulders as he drove back to London, the awful realisation dawning on him that the Manor no longer felt like a home to him anymore.

*

He arrived in Edinburgh on a cold damp Monday afternoon, his train pulling into Waverley just before two-thirty. After picking up Alain-Fournier's novel that lay on the table in front of him, he stood up, draping his trench coat over his arm before pulling his case down from the luggage rack. When the train came to a stop, the doors unlocked, and he followed the other passengers out of the carriage.

Once on the platform, he took his pocket watch out of his waistcoat pocket and glanced at the time. He wasn't due to check-in until three but was sure arriving twenty minutes early wouldn't make much of a difference. Although it was not yet rush hour, the station was full of people rushing to catch trains. He navigated his way through the crowd, leaving the station by climbing the Waverley steps up to Princess Street, a bitter wind greeting him when he reached the top, his destination, the Balmoral Hotel, looming before him.

Seeing him approach, a kilted doorman greeted him cordially and took his luggage for him. James then passed through the revolving door and stepped into the hotel. Before him, a grand staircase led to a mezzanine overlooking the lobby. At the reception desk, a young woman welcomed him to the hotel. He introduced himself and told her he'd booked a suite for the week. She immediately called for the concierge, who appeared moments later to escort him to his rooms.

Even on a dull day, the spacious suite looked light and airy. The furniture faced a working fireplace and appeared comfortable and inviting. He glanced out of the window, taking in the views of Edinburgh Castle and Princes Street Gardens. He'd never been to Edinburgh before and was keen to see the city. The concierge pointed out the other rooms. A king-sized bed big enough for three filled the bedroom, and the bathroom had been decked out in Italian marble.

He asked where he could hire a car, explaining he'd be house hunting during his stay with them, though he didn't go into the details. The concierge told him he could contact a car rental company on his behalf.

'Better make it a four-by-four,' he said. 'I don't know how far off the beaten track I'll be going.'

Before he left, the concierge asked him if he would be dining with them that evening. He told him he wouldn't. He'd probably just grab something to eat in the bar later. He didn't like to eat alone in restaurants. Somebody, undoubtedly an older couple bored with each other's company, would take pity on him and invite him to join them. He didn't feel in a particularly sociable mood that day and did not care to meet any of the other guests staying at the hotel.

Finding his clothes had been unpacked for him in the dressing room, he decided to change out of his suit into something a little more casual, opting for a blazer and chinos. He left the hotel a little after four and wandered aimlessly through the streets, not knowing where he was or where he was going. By five o'clock he started feeling hungry so began looking for somewhere to eat and found an old Edwardian pub called *The Bride of Lammermoor* down a narrow pedestrianised street.

Except for an attractive girl with auburn hair standing behind the bar, the place appeared empty, so he pulled open one of the double doors and stepped inside. When the girl glanced up, her eyebrows raised slightly at the sight of him. She greeted him warmly, probably glad of the company, her large hazel eyes meeting his. Drawing nearer, he saw she was wearing a drab polo shirt two sizes too big for her petite frame, and tight jeans that emphasised the curves of her hips.

He asked her if it was too early to get something to eat.

'We serve food all day,' she said, handing him a menu. She noticed his deep tan and asked him if he'd recently returned from a holiday.

'I've been living in Italy for the last year and a half or so.'

She seemed interested so he continued. He told her he travelled all over Italy but spent most of his time in Capri. She'd always wanted to visit the Bay of Naples and the Amalfi Coast and was very envious of him. She'd only ever been abroad once when she'd spent a two-week holiday in Barcelona shortly before starting university.

'So, what brings you to Edinburgh?'

'I'm looking for a house.'

'In the city?'

James shook his head. 'No, further south. In the Borders.'

He told her the house had once belonged to his family.

'Are you planning on living there?'

'No one's lived there in years. The house may no longer be habitable. I'm not entirely sure where it is. The directions I've been given are a little vague, to say the least. Apparently, it lies about five miles from Selkirk in the Ettrick Valley and can be reached from a village where gatehouses marking the entrance to the estate are to be found.'

'The estate?' she exclaimed, her eyes opening wide. 'How big is this house?'

'I've no idea. I've never even seen a photograph of it.'

As a boy, he'd pictured the house so vividly in his mind, almost as if he had grown up there, he'd always believed he'd recognise the village as though he'd driven through it many times.

'Well, I hope you find it okay.' After taking his order she disappeared into the kitchen.

He wasn't entirely sure she believed his story. He couldn't blame her - he hardly believed it himself.

When she returned from the kitchen, she asked him how long he would be in Edinburgh.

'Until Friday. I'm staying at the Balmoral.'

'I've heard the restaurants there are very good, though I've never been myself. I believe one was awarded a Michelin star.' Her eyes narrowed. 'If you are staying there, why would you want to eat here?'

'I don't like dining alone.'

'You'll be dining alone in more ways than one here.'

'I won't be if you keep me company.'

She smiled. 'Until we get another customer,' she said, 'I'm all yours.'

They spent the evening getting to know each other better. He learnt her name was Tessa and she was in the second year of an Earth Science degree at Edinburgh University. He told her he went to Oxford, though failed to mention he'd left after his first year. Although she'd been born in Edinburgh and had grown up there, she'd moved to a small fishing village in the East Neuk of Fife when she was thirteen. James wasn't entirely sure what Neuk meant but assumed it roughly translated as nook. Her parents had opened a B&B there, and although a beautiful place, with views over the Firth of Forth, there wasn't much for a teenager to do - except help her parents run their business. Fortunately, her grandmother still lived in Morningside, so she was able to visit the city during the school holidays, though it wasn't the same as living there.

The pub filled up as the evening progressed. By the time he went to leave, Tessa was busy behind the bar, and he didn't get a chance to say goodbye. He'd hoped to get her number before leaving. He wanted to invite her to have dinner with him at one of the restaurants at the Balmoral - ideally the one that had been awarded a Michelin star.

The following morning, he woke early to find rain streaming incessantly from dark leaden skies. He decided to wait until the rain had eased before setting off, so went for a swim in the hotel's pool, before enjoying a leisurely breakfast in his suite. But as the day went on the weather only got worse. The skies grew darker, the rain fell heavier. He decided to postpone his search for Wychwood House, spending the morning in the National Gallery. Around midday, he'd returned to *The Bride of Lammermoor*. To his disappointment, he learnt Tessa wasn't working that day. He learnt she only usually worked weekends and had only been in on Monday to cover for a friend who'd called in sick. Only when he turned to leave was he told she would be working Wednesday night. They had a folk band playing and expected the place to be busy.

That evening he rang his mother to let her know he'd arrived safely, before turning in early for the night. He woke the next morning to clear skies. When he went down to the lobby the doorman collected his Range Rover for him, pulling up outside the hotel, and he was soon on his way, heading south out of Edinburgh to the Scottish Borders. The drive was due to take about an hour and a half. He hoped to reach the house before midday, which would give him plenty of time to explore the old place, though he grew increasingly nervous as his journey progressed. When he reached Selkirk, he decided to take a break. He needed time to get his bearings and figure out where to go next, so he grabbed a drink in a little coffee shop in the marketplace before proceeding.

Leaving Selkirk, he headed west, following the Ettrick Water. After about four miles he passed a tower house and slowed the Range Rover expecting to reach a village, but none appeared. He continued driving and after about seven miles came to the village of Ettrickbridge. Ettrickbridge was the only village in the area that showed up on the basic road map he'd picked up from a service station on the way down. The village he was looking for was probably far too small to show up on such a map. Now that he discovered it wasn't where he'd hoped it would be, he realised how ill-prepared he was for his search. He should have picked up an Ordnance Survey map in Selkirk before setting off.

Nevertheless, he decided to persevere, continuing down the valley. After all, the directions his grandmother had given him were uncertain. For all he knew the village could be fifteen, even twenty miles from Selkirk. He saw no harm in looking. But no villages matching the description he'd been given materialised and eventually he reached a T-junction. He could head either south or west. According to his map, the road west circled back to Selkirk, so he took that one, the road soon leading him north. After crossing the Yarrow, he came to an old coaching inn beside a crossroad.

Leaving the road, he pulled up into the car park and headed inside the inn, hoping someone there would be able to help him. The only person working there that afternoon was a young man who'd never heard of Wychwood House. Before leaving, he asked where the nearest petrol station was. He had a feeling he was going to be driving around for some time yet. The young man told him to head up to Innerleithen. There was a Shell station on the

Innerleithen Road just outside of Peebles. He couldn't miss it.

Once back in the Range Rover, James returned to the valley road, coming to a stop at the crossroads. Eager to resume his search, he briefly considered returning to Selkirk - there was bound to be a petrol station there, though he couldn't remember passing one on the way down - before heading up to Innerleithen. He left the Yarrow Valley and headed north, following the winding road past a managed forest of coniferous trees. Blackface sheep, fenced in by drystone dykes, grazed on fields of rough grass and open moorland.

From Innerleithen, he drove on to Peebles, the petrol station appearing on the outskirts of the town. He drove on, deciding to stop for lunch before filling up. From a café on the High Street, he bought a sandwich before going for a walk along the riverbank where he stumbled upon the ruins of an ancient castle. Under crisp blue skies, sitting among crocuses and daffodils on a steep grassy bank overlooking the Tweed, he ate his lunch. After about an hour he returned to the Range Rover and drove out of Peebles, stopping at a petrol station before proceeding.

When he went inside to pay, he asked the woman behind the counter if she'd heard of Wychwood House. She looked up slowly, her eyes coming to rest on him as he removed his credit card from his wallet.

'It's an old house,' he continued when she didn't reply. He slipped his card into a handset and entered his PIN. 'It's most likely deserted.'

The woman brushed her dark hair away from her face and stared at him blankly. She was in her late thirties, early forties. A silver name necklace that bore the name Ethan hung round her neck. James assumed it was the name of her son.

'Are you sure you're in the right place?' she asked after a pause.

'All I know is it lies about five miles from Selkirk in the Ettrick Valley.'

The woman handed him his receipt. 'I'm sorry I can't be of more help.'

'I'm sure I'll find it,' said James, turning to leave.

'Did you say it's deserted?'

James nodded.

'I haven't heard of Wychwood House, but I have heard of the Witches' Wood.'

'I haven't seen a wood on the map with that name.'

'That's just what the locals call it. I don't think it has a name - it's part of the Ettrick Forest. There's a house in the wood. As far as I know, no one's lived there for over fifty-odd years. I'm afraid it's something of a ruin.'

'Sounds like the place.'

'You know,' said the woman, after a pause, 'there are other houses in the area you can visit. Traquair, Abbotsford, Bowhill -'

'I'm not a tourist.'

'No, you don't look like one.'

'Where is this wood?'

'There's a turning off the main road just before the first of two bridges that cross the Yarrow. There's no signpost to mark the way, but I believe there's a cottage on the corner. Follow the road up a hill and you'll come to a village.'

The village lay in the Yarrow valley, not the Ettrick. He'd been following the wrong river ...

'At the end of the street, before you reach the kirk, you'll come to a lane. Follow the lane into the wood and up a hill and you'll reach the house.'

'Thanks,' said James. 'I'll take a look.'

As he pulled open the garage door and stepped outside, he heard the woman say, 'Watch out for yourself up there.'

Crossing the forecourt, he noticed the once-crisp blue sky was turning red as the sun began to set. He slipped inside his Range Rover, drove across the forecourt, and pulled out into the road. He headed east, leaving Peebles behind him, driving quickly, the countryside racing past him.

Returning to the crossroads, he followed the Yarrow Water east towards Selkirk, the low sun silhouetting the trees behind him. He slowed the Range Rover as he came to the first bridge. When he crossed the second, he saw the cottage on the corner and turned off the main road, following a single-track road up a slight hill. He drove to the end of the street, stopping just before the church, but when he couldn't find any buildings resembling gatehouses, or a drive that looked like it led to a country house, he assumed he was in the wrong place. Only then, when he looked for someone to ask directions from, did he realise he hadn't passed anyone as he'd driven through the village.

After parking the Range Rover, he approached one of the

houses. The paintwork on the window frames and door was blistering and cracking. Drab, worn curtains hung at the windows. He rang the bell but didn't receive a reply. He tried knocking, but there was still no answer. He approached other houses but without success. No faces appeared at the windows. No one answered his call.

He suddenly felt very alone.

Retracing his steps, he wandered up to the two derelict cottages and wondered if they had once been the gatehouses that marked the entrance to the estate. The lane that led into the wood did not look like a drive leading to a large country house. If he drove down the lane, would he be able to get out again? There was only one way to find out.

Without any further delay, he returned to the Range Rover, turned down the rutted, potholed lane and headed into the dark wood. He switched on his headlights and crossed the balustraded bridge. Ahead an uprooted tree lay across the track, blocking his way. He slowed the Range Rover, yanking up the handbrake when he came to a stop. He had no choice but to walk the rest of the way on foot. He set off briskly, climbing over the uprooted tree, its dark, scaly bark covered in lichen and moss.

Bare trees, stunted and twisted into deformed shapes, resembled old hags with bent backs. He wondered if that was how the wood got its name. High up in the branches of the trees, rooks were building their nests. Hearing leaves rustling behind him, he turned, pausing to see what was moving in the undergrowth, but couldn't see anything. He realised, except the cawing of the rooks in the trees, he couldn't hear any birdsong. A sharp, bitter wind blew through the trees, sending a shiver down his spine. He walked on, moving slowly, cautiously, the trees crowding round him, the wood growing darker with every step he took.

When the gates, red with rust and drooping on their hinges, came into view, he felt his heart pounding in his chest. A heavy iron chain, held together by a sturdy padlock, had been wrapped tightly round them. He couldn't see the house, his view obscured by overgrown bushes and brambles that spilled out onto the drive from the borders. He glanced up at one of the griffins adorning the gates, his gaze drifting to the shield held in its claws. Although faint in the gathering darkness, he could just make out his family's coat of arms emblazoned on the stone.

He had found Wychwood House. At last, his journey was over.

He grabbed a rock from the ground and struck the padlock repeatedly, but it held fast. If he wanted to get into the grounds, he was going to have to climb the gates. He hesitated before proceeding. Night was drawing in. It would be dark by the time he began exploring the house.

Wisps of drifting mist weaved their way down the drive towards him. He suddenly found himself gripped by a feeling that someone, or something, was watching him from the grounds of the house.

'Hello,' he cried out. 'Is there anybody there?'

There was no reply.

He leant forward, his eyes struggling to penetrate the gloom. Through the swirling mist, he thought he saw a shadowy, indistinct figure moving through the bushes and brambles towards him. At first, he thought it was an animal - he could have sworn he'd seen horns or antlers - but realised it couldn't have been, for when he looked closer, he saw the figure was standing upright on two feet. Beads of sweat broke out on his forehead. Was there someone there, or was it simply a trick of the light?

'Is anybody there?' he repeated, wiping his forehead with the back of his hand.

Again, there was no reply. Whoever, or whatever, had been there was gone - if they had ever really been there in the first place. The mist had reached him and was now encircling his feet. Terror gripped his heart. He had to get out of there. Get far away and not look back ...

Turning quickly, he hurried back down the track. As he climbed over the uprooted tree, he saw the Range Rover wrapped in the thickening mist. He pulled open the door, climbed inside, and began reversing carefully down the muddy track, not daring to glance back towards the house for fear of what he might see coming down the track after him. After crossing the bridge, he turned the Range Rover round. Thorns scraped against the side of the vehicle as he headed down the narrow lane. When he reached the street, he pressed his foot down hard on the accelerator, the village disappearing from view in his rear-view mirror as he drove away.

*

By the time he reached Edinburgh darkness had fallen. He pulled up outside the Balmoral, handed the keys to the doorman, and headed straight to his suite. Once inside, he switched on all the lights and was about to turn on the television, when, out of the corner of his eye, he caught sight of a dark figure across the other side of the room. He turned suddenly to see it was nothing more than his own frightened reflection staring back at him from a mirror hanging on a far wall. He looked like a frightened rabbit caught in the headlights of an oncoming car, his eyes anxious and scared.

He knew he was being ridiculous. No one had been watching him from the grounds of the house. In running away like he did he'd acted like a child frightened by his own shadow. There was nothing there for him to be afraid of.

'The first thing tomorrow,' he told himself, 'you're going to buy some bolt cutters, break the padlock and go inside the house.'

Unable to shake his feeling of unease, he decided to get out of his suite and be amongst people. According to his watch, it was just after eight. Still early. He could get something to eat in the city. He glanced out of the window, his gaze drifting from Edinburgh Castle to the New Town.

*

Music floating through the night air greeted him as he emerged from an alley into Rose Street. *The Bride of Lammermoor*, as expected, was teeming with people listening to the folk band, which meant he wouldn't get to speak to Tessa for long. He found her leaning against the bar, swaying gently to the rhythm of the music. When the band came to the end of a song, she glanced in his direction, her eyes widening when she saw him approach.

'I wondered if you'd be joining us tonight,' she said, her voice soft and gentle. She picked up an empty pint glass. 'Have you had any luck finding your house yet?'

He nodded and was about to tell her all about his day when the band began another song.

'Is it too late to get something to eat?' he asked, raising his voice so he could be heard over the music.

Tessa pulled on the blue porcelain handle of a pump and began filling the glass with beer. 'We serve food until ten,' she said, placing his pint on the bar. 'What would you like?'

James glanced at a menu and placed his order.

Tessa gestured to an empty table. 'Why don't you grab a table and I'll bring it over to you.'

James thanked her, and with his pint in hand, forced his way through the crowd. He sat at the table and listened to the band, the singer's voice sweeping across the crowded room.

"O I forbid you, maidens a',
That wear gowd on your hair,
To come or gae by Carterhaugh,
For young Tam Lin is there ...'

His thoughts turned to Wychwood House. He hoped the house was in a better state than the desolate gatehouses at the entrance of the estate. He'd always assumed once he found the house that would be the end of his journey. He was beginning to realise it was just the start. There was a long way to go yet.

He saw Tessa navigating her way towards him, a plate in one hand, a knife and fork wrapped in a serviette in the other. She set the plate and cutlery down in front of him. James thanked her and rolled up the sleeves of his blue Oxford shirt.

'Are you enjoying the music?'

James nodded. 'What song are they playing?'

'Tam Lin. It's an old Border Ballad.'

'You know it well?'

Tessa brushed stray wisps of her long reddish-brown hair out of her face. 'Only because they perform here at least once a month and always play this song.' She perched herself on the edge of his table.

He told her how it had taken him all day to find the house and had been too dark to go inside. She listened with interest, though he still wasn't sure she believed him.

Before she left him, she said, 'We're going out after work. It's student night at the Liquid Rooms. I wondered if you'd like to join us.'

'Thanks for the offer,' he said. 'I'd love to, but I've got an early start tomorrow. I have to get back to the house.'

'Well, you'd better take my number in case you change your mind.' She pulled a pad out of her back pocket and wrote her number down for him. As she rose to her feet, she placed her hand on his before making her way back to the bar.

James, unable to take his eyes off her, watched her walk across the room. She stopped momentarily to speak to one of the bartenders, before glancing back at him over her shoulder. When she saw he was looking in her direction, she smiled before disappearing from view. After finishing his dinner, he decided to return home. He really did need to get an early start the next day. Once again Tessa was nowhere to be seen and he didn't get a chance to say goodbye.

The streets were quieter as he made his way back through the city. A group of students passed him, the orange street lights reflecting off their pale faces. He wondered if they were on their way to a club. Remembering the touch of Tessa's hand on his, he contemplated whether to join her after she finished work. To hell with it, he thought. The house wasn't going anywhere. He could shower, change, and still have plenty of time to meet her before she left work. He'd still be able to visit the house tomorrow - even if he arrived a little later than planned.

Only when he appeared from the bathroom wrapped in the hotel's bathrobe did he notice someone had left him a message on his voicemail. His heart sank when he listened to the message and heard his father's voice.

'James, your mother wants to know if you'll be staying in Scotland this weekend or spending Easter with us. Personally, I think you're wasting your time and money searching for a house that no longer exists, but then you've made it abundantly clear you couldn't care less what I think.'

James put the phone down. He didn't want to hear any more of the message. Once again, his father was attempting to sow seeds of doubt in his mind, leading him to believe there was a reason he didn't want him finding Wychwood House. Whatever the reason was, he'd find out soon enough. He briefly considered ringing him back and telling him his search hadn't been such a waste of time after all, but thought better of it, deciding to wait until he'd seen the state of the house.

Hearing his father's voice made him dismiss all thoughts of going to the club with Tessa. He wasn't there on holiday. He had to focus on the task in hand. After deleting the message, he made his way to his bedroom. Although not yet ten, he decided to turn in for the night. He'd need a good night's sleep if he wanted to get an early start the next day.

*

The following morning, drizzling rain fell from dull grey skies as he left Edinburgh. By the time he reached Galashiels the rain had eased. There he found a DIY store, where he purchased some bolt cutters. He didn't see anyone as he drove through the village, the street being as deserted as it had been the previous day. Only when he turned down the track did he catch a brief, fleeting glimpse of a white-haired man standing outside the kirk. He appeared to be watching him intently, his eyes remaining fixed on James as he drove into the wood.

Gripping the steering wheel, James followed the curving, mysterious lane that beckoned him up the hill, coming to a stop before the fallen tree. He grabbed his set of keys, a torch and the bolt cutters, slipped out of the Range Rover, and began his ascent of the hill. Upon reaching the gates, he placed the hasp of the padlock between the jaws of the bolt cutters, gripped the arms, and pushed them together. The hasp snapped and the padlock fell to the ground. Discarding the bolt cutters, he unwrapped the chain and pushed at the gates. One came free of its hinges and fell with a mighty clunk onto the drive.

The way through the brambles and bushes that covered the drive was easier than he'd anticipated, and it wasn't long before he saw the house properly for the first time. Ivy hid the doors and windows from view. Ancient trees bent and twisted into grotesque forms by harsh winds they'd withstood for centuries, surrounded the house, their branches intertwining above the steeply pitched roof in places as though sheltering the house from the elements. The strange eerie silence of the wood seemed even more intense now. By the time he reached the house, he couldn't even hear the cawing of the rooks nesting in the trees.

Unable to contain his excitement any longer, he wrenched open the entrance gate, hurried through the gateway and raced across the courtyard, ivy tendrils brushing against his face as he ducked into the entrance porch. Patches of mildew and moss were growing on the damp walls. Stopping before a nail-studded door, he placed one of the larger keys on the key ring into the lock. The key turned and he pushed against the heavy door. A horrendous screeching sound echoed throughout the great hall as the bottom of the door grated against the stone floor.

He switched on his torch; the daylight unable to penetrate the gloomy depths of the dark panelled room. Plaster had fallen from the ceiling covering the stone floor in dust and rubble. Sofas, an oriental folding screen and a grand piano furnished the room. Stepping over the crumbling stone and fallen masonry, he saw there were also several brass jardinières embossed with copper and silver Arabic writing. A portrait that had once hung above the fireplace lay facc down on the floor below.

Seized by a feeling of intense cold, he shivered and buttoned up his blazer. The wide staircase loomed before him, and he shone his torch up its old, warped steps to the gallery above. The house was profoundly quiet, his heavy, laboured breaths only making the silence more apparent.

There were three arches in the wall to his left. The middle arch led to a long stone passageway that disappeared into darkness. He assumed it led to the servants' quarters. He tried the nearest door enclosed within the first arch but found it locked. All the doors leading from the old medieval hall were shut. Only the door enclosed within the third arch had been left open.

Leaving the great hall, he stepped through the open doorway and entered the drawing room, the beam of his torch dancing over the flower-patterned wallpaper, coming to rest on the cream sofa and matching armchairs arranged round the marble fireplace. Beside them, strewn across the floor, lay the dust sheets that had once covered the furniture. All the curtains in the room were open. Shutters covered the windows and thick, heavy planks of wood had been nailed to the outside of the French window.

Drawing nearer, he saw one of the doors of the French window had been left slightly open. The key was still in the lock and one of the panes had been smashed. Shards of broken glass lay on the floor below. Pulling the doors open, he began kicking at the planks, prising them loose, filling the room with light, sending dust motes dancing in the air. Overhead, cobwebs festooned an enormous gilt chandelier.

An empty whisky glass and a cocktail glass stood on a walnut coffee table next to copies of *Country Life* and *Tatler* magazines. A packet of Player's No 6 cigarettes lay next to an ashtray filled to the brim with cigarette stubs. Another cocktail glass lay on the carpet below. On closer inspection, he saw there were pink lipstick smudges on the cocktail glass. A second whisky glass stood on the mirrored sliding tray of the cocktail cabinet.

Four glasses. Four people. Probably teenagers from the village. Whoever they were, they were long gone. Apart from smashing a pane of glass, they didn't appear to have done any damage. Fortunately, the planks nailed outside the French window had kept others out.

The lid of the gramophone had been lifted and a record lay on the turntable. He read the gold lettering on the red label: "The Very Thought of You" by The Ray Noble Orchestra featuring Al Bowlly. Before leaving the room, he locked the doors of the French window, pocketing the key, and made his way back to the great hall where he began exploring the other rooms on the ground floor.

In the dining room, ugly cracks ran across the aged walls. A Victorian gilt mirror hung above the mantelpiece, its warped glass reflecting a distorted image of the room. He explored the library next, the beam of his torch slowly revealing the room to him. Bookshelves filled with expensively bound volumes, separated by a second-floor gallery, stretched up from the floor to a high beamed, coffered ceiling. Elaborately carved oak panels covered the lower half of the walls. Displayed above were paintings of huntsmen and horses. In contrast to the drawing room, the library seemed austere, conservative, and had the air of a gentlemen's club about it. There were also several rather beautiful oil lamps with opaline white glass shades dotted about the room.

The library had a second door that was also closed. He tried the handle but found it locked. Eager to know what was on the other side of the door, he selected a small key that looked about the right size to fit in the keyhole. As he went to unlock the door, he was overcome by the feeling he was being watched. Momentarily distracted, he fumbled with his keys, and they slipped from his hand, falling to the floor.

When he bent down to pick them up, out of the corner of his eye, he thought he glimpsed something moving across the room. Goose pimples covered his arms, and he froze in absolute terror. Someone or something was moving stealthily across the room towards him.

He spun round suddenly, his torch held high.

There was no one there, but he stood frozen to the spot, his eyes fixed on the open door as though expecting someone to appear.

'Is there anybody there?' he asked.

When he didn't receive a reply, he shone his torch round the room. The library appeared to be empty. Had he imagined the whole thing? Someone might have been living there without permission. After all, the house hadn't been visited in years, not since the caretaker retired. There was no chance of being discovered there - the perfect place to hide out. They'd probably heard him moving about the house and had come to investigate, promptly beating a hasty retreat when they discovered him there. Was this the same person he'd seen the day before, watching him from the drive as he'd stood outside the gates?

He hurried out of the library, closing the door behind him. In the dust and rubble that covered the floor of the great hall, he saw only his own footprints. His squatter must have headed upstairs. He climbed the staircase, the warped boards creaking underfoot. Once on the landing, he followed the stairs that branched off to the right and reached the gallery where he came to the flaking portraits of his ancestors, their faces hidden under decades of dust and dirt.

Stopping at the first portrait he came to, he wiped away the grime to reveal a painting of a young man wearing a knee-length tailcoat, high-collared linen shirt and a perfectly tied cravat. James didn't know who he was but was eager to find out. He felt a tingle of excitement at the thought of learning about the lives of the men who had lived in the house and wondered what dark secrets he would uncover.

Leaving the gallery, he passed down the corridor to the bedrooms. The door to the first bedroom was ajar, so he entered the room. A feeble light straggling in through a gap in the shutters revealed a four-poster bed. The bed was made, and it didn't look like anyone had slept in it in years. He returned to the gallery and continued down the corridor on the other side of the house, passing empty, shuttered, forgotten rooms, until he came to a green baize door. Opening the door, he followed a staircase up to the second floor. Passing through another green baize door he was greeted by the almost unbearable smell of damp and decay. Flies swarmed round him as he walked on, and he found mould growing on the walls in one of the rooms further down the corridor. To his horror, he saw there was a hole in the ceiling where water had seeped into the room.

Clearly, no one was living in this part of the house.

Returning to the servants' staircase he ascended the steps and eventually reached a wooden door that he assumed led to the attic rooms. He tried the handle but found the door locked. Only then did he realise he'd left his keys where he'd dropped them in the library. Cursing himself, he hurried back downstairs. They were the only set he had - the only set he knew existed.

Upon entering the great hall, the light of his torch fell upon an old transistor radio lying in pieces at the foot of the staircase. There were no transistor radios in the nineteen-thirties, which meant it couldn't have been his great-uncle's. It must have belonged to whoever had broken into the house. Had something happened to the person who dropped it? Had they slipped and fallen down the rickety old staircase?

The thought sent a shiver running down his spine.

After retrieving the keys from the library, he opened the locked door and entered what appeared to be a study. In the centre of the room stood a rosewood desk. Reproductions of nineteenth-century paintings of fairy worlds hung on oak panelled walls. In one, fairies, goblins and elves had gathered in a giant wood. Others depicted scenes from Shakespeare's *A Midsummer Night's Dream.* The shutters covering the window in the room had been left open. On a table below the window, mounted on an octagonal brass base, were a series of interlocking and overlapping brass rings surrounding a wooden model of the Earth. On the desk stood an oil lamp with the same opaline white glass shade as the ones in the library.

Placing the keys down on the desk, he tried the desk's drawers but found them locked. A letter opener lay on a crested leather blotter next to a slightly rusty bronze desk calendar. The date shown on the calendar was the thirty-first of October. There was no year. He briefly considered using the letter opener to force open the drawers but thought better of it - he didn't want to damage the desk. He'd come across the keys eventually.

He remained at the house all day, exploring the rooms until the light started to fade. Through the door under the first arch, he discovered what looked like a sitting or reading room. Red curtains hung at the window and faded red damask wallpaper covered the walls. A Chippendale circular tea table stood below the window, and he discovered a two-seater chenille Chesterfield sofa hidden under a dust sheet.

At the end of the passageway, he came to another study. The room seemed slightly larger than the study next to the library, and he imagined it to be a lighter, airier room when its windows weren't shuttered. However, this room was not as well furnished as the other one, its desk wasn't as grand as its counterpart, being more functional than ornate. Solid mahogany bookcases, cabinets and a bureau lined the walls. The doors of the cabinets were locked, and business, finance and law books filled the shelves of the bookcases. Despite being built to replace the other study, he came to the conclusion it had ended up being used as an office, perhaps due to its proximity to the servants' quarters, and had probably been used by a secretary to manage the estate.

Moving on, he explored the rooms in the servants' quarters. Although this part of the house appeared to have been built more recently than the rest of the house, it seemed to have fallen into a state of disrepair earlier, long before his great-uncle had left the house. Chunks of plaster had fallen from the walls, leaving them bare. All the exterior doors in this part of the house were locked and the windows firmly secured. Again, he found no evidence to suggest anyone was living there, though he couldn't shake the feeling he was being watched as he made his way through the house.

As dusk fell, he explored the grounds and soon discovered the dilapidated stable block. The coaching house and cottage were no longer habitable, their roofs having caved in years ago. Passing through an open gate he walked onto a cobbled courtyard and saw part of the stable block had been converted into a garage. There, left to rust under a canvas tarpaulin, he found a Daimler limousine that he assumed had once belonged to his great-uncle. Apart from the car, a couple of rusting cans of Rimer's oil and some rags, the outbuilding was empty. Again, he found no evidence to suggest it had ever been occupied. Hidden away amongst oily rags he found a toolbox, in which he discovered, amongst other tools, a hammer. After deciding it would be best to replace the wooden planks he'd prised loose from outside the French window before leaving, he lifted out the hammer and made his way back up the winding track to the house, passing through the wood, the ancient trees creaking and groaning as they swayed in the wind.

By the time he left the house, twilight had turned to night. He would have liked to have stayed longer, but only had one night left at the Balmoral; he was booked on a train back to London in the morning. Reluctantly he made his way through the silent, pitch-black wood to the Range Rover and began his journey back to Edinburgh.

CHAPTER FIVE

Jolted from a nightmare, Will opened his eyes and glanced round the bedroom. Overhead, the uneven ceiling sagged through heavy oak beams. A draught stirred the heavy, moth-eaten curtains that hung at the window. He lay motionless, listening intently for a few minutes. The only sound he could hear was Miriam breathing gently as she slept in the bed next to his. The house seemed too quiet - eerily quiet.

Images from his nightmare filled his mind. Lost in a dark labyrinth of corridors and winding passageways, he glimpsed bare, unfurnished rooms. Empty windows looked out onto a barren landscape and bleak night sky. Hearing a scream echo throughout the house, he followed the cry down a spiral stone staircase and along a narrow passageway. Flickering torches illuminated the way. Many had burnt out leaving parts of the corridor hidden in dark shadows.

At the end of the corridor, a flight of steep steps led down into darkness. After removing one of the flaming torches from its wrought-iron bracket, he continued down the steps. Ahead, a heavy oak door with a barred window stood ajar. Pushing open the door, he stepped onto damp flagstones. Cracks ran across the bare, crumbling walls of a dark chamber. The light from the torch revealed a manacled prisoner hanging on the wall. His clothes were little more than rags that clung to his emancipated, skeletal body. Hearing him approach, the prisoner glanced up, the light from the torch hurting his eyes. A thick beard and matted hair concealed his bruised and bloodied face, but Will instantly recognised his friend's dark eyes.

'James!' he cried, his voice echoing round the chamber.

James tried to speak but his words were barely audible.

'It's all right,' said Will. 'I'm going to get you out of here.' He reached for one of the manacles in a vain effort to release his friend, but the shackle held tight. 'I'll go and get help.'

James shook his head. 'No,' he whispered. 'Get out of here before they come back.'

'Before who comes back?'

Footsteps echoed down the passageway outside. Terrified, Will turned to leave, stumbling on the uneven flagstones underfoot, the torch falling from his grip, the flame extinguishing as it hit the ground. Regaining his balance, he made for the open doorway, only to see the door swing shut on him. Realising he was a prisoner now too, he fell to his knees, the darkness engulfing him until there was nothing but silence.

The memory sent a shiver running down his spine.

Flinging aside his sheets, he sat up, dropping his legs over the side of his bed. According to his phone on the bedside table, it was a few minutes past eight. The fire had long burnt itself out, and although the radiator was warm to the touch, the room felt cold. Shivering, he dressed quickly, leaving before Miriam woke so as not to suffer the indignation of being asked to leave again.

Once on the gallery, he saw that even in daylight shadows draped the thick stone walls of the old medieval hall. The small-paned windows cut deeply into the walls let in very little light. Stepping off the staircase, he hurried across the hall's stone floor and entered the drawing room to find a table had been set before the bay window.

Moments later, Hodgson, carrying a breakfast tray piled with cutlery and plates, appeared through the other door.

'Good morning, sir,' he said. 'Did you sleep well?'

'Not particularly.' He found it hard to imagine anyone ever slept well there.

'I'm sorry to hear that.'

Will crossed the room, hoping to see the gardens, but instead was disappointed to find the house shrouded in an early morning mist. He could only see as far as the terrace. Puddles of water had formed from all the rain that had fallen overnight.

Hodgson placed the tray on a sideboard. 'Although the trees block out the sun in the morning,' he said, 'this is the warmest room in the house at this time of day. Once it had been two rooms; the breakfast room and dining room - the drawing room being where the current dining room is now.'

'Why doesn't James have the trees cut back?'

'Believe me, I have suggested it. The garden is at its best in the spring when the azaleas are in bloom.'

Will warmed himself before a crackling fire. 'I'll take your word for it,' he said. After a pause, he added, 'I don't know how you live in such a place. I wouldn't care to myself.'

Hodgson smiled. 'Over the years, I have become accustomed to living in draughty old houses. You'll find the house grows on you.' He turned to leave the room, pausing briefly in the doorway. 'You had similar reservations about the Manor once, didn't you? You soon grew to love it there.'

Yes, I did, thought Will.

During their first summer together, Will met James almost every day, but one morning, when he stood waiting under the oak tree, its heavy shade keeping him hidden from view, his friend didn't appear. After waiting for about an hour he decided he must have gone out with his parents and reluctantly returned home, vowing to return the following day. But the next day, when James failed to appear for a second time, he began to wonder if something had happened to him. That night, unable to sleep, he lay in bed worrying about his friend. If James didn't appear tomorrow, he told himself, he'd go to the house to make sure he was all right.

By then he'd had to confess to his parents where he was spending his days. He hadn't wanted to - they'd always told him to stay away from the Manor. To avoid getting into trouble, he casually mentioned he'd met James in the village one day. After introducing himself, he'd been invited to the house. The truth was he'd never been inside the house, even going so far as to hide from the gardener whenever he saw him, worried what would happen when James's parents found out who he was.

The following morning, he woke early to find the village still sleeping, warm and snug under a thick blanket of grey cloud. When James didn't appear for the third time, he decided to go to the house to check on him. He knew he couldn't just walk up to the house from the gardens. He'd have to approach the house from the drive. The thought filled him with dread. He wondered what James's parents would say to him when he turned up on their doorstep.

The first drops of rain had begun to fall as he hurried past his cottage and headed into the graveyard. By the time he reached the High Street, the rain began falling heavily. A young couple ran past him, seeking shelter in the doorway of the village shop. Quickening his pace, he ran down the road that led to an old farm, avoiding the puddles that were beginning to form, and stepped over a stile into a field. From the road, he heard cars hum past, but he paid them no attention as he ran across the field, his eyes fixed on the gates to the Manor visible at the far end of the enclosure.

When he saw they were open he swallowed convulsively, pausing momentarily before continuing down the drive. He stopped before the iron railings, his eyes scanning the gardens. The gardener was nowhere to be seen so he pushed open the gate and stepped onto the lavender lined path that led to the house.

'Who are you? What do you want here?'

Spinning round, he saw the gardener standing in the shade of a tree, a wheelbarrow at his side, a cigarette dangling out of his mouth.

'I'm James's friend from the village,' he said.

The old man left the shelter of the tree. 'Master Roxburgh doesn't have any friends in the village,' he said, lurching forward as Will turned to leave, grabbing his arm. 'Wait a minute, I know you. I've seen you sneaking through the gardens.'

Will glanced up at his face. He had red cheeks and a bulbous nose. His teeth were stained, and his breath smelt of stale tobacco.

'Let go of me!'

'You're not going anywhere -' He paused when he saw a woman appear from the house.

Will considered running away but the gardener still had a hold of him.

She asked him his name, but Will, too scared to reply, fell silent.

The gardener tightened his grip. 'Answer the lady.'

'That's all right, Reg. You can get back to work now.'

'Yes, ma'am.' He released Will's arm and made his way back towards his wheelbarrow, grumbling to himself as he went.

Will rubbed his arm. 'I've come to see James,' he said.

James's mother smiled at him kindly. 'He's not well, I'm afraid.'

'What's wrong with him? He's not contagious, is he?'

James's mother shook her head. 'No. You don't have to worry about that. Would you like to see him?'

Will nodded and she led the way into the house.

James's bedroom was in darkness, the curtains pulled too, although Will could just make out his friend lying in his bed. Sat at his side was a grey-haired man he assumed was his father.

When James saw Will he became upset and started screaming at his mother. 'Get out of here!' he cried, rolling over in his bed, hiding in the covers.

Before Will knew what was happening, Jamcs's mother ushered him out of the room. He could hear his friend crying into his pillow as his mother pulled the door too. She apologised to him, and when they made their way downstairs, he noticed there were tears in her eyes. He didn't understand what was going on. He thought it was something he'd done, though James's mother assured him it wasn't his fault.

The rain had stopped by the time Will left the house. As he made his way back down the lavender lined path, he heard James calling to him and turned to see his friend step out of the house. He'd dressed, though his hair was ruffled, and his cheeks were still stained with tears.

'Wait for me,' he said casually, following his friend down the path.

Will glanced at James's mother who nodded and gave a faint smile.

James gestured for Will to follow him into the gardens. 'What are you waiting for?' he said.

Will ran after his friend. 'Where are we going?' he asked.

But James didn't reply, running on through the gardens until their voices could no longer be heard by his mother.

Will hadn't been back to the village since leaving almost six years before, and in that time hadn't given it much thought. He wondered if the village had changed since he was last there. It seemed unlikely - it hadn't changed in decades. Another family now lived in the cottage he grew up in. He wondered if a young boy was living there now who was as curious as he'd been about the Manor. Had he found the tree stump down the path, hidden away amongst the weeds and brambles? Had he climbed over the wall and explored the grounds as he had?

When Hodgson returned, Will asked him about the old gardener, curious to know what happened to him.

'He retired years ago,' said Hodgson. 'He still visits occasionally, getting in the way of the other gardeners and generally making a nuisance of himself.'

Will glanced out of the French window. Through the swirling mist, he caught sight of a vague, indistinct figure of a man in the garden, not far from the house. For a moment he thought he might be James, but it seemed unlikely he was up and about at such an early hour. Then he remembered the man at the lodge who let them through the gates. It had to be him. The man disappeared from view and Will thought no more about him.

'How long was James alone in the house?' he asked.

'I left in the middle of August and returned towards the end of September. I had to leave so suddenly there wasn't time to arrange for someone to take my place.'

'What happened to James wasn't your fault,' said Will. He's not a child, he thought. He should be able to fend for himself.

'Upon my return, I tried to convince him to leave. Of course, he refused. He wouldn't even contact his parents. It was then that I reminded him of the promise he made to you. Your presence always seemed to reassure him when he wasn't feeling well.'

Will had come to realise that was why, despite their different backgrounds, their friendship had been encouraged. Whenever James was feeling depressed, he'd been said to have been 'not feeling well' for as long as he could remember. He suspected it was for the benefit of his mother who blamed herself for the way he was. His father had always coped better than she had. Will had, however, considered it a mistake. In later years James had found it difficult to discuss his condition, never admitting to anyone how he was feeling, which had only made matters worse.

After pouring coffee from a large chrome cafetière into a cup, he sat himself down at the breakfast table and waited for the others to join him.

*

Alexander pulled a Harris Tweed jacket over his tattersall check shirt and turned to admire himself in a mirror. He straightened his tie, pausing momentarily to admire the stags' heads embroidered onto the fabric. Behind him, Jemima slept peacefully in their bed, her face buried in a pillowcase.

Alexander shook her foot that stuck out from under the sheets. 'Wake up, Jemima.'

She turned sleepily on her pillow, her large dark eyes opening slowly. 'What time is it?'

'It's almost nine. You'd better get a move on, or we'll miss breakfast.'

Jemima pulled the sheets over her head. 'Don't wait for me. I'll follow you down in a bit.'

'Make sure you do.'

Alexander left the room, closing the door behind him. Before starting down the corridor, he paused briefly outside Will and Miriam's room. No sound came from within. They've probably gone down to breakfast already, he told himself.

As he descended the staircase, he began singing a song to himself.

"The Stately Homes of England,
How beautiful they stand,
To prove the upper classes
Have still the upper hand …"

When he entered the drawing room, Hodgson bid him a good morning. 'Did you have a good night's sleep, sir?'

'I'm afraid so.'

Will glanced up at him from the breakfast table, his attention drawn to the breeks, long socks and country brogues he was wearing.

'Why on earth are you dressed like that?' he asked.

'These are my hunting tweeds,' replied Alexander. He glanced at Will and saw he was wearing chinos and a shawl collar cardigan. 'I'd ask you why you aren't wearing yours, but there wouldn't be much point.'

Will sipped his coffee. 'What were you planning on hunting?'

'Lagopus lagopus scotica,' said Alexander proudly. Seeing Will stare blankly at him, he added, 'Red grouse man!'

'You've arranged a day's shooting in the area?' asked Hodgson.

'I was under the impression the estate included a grouse moor.'

'I'm afraid not, sir.'

'Well, I'll just have to settle for pheasant.'

'Pheasant hasn't been reared on the estate for over seventy years.'

'Partridge?' said Alexander hopefully.

'Master James has yet to employ the services of a gamekeeper.'

'How very remiss of Master James.'

Out in the great hall, a grandfather clock chimed the hour.

'If you'll excuse me,' said Hodgson. 'I'll see to breakfast.' Turning on his heels, he left the room.

Alexander poured himself a cup of coffee and joined Will at the breakfast table. 'I was expecting two days of hard shooting.'

'Well, you'll just have to find other ways to amuse yourself.'

'Yes, I suppose I will.'

Miriam, wearing a fleece gilet and long country tweed skirt, silently entered the room. Both Will and Alexander thought better of asking her if she'd slept well. She sat down at the breakfast table without saying a word and looked expectantly across the room.

'What are you waiting for?' asked Alexander.

'Breakfast …'

'Hodgson's in the kitchen,' said Will. 'He'll be through in a minute. There's coffee if you want it. You'll have to get it yourself.'

'Has James no other staff?' grumbled Miriam.

'This isn't a hotel, Miriam,' said Alexander.

Miriam sighed and said, 'Why does everyone insist on telling me that?' She rose from her seat and crossed to the sideboard. 'I am all too aware of the fact.'

Alexander marmaladed some toast. 'Jemima didn't get a wink of sleep last night,' he said. 'Claimed she kept hearing things in the middle of the night. This old place petrifies her. She was a nervous wreck when we went to bed last night. Certainly spoilt my plans for the evening, I don't mind telling you.'

'We don't wish to know, Alexander,' snapped Miriam.

Moments later, Jemima entered the room wearing Alexander's monogrammed silk pyjamas.

'Good morning,' she said drowsily. She sat down next to Alexander, snuggling up to him. 'It's chilly in here. I'm freezing.'

Miriam looked at her with disdain. 'Then I suggest in future you dress for breakfast like the rest of us.'

Jemima brushed the untidy curls of her hair away from her face and glanced at Miriam. 'While you're there,' she said, 'could you be a sweetie and grab me a cup of coffee?'

Miriam glared back at her, huffed and proceeded to pour out a further cup of coffee. When she returned to the table, she asked what their plans were for the day.

'Apparently,' said Alexander, 'there's no grouse.'

'No grouse?' said Miriam incredulously.

'No pheasant or partridge either. There's not even any blasted woodcock!' He saw Hodgson enter the room pushing a hostess trolley. 'There's no woodcock, is there Hodgson?'

Hodgson parked the trolley before the sideboard. 'I'm afraid not, sir.'

'Miriam Crenshaw,' said Alexander, 'you brought me here under false pretences.'

'When one is invited to a country estate,' said Miriam, 'one naturally assumes they will be spending the weekend shooting.'

'You shoot, Miriam?' asked Will.

'And how!' said Alexander. 'She once bagged fifty-seven pheasants for sixty-four cartridges.'

'Am I supposed to be impressed by that?'

'I certainly was,' said Alexander. 'She's a sight to behold with a 12-bore in her hand. I was looking forward to seeing her in action again.' He sighed. 'Oh well,' he continued, 'you're never far from a decent golf course in Scotland.' He glanced at his watch. 'If I hurry, I could be teeing off before lunch.'

Jemima sipped her coffee. 'You're not planning on spending the weekend playing golf, are you?'

'No, of course not. Tomorrow I think I'll try my hand at fishing. Hodgson, do you know where I could hire a decent ghillie for the day?'

'I'm afraid not, sir.'

'I am not spending the day fishing,' said Jemima.

'I didn't think for one moment that *you* would,' said Alexander.

'I imagine there are lots of nice walks in the area,' said Will. 'How about heading up onto the moors instead?'

'No golf, fishing or walking!' cried Jemima. 'I want to have some fun this weekend!'

'Can you play bridge?' asked Miriam. 'We need a fourth.'

'I'm sorry,' said Jemima sweetly. 'I don't play. Why don't we have a party tonight? We could drink cocktails, listen to music on that old gramophone, dance -'

Miriam stared icily at Jemima. 'Dance …'

Undeterred, Jemima continued. 'Why not?' she asked.

'Well, for a start,' said Alexander, 'there's not even enough of us for a decent Scottish reel.'

'I'm sure we'll cope. Come on, let's see if we can breathe some life into this old place.'

'Someone should try breathing some life into James. What's wrong with him anyway? He looks terrible.'

'He hasn't been well,' said Will.

'Clearly,' said Miriam. 'Will he be gracing us with his presence this morning?'

'I'm afraid Master James will not be joining you for breakfast,' said Hodgson. 'He hopes to join you for lunch.'

'Is he all right?' asked Will with concern in his voice. 'Can I see him?'

Hodgson shook his head. 'He doesn't wish to be disturbed.'

'Just like James,' said Alexander. 'Never was an early riser. At university, you could never get him out of bed before midday. He always was a creature of the night.'

'He's not the only one,' said Jemima. 'Isobel's not up yet either.'

*

Upstairs in her bedroom, Isobel woke suddenly, her eyes flicking open. Disorientated, it took her a moment or two to realise where she was. Then, from somewhere in the house, a clock chimed the hour. She lay in bed listening to the chimes, counting ten in all.

She sat up suddenly. It was ten o'clock!

She slipped out from under the covers and shivered. The room was cold, the windows covered in condensation. She dressed quickly, slipping on her jeans and a chunky cable knit jumper, before hurrying downstairs.

In the drawing room she found Will standing by the sideboard. He smiled when he saw her.

'Sorry I'm late,' she said, neatening up her dishevelled hair. 'I must look terrible.' She hoped it didn't look too obvious she'd dressed in a hurry.

'Not in the slightest,' said Will. 'Would you like some coffee?'

'Yes, please.' She glanced round the room. Alexander, Miriam and Jemima were sitting at the table, talking amongst themselves. They hadn't noticed her slip into the room. 'Where's James?'

'He's … resting. He hopes to join us for lunch.'

'How did you get on with him last night?'

'He refused to leave the house until it's finished. How long that will take is anyone's guess.'

'Well,' said Isobel, 'you'll just have to persevere with him.'

'Why me?'

'Because he'll listen to you - he always did.'

Will looked doubtful. 'Maybe once. Not anymore.' After pouring some coffee from the cafetière into a cup, he led Isobel over to the table to join the others.

When Jemima saw her approach, she said, 'We're going to have a party.' Her enthusiasm was childlike and infectious.

Isobel glanced across the table at Will. 'We are?'

'Apparently,' he said, sitting down.

'It's a shame we don't have any fancy-dress costumes to wear,' said Jemima.

'On the contrary,' replied Miriam, 'I would have thought it rather fortunate.'

Alexander frowned. 'What do you want to dress up for?' he asked tentatively, dreading the answer.

'Because it's Halloween tomorrow,' said Jemima.

Embarrassed, Alexander made a dull grunting sound.

'There's bound to be a dressing up box somewhere in this house,' said Will.

Miriam looked at him with undisguised distaste.

'I found some old dresses in my wardrobe,' said Isobel. 'They're in remarkably good condition. Some look as though they date back to the nineteen twenties.'

Jemima's face lit up. 'You must show me them.'

'I'll show you them after breakfast if you like.'

Miriam cast her a withering look. 'We finished breakfast ten minutes ago.'

*

When Hodgson went to clear away the dishes, Isobel, Jemima and Will insisted on being allowed to help him wash up. Reluctantly he agreed, and leaving the drawing room, led them to the kitchen.

'The first room we'll come to is the butler's pantry,' he said. 'It separates the family rooms from the servant's quarters.'

Pausing to investigate the room, Jemima asked Hodgson how long he'd been working for James's family.

'It must be almost twenty years now,' he said. 'Initially, I was employed by James's grandfather to help him put his affairs in order during his illness. Following his death, I managed the Manor for James's grandmother who wasn't quite up to the task herself at the time.'

Both Will and Isobel listened with interest. These were questions they'd wanted to know the answers to for years, questions they'd thought too impertinent to ask as children.

'She'd planned to sell the property until James's father announced his intention to live there, moving from Belgravia with his family in '93. I've been with them ever since.'

'Hodgson had the unfortunate task of trying to supervise us as we ran riot through the house,' said Isobel.

'They'd disappear for hours without telling me where they were going, or what time they would be back.'

'I'm afraid to say we were often very badly behaved,' added Will.

'You must have thought us quite impossible,' said Isobel.

Hodgson smiled and said, 'I've only fond memories of our time together.'

Isobel noticed a set of black cast iron skeleton keys hanging on the wall. 'Are those the keys James found in the attic?' she asked.

'A room they were expressly told to stay out of,' Hodgson told Jemima. He glanced back at Isobel. 'They're all we have,' he said. 'The caretaker would have had a set, but we didn't find any others in the house. If there were any more, they were lost years ago.'

Faded black and white photographs lined the walls. In one an elderly man posed with a hunting rifle in his hand, his wolfhounds sat obediently at his side. A gamekeeper lingered in the background.

'I assume that's James's great-grandfather, George Roxburgh,' said Will.

Hodgson nodded and said, 'He owned the house at the turn of the century - the last century that is. There's another photograph of him here somewhere, taken during one of the hunting parties held here.' He found the photograph on the opposite wall and pointed out a young man. 'That's Edward, the son he lost in the First World War.'

In another photograph, the servants were assembled outside the house. The housekeeper, sitting on a seat with a large bunch of keys in her hand, took centre stage. Maids in starched uniforms sat alongside her, a young boy at their feet. Behind them stood the stern-faced butler, the groom, and a footman holding a silver salver.

'My grandfather worked in many houses like this one during his life,' said Hodgson, 'moving up the ranks from hall boy to butler. The hours were long and the work was hard. Both his employers and co-workers could be cruel. He used to tell me awful stories, though admitted there were perks to the job - as if that somehow made it all right. Your laundry was done for you, coal fires kept you warm and you had your meals provided, including vegetables and fruit from the garden - which was considerably better than what many were living on at the time.'

Will studied the other photographs of the servants and wondered how many that worked there dreamt of a better life, but, through an accident of birth, found themselves forced into a life of servitude.

'The Second World War saw the demise of the landed gentry in England,' said Hodgson. 'My grandfather's generation was the last to work in their country houses. Only in the largest homes did service survive.'

Leaving the pantry, they followed the corridor past the laundry and a cramped scullery with a sink and wooden draining racks. The workrooms had thin narrow windows that overlooked a small, enclosed courtyard.

'My father,' continued Hodgson, 'who had been raised into service, had to find work elsewhere. He became a gentleman's gentleman, a valet to a wealthy bachelor living in London, though his career as a manservant came to an end with the outbreak of the Second World War. When he returned to Civvy Street he found the world he'd known had all but disappeared. Bewildered by the cultural and social changes that took place in post-war Britain, both my father and grandfather often became nostalgic for the ordered world they'd once been a part of.'

They reached a small flight of stairs leading down to the

cavernous kitchen. Before descending the stairs, Hodgson pointed out the servant's hall opposite. At the far end of the kitchen, under a giant chimney arch, stood a blackened range. Through the high windows, a shaft of sunlight fell onto the polished surface of a solid work table that stood in the centre of the room. Copper pans and moulds, their sheens tarnished, sat on the shelves of a sturdy dresser. On the wall beside the dresser hung a calendar from 1938.

Once everything had been cleaned and put away, they left the kitchen and headed back through the old house, Will returning to the drawing room to rejoin Miriam and Alexander. He expected Isobel and Jemima to accompany him, but they skirted past the room, continuing down a passageway that led to the great hall.

As they crossed the stone floor and headed for the staircase, Jemima took Isobel's hand in hers, her eyes fixed on the way ahead. Once they were on the gallery, she avoided the shadows, never once glancing at the portraits hanging on the walls. Since arriving at the house, Isobel had felt unwelcome, not just by their host, but by the house too, almost as if it resented her presence there. She found it oddly reassuring to find Jemima shared her sense of unease.

Only when they were in the bedroom did she let go of her hand.

'What a gorgeous room,' she said, her eyes wide with awe.

'I feel a bit guilty sleeping in here by myself,' replied Isobel. 'The bed's far too big for just one person.'

Jemima's astonished gaze came to rest on the four-poster bed. 'I've never slept on a four-poster before. It looks very comfortable,' she said enviously. 'We could always swap rooms if you like.'

'Thanks, but I don't feel that guilty.' Isobel led her over to the wardrobe. 'The dresses are in here.'

Jemima opened the doors and looked at the gowns and dresses hanging inside. 'I didn't realise there would be so many,' she said, her eyes coming to rest on a shimmering gold brocade evening gown.

'Why don't you try it on?'

The long flowing dress tumbled to the floor as Jemima removed it from the wardrobe.

'You don't think James would mind?' she asked.

Isobel shook her head. 'Of course not,' she said. 'You can

change in the bathroom if you like.'

Whilst changing, Jemima told Isobel all about her life as a background dancer. She'd started her career when she was still a teenager and soon learnt that life as a dancer wasn't as glamorous as she'd imagined. The industry proved competitive and ruthless, but, undaunted, she'd worked hard, appearing on television and in music videos before eventually making it to the West End. Isobel admired her confidence. She couldn't imagine how she plucked up the courage to audition on a bare stage, especially at such a young age.

She appeared from the bathroom wearing the gown. It was just the right length and fitted her perfectly.

'It's like something out of a Hollywood film,' she said, turning to look at herself in the mirror. 'When I was a little girl, I used to watch old films with my grandmother. She loved the lavish MGM musicals, but my favourites were the black and white films Fred Astaire and Ginger Rogers made for RKO. They danced so elegantly and gracefully together … I hope Alexander knows how to dance.'

Isobel pictured a young Alexander lumbering across a dance floor, his arms flying all over the place.

'You haven't known him very long, have you?' she asked.

'No,' said Jemima hesitantly.

She admitted to Isobel that she didn't usually make a habit of spending the weekend away with men she'd just met but needed to get out of London for a couple of days. Ever since she'd split up with her boyfriend, she'd been finding it hard to get work. She seemed to be stuck in a rut, spending her days going from one audition to another, joining longer and longer queues of younger and younger girls.

'I guess my heart's just not in it at the moment,' she continued. 'I couldn't face another weekend alone, wondering if I should just jack it all in and look for work elsewhere … which was why when Alexander invited me here, I jumped at the chance.'

Isobel couldn't help but sympathise with her. She'd spent all summer going from one interview to another alongside dozens of others all vying for a place as an unpaid intern. When she left university, she'd thought she was going to be the next big thing in the fashion industry. Now she was beginning to wonder if she'd even get her foot in the door.

'To tell the truth,' continued Jemima, 'I don't usually go for men like Alexander.' She preferred actors and musicians - or rather she did. 'The problem with creative types is they're too impulsive, not to mention unreliable.' Although neither of their careers was conducive to a successful relationship, she thought she could build a future with her boyfriend. 'I should have known better.' After a pause, she continued. 'I made myself a promise I'd only see normal men from now on.'

'I don't think you could describe Alexander as normal.'

'He works regular hours and has a steady income. That's normal enough for me.'

Isobel had always been wary of men like Alexander. She'd met far too many like him during her time in London. While she envied Jemima's ability to throw caution to the wind, she wouldn't have accepted Alexander's invitation after only knowing him for a short time, preferring to take a more cautious approach to relationships.

Jemima sat herself down on the chaise-longue, curving her long legs under her. 'So, are you seeing anyone at the moment?' she asked.

It was the inevitable question. The one she was always asked without fail, and the one she always dreaded answering.

'No, I'm not,' she said, 'Despite the best efforts of my friends, I'm still single. Between announcing their engagements and planning their weddings, they seem to spend their time trying to set me up with someone. You'd think they had better things to do with their time. Is it so hard to believe I'm just not interested in seeing anyone right now? You know, one of my friends even accused me of having an affair with a married man.'

'Are you?' said Jemima teasingly.

Isobel smiled. 'No, I'm not,' she said. 'I prefer unmarried, single men.'

'James doesn't appear to be seeing anyone at the moment.'

'Not at the moment - but he was never single when I knew him. He had a girlfriend from about the age of fifteen until just before he left home for university.'

'That's a shame,' said Jemima. 'I imagine you two would have made a very handsome couple.'

'They made a more handsome one, believe me,' said Isobel. 'Anyway, James has always been like a brother to me, and I a sister to him. We were very close … once,' she added, remembering the awkwardness of their meeting.

'Once? Not anymore?'

'I haven't seen him in years. I was in two minds about accepting his invitation.'

'Why did you?'

'Because the time I spent with James and Will at the Manor was the happiest of my life. That sounds so sad, doesn't it? As though my life had been awful ever since then. It hasn't, of course, but I have very fond memories of my time at the Manor.' Turning, she glanced out of the bay window and stared at the horizon. 'I can still remember sneaking out of the house with James, our excitement building as we ran to meet Will. We'd always find him waiting for us under the oak tree at the bottom of the garden every day without fail, ready to take us on another adventure.'

'Will? Really?'

'You seem surprised.'

'He seems a little stuffy to me.'

'He wasn't when I knew him.'

She suddenly felt a pang of regret. So much had happened since they were last together. She had her own life now and a whole different circle of friends. The summers they'd spent together were becoming a distant memory to her.

CHAPTER SIX

They were halfway through eating lunch when it became apparent that James would not be joining them. Hodgson hadn't set a place for him at the table and this time provided no explanation for his absence. Only Will and Isobel seemed to notice he wasn't present; the others having grown accustomed to him not being around.

'People are always extolling the virtues of the countryside,' said Alexander, swallowing down the last mouthful of his pork pie before continuing. 'Emphasizing the fresh air and wide open spaces.' He finished off a second glass of wine. 'Since arriving, I've done nothing but eat, drink and smoke. I'm beginning to feel decidedly unhealthy.'

He remained dressed in his hunting tweeds, while Miriam had changed out of hers, reverting to her customary twin set and pearls.

'Can we try to have an intelligent conversation for once?' she suggested.

'I'd rather we didn't,' said Alexander. 'Intelligent conversations are invariably dull.'

Jemima twirled a lock of her hair round her finger. 'Does Hodgson know we're going to have a party tonight?'

Isobel nodded and said, 'He's going to prepare a light dinner for us.'

'Did you find something to wear tonight?' asked Will.

'Yes, we both did,' replied Jemima. 'Are you sure you won't reconsider wearing one of the dresses, Miriam?'

'I'm sure,' said Miriam coldly.

When everyone had finished eating, Isobel suggested they go through to the drawing room. Jemima leapt nimbly to her feet, took Isobel's arm and led her out of the room.

When they were out of earshot, Miriam sighed. 'Oh, God,' she said, standing up, 'this evening is going to be unbearable.'

'You never know,' replied Alexander, 'you might enjoy yourself.'

She fixed him with a withering stare. 'It seems highly unlikely,' she said, before promptly leaving the room.

Alexander shivered. 'Now I know what it felt to stare into the eyes of Medusa.' He followed the others out of the room.

Will offered to help clear away, but this time Hodgson refused his assistance.

When he joined the others in the drawing room, he saw Miriam had sat herself down in one of the armchairs, a book in hand, a pair of half-moon glasses perched on the end of her nose. Isobel sat cross-legged on the floor, flicking through a pile of old 78s she'd found stored inside the gramophone cabinet while chatting to Jemima who lay on the sofa.

Alexander had made his way over to the drinks cabinet.

'Care to join me?' he asked.

Will declined courteously. 'Bit early for me yet,' he said. 'But you go ahead.'

'Don't mind if I do,' he said. 'Keeps out the cold.' As he fixed himself a whisky and soda he glanced round the room. 'Are there any papers?'

'I haven't seen any.'

'No papers, no radio, just that old gramophone,' said Alexander despondently. He sat down on the sofa next to Jemima. 'What on earth does James do with himself? I've been here less than a day and already I am bored out of my mind.'

Miriam glanced at him over the top of her glasses. 'Perhaps he reads,' she said. 'Why don't you try reading a book?'

Alexander gave a derisive grunt. 'Never read a book for pleasure in my life. Not going to start now.'

'You surprise me.'

Will wandered over to the French window. The mist was lifting, and the trees were taking shape beyond the lawns. He could just make out an indistinct, dim figure raking up leaves.

Isobel joined him at the window. 'It's clearing up out there,' she said. 'We should be able to go out for a walk soon.'

Will nodded in agreement.

Since arriving, he'd been eager to speak to her. He wanted to know what she'd been up to in the six years since he last saw her. But now he had the opportunity to talk to her he found himself speechless, not knowing what to say. Once they had been close; now they were as distant as strangers. He'd expected nothing less. After all, they hadn't seen each other in years. She'd probably forgotten all about him.

But then not a day had gone by when he hadn't thought about her.

She asked after his mother, and he told her she was living on the coast near her sister.

After a pause, he said, 'So you're living in London now?'

Isobel nodded. 'At my aunt's flat in a mews near Grosvenor Square,' she said. 'She hasn't been back to England in years. When she learnt I was looking for a place to live after I finished university, she offered it to me.'

'Where did you go in the end?'

'I studied fashion design at the Istituto Marangoni.'

'Is that in London?'

'The one I went to is, though I spent my placement year in Milan. Whilst there, I took the opportunity to see as much of Italy as I could. Did you ever get to go travelling?'

Will shook his head. 'No, I didn't,' he replied. 'I never found the time.' Or the money, he thought.

'I'm sure you will, one day.'

Considering how much debt he was in - added to the fact he was spending a third of his income on rent - he thought it unlikely. Out of the corner of his eye, he noticed Miriam eyeing them suspiciously from across the room.

Alexander fidgeted uncomfortably on the sofa and let out a long-drawn-out sigh.

Miriam put down her book and glared at him. 'For heaven's sake, Alexander, will you please sit still!'

'I've been sitting still all morning. I want to do something.'

'How about a walk?' suggested Isobel. 'We could explore the gardens …'

Jemima sprang to her feet. 'Well, I'm game,' she said enthusiastically. 'Aren't you going to join us, Alexander?'

Alexander glanced at Miriam. 'How about a tour of the gardens and a leisurely stroll across the lawns, Miriam?'

Removing her glasses, Miriam polished them with a cloth. 'It's cold enough inside,' she said, replacing them on her thin, narrow nose. 'I imagine it will be even more unbearable outside.'

Alexander stretched himself out on the sofa. 'Having just warmed myself up,' he said, 'I'm inclined to agree.'

'Then it's just the three of us,' said Jemima, ushering Will and Isobel out of the room.

*

After collecting their coats from their bedrooms, they ventured outside, leaving the house through the entrance porch, a cold northerly wind blowing upon them as they crossed the courtyard.

Zipping up her gilet, Jemima asked Will how long Alexander and Miriam had known each other.

'For a couple of years now,' he said, leading the way across the sunken lawn. 'Ever since Alexander started working at Crenshaw, Willoughby and Stern.'

'Does Miriam work for the firm too?'

'No,' replied Will. 'She's a barrister.'

'Is that why she was so reluctant to make me a coffee?'

'No, that was for a completely different reason. She's a barrist*er*, working in chambers in Lincoln's Inn, but she has her sights set on becoming a judge.' Something Will secretly considered a terrifying prospect. 'They may have known each other at Marlborough. I'm not really sure.'

He noticed the roses had yet to be pruned back ready for winter.

'Have they ever been in a relationship together?'

'Not that I'm aware of. If they did, it didn't last for long. Alexander's relationships are invariably brief - though I'm sure you'll be the exception,' he added hastily.

Jemima smiled. 'I'm sure I won't,' she said.

Will turned to Isobel. 'I've been meaning to ask - how does your brother know Miriam?'

'I think they were in the same year at Marlborough.'

Will tried to remember how old Isobel's brothers were. 'Which one? Tom?'

'No … Philip.'

'How much older is your older brother Philip?'

Isobel hesitated. 'Older,' she said tactfully.

'You have older brothers?' asked Jemima.

'Half-brothers,' explained Isobel. 'From Clive's - my father's - first marriage. I'm afraid I hardly ever see them. Philip followed in his father's footsteps and joined the Royal Navy, and Tom works for a hedge fund management firm in New York.'

Jemima told them she was from a large family and had two older sisters and a younger brother. She asked Will if he had any siblings.

'Not that I'm aware of,' said Will. 'I was adopted at an early age. I never knew my birth parents. Unfortunately, my adoptive parents couldn't tell me anything about them.'

'When we were younger,' said Isobel, 'James and I believed Will to be an exiled prince who'd been smuggled out of his country when a violent revolution had taken place. We fantasised about how, when he'd grown up, he'd return to his kingdom, overthrow those who had deposed him and take his rightful place as king of his realm.'

Will smiled and said, 'I must get round to that one day.'

Passing through an open gateway they wandered into the walled garden. Impenetrable barriers of brambles barred their way. The borders and flowerbeds were lost to weeds and wildflowers. Saplings grew up against crumbling stone walls overrun with moss and lichen.

When Isobel suggested a walk down to the river instead, they retraced their steps, making their way back across the sunken lawn.

*

From the sofa, Alexander glanced listlessly in Miriam's direction to find her engrossed in her novel.

'What are you reading anyway?' he asked.

She held up the book and he read the title: Georgette Heyer's *Regency Buck*.

'I found it over there,' she explained, gesturing to a bookcase behind him.

'Looks like one of those ghastly romantic novels. What's it about?' He held up his hand. 'No, don't tell me, let me guess. A virtuous young woman falls head over heels in love with a womanising cad who doesn't even know she exists.' He paused for a moment and then went on thoughtfully. 'For some convoluted reason they are thrown together, then over the course of the novel, he realises he's in love with her and she forgives his wicked ways. Am I right?'

'Really,' said Miriam, without batting an eyelid, 'you've spoilt the ending for me now.'

'I don't know why you read that rot. Nothing but a load of old nonsense - has no bearing on real-life whatsoever.'

'Oh, you'd be surprised …'

Out of the corner of her eye, she noticed Alexander lean forward, open a humidor and lift out a cigar.

'You're not going to smoke that in here, are you?' she said, without turning to face him.

'Apparently not.' Alexander returned the cigar to its box, snapping the lid shut.

He recalled a conversation he'd had with her father not long after he'd started working for Crenshaw, Willoughby and Stern. One night, after a long day at the office, they'd gone for a drink at their club together. Bill had a few too many whisky and sodas and had revealed more about his personal life than Alexander had cared to know. Thankfully, the details were a little sketchy as he'd been sailing three sheets to the wind himself. Apparently, her mother had left or died - he couldn't remember which - when Miriam was just a few years old. Unable to raise her alone, Bill had left her in the care of others until she was old enough to be packed off to boarding school. Naturally, he'd wanted to be there for her, but it had been a busy time in his life. If he hadn't put the hours in then he wouldn't be the director of a prestigious law firm. It was a decision he'd grown to regret.

'I know you are going to tell me it's none of my business,' said Alexander, 'but I've noticed you've become increasingly cold towards young William over the last week or so.'

Theirs had never been the most passionate relationship he'd known. The only time he'd seen them kiss was when she'd dragged them to an awful Tapas restaurant after a particularly steamy production of Bizet's *Carmen*, had one too many glasses of Amontillado sherry, and got carried away with herself.

'Since arriving here your behaviour towards your young beau

has bordered on the downright frosty.'

'You're right,' said Miriam. 'It is none of your business.'

Bill had been the one who'd introduced Miriam to Will. Worried she was becoming increasingly cold and distant, and fearing she'd end up a spinster, he'd often introduce her to the young trainees who passed through the office. Miriam, resenting her father's interference in her personal life, paid them scant regard. Will was no exception. During his first nine months at the firm, Miriam took no notice of him, or he of her for that matter, when she'd popped into the office to see her father, going out of her way to appear aloof. So, it came as some surprise when, at Bill's sixtieth, she invited Will to the theatre. Alexander remembered she'd been due to go with him, but he'd made other arrangements, leaving her with an extra ticket.

On the following Monday, when they were back at work, Will told him they'd had a pleasant enough evening, but nothing more. Alexander thought that was that until the following week when Miriam told him she'd invited him to join them for dinner. He was taking someone with him so didn't see why not. Their relationship moved slowly - too slowly in his opinion - and had seemed destined to fizzle out due to a lack of enthusiasm from both parties. Had it not been for Bill's intervention they probably would have stopped seeing each other. He'd been the one who suggested they spend a weekend away together, preferably at a nice hotel in the country somewhere, the further away from London the better.

Will, who couldn't afford a stay in the type of hotel Miriam was accustomed to, dismissed the idea. He was sure she would refuse anyway. It was only when he received James's invitation to Wychwood House that he changed his mind. Miriam seemed reluctant to join him, making up all sorts of excuses why she couldn't go, though eventually agreed, probably at the insistence of her father.

Alexander wondered if Miriam was taking things slow because she was being cautious, getting to know Will before taking things further. Others had questioned his motives for seeing her - maybe she too had suspicions. They were probably being unfair to him. He thought Will a genuine, amiable, decent enough person, if a little dull.

But then, as he knew only too well, appearances could be deceptive.

'I know his upbringing and deplorable lack of a decent education leaves a lot to be desired,' he continued, 'but the way he's managed to pull himself up by his bootstraps has been quite admirable.'

'Please,' said Miriam, 'I had enough of my father singing his praises yesterday.'

A look of concern crossed Alexander's face. 'He was?'

Miriam suppressed a smile. 'Apparently, William has a bright future ahead of him.'

'He does?'

'I admit I had reservations about him, to begin with, but lately, I've grown quite fond of him.'

'So why the cold shoulder?'

'To discourage any expectations he may have for this weekend. Despite my growing affection for him, a relationship can only be truly successful if both parties share the same values, beliefs and common interests. I'm afraid to say William holds some very dubious opinions.'

'Life would be very dull if we all shared the same opinions, Miriam. Personally, I couldn't care less what the women I see think.'

'Having had the misfortune of meeting the majority of the women you've been out with, I can assure you it wasn't much.'

'If I'm attracted to a gel, I ask them out, it's as simple as that.'

'"Simple" being the operative word here. Do you ever wonder why your relationships never last longer than a few weeks?'

'I know exactly why they don't - I don't want them to.'

'Why not go out with someone whose company you enjoy for a change?'

Alexander harrumphed. 'I'm not looking to find Miss Right just yet, Miriam. I'm still young. I want to embrace life and all it has to offer. And so should you.'

'We can't all have your epicurean tastes.'

Rising to his feet, Alexander crossed to the bookcase.

'Everyone - even you Miriam Crenshaw - needs to let their hair down once in a while and go a bit wild,' he said, pulling out a book at random. 'Tonight, I want you to put on one of those dresses Isobel found in her room, have a glass or two of champagne, and dance until the early hours. Who knows where the night may lead ...'

Seeing he was holding a copy of *Forbidden Territory* by Dennis Wheatley, he promptly replaced the novel on the shelf.

Miriam felt her face flush. 'I'll tell you where it will lead,' she snapped. 'It will lead to a painful hangover tomorrow morning, coupled with overwhelming feelings of regret and self-loathing.'

'No one's going to think any less of you for enjoying a night of revelry, Miriam.'

No, she thought, they probably wouldn't. But she would think less of herself.

*

Will breathed in the air heavy with the smell of lichen, moss and damp wood, the fallen leaves crunching under his boots.

'He didn't do a particularly good job,' he said, kicking up the leaves.

'Who?' asked Isobel.

'The gardener. I saw him raking up the leaves earlier.'

'He probably realised he was fighting a lost cause and gave up.'

They continued down the garden until the unkempt lawns turned into rough grass. Bracken and weeds covered the final stretch. Will beat a path to a wooden door that hung on rusted iron hinges. He turned the handle but found it locked.

'Well, that's that,' he said.

'We can't give up that easily,' said Isobel.

Jemima glanced up at the house. 'I could go and see if Hodgson has a key ...'

'That will take too long,' said Isobel. 'We'll just have to climb over the wall.' She turned to Will. 'Give me a leg up.'

Will linked his fingers together and steadied his legs. Isobel placed her right boot in his hands and vaulted lightly up, swinging one leg over the lichen-encrusted wall.

'I didn't realise there would be climbing,' said Jemima warily. She glanced down at the black tights and short winter skirt she was wearing.

Isobel sat astride the wall. 'We can't turn back now.'

'You two go ahead. You probably have lots of catching up to do anyway.'

'Are you sure?' asked Isobel.

Jemima nodded. 'You know what they say about three being a

crowd …' Turning, she headed back to the house.

Will glanced up at Isobel. 'We should go back with her.'

'She'll be fine.' Lifting her tweed cape, she reached out her hand to him. 'Here, I'll help you up.'

Uncertainly, he placed his hand in hers, found a footing on the old crumbling wall, and hauled himself up next to her.

'This reminds me of all those times I used to climb over the wall at the Manor,' he said, straddling the wall. 'I see now why my mother didn't want me going near the place. I really should have listened to her.' He dropped down behind the wall.

'Well, I'm glad you didn't,' said Isobel, slipping down beside him.

They followed an old, neglected path that led down to the river's edge. Pausing to take in the view, they stood listening to the gentle ripple of the water washing over pebbles.

Isobel followed the river downstream. 'You know,' she said, 'before you came along, James couldn't stand the sight of me. He regarded me as nothing more than an annoying little brat to be avoided at all cost.'

Will fell into step beside her. 'I'm sure he didn't.'

'Do you remember the day I followed him to the woods and saw you two playing together for the first time?'

'He started yelling at you to go away.'

'If you hadn't calmed him down and invited me to join you, I think he would have chased me away.'

Will remembered she had a ring of daisies in her hair. He'd thought her about the prettiest thing he'd ever seen.

'Afterwards,' continued Isobel, her eyes straying towards the river, 'as we made our way back to the house, I asked him where you were from. He told me you lived in the wood, and said, "Adults can't see him, so don't tell anyone about him or you'll get in trouble for telling tales."'

'Did he really say that?'

Isobel nodded. 'We only became friends because of you.'

Eventually, they came to the edge of the wood. An enormous canopy of twisted branches stretched out above their heads, their yellow and orange-brown leaves bringing out the warm tints of red in Isobel's chestnut hair.

Will suggested heading back, but Isobel disagreed.

She gestured to a vague, ill-defined path that disappeared into the wood. 'Let's see where this leads.' She stepped onto the path, treading over a shroud of dead leaves.

Will had a pretty good idea where it would lead but followed her anyway.

Isobel moved round a tree entwined with ivy. 'Visiting the Manor was a lot more fun when you were there,' she said.

'I don't know about fun. I remember getting us into a lot of trouble.'

'Like the time that old gardener caught us stealing apples from the orchard and chased after us …' She laughed. 'His face turned so red I thought it was going to explode.'

'If I remember rightly, you had nightmares for weeks after that. I behaved irresponsibly - I should have known better. I'm beginning to see why your father didn't like me. I was a bad influence on you.'

'You certainly were. I had to lie to my parents all summer so we could be together.'

'You did?'

'I didn't want to - but they gave me little choice. Clive forbid me from seeing you.'

'You never told me that.'

'I guess I was too embarrassed.' In the middle of a field, on the other side of the valley, she saw the ruins of a desolate cottage. 'I was already mad at them for not being there to welcome me when I arrived home from school that summer. I'd tried to stay awake long enough to see them but had fallen asleep before they returned home. The following morning, when I went down to breakfast, Clive didn't even ask me how I was. When I asked him where my mother was, he told me she'd already gone out for the day and wouldn't be back until the evening. I'd come to expect as much from them, but it still upset me. The Manor always felt more like home to me than my parents' house ever did. I was eager to see the old place again, but when I told Clive, he reminded me James was on holiday with his parents. That was when I told him I wanted to see you.'

She remembered his words: 'You're to stay away from that boy, young lady.'

'I'm afraid to say, he didn't want me to have anything to do with you.'

'Why not?' asked Will.

'I guess he was worried about what we'd get up to together.'

'Was he indeed …'

'I had to wait until he left the house before making my way to the village …'

Dressed in cut off jean shorts, a white cami and sandals, her sunglasses in her bag, she began the twenty-minute walk to the city centre bus stop. From there, she'd caught a bus to Devizes, which took over an hour to reach its destination. After changing buses, it took her a further thirty minutes to reach the village. When the bus pulled up outside the Red Lion pub just after twelve, the garden was already packed with locals and tourists enjoying the midday sun. She made her way down the busy High Street, passing through the lychgate into the churchyard. Will's cottage stood to the left of the churchyard. When she saw the windows were open, her spirits lifted. She hadn't known if anybody would be home.

The door was opened by Will's mother, who greeted her warmly.

'Your mother had been baking. The kitchen was in a real mess. You were at the garage but were coming home for lunch.'

Every corner of the cluttered sitting room was filled. Novels, books on folklore and mythology filled the shelves of an old bookcase. Framed photographs covered the walls and vases overflowing with flowers were dotted about the small room. She pictured their cat Ronald, stretched out on a windowsill, enjoying the warm sun that came in through the window. She'd always thought it a happy house, filled with memories. It felt like a home should to her.

'She liked to bake in the holidays,' said Will. 'She never managed to find the time when she was teaching.'

After lunch, his mother had suggested Will take Isobel for a drive in his car.

'You'd just finished restoring your Mini and took me to the garage to see it.'

Will, thinking she looked dressed for the beach, had suggested driving to the coast. They'd headed west for almost two hours, passing through small, pretty villages full of cottages with thatched roofs.

Isobel was beginning to think he'd lost his way, but he assured her he knew the area.

'My aunt lives around here somewhere,' he'd told her. 'I know where I'm going.'

When they eventually reached the coast, Will parked on the beach. He wanted to show her the wreck of a barque.

'It ran aground at the end of the nineteenth-century,' he'd explained, leading her along the beach, 'driven onto the sands by a ferocious, south-westerly gale that blew up the Bristol Channel. They'd tried to ride out the storm but soon found themselves powerless against the forces of nature. The waves hammered and beat the ship, smashing both it and their hopes and dreams to pieces.'

When he was a boy, he used to play amongst its timbers. To his disappointment, the tide was in and they couldn't see anything, so instead they walked barefoot along a stretch of golden sand and dunes, the water sparkling with golden flecks.

They remained there all afternoon, neither wanting to go back. Will suggested staying out all night.

'Clive would be furious,' Isobel told him.

'Then we'll never go back. We could drive to Europe, find work, spend the summer in France and Italy.'

'Are you asking me to run away with you?'

'If that's what you want.'

'Maybe one day,' she'd said, kissing him gently on the lips.

It was almost dark when they returned to Bath. They parked in a quiet cul-de-sac not far from Isobel's house on the Royal Crescent so as not to be seen.

Will had asked if he could see her the next day. 'We could go to the cinema together, or for something to eat. It's up to you. I don't mind which …'

Isobel knew she wasn't the first girl he'd ever asked out and wondered why he was acting so awkwardly. Initially, she'd hesitated, unsure if it was a good idea. After thanking him for a lovely day, she'd kissed him again, this time for longer.

Despite her initial uncertainty, they continued to see each other, meeting up most evenings and on Sundays when Will wasn't working at his dad's garage, though they never returned to the beach.

Not together, anyway.

Will gestured to a clearing ahead of them. 'Look over there,' he said.

Isobel followed his gaze down a rocky, heather covered slope of a hillside to a circle of ancient stones crowing a field ahead of them. Grabbing Will's arm, she dragged him down the hillside, stepping over grey stones covered in lichen and green moss. The slope levelled off and they crossed the trackless, untrodden field. Ahead, the last wisps of mist curled round the ancient stones. Only one still stood upright. Two others were lying on the ground, one of which had been broken in two.

Isobel ran her hand over the hard surfaces of the stones. 'I'm surprised James didn't tell us about them,' she said. 'He must have been thrilled when he found them. What was it he used to say about them?'

Will perched himself on one of the monoliths. 'By aligning them with the moon, the sun and the stars, our ancient ancestors were trying to make sense of their place in time and the universe. He believed it may have even been where they first conceived of the idea of a heaven.'

Isobel sat down on the damp grass and rested her back on the upright stone. She wondered what ceremonies were held there by their ancient ancestors. She imagined them lighting fires within the circle to drive back the darkness, the flames reaching high up into the night sky. She could almost hear the chants of their distant ancestral voices and see them dancing within the circle.

A brisk, bitter wind blew through the valley. Isobel's face darkened as she watched white clouds drift across the sky. Will instinctively knew she was thinking about James.

'What happened to him at Oxford?' she asked. 'The last time I saw him he was so excited to be going. Why did he leave before the end of his first year?'

Will shrugged. 'I'm afraid James's life at Oxford was very different from mine. We went to different colleges and were on different courses. He spent time with Alexander and others he knew from Marlborough, and I soon made friends of my own. Whenever I went to see him, I always found him distant and unwelcoming. He never once sought me out or came to see me. He didn't even attend my father's funeral. When I went to see him following my return to university, he offered no explanation for his absence and made no apology. We argued and I walked out on him. After that, I only saw him in passing, though we never spoke. I only learnt he'd left Oxford from Felicity - a friend of his.

'I never thought I'd see him again. Then, years later when I was in London, he came to see me. He told me he'd been up to Scotland and had found Wychwood House, acting as though we'd never fallen out and were still the best of friends. For a while, things were just like old times. Even when he moved to Scotland we kept in contact. He'd often call me to tell me how he was getting on. At the time, I was happy for him.'

'You were?'

'I thought he might find what he was looking for.'

'What could he hope to find here?'

'A connection with his ancestors that he never had with his own family. A sense of belonging. A home.'

'Do you think he's found that?'

Will shook his head. 'No, I don't. He wouldn't be like he is if he had.' After a pause, he continued. 'I knew when I received his invitation to the house something was wrong.' He sighed. 'I should have come up then.'

'Why didn't you?'

'I kept telling myself I was too busy at work to visit him, but the truth is I just couldn't face going through it all again.' He glanced down at Isobel. 'That must sound rather callous.'

Isobel pulled her knees up and wrapped her arms round her legs. 'No, I felt the same way,' she said. 'I was in two minds about making the journey myself.' She stared out across the valley. 'When I arrived yesterday, James didn't seem to recognise me. When he did, he became quite furious and seemed to have no recollection of inviting me to the house. Eventually, he calmed himself down, though seemed on edge for the rest of our very brief conversation.'

Will crouched down next to her. 'I wish there was something I could say or do,' he said, placing his hand on hers, 'but there isn't. Maybe our being here will make a difference. I don't know. But I do know I'm not going to give up on him, Isobel. I promise.'

Glancing down, she saw their fingers had intertwined.

A large black bird perched itself on one of the stones behind them, startling Isobel.

'It's just a crow,' said Will, turning. He shooed it away.

With a sudden flapping of wings, the bird flew off into the sky.

'That wasn't a crow,' said Isobel. 'It was a raven.'

CHAPTER SEVEN

Seventeen Months Earlier

James remained in London for two months following his first visit to Wychwood House. Believing it could be months, maybe longer, before the house would be habitable again, he decided to live in Edinburgh whilst the renovations were undertaken on his ancestral home. During his first visit to the city, he'd stumbled upon a townhouse that was up for sale whilst exploring the New Town and had Bill put in an offer before he'd even returned to London. Bill had negotiated the conditions of the sale on his behalf, James remaining in his apartment in the Albany until the missives were concluded - whatever that meant.

He returned to Edinburgh on the last Friday in May, a warm, clear day, the sun behind him as he drove north in his old Land Rover Defender, the boot filled with his bags and suitcases. He'd left London in the early hours of the morning and had driven straight up to Scotland, only stopping for petrol, eager to reach his destination. Once in the Borders, he had to stop himself from heading to Selkirk, so strong was his desire to see his ancestral home again.

There was, of course, another reason for him to return to Edinburgh. During the two months he'd been away he'd stayed in touch with Tessa and was looking forward to seeing her again. She'd never been far from his thoughts throughout their time apart. He arrived at his destination just after eleven and pulled up outside a row of Georgian terraced townhouses. Moray Place looked even more impressive than he remembered, the bright sun shining on the stone-built townhouses that stretched five stories high. The green luxurious grounds of Moray Place Gardens, enclosed by wrought iron gates and railings, lay hidden in deep shadows. Sunlight dappled on the lawns and birds sang in the trees and hedgerows.

Glancing at his watch, he saw it was just after eleven. He'd made good time, arriving earlier than planned. He let the estate agent, a Mr J.H. Marriott, know he'd arrived. He didn't have to wait long for him to appear. Ten minutes later a BMW pulled up next to his Land Rover and a well-dressed man in his late fifties appeared.

'Mr Roxburgh,' he said, stepping out of his car, 'it's nice to finally meet you.'

'And you,' replied James.

They shook hands and Mr Marriott congratulated him on his purchase.

'The Moray Feu is one of the most exclusive and upmarket residences in Scotland. Properties here don't often come onto the market.'

He had some paperwork for James to sign and led the way into the townhouse.

'I'm sorry we weren't able to arrange a viewing of the house before you left,' he said, stepping into the entrance hall.

'The brochure you sent me told me all I needed to know,' replied James.

'I'm afraid it hardly does justice to the property.' Portraits of previous owners hung on the walls. 'The estate was designed by the architect James Gillespie Graham in 1822 for the tenth Earl of Moray and took over thirty years to complete. The earl himself lived in number twenty-eight, the largest house in the feu. Unfortunately for him, it proved a little too large, even for an earl living in the nineteenth-century. Within five years he'd put it on the market. He'd hoped the property would become a hotel, but after it was sold the house was split into five flats instead.'

The estate agent showed James into the drawing room first, then the study. There was no furniture in the drawing room. A Westminster desk had been left in the study, though there was no chair. The walls were lined with burr walnut panelling, display cabinets and bookcases, their shelves empty. James thought a couple of bergère armchairs would finish the room off nicely.

Mr Marriott led him over to the tall sash windows to show him the view over the central gardens.

'You have to apply to the management committee for a key to the gardens, I'm afraid.'

James thought it unlikely he'd ever get round to doing that but thanked the agent for letting him know. They left the study and Mr Marriott pointed out the family room at the end of the hall but didn't go inside, opting to show his client the Clive Christian kitchen instead.

'There's a gas Aga,' said the agent, leading James into the room, 'and over here is the Miele fridge-freezer.'

A Baccarat chandelier hung over the kitchen island. The estate agent produced the forms for James to sign, laying them down on the polished granite surface of the island. He duly signed the forms and Mr Marriott handed him the keys to the property, telling his client he hoped he would be happy in the house. James assured him he would. When he followed Mr Marriott outside, he felt the phone in the breast pocket of his jacket vibrate. Removing the phone, he saw he'd received a message from Tessa wanting to know if he'd arrived safely.

They arranged to meet at the National Gallery on the following Sunday around lunchtime before Tessa started work that afternoon. He would have liked to have seen her sooner but there was too much to do. He briefly considered going to see her at *The Bride of Lammermoor* that evening, but quickly dismissed the thought from his mind. The pub would be busy, and he thought it unlikely he'd get much of a chance to talk to her. He decided to wait until he had her to himself.

When Mr Marriott had gone, he returned to his Land Rover and began unpacking the boot, carrying his suitcases into his new home.

*

Although James thought it was only slightly warmer than when he'd left Edinburgh in March, Tessa appeared wearing a floral print dress. She looked younger and more relaxed than he remembered, her auburn hair fuller, redder, her complexion rosier. She greeted him with a kiss on the cheek and they headed straight to the café on the ground floor of the gallery, where she asked him about Wychwood House. He told her he'd hired a local firm of builders to undertake the restoration of the property.

Over coffee, he asked her what her plans were for the summer.

She told him she didn't have any. 'I just want to get as many hours working in the pub as I can. I could do with the extra money.'

'So, no trips abroad planned?'

'No, not this year. How about you?'

'No, not for the foreseeable future. Not until the work on Wychwood House is complete.'

When they had finished their drinks, they looked round the gallery together. They stopped by a portrait of the young James VI by Bronckorst and Tessa said she needed to be making a move.

Before she left, James asked her to have dinner with him one night that week.

'Where did you have in mind?' she asked.

'I thought we could go to the Balmoral.'

'You're staying at the Balmoral again?'

James shook his head. 'No,' he said. 'I've found somewhere to live in the New Town.'

'Whereabouts?'

'In Moray Place.'

'You're renting a flat there?'

'No, I bought a house there. I noticed it was up for sale the last time I was here. I thought it unlikely it would be on the market for long, so I put in an offer as soon as I returned to London.'

'Just like that?'

James smiled. 'Just like that.'

Tessa's soft hazel eyes met his. 'Are you always so decisive?'

'Only when I really want something.'

He sensed she was a little hesitant to accept his offer.

'Are you seeing anyone at the moment?' he asked.

'I wouldn't have thought that would have made a difference to someone like you.'

He was slightly taken aback by her words. 'Why do you think that?' he asked.

'Because you are so used to getting what you want.'

'It may not have mattered to me in the past,' he replied, after a pause. 'But it does now.'

'I'm not seeing anyone. I haven't for a long time now.'

She asked him if he had a girlfriend back in London.

He told her he didn't, which was true. He wasn't sure she believed him.

'We come from very different backgrounds,' she said, 'and have lived very different lives.'

'That shouldn't be a reason why we can't be together.'

'No, it shouldn't,' she said thoughtfully, 'but it probably will.'

James didn't understand what she meant. He thought perhaps it was because she didn't quite trust him. He wanted to reassure her his feelings were genuine and tell her he hadn't stopped thinking about her since he'd first laid eyes on her - but he didn't.

'I'm working next weekend,' said Tessa, after a pause, 'but at the moment I'm free all week.'

He suggested Thursday.

'I look forward to it,' she said. After kissing him on the cheek, she turned and left.

He watched her go, expecting her to glance over her shoulder at him before disappearing from sight, as she had in the pub, but this time she didn't look back.

*

The following morning, he left Edinburgh early to avoid being caught in traffic and headed south to Wychwood House. After being on the road for almost an hour, he realised the journey was going to take him longer than anticipated. There was no way he was going to be able to drive to the house every day, which meant he was going to have to leave the keys with his builders - something he hadn't wanted to do. There only appeared to be one set of keys to the house and he didn't want them to be misplaced.

The caretaker must have had a set, but he'd retired years ago, and they were most likely lost. He didn't want his set to suffer the same fate. He knew he was being ridiculous - he was sure his builders would keep them safe - but they'd been in his possession for so long he found himself reluctant to part with them.

He arrived to find two white vans parked on the courtyard outside the servants' entrance. The lettering on the side of the vans read, *K J Turnball Building Contractors Ltd, Selkirk*. His builders were sitting in their vehicles waiting for him. One was leaning against the house smoking a cigarette. James apologised for being late, explaining he'd driven down from Edinburgh, and quickly introduced himself. The oldest man in the group stepped forward and introduced himself as Mr Turnball and shook his employer's hand. Not wanting to keep them waiting any longer, James unlocked the door to the servants' entrance and led Mr Turnball and his men inside. He pointed out the kitchen, informing them there was no gas or electricity in the house, before proceeding on to the great hall. Mr Turnball and his men looked round the cavernous room in awe, clearly overwhelmed by the task ahead of him.

'We've got our work cut out for us here,' Mr Turnball muttered under his breath.

'This isn't the worst of it, I'm afraid,' said James. He led them up to the first floor and showed them the hole in the ceiling.

The smell of damp and decay was still present on the second floor and there seemed to be even more flies than before. Unable to bear the stench for long, James promptly left his builders to inspect the damage. He returned downstairs to the library where he began searching for books containing information on his ancestors. It wasn't long before he stumbled across a copy of George Ridpath's *The Border History of England and Scotland,* from which he learnt two of his ancestors were Wardens of the Middle Marches. He was reading Howard Pease's *The Lord Wardens of the Marches of England and Scotland* when he heard Mr Turnball calling to him from the great hall.

'I'm in here,' he replied, his voice echoing round the room.

His builder appeared in the doorway.

'We've just been up on the roof taking a look about,' he said gravely. 'The chimney stacks are unstable, and parts of the roof are going to need to be completely replaced. Unfortunately, where the roof has leaked there's considerable damage to the attic and upper floors.'

'Can they be repaired?'

'We don't know the extent of the damage yet, but we'll keep you posted. While we were up there, we found some old suitcases and boxes. We're going to have to bring them downstairs.'

'Put them in the drawing room for now. I'll have a look through them later.'

When Mr Turnball stepped out of the room, James went into the study to continue reading, remaining there all day. He left when his builders did, handing the keys to Mr Turnball, telling them he'd be back the following day should they need him.

*

Work on the house moved slowly. The days he spent at the house were long and the nights in his townhouse lonely. After what seemed like an age, Thursday arrived. He didn't visit Wychwood House that day, opting instead for a lie in so he'd feel refreshed after a good night's sleep. In the afternoon he visited a local barber for a haircut and shave, and on his way home he picked up a small bunch of flowers from a florist. He decided to wear a two-piece rather than a three-piece suit that evening, so as not to appear too formal.

He picked Tessa up at the house near the Meadows that she shared with three other students on her course. The front door was opened by one of her housemates who informed him she'd be down shortly. He felt his heart beat a little faster when she appeared wearing a little black dress, a simple but effective outfit. She was wearing her hair down, her eyes dark and smoky, her lips painted a rosy pink. Her hair was longer than he'd imagined, falling over her shoulders, curling round her neck and down her back. At work, she wore very little make-up and always tied her hair up.

Handing her the flowers he'd bought her, he told her she looked beautiful. After she thanked him, one of her friends agreed to put them into water for her. She promptly introduced him to two of her housemates; the third had yet to return for the evening. When they left one of her friends teased her about not staying out too late.

They made their way through the city to a restaurant near the gates of Edinburgh Castle. Both appeared a little nervous to begin with but soon relaxed, their conversation flowing naturally, both enjoying the other's company. At dinner, she admitted she hadn't believed him when he told her he was looking for his ancestral home, just as he suspected. She made him promise to let her see the house. He agreed, though told her she'd have to wait until his builders had tidied it up a bit. She didn't seem too disappointed by this. She seemed far more interested in his townhouse than she did in Wychwood House, telling him she'd dreamt of living in one of the houses in the area ever since she was a little girl. She'd always wanted to play in the private gardens, but the wrought-iron railings and locked gates had kept her out.

They left the restaurant just after ten and took a leisurely walk through the city to the New Town. Tessa pointed out some of the city's landmarks and monuments as they made their way down the Royal Mile, including the Witches' Well on Castlehill. Their tour ended at Moray Place. He wanted to show her the gardens but didn't have a key to unlock the gates. Instead, he invited her inside to see the house for herself. She eagerly accepted his invitation and they stepped inside the townhouse, her heels echoing on the mosaic floor as he led her through the entrance hall. He showed her the drawing room first. There was no furniture, and the walls were bare. On the mantelpiece were two photo frames given to him by his mother before he'd left London. In the first, taken on a holiday when he was a boy, he was standing on a beach between his mother and father.

'I believe we were in France at the time, somewhere in the Côte d'Azur.'

When Tessa picked up the second photo frame, he moved up behind her, placing his hand on the small of her back, breathing in the scent of her perfume. The photo had been taken in the garden at the Manor when he was about fifteen or sixteen and showed him with Isobel and Will. He told her he'd moved to the Manor when he was eight and that Isobel and Will had been his closest friends when he was growing up. He mentioned he was still in touch with Will but hadn't seen Isobel in years.

'You must miss London,' said Tessa. 'You're so far from your friends and family here.'

He told her he'd initially moved to London when the summer social season was in full swing. Invitations to dull parties held by friends of his parents soon reached him. 'I found myself being introduced to lots of young women fresh from their debutante balls, who'd spent too much time at Pony Club for my liking. Like young Dombey, "my way in life was clear and prepared and marked out before I existed."' The sentence had stuck with him ever since he'd read Dickens's novel.

'Is that why you moved abroad?'

'It's one of the reasons I didn't come back when I should have.'

She lifted her head to his, their lips almost touching. He felt she was trembling slightly and realised his mouth was dry.

'Would you care for a glass of wine?' he asked, taking the frame from her and placing it back on the mantelpiece.

'I'd like that.'

He took her hand and led her out of the room.

'I always wondered what these houses looked like on the inside,' said Tessa. 'This wasn't quite what I imagined. It's very … modern.'

'The house retains some period features, though I doubt any are original to the house.'

'How many floors are there?' she asked as they passed the staircase.

'Just two. There are three bedrooms upstairs, a family room at the end of the hall and the kitchen's in here.'

'It's a lovely house. I like it a lot.'

'I'm glad.'

He smiled and led her into the kitchen where he opened a bottle of wine.

'It's nothing special,' he said apologetically.

'I'm sure it will suffice.'

He handed Tessa her glass of wine. 'I had hoped to furnish the house before inviting you over,' he said. 'I'm afraid the only piece of furniture I've managed to buy so far is a mattress for the bed.'

Tessa put the glass to her lips and took a sip of wine. 'Well, right now,' she said, 'that's all we need.'

*

The following morning the sound of rain drumming against the windows woke him. Pulling back his quilted satin eiderdown, he rose from his bed, padded barefoot across the room, the carpet soft and luxurious underfoot, and opened the heavy curtains hanging at the window. Rain fell from dark leaden clouds that hung heavily in the sky above Edinburgh. He glanced over his shoulder at Tessa who lay on her back sound asleep, her head resting on a soft plump pillow, her face turned toward the window. One of her arms rested above her head, the other lay languidly at her side under the eiderdown.

Although faint, the light coming in through the window hurt

her eyes and she rolled over onto her side, so James promptly closed the curtains so as not to wake her. He decided to shower in the main bathroom, rather than in the en-suite shower room to avoid disturbing her again. According to his watch, it was a quarter to six. They hadn't fallen asleep until the early hours of the morning. He wasn't sure of the exact time, but he couldn't have had more than a few hours' sleep.

Feeling tired, he wanted nothing more than to get back in bed but knew he should get to Wychwood House and see how his builders were getting on. Seeing Tessa's black dress lying crumpled on the floor, he picked it up and lay it over the foot of the four-poster bed. The bed had no drapes or dressings, but she didn't appear to have minded, or even have noticed. He then hung his suit in the fitted wardrobe before grabbing some clean clothes and slipping quietly out of the room.

By the time he made his way downstairs to the kitchen, the rain had eased a little. He filled his kettle and stood staring absently out of a window whilst waiting for it to boil. The previous summer had seen some of the worst flooding in Britain for years. He was beginning to wonder if they were in for the same again that year. He hoped not. It would only delay the work on Wychwood House. As he spooned a teaspoon of instant coffee into a mug his mind wandered and he soon found his thoughts drifting to their night together, thoughts he probably shouldn't have while she was still lying in his bed.

He hadn't expected their evening together to go as well as it had. He certainly hadn't expected them to spend the night together. He couldn't help but wonder if he was doing the right thing. Now wasn't exactly the best time to start seeing someone. He was probably worrying unduly. For all he knew she might not want to see him again - though he thought that unlikely considering how well their evening had gone.

The kettle came to the boil, steaming up the room. He filled the mugs with hot water and made his way back upstairs. Crossing the hall, he heard what he thought was the rain, until halfway up the staircase, he realised the shower was running. Once in the bedroom he glanced through the open doorway into his shower room and saw Tessa step out of the shower, her skin wet and glistening as she reached for a towel. Water from her dripping hair ran in droplets down her back, rolling over the soft curves of her body.

He knocked gently on the shower room door. 'I made you some coffee.'

She thanked him and patted herself off with a towel, her skin still pink from the heat of the shower.

Crossing the room, he placed the mug down on a bedside table next to a pile of books as Tessa appeared from the shower room wrapped in a cotton towelling robe.

'It's hammering it down out there,' he said.

'You'll get used to it living in Edinburgh.' She dried her wet hair with a towel. 'What time is it?' she asked.

'Just after seven. I'm going to head off in a minute.'

'So early?'

James nodded. 'I like to leave early to avoid the rush hour traffic,' he said. 'I wasn't at the house yesterday and would like to see how my builders are getting on before they finish for the weekend. But feel free to stay here for as long as you like.'

Tessa reached for her mug of coffee and glanced at the books on the bedside table. 'So, who exactly were your ancestors?'

'The Earls of Leithen.' He held up John Buchan's *The Marquis of Montrose*. 'You've heard of James Graham -'

Tessa's eyes widened. 'You're related to the Great Montrose?'

'No, but according to this book, the first Earl of Leithen stood alongside him when he signed a copy of the National Covenant in 1638.' He turned to a marked page in the book. 'Our families maintained close links ever since the first earl's great grandfather and William Graham, the second Earl of Montrose, fought alongside each other at the Battle of Solway Moss in 1542. Following the Scots defeat, my ancestor and many other nobles were captured.' Laying the book down on his lap, he glanced round the room. 'I have a copy of the schedule of prisoners from the time round here somewhere.'

'I'll take your word for it.'

'He was released five years later by Henry VIII, only to be killed at the Battle of Pinkie Cleugh in the same year, alongside Montrose's son, Robert.'

'That's awful.'

'They were both slaughtered while retreating after coming under heavy fire from English ships offshore ...'

Removing the towel from her head, Tessa cosied up to him, resting her chin on his right shoulder, her arms curling round him.

'And how big is this estate you've inherited?'

James could feel the warmth from her body on his back. 'I'm not sure,' he said. 'Once it must have been quite substantial, though it could never have been as vast as the Scot and Kerr clans. If it had been, we'd still be one of the richest families in the country.'

'Well, you don't seem to be doing too badly for yourself.' She nuzzled her face against the back of his neck.

'Don't you have lectures to go to?'

'I finished last week,' she whispered, her soft lips brushing his ear. 'And I'm not due at work until this evening …'

Turning to face her, James saw her robe had fallen open slightly. She reached for his face, pulling him towards her, her lips meeting his. She kissed him deeply, hungrily, leaving him breathless.

'I told them I'd be there first thing,' he murmured, his eyes meeting hers.

'Do they know about our date?' she asked.

James nodded.

Tessa lay back on the bed, resting her head on a soft pillow. 'Then they'll understand.'

*

The rain had stopped by the time James reached Wychwood House. Passing an empty skip, he made his way under the crenellated gateway, crossing the quadrangular courtyard. Stepping into the great hall, he saw one of Mr Turnball's workmen, a broom in hand, standing next to a wheelbarrow, sweeping up the dust and crumbled plaster that littered the floor, uncovering a Turkish carpet in the process.

Mr Turnball appeared from the drawing room and greeted his employer with a warm smile that emphasised the lines on his weather-beaten face.

'I take it your evening with your young lass went well,' he said.

'Very well, thank you.'

'Once we've tidied up in here, I'll bring in an electrician to rewire the house. The round pin sockets are going to have to be replaced and you're going to need a new fuse box.'

James led his builder across the great hall towards the study. 'I'll leave it in your capable hands.'

Stepping into the low-ceiling room, he flicked a dolly switch. The lights didn't come on.

'A replacement generator should be with us in the next couple of days,' explained Mr Turnball. 'Which should suffice until we can get the house connected to the mains.'

James made his way round the dimly lit room, pulling open the heavy damask curtains that hung at the windows. A dull light filled the room.

Mr Turnball gestured to the rosewood desk. 'Have you found the keys for your desk yet?'

'Not yet.' James sat himself down on the swivel chair before the desk. 'They'll turn up eventually.'

Mr Turnball spotted the transistor radio lying on the crested leather blotter. 'I haven't seen one of those since I was a kid,' he said, stepping forward. He picked up the old Binatone 8 radio. 'Where on earth did you find it?'

'At the foot of the staircase, out in the hall.'

Mr Turnball's face turned pale. Repressing a shudder, he placed the radio back on the desk.

'What's wrong?'

His builder shook his head. 'Nothing,' he said quickly.

'I keep wondering how it found its way into the house.'

'I wouldn't know, I'm afraid,' his builder insisted, though he clearly knew more than he was willing to say. 'Well, I won't keep you any longer. Looks like you've got your work cut out for you today.' He gestured to the books on the desk.

'That I have,' said James, sitting back in his chair.

Turning, Mr Turnball slipped out of the room, pulling the door too behind him.

James glanced down at the transistor radio. He wondered if something had happened to the people who'd broken into the house. Although eager to find out more, he had more than enough to be getting on with. He spent the rest of the day trawling through the books on his desk, copying out passages into his notebook, not even stopping to eat the sandwiches Tessa had made him for lunch. He became so engrossed in his task, he only realised the time when Mr Turnball stuck his head round the door and told him they were finishing for the day.

James told him he planned to stay for a bit longer.

'I'll leave these with you then.' Mr Turnball set the keys down on the desk before his employer. 'We've emptied the attic and put everything in the drawing room as instructed.'

James thanked him, and Mr Turnball left the study, his men following him across the hall, their voices fading away as they made their way out of the house.

The hours passed and the evening drew on. James, his eyes tired, found himself struggling to read the words on the page of the book that lay open on the desk before him. Glancing at his wristwatch, he saw it was a quarter past nine. He wasn't due to meet Tessa from work until half eleven. He had about fifteen minutes before he had to leave.

Rising from his chair, he stretched out his aching body and made his way into the drawing room to see for himself what had been brought down from the attic. Trunks of all shapes and sizes, storage boxes, and suitcases lay spread out on the floor. Before the fireplace stood a Victorian blanket box riddled with woodworm. By the door, propped against a wooden chest were some paintings by Bouguereau of gypsy girls and shepherdesses. Amongst them, he found a Pénot nude and a portrait of an elderly lady in an austere Victorian dress. The gathering darkness made it difficult for him to see the portrait in any detail, so he propped it carefully back against the chest.

Glancing round for a candelabra, he saw there were only electric lamps in the room. Without power, they weren't much use to him. After retrieving a three-branched candelabra from a small oak table in the great hall, he made his way back into the drawing room where he discovered an old box of Swan Vestas in a drawer of the sideboard. After lighting the candles, he set the candelabra down on the side table next to the sofa. A hand-stitched tan leather suitcase inscribed with the initials H.J.R. lay on top of an old wardrobe trunk. Opening the case, revealing its calico interior lining, he saw it was empty, which didn't surprise him; he'd found Henry's clothes in the room next to Emily's bedroom.

Closing the suitcase, he turned his attention to the wardrobe trunk, the largest of all the trunks in the room. Inside were four drawers. Victorian and Edwardian gowns and dresses hung from a hanging rail; old clothes packed away when they weren't wanted anymore. Nearby stood a steamer trunk. A name had been stencilled on one end of the trunk - though he couldn't make out the faint letters. Crouching down, he traced the stencil with his finger, revealing the name Emily Knight to him. Until then he hadn't known the maiden name of his great-uncle's wife.

He was about to open the trunk when he became aware of the smell of rotten eggs in the room, a pungent smell that almost choked him as it filled his lungs. At first, he attributed it to a gas leak somewhere in the house, until, once again, he felt he was being watched. There was someone in the room with him. The shadows seemed to grow darker, the candlelight struggling to penetrate the gloom.

Terrified, he stood rooted to the spot, his body tensing up, the hairs on the back of his neck rising. Turning his head slowly, he glanced over his shoulder and watched in horror as a shadow shaped itself into the form of a large black dog. He reached for the candelabra on the side table next to the wooden chest, his eyes remaining fixed on the dog as it prowled towards him, its eyes reflecting the candlelight. He couldn't identify the breed in the darkness. As it drew nearer, he saw its ribs were exposed. Clearly, it was malnourished and hungry. Hungry enough to attack a man?

The dog snarled at him, baring its teeth, its fangs long and sharp. Seeing the dog crouch low, ready to pounce, James hurled the candelabra at the beast, its flames extinguishing as it hit the floor. Without glancing back, he ran from the room, grabbing the handle of the door as he went, slamming it shut behind him. In total darkness, he ran across the great hall, his eyes fixed on the way ahead. He prayed the builders had left the front door open.

When he was halfway across the hall, he caught his foot on something, tripped and hit the floor hard, falling into a pile of rubble that lay uncollected on the floor. Looking up, his eyes now accustomed to the darkness, he glanced back to see the drawing room door swing open behind him. For a moment he lay on the floor stock-still, expecting the creature to appear and intercept him before he had a chance to escape, but soon came to his senses. Scrambling to his feet, he ran for the exit.

A sense of relief swept over him when he saw moonlight shining through the open doorway, illuminating the front porch. He decided to leave it open. The door still grated against the floor and could not be closed quickly. Once outside, he stumbled down the stone steps, falling onto the gravel below. Without pausing for breath, he picked himself up and ran towards the entrance gate, not daring to look back as he headed for the Land Rover. He climbed inside and locked the doors, his hands fumbling with the key in the ignition. The engine started, and he slammed his foot down on the accelerator, the tyres gouging the gravel as he reversed. Yanking the steering wheel round, he nudged the Land Rover into first gear, and sped down the drive, only slowing when he passed through the gates.

He drove fast, arriving in Edinburgh with plenty of time to spare before Tessa finished work. Parking outside his apartment, he walked into the city to meet her. That night, he didn't feel like going inside the pub. Instead, he waited for her in the street.

Tessa knew as soon as she saw him something was wrong. 'You look dreadful,' she said. 'Is everything all right?'

'I had a bit of a scare, that's all.'

'Have you eaten?'

James shook his head.

Taking him by the arm, she led him up Frederick Street. 'Come on, I'll make us some dinner.'

As they made their way through the city, he told her about his encounter with the dog. 'It appeared quite emaciated,' he said.

'The poor thing.'

'I wouldn't waste your sympathy on the creature. I'm sure, given the opportunity, it would have attacked me.'

'Where do you think it came from?'

'I have a feeling it's been living there for a while. The first time I visited the house I thought I caught a glimpse of someone or rather something in the library. At first, I thought I had a squatter.'

'Looks like you do.'

When they reached Moray Place Tessa asked him what he planned to do about it.

James unlocked his front door and held it open for her.

'If it's still there in the morning I'll call the RSPCA,' he said, 'though I have a feeling it may have fled.'

'Why, what did you do to it?'

'I threw a candelabra at the beast.'

Tessa stepped into the apartment. 'Did you hit it?' she asked.

James shook his head. 'I don't think so,' he said, flicking on a light switch. 'I didn't hear it whimper.'

The lights came on, reflecting off the tiled floor.

'You must have scared the life out of it.'

'Well, it certainly scared the life out of me.' He dropped his car keys on the console table, and they made their way towards the kitchen. 'I left in such a hurry I didn't lock up. The keys to the house are still on the desk in the study.'

Tessa wandered over to the fridge. 'Well, it's too late to go back tonight.' She opened the fridge to find the shelves sparse. 'You really need to go shopping. When did you buy these eggs?'

'A couple of days ago.'

'I was hoping for something a little bit more exciting than an omelette for dinner.'

She grabbed the box of eggs, some butter and cheese, and carried them over to the Aga, whilst James poured them out some wine from the bottle they'd opened the previous night. When Tessa had finished cooking, they sat down at the kitchen table together. She asked how the builders were getting on at the house.

'They've discovered the roof has leaked. We don't know the extent of the damage yet, but even if it's minimal it's going to set us back weeks.'

She seemed pleased by the news but didn't say anything.

*

The following morning, James rose before six, leaving Tessa asleep in his bed, hurrying out of the house before she woke. Upon arriving at Wychwood House he headed straight to the study, where, to his great relief, he found the keys to the house lying on the desk where Mr Turnball had placed them. The door to the drawing room stood wide open. Upon entering the room, he saw the dog had gone. He hadn't expected it to still be there. It must have followed him out of the house and was probably miles away by now. He picked the candelabra off the floor and carried it back to the great hall where he returned it to the small table he'd taken it from.

Before leaving, he decided to call Tessa to let her know where he was.

'I haven't woken you, have I?' he asked when she answered her phone.

She told him she was in the kitchen eating breakfast.

'Any sign of the dog?' she asked.

'Not so far.'

No, there was no sign of the creature anywhere.

The dust lay heavily outside the drawing room. Although there were plenty of footprints in the dust, there were no discernible paw prints.

'There's not one,' he told Tessa. 'Not even a partial print. The only way out of the house is through the front door. It could only get out by crossing the hall.'

'Is there any other way out of the drawing room?'

'No, the French window is locked. There's another door, but that's locked too.'

As he scoured the room for signs of the dog, he noticed a pentagram had been drawn on the ancient flagstones.

'I've found something.'

'A paw print?'

'No, something else.'

The five-pointed star had been uncovered when he'd tripped over the large Turkish carpet the night before. It had been drawn onto the floor with black paint and appeared to form part of a much larger design.

'Words I can't quite make out,' he explained, gently pulling back the carpet to reveal the whole design, 'that seem to be written in some ancient language, have been drawn on the floor between two concentric circles that measure somewhere between eight and nine feet across.'

Placed in the centre of the circle was a square, which had been painted red, with the word *maister* written within it. Surrounding the square were four hexagrams placed at the cardinal points of the compass. A T-shaped cross had been drawn within the hexagram and the letters *a, d, o, n, a, i* had been written inside the six-pointed stars.

'Adonai is the Hebrew name of God,' he said. 'Which means the words within the circle must be written in Hebrew too.'

In addition to the pentagram he'd inadvertently uncovered, there were three other five-pointed stars positioned round the outside of the circle.

'The hexagrams, pentagrams and the space between the circles are all painted yellow.'

Finally, at the head of the circle was another, smaller circle. This one had been drawn within a triangle and painted black.

'The design's definitely of an occult nature,' he said. 'The type used in ceremonial magic.'

Although he only had limited knowledge of the subject, he was almost certain his surmise was correct.

'I can't hear you,' said Tessa, her voice muffled and distant. 'You're breaking up.'

James decided to finish the call out on the terrace.

When he had stepped out of the house, he said, 'Whoever broke into the house in the sixties must have drawn it there.'

'Why do you think that?'

'Because I found the transistor radio at the bottom of the staircase not far from where I discovered the pentagram.'

'Did you ever ask Mr Turnball if he knew what happened at the house?'

'I haven't spoken to him about it since.'

'Well, you could always ask in the village.'

'All I'd learn there is local gossip. I'd rather learn the truth.'

'Then go to the local library,' said Tessa. 'They'll have copies of old newspapers on microfilm. If something happened at the house it would have made the local papers.'

Before he left, he grabbed a notebook and pencil from the study and began drawing the design of the circle onto a blank page, copying the letters as best he could. When he'd finished, he ripped out the page, slipping it into his inside jacket pocket, before making his way to the kitchen in search of a bucket and brush. He didn't want the builders, or anyone else for that matter, seeing what had been painted on the floor of the great hall. He found a bucket and cloth, and after filling the bucket with water, began wiping the design off the floor.

When all the paint was gone, he replaced the carpet and made his way through the house, checking all the doors and windows were secure before leaving. He found no trace of the dog and prayed it would be the last he saw of the terrible creature.

*

Parking in Chapel Street car park, he made his way along Ettrick Terrace, stopping at an archway where he read the words, 'Public Library and Reading Room 1888' inscribed above the arch. A short flight of steps led up to the building. Once inside he made his way up another flight of stairs to the library. Standing behind the reception desk was a middle-aged woman who greeted him with a smile. Thin framed cherry red glasses hung from a chain round her neck.

'How can I help you?' she asked.

'I was wondering if you have any local newspapers from the sixties held on microfilm.'

'We do. The microfilm readers are kept in the reading room.' She gestured across the library. 'We have the Kelso Chronicle, Southern Reporter and Selkirk Advertiser on file from that time. Do you have a specific date or event you're searching for?'

'No, I don't.'

'I'm afraid the newspapers aren't indexed,' said the librarian regretfully. 'You'll likely have a long trawl before you find what you're looking for. Your search will be a lot easier if you had a rough idea of the date. What exactly was it you were looking for information about?'

'Have you heard of Wychwood House?' said James, after a pause. 'You may know it better as the House in the Witches' Wood.'

The librarian stared absently down at a pile of books on the desk. 'I haven't heard that name in over thirty years.'

'So, you've heard of the place?'

'Everybody round here's heard of the House in the Witches' Wood.'

James sensed a hint of regret in her voice. 'I think something happened there in the sixties …'

The librarian lifted her gaze. 'In the summer of '66,' she said confidently. 'Early August, to be exact, shortly before the schools went back. The girls involved, Hazel Anderson and Veronica Scott, were from Selkirk. They were in the year above me at the grammar school - now I am showing my age,' she added, blushing slightly.

'What happened to them?'

'What is your interest in the house if you don't mind me asking?'

'My name is James Roxburgh. My great-uncle, Henry Roxburgh, lived at Wychwood House during the nineteen-thirties. I own the house now. If something happened there, I'd like to know.'

Lifting her glasses, the librarian placed them on her nose and stared intently at James. 'You're a Roxburgh?'

James nodded.

'I can only tell you what I know.' She moved out from behind the reception desk. 'I believe it was Hazel's grandmother that used to live in the village. She would visit her every fortnight, sometimes taking Veronica with her. During their visits they came to know two brothers - I'm afraid I don't remember their names - who lived in the village with their mother.' She perched herself on the edge of a nearby desk. 'One afternoon, despite being told to stay out of the wood, the two brothers took Veronica and Hazel up to the house. That was the last anybody saw of them. The younger brother, I think his name was Tim or John - it could have been Tom - appeared from the wood the following morning, raving like a madman. He claimed they'd been attacked by some sort of creature - a hellhound I think it was.'

James felt his stomach sink at the mention of the hound but didn't say anything, allowing the librarian to continue.

'It dragged one of the girls - I can't remember which one - into the darkness after she tried to flee the house, before turning on his brother. The other girl was wrenched from Tom's hand as they fled the house. Naturally, suspicions were raised about his story. Nobody could understand how it had taken him all night to reach the village. Many believed he was smitten with Hazel - she was a very pretty girl - and had become jealous when his older brother had shown an interest in her. Some suggested he'd attacked his brother in a fit of rage, hunted down the girls when they'd run for fear of their lives, and murdered them both, burying all three bodies in the wood. An axe, bearing Tom's fingerprints, was discovered at the scene. The police conducted a thorough search of the woodland but no trace of any of them was ever found. Due to the lack of evidence, Tom was never convicted, though he never recovered from his ordeal. He spent the next thirty years in Woodilee asylum.'

James, still in shock, said, 'I'd like to see the local news reports, if I may.'

The librarian showed him through to the reading room and he began searching through the old newspapers. He learnt the brothers were called Thomas and Andrew Rutherford. They'd lived in the village with their mother. The whereabouts of their father was unknown. Tom was sixteen at the time, Andy twenty. There were photographs of Veronica and Hazel. The librarian was right - Hazel had been a pretty girl. He found a photograph of Tom and noticed he bore a vague resemblance to the white-haired man he'd seen in the village. If he'd been sixteen in 1966, he'd be fifty-eight now. The man in the village looked ten years older. He found no mention of the occult design that had been drawn on the floor of the great hall.

When he left the library, he rang Tessa and asked her where he could access a computer. She told him to meet her at a café in an arts centre popular with students. They had computers with internet access there.

*

Arriving at Bristo Place, he pulled open the doors of the former Congressional Church and stepped inside the arts centre. He headed for the café, making his way to the counter, where he ordered a coffee and asked to use one of the computers. He sat in a quiet corner of the room, away from others, and logged on to a computer. He searched for images of occult circles. Illustrations of various designs flashed on his screen.

Reaching into his jacket pocket, he pulled out the piece of paper on which he'd drawn the circle. Unfolding it, he saw two of the images displayed matched his drawing. He clicked on the first and was redirected to a website. The image was of the Magical Circle of King Solomon and appeared in *The Book of the Goetia of Solomon the King* by Aleister Crowley. Although similar, the words written between the outer and inner circles were drawn within a coiled serpent. The version on the floor of the great hall had not included the serpent.

'Is that what you found drawn on the floor of the hall?'

Glancing over his shoulder, James found Tessa standing behind him. She kissed him gently on the lips, pulled up a chair and sat down next to him.

'According to this site, the book the circle appears in contains diagrams and seals for the invocation of spirits.'

'What did you find out at the library?'

'In the summer of '66, two brothers from the village took a couple of girls up to the house.' James paused, unsure whether to continue.

'What happened to them?'

'The eldest brother and the two girls were never seen again. The younger brother, Thomas Rutherford, claimed they were attacked by a large black dog.'

'Please tell me you're joking …'

James shook his head. 'The bodies of the oldest brother and the two girls were never discovered, and Tom spent the next thirty years in an asylum.'

'A large black dog … that's some coincidence.'

'At the time Tom claimed the creature was a hound from Hell.'

'You think they were the ones responsible for drawing the occult circle on the floor of the hall?'

'It would appear so.'

James wondered if they'd inadvertently raised the hound from Hell - but immediately dismissed the idea as ridiculous.

'I'm sure the dog you encountered was nothing more than a stray looking for food and shelter,' said Tessa.

When she saw he didn't look convinced, she took the keyboard from him and typed the word hellhound into the image search. Artists' impressions of hounds from Hell, including several drawings of Cerberus, the three-headed dog that guarded the entrance to Hades, appeared on the screen. All were monstrous creatures pictured snarling, bearing their long fangs, their eyes glowing red. Some were shown breathing fire.

'Did your dog look like any of those?'

'No, of course not.'

Tessa clicked on one of the images and was redirected to a website. James read the text that accompanied the illustration and noticed a reference to hellhounds giving off a sulphur like odour. He hadn't mentioned the smell of sulphur in the room to Tessa and decided to keep quiet about it. If what he had encountered was a hound from Hell, why hadn't it attacked any of the builders working in the house? Maybe, he told himself, it only appeared at night, after they'd left the house. Then he remembered that Thomas and his brother had visited the house with the girls during the day. He was being ridiculous and he knew it. There had to be a rational explanation for it all.

After logging off the computer, Tessa asked him if he'd eaten that day. James shook his head and told her he hadn't.

'I didn't think so. Come on, I'll buy you something to eat.'

Leaving Bristo Place, they made their way along George IV Bridge to an Italian restaurant. Neither spoke about the incident at lunch, only later when they'd returned to his apartment did James raise the subject again, telling her he thought the whole thing had been a practical joke.

'I think someone's having a little fun at my expense,' he said.

He was standing shaving at the sink, a towel wrapped round his waist, his thick black hair combed away from his face.

'The librarian told me everyone in the area has heard of the House in the Witches' Wood,' he said, running a straight razor over his lathered jaw. 'Whoever's responsible must have known it was only a matter of time before I found out too, so they decided to play a prank on me.'

Before Tessa had a chance to reply, he continued.

'They must have slipped the dog in through the French window,' he said, pausing to wash his blade in the sink, 'and taken him out the same way. That's why there were no paw prints in the hall.'

And the odour of the hellhound was nothing more than an ammonium sulphide stink bomb picked up in a toy shop.

Tessa sat on the edge of the roll-top bath and turned on the taps. 'I thought you said the French window was locked.' She poured a generous amount of bubble bath into the water.

She was wearing a silk dressing gown, her hair piled on top of her head and held in place by a clip.

'It was this morning,' said James. 'But that doesn't mean it was last night. The key is always in the lock. Men are in and out of the house all day.'

Tessa moved round the bathroom, lighting scented candles. When she had finished, she pulled open a linen cabinet, removed two towels and placed them down on a rattan chair before moving back to the bath.

'Anyone could have pocketed the key,' murmured James, staring at himself in the mirror.

In the reflection of the mirror, he watched Tessa slip off her robe, allowing it to fall to the floor at her feet. Momentarily distracted as he watched her step into the bath, he almost cut himself with his razor. She eased herself slowly down into the bath, sliding through the bubbles, the hot water enveloping her body.

'Who would do such a thing?' she said, laying her head back on the edge of the bath.

'Someone from the village.'

Tessa reached her toe up and out of the water, rotating the taps until the running water trickled to a stop. 'Why?' she asked before closing her eyes and taking a deep relaxing breath.

'Who knows,' said James. 'Maybe the locals don't like the idea of a Roxburgh returning to Wychwood House and are trying to scare me away.' Patting his face dry with a towel, he switched off the lights and made his way over to the bath.

Tessa lay with her head tilted back over the edge of the bath, the flickering candlelight reflecting off her wet skin.

'May I join you?'

She opened her eyes and glanced up at him.

'Of course,' she said dreamily, a faint smile curving her lips, her eyes meeting his before trailing down to his bare chest.

'It may even be one of my builders envious of the life I lead,' he said, removing his towel and throwing it over the rattan chair.

He stepped into the bath behind her, his legs sliding next to hers as he settled himself down into the warm water.

She leant back against him, resting against his chest, her head on his shoulder. 'Aren't we all?' she said.

Smoothing away stray strands of her hair, James placed a kiss on her neck, his soft lips lightly brushing her ear.

'At least you get to enjoy it with me,' he whispered.

'For that,' she murmured, 'I am very grateful.'

Without saying another word, she turned in his arms, the water sloshing over the sides of the bath as she moved round to face him, her eyes meeting his. Looking deeply into his eyes, she wrapped her arms round his neck, her mouth meeting his as she threaded her fingers into his hair. James then reached for her hips, her legs sliding round his waist, their kisses deepening as he pulled her wet soapy body against his.

CHAPTER EIGHT

Isobel and Will remained at the stone circle until the sun disappeared behind the far hills. When they returned to the house, they found the others in the drawing room enjoying afternoon tea.

Jemima was the first to notice them enter the room. She asked them if they'd had a nice walk.

'Yes, thank you,' replied Isobel, sitting down at the table. 'We found a stone circle not far from here.'

Miriam poured herself out some tea from a silver teapot. 'Growing up in Wiltshire,' she said, 'I'd have thought you'd be bored of stone circles by now.'

Will sat down next to her and reached for a sandwich. 'Oh, they're nothing like the stone circles and henges in Wiltshire.'

'Then surely they would have held even less interest for you.'

'Well, I've decided which dress I'm going to wear,' said Jemima, smiling proudly.

Alexander sighed. 'Finally,' he said despairingly. 'It's taken her all afternoon.'

'The preparation for a party is the best part,' explained Jemima.

'Which dress did you decide on?' asked Isobel.

'I'll show you later. I want it to be a surprise.'

Miriam pushed back her chair and stood up. 'Well, I'd better go and prepare myself for the party tonight.' She paused, then added, 'Which I've no doubt will be the best part of the evening for me too.'

Jemima laughed. 'Oh, Miriam, you're so funny,' she said. 'I can never think of anything amusing to say … not until it's too late anyway.'

'Even then, I imagine you struggle,' muttered Miriam, crossing the room.

When she had left, Jemima said, 'Maybe she's looking forward to the party more than we thought.'

'Yes, she can hardly contain her excitement,' said Alexander doubtfully, raising his eyebrows.

Jemima then led Isobel upstairs to show her the dress she'd decided to wear, leaving Will alone with Alexander.

'You were a long time this afternoon,' he said, pacing back and forth before the fireplace.

'We went for a long walk.'

'Rather mean of you to leave me with Miriam.'

'That was your choice. Anyway, Jemima was with you.'

'Jemima's been upstairs all afternoon trying on dresses,' said Alexander irritably. 'She wouldn't even let me in to see her.' He took a cigar out of the humidor on the coffee table and amputated the tip. 'I hope the results are worth the effort.'

'I'm sure they will be.' Will settled himself down into an armchair. 'Do you have to smoke that in here?'

'What else do you suggest I do with it?' said Alexander, lighting the cigar. Smoke curled up into the air.

'Why don't you go out onto the terrace?'

'Why don't you?'

Will had known Alexander since they were at Oxford, and although they now worked closely together at Crenshaw, Willoughby and Stern, he knew very little about him. Alexander never spoke about his family. Will had learnt they owned a Palladian mansion not far from Marlborough but had never visited the house himself. Bill had mentioned he was one of four, having two older brothers and a sister, though he didn't know if she was younger or older than him. On more than one occasion, he'd overheard him claim - usually to impress some young woman he'd just met - to be descended from a prestigious aristocratic family from Provence-Alpes-Côte d'Azur region in the South of France. Émigrés from revolutionary France, they'd been rescued from Madame Guillotine by none other than the Scarlet Pimpernel. To his dismay, more often than not, he'd been believed. The truth was, of course, slightly less romantic, the de Villeneuves being a French banking family that moved to England in the mid-nineteenth-century to expand their business.

Will regarded him thoughtfully. 'You never told me you knew Isobel.'

'Didn't I?' Alexander blew out a soft smoke ring. 'I bumped into her at Glyndebourne. She was there with her mother. I knew her before then, of course. She came to my eighteenth the summer before I started at Oxford.'

'That was your party?' Will stifled a chuckle, a grin appearing on his face. 'So you're the awful bore she spent the whole night trying to avoid.'

'I am? I mean, I was?'

Will nodded. 'James told me, to avoid an embarrassing scene, he had Hodgson drive her home around ten.'

'So that's where the little minx went. Can't blame her, I did come on a bit too strong.'

'Don't you always?'

Alexander wandered over to the fireplace. 'Well, she didn't appear to harbour any bad feelings towards me when I saw her again.' He knelt down and began prodding the remnants of the fire with a poker, stirring the glowing embers. 'She'd just moved into her aunt's flat. As she didn't know anyone in the area, I took it upon myself to present her to society. At the time, my intentions were purely honourable.'

Will was sure they weren't.

'And you never thought to introduce her to me?'

Alexander placed a log on the fire, stood up and turned to face Will. 'Why on earth would I want to do that?'

'Because we're old friends.'

'Who you've been spending far too much time getting reacquainted with.' He puffed contemptuously on his cigar. 'Quite something, isn't she? I noticed you haven't been able to keep your eyes off her since we arrived. I'm beginning to regret bringing Joanna with me.'

'Jemima.'

'Her too.' He mixed himself a whisky and soda before sitting himself down in the armchair opposite Will. 'She seems to think something once happened between you two. After seeing you together earlier, I'm inclined to agree.'

The log fell in the grate and hissed for a moment.

'I remember the first time we met,' continued Alexander. 'It was at that party James's parents held just before we all left for Oxford. If I remember correctly, you spent most of the night dancing with Isobel. In fact, you didn't leave each other's sides. Did something happen between you two that night?'

Will stood up and walked towards the French window. 'The three of us were very close then.'

'I didn't see her dancing with James.'

'James doesn't dance.'

The fire began to spit angrily.

Alexander huffed. 'She's a bit out of your league, don't you think? Her father's a baronet.'

'I know who her father is,' Will said sharply. He pulled back the thick curtains, turned the handle and opened the doors of the French window. A cool, refreshing breeze blew into the room.

Alexander drew deeply on his cigar. 'I'd pay a little bit more attention to Miriam if I were you.' His voice held a threatening note.

'I don't see how that is any of your business.'

After blowing out a cloud of smoke, Alexander held up a protesting hand. 'It is my business while you are seeing Miriam. I don't want to see the old girl get hurt.'

Will sank back down in his seat. 'We're just friends. Miriam said as much to me yesterday.'

'I don't know about that. She spoke quite fondly of you earlier. You may be burrowing your way into her heart after all. Bill's been trying to marry her off for years. I think he expected me to step up to the crease - made things a bit awkward for a while. Thankfully, you came along and saved the day.'

'I've no intention of asking Miriam to marry me!'

'Maybe not, but you know as well as I do, she's the only reason you have a snowball's chance in hell of being kept on at the firm once you've qualified.'

Will hated to admit it, but Alexander was right on all counts.

Since the banking crisis Messrs Crenshaw, Willoughby and Stern hadn't retained as many trainees as they had in previous years. Until he'd started seeing Miriam, he felt he was being overlooked in favour of other trainees, and it seemed increasingly unlikely he'd be kept on at the firm once he'd qualified. Of course, that changed once they'd been out a couple of times and Bill began taking an interest in him, introducing him to some of his most important clients. He'd even gone so far as to suggest he had a promising future with the firm.

Will was well aware his 'promising future' depended on him continuing to see Miriam. He wasn't proud of the fact, but he had to look out for himself.

'I'm going to be kept on at the firm,' he insisted, 'because I work damn hard and will make a great lawyer.'

'If that's the case, then why are you continuing to see Miriam, someone you seem to have little affection for?'

'Because …' Will paused thoughtfully.

'I'm waiting …'

'I happen to think she's quite beautiful.'

Alexander's enormous laugh rang through the room. 'Now I know you're lying!' he cried.

*

Isobel, dressed in a pale pink satin sheath dress, stood admiring herself in the cheval mirror.

Jemima, sitting on the chaise-longue beside her, had opted to wear a beaded champagne flapper dress that left her arms bare, her skirt rising just below the knee. For added authenticity, she was wearing silk stockings, a suspender belt and a pair of high heels.

'It looks great on you,' she said, glancing up at the dress Isobel was wearing.

Isobel agreed. She thought the gown an elegant, timeless dress that probably dated from the early 1930s when the bias-cut came into fashion - though it looked a bit too much like a wedding dress for her liking.

They heard a knock on the door, and both turned to see Miriam enter the room. Much to their surprise, she asked to see the dresses they'd found in the wardrobe. Neither knew what had prompted this change of heart in her and didn't dare ask.

As Jemima fastened the clip of her suspender belt onto the silk stockings she was wearing, she asked Miriam what she thought of Isobel's dress.

Miriam regarded the gown that clung to the curves of Isobel's Junoesque figure. 'Looks a little tight to me,' she said.

'Maybe a little,' said Isobel, opening the wardrobe doors, 'but I think I can get away with it.'

Miriam promptly selected three dresses before disappearing into the en-suite bathroom to try them on for size. She did not reappear to ask their opinion, remaining locked in the bathroom whilst changing.

Isobel sat herself down at the dressing table. 'Now I've chosen which dress I'm going to wear,' she said. 'I just have to choose the jewellery to match.'

Jemima rose to her feet. 'There's jewellery too?'

Isobel nodded and opened a jewellery box. There were diamonds everywhere; they covered necklaces, bangles and bracelets.

Jemima's attention was drawn to a long string of freshwater pearls. 'Are they yours?' she asked, lifting out the necklace.

Isobel shook her head regretfully. 'No, they also belonged to Emily.'

Jemima hung the pearls round her neck. 'She must have had quite a time living in London in the twenties,' she said, 'spending her evenings attending one fashionable party after another, being adored by all those men.'

'Oh, I don't know,' said Isobel. 'I imagine she would have grown tired of it all very quickly.'

'Even so, it couldn't have been easy leaving life in the city to come and live here.'

'No, it couldn't have been.'

Jemima lay back down on the chaise-longue. 'Personally,' she said, stretching out her legs, 'I'd jump at the chance to marry an earl.'

'Henry wasn't an earl.'

'Still, I imagine he had money.'

'Probably not as much as you'd think. Not back then, anyway.'

'Then why did Emily marry him?'

'She may not have had much of a choice,' said Isobel. 'If my mother had her way, I'd be married to James by now.' She paused thoughtfully. 'Fortunately for me, things are a bit different now than they were in the thirties.' She wondered how true that was. 'Sometimes,' she continued, 'I think my mother only married my father because he was due to inherit a baronetcy. Their marriage is not a happy one.'

'That can't be the only reason she married him …'

'Well, I can't think of another. They have nothing in common. The only time they spend with each other is in the company of others. That's not the sort of marriage I want.' She turned to face Jemima. 'You know, I'm not so sure about this dress. I think I prefer the green one. Could you help me off with it, please?

Jemima eased the gown carefully up over Isobel's upstretched arms, and said, 'So you do want to get married.'

Isobel smiled. 'Maybe one day,' she said, slipping on a robe. 'Just not right now.'

*

When Will went upstairs he expected to find Miriam in their bedroom, but she was nowhere to be found, so he took the opportunity to dress for the evening, changing into his dinner suit once again. He knew he should heed Alexander's warning but was enjoying spending time with Isobel again. They'd been friends for a long time, and he'd missed her company over the last six years. His fondest memories of their time together were when she visited him at his cottage. On rainy afternoons, they'd spend hours in his bedroom while his mother busied herself downstairs, often looking in on them to make sure they weren't getting up to anything they shouldn't, Isobel being only sixteen at the time.

He realised then he had to tell Miriam about his relationship with Isobel, admit to her that feelings he'd buried deep down inside him were in danger of resurfacing. Feelings he knew he would never have for her. But how could he tell her? He'd never told anyone. Not even James. He'd wanted to, but had always hesitated, never feeling the time was right. He hadn't told him when his friend had returned from his holiday with his parents, and he hadn't told him once they were at university - though that was for a different reason.

After he finished dressing, he left the room and knocked on the door to Alexander and Jemima's room. When there was no reply, he made his way over to Isobel's room on the other side of the house where he was sure he'd find Miriam and Jemima. He was going to have to wait to speak to Miriam - a prospect he didn't relish.

He came to Isobel's bedroom and knocked gently on the door.

'Can I come in?' he asked.

The door swung open to reveal Isobel standing in the doorway. Without saying a word, she took his arm and dragged him into the room.

'I need your opinion,' she said. 'I can't decide between gowns.' She held up both in front of her. 'Which one do you prefer?'

'The pale pink one.'

'The pink one it is then.' She hung the gowns on the wardrobe door.

Will glanced round the bedroom. 'This is a beautiful room,' he said.

Turning, he saw the portrait of Lady Roxburgh on the wall behind him. Her proud face seemed to be staring down at him disapprovingly.

'She even gets her own bathroom,' said Jemima from the chaise-longue. Her hair was set in finger waves and pin curls.

'I was looking for Miriam.'

Isobel sat down on her bed. 'She's in the bathroom.' She gestured to the closed door. 'She's decided to wear one of the dresses after all.'

'She has?' said Will, surprised.

Isobel nodded, a smile playing on her lips.

Will knocked gently on the door to the bathroom. 'Miriam, are you ready to go downstairs yet?'

'No, I am not,' she replied without opening the door. 'Go down without me. I shan't be much longer.'

'You can escort us down if you like,' said Jemima.

'It would be my pleasure,' said Will.

Isobel picked up the satin sheath gown she'd draped across the four-poster bed. 'Just give me a minute, and I'll be right with you.'

'I'll go and see if James is ready,' said Will, making for the door. 'We'll wait for you on the gallery.'

To his surprise, when he knocked on James's bedroom door, it swung open almost immediately. His host appeared dressed for the party. He'd tidied up his hair and even trimmed his beard.

'You look better,' said Will.

'Thank you,' his friend said, leading the way back down the corridor to the gallery. 'I feel better. Shall we go downstairs?'

'Not just yet. We're to escort Isobel and Jemima down.'

'Then while we're waiting, I'll introduce you to my ancestors.' He gestured to the portraits behind him. 'I like to think the paintings are by Gainsborough and Reynolds, though it's unlikely. I know the ninth earl's portrait was painted by Hoppner, and the portrait of Edward Roxburgh, who was killed at the Somme, is by William Orpen. It's hanging in the library alongside the Heywood Hardy hunt scenes.' He drew his friend's attention to a faded, blackened portrait hanging on the wall behind him. 'This is the earliest surviving portrait I have and shows the first Earl of Leithen as a young man.'

The earl was wearing an embroidered jacket, short, padded trousers and a white lace ruff. On his right hand was a ring. Will glanced at a portrait of another of the earls dressed in an exquisitely tailored plain dark coat with a frilled cuffed, high-collared linen shirt and a perfectly tied cravat.

'I didn't realise you were related to Beau Brummell,' he said.

James smiled. 'That's the ninth Earl of Leithen.'

'He's quite the dandy,' said Will. 'This is the portrait painted by Hoppner?'

His friend nodded. 'As a young man, he moved within the highest social circles of Regency London, though I'm afraid he was no Mr Darcy. He lived an extravagant lifestyle, spending most of his time womanising and gambling. Like the Prince Regent, he paid little regard to the plight of the poor, many of whom were dying of starvation and freezing to death on the streets of London at the time. He was probably too busy polishing his boots with champagne.'

'They really did that?'

'Brummell wouldn't clean his boots with anything else. After falling heavily into debt, the earl decided to marry, setting his sights on the daughter of a Scottish tobacco merchant. They were married in the parish kirk, and he remained here briefly with his young bride, leaving soon after she fell pregnant. Alone in London, he soon reverted to his wicked ways. I've found letters from him begging his wife for money. I doubt he would have ever returned to Scotland again had it not been for George IV's visit to Scotland in 1823. Having been an associate of the king when he was Prince Regent, the earl was keen to take part in the celebrations orchestrated by Sir Walter Scott.

'Scotland was reborn in a grand pageant of the clan chieftains, with George IV decked out in full Highland regalia, complete with kilt and pink tights. Inspired by the celebrations, the earl decided to settle in Scotland. He was approaching fifty by this point, his womanising days behind him, and set about building his own medieval castle. Despite the stock market crash of 1825, which wiped out a considerable part of his wife's fortune, he continued with his extravagant plans. He died four years later, a year before the house was completed. After his death, though she received some financial assistance from her mother's family, his daughter, Lady Roxburgh, was forced to sell furniture, clothes and some of her personal belongings.'

'Is that a portrait of Lady Roxburgh hanging in Isobel's bedroom?'

James nodded. 'I believe so.'

Hearing voices echo down the corridor, they turned to see Isobel step onto the gallery with Jemima on her arm. She was about to comment on James's appearance when Jemima stepped forward.

'Well, what do you think?' she said, a wide grin on her face. Giggling nervously, she twisted and turned to allow herself to be admired.

'You look very beautiful,' said James perfunctorily, casting a brief cursory glance at her dress before looking at Isobel. 'You both do.'

Isobel found it was Will's reaction she sought. Their eyes met but he dropped her gaze and glanced down at the floor.

'Are there any portraits of William Roxburgh in his Scot's Grey uniform?' she asked.

Taking her hand, James drew it through his arm. 'I'm afraid not,' he said, leading the way downstairs. 'I have yet to unearth any portraits of him.'

Will extended the crook of his elbow to Jemima and they followed on behind.

'Were the debts she incurred by her father the reason Lady Roxburgh never married?' asked Isobel.

'I'm afraid so,' said James. 'Unable to afford servants, she lived here alone. In later years, she became paranoid the house was going to be taken from her, driving away anyone who came to visit.'

'How sad.'

As they crossed the old medieval hall, Jemima looked up at the portrait above the fireplace. 'Is he another of your ancestors?' she asked.

'Unfortunately not,' said James. 'That's James IV.'

They found Alexander in the drawing room, a sight to behold in full Highland dress, complete with Prince Charles jacket with gleaming silver buttons, kilt, sporran, kilt hose and ghillie brogues. Seeing them enter the room, he crushed the stump of his cigar into an ashtray, his glance wandering appreciatively over Isobel and Jemima.

'You certainly look the part,' said Will.

'I thought one of us should,' replied Alexander. 'Miriam not joining us?'

'She'll be down soon,' said Isobel.

'Then let's clear a space to dance whilst we're waiting,' said Jemima eagerly.

Alexander and Will carried the sofa and armchairs to the sides of the room, whilst Isobel and Jemima moved the vases and ornaments out of harm's way. Once the room was cleared, Jemima put a record on the gramophone, wound the handle, and a quickstep by Joe Daniels and his Hotshots began to play. She dragged Alexander into the middle of the room, his arm snaking slowly round her waist, and they began to dance to the fast-paced music.

Although energetic, Alexander was uncoordinated, and lumbered about the floor, treading clumsily on Jemima's small feet.

'I've no formal training,' he announced proudly. 'I simply have natural rhythm.'

The song ended and Will made his way over to the gramophone. 'How about something a little less energetic?' he said, changing the record. 'Before Jemima's feet get broken.'

Placing a record on the turntable, he set the needle in the groove, and a waltz began to play.

Out of the corner of her eye, Isobel became aware of Alexander's gaze upon her and turned her head to see him prowling towards her. Turning her back to him, she glanced anxiously about the room. Will had remained by the gramophone flicking through the records. Alexander would intercept her before she reached him.

James extended his hand to her. 'Would you care to dance?'

Isobel smiled, and nodding appreciatively, took his hand. Alexander grunted disapprovingly and resumed dancing with Jemima.

James placed his hand lightly on Isobel's back as they began to waltz across the room.

'I hope you don't mind that we decided to have a party tonight,' said Isobel.

'Of course I don't mind,' replied James. 'You know how I love watching Alexander make a fool of himself on the dance floor.'

'Do you remember the first party your parents allowed us to attend at the Manor? I was allowed my sip of champagne that night. I remember thinking then I wanted to spend my life going from one party to the next. At the time I didn't realise not all parties are like the ones held by your mother.'

'You miss the Manor, don't you?'

Isobel nodded. 'Of course. Don't you?'

'This is my home now,' James said flatly. After a pause, he added, 'I've been looking forward to your visit for a long time now. I just wish it could have been under different circumstances.' Once again, he paused before continuing. 'Do you remember our last weekend together?'

'At the party?'

James shook his head. 'Before then when it was just the three of us.'

'The weather was glorious that weekend.'

'We had a picnic down by the pond. It was always cooler there than anywhere else in the garden.'

Isobel remembered it was there James had told them his mother had decided to hold a party before he left for university. They lay amongst the ferns, shaded by a Swamp Cyprus and a wide-spreading yew. Water lilies floated on the still surface of the pond, their flowers in bloom.

'I had hoped,' said James, 'it would just be the three of us this weekend as it was then.'

'Me too.'

The waltz faded and Will put on another foxtrot. Alexander grabbed Jemima and propelled her into the air. Whirling her about, he almost collided with Miriam as she entered the room.

'Terribly sorry!' he cried.

He didn't seem to recognise her. She was dressed in a black satin floor-length gown that trailed across the floor behind her. Her hair was down, and she'd applied some rouge to her cheeks.

Alexander swung Jemima in a graceful pirouette before her. 'Miriam, you *are* beautiful,' he said.

Miriam's cheeks turned crimson.

Alexander extended his hand towards her. 'Would you care to dance?' he asked.

To everyone's surprise, she took his hand. Alexander placed his right arm firmly round her waist and swept her across the floor.

Jemima hobbled across the room and fell slackly into an armchair. 'You're not dancing?' she asked Will, who was still flicking through the gramophone records.

'Did you know records used to be labelled by the type of dance they were?' He held up a record. 'See this is a quick step.' He picked up another. 'This one's a waltz.'

Jemima pretended to yawn. 'Are you always this fascinating at parties?'

Will placed the records back on the pile. 'I don't get invited to many parties.'

'I think I've figured out why.' Jemima grinned and slumped back in her seat, stretching her legs out in front of her. 'Have you found any music we can dance a reel to?'

'I wouldn't know where to start.'

'Look for music with a time signature of 4/4, like Gay Gordons or the Dashing White Sergeant.'

'You seem to be quite the expert on Scottish Country Dancing.'

'I played Meg Brockie in a production of Brigadoon at the Queen's Theatre.'

'On Shaftesbury Avenue?'

Jemima shook her head. 'Billet Lane, Hornchurch.' Her gaze drifted across the room. 'Isobel will be disappointed if you don't ask her to dance.'

'She seems quite happy dancing with James,' replied Will, rising to his feet.

'She'd rather be dancing with you.'

Will picked up his glass of whisky and sat himself down in the other armchair. 'She wouldn't if she had any sense. I could hardly keep her in the manner to which she has become accustomed.'

'You've done all right for yourself. Anyway, I'm sure she's more than capable of keeping herself in any way she chooses.'

'She should be with someone who can afford to buy her diamond necklaces … not cheap costume jewellery.'

Jemima lent towards him. 'Don't let this become common knowledge,' she whispered into his ear, 'but not all women are after rich men to keep them in stunning dresses and sparkling jewellery. Some are looking for true love.'

Will's eyebrows rose. 'Really? Even you?'

'I said some, not all. I look far too fabulous in this necklace. Why don't you stop sitting here feeling sorry for yourself and go and dance with her?'

'I'm sure it hasn't escaped your notice, but I came here with Miriam.'

Jemima brushed a stray hair from her eyes and glanced over at Miriam and Alexander dancing together. 'I wouldn't worry about her.' She nudged Will forward. 'Go on, Will. It's only a dance.'

'I know what dancing can lead to.' He rose to his feet. 'You must be thirsty. What would you like to drink?'

Jemima glanced towards the door. 'Looks like we're drinking champagne tonight.'

Hodgson had entered the drawing room carrying a tray of crystal flutes and a bottle of champagne. After placing them gently down on the sideboard, he removed the foil from the neck of the bottle and began to untwist the wire that caged the cork. The music stopped and everyone gathered round as he popped the cork and began filling the crystal flutes with champagne.

When they all had glasses in their hands, Alexander made a toast.

'To renewed acquaintances,' he said with a grin. He winked at Will who shot him a vicious look back.

They clinked glasses and sipped their champagne.

CHAPTER NINE

The party was over by ten. Their host had left them early in the evening, disappearing without telling anyone where he was going. Isobel, who'd been the first to notice his absence, had gone upstairs to tempt him back down. Not long afterwards, when Alexander and Miriam, who'd spent the evening talking together in a darkened corner of the room, ignoring the others, realised they were down to the last of the champagne, they promptly left the room in search of Hodgson to see if he could furnish them with another bottle or two.

When, after about ten minutes, they hadn't returned, Jemima decided to go and find them. 'It's easy to get lost in this house,' she said to Will, before hurrying out the door.

Finding himself alone, Will pulled his armchair closer to the fireplace and sunk himself down into its deep seat.

The evening had been a disappointment. He'd hoped they'd manage to capture some of the magic of the party held at the Manor, though knew deep down they never would.

No night, before or since, had been as magical as that one.

He could almost hear the string quartet playing in the garden, the soft music drifting through the air, drawing him back to the house. Closing his eyes, he recalled stepping into the Manor to find the parlour filled with James's friends from Marlborough. Boys wearing expensive dinner suits and girls in lavish ball gowns stood in groups chatting. He pictured Isobel descending the staircase on James's arm and remembered thinking how radiant and elegant she'd looked in a long backless gown she'd thought far too revealing, all eyes turning on her as James led her across the room towards him.

As the evening drew on couples began to dance on the lawn, and it wasn't long before he and Isobel joined them, holding each other close as they danced. Many of James's friends approached Isobel requesting a dance, but she refused them all, unwilling to leave his side, as though worried if she let him go, she'd lose him.

Will noticed Isobel's mother trying to attract her attention. She seemed to want Isobel to dance with someone else.

Isobel rested her head on his chest and said, 'I don't want to dance with anyone but you.'

Seeing her mother making her way through the dancing couples towards them, Isobel, keeping a tight hold on his hand, led him towards the main lawn where a few guests had convened. When they saw her father Clive amongst them, they turned and slipped through a narrow gap in the yew hedge, making their way down a flagged path to the water garden. Will knew where Isobel was taking him. There was a deep arbour of yew overlooking the lily pond where they could stay hidden from her parents.

To their disappointment, they found it occupied. Other guests had convened round the pond, so they sat on the low stone wall, their backs to the house. A waiter carrying a tray of champagne flutes approached them. Will shook his head, refusing the offer.

Isobel reached for a flute, drank down its contents, and placed the empty glass down on the wall beside her. 'Will, I don't want this evening to end,' she said.

'Nor do I.'

Behind him, Will heard Isobel's mother say, 'It's getting late. Say goodnight to William, dear.'

He turned to see her reach for Isobel's hand.

'Goodnight to William dear.' As she was pulled to her feet, she whispered into Will's ear, 'Meet me in the wood.'

'Under the oak tree were I always used to wait for you?'

Isobel nodded, kissed him gently on the cheek, and walked away, the scent of her perfume lingering in the air after she was gone.

'Are you asleep?'

From his armchair, Will glanced up at Isobel with half-closed eyes. 'I was having a most wonderful dream,' he said, promptly shutting his eyes.

Isobel dragged an armchair across the room. 'I can't find James anywhere.'

'He's probably in the kitchen with Hodgson. Alexander and Miriam may find him yet.'

Isobel glanced at the bottle on the table beside Will. 'Is there any champagne left in that bottle?'

Will gave a slight shrug and reached over to the bottle. 'Looks like there is.' He lifted it off the table. 'Care to finish it off?'

Isobel nodded and grabbed her flute from the mantelpiece. Will filled the glass and topped up his own with the little that was left.

'How many glasses have you had?' asked Isobel.

'Only a couple -'

'A couple too many. You never used to drink.'

I never used to need to, he thought. 'How else do you expect me to make it through this *frightfully* dull evening?' he said.

Isobel sighed regretfully. 'All the parties I go to nowadays are frightfully dull.'

Will's eyes narrowed. 'Even the ones you go to with Alexander?'

'Is that a hint of jealousy I detect in your voice?'

Will regarded her thoughtfully. Had she really fallen for Alexander's dubious charms? He hoped not. Surely, she had more sense. 'I've never understood why so many women seem to find him irresistible,' he said.

'Maybe it's because he has an apartment in Jermyn Street, or it could be because he's an expert on fine wines and can afford tables at the best restaurants London has to offer.'

'I think that's enough examples for now. You know his money's not his own …'

'It never is,' said Isobel ruefully. She lifted her champagne flute to her lips and took a sip. 'I had dinner with him once and only went to a couple of parties with him because he told me you and James were going to be there.'

'He did?' said Will, surprised.

Isobel nodded. 'Nothing happened between us - I can assure you of that.'

'I don't get invited to many parties, but from now on I'll attend all the ones I'm invited to and gatecrash all the ones I'm not.'

'I wouldn't bother if I were you,' said Isobel. 'They were very dull parties.' After a pause, she said, 'Alexander mentioned you're a trainee at Crenshaw, Willoughby and Stern.'

Will grimaced. 'How good of him,' he said. 'It's not the type of law firm I wanted to work for, but you have to take what you can get nowadays.'

'And how long have you been seeing Miriam?'

'Is that a hint of jealousy I detect in *your* voice?'

'Alexander told me things were quite serious between you.'

'Did he now? I didn't realise I was such a popular topic with him. Well, they're not … I can assure *you* of that.' After a pause, he said, 'So is there anyone in your life?'

Isobel kept her eyes fixed on the champagne glass she was caressing in her hands, watching the last of the bubbles fizzle away. Champagne goes flat so quickly, she thought.

'There was,' she said regretfully, 'but he made promises he didn't keep and then forgot all about me. He broke my heart, I'm afraid. I've never believed a word a man has told me since.'

Will felt a pang of jealousy. 'A very wise policy,' he said.

Isobel kicked off her shoes and pulled out a hairpin, her long chestnut brown hair cascading down over her shoulders. 'I didn't see you dancing earlier.'

'No one asked me.'

Isobel drank down his champagne and set her empty glass down on the floor. 'Well, I'm asking you now,' she said, standing up.

Will allowed her to pull him to his feet.

Isobel smoothed out the wrinkles on her gown. 'We'll need music,' she said.

Will crossed to the gramophone, replacing the last record played, the "Duke of Perth", with "The Very Thought of You".

After winding the handle at the side, he set the needle in the groove. When the record began to play, he closed the lid and crossed the room to where Isobel stood waiting for him. Placing one hand in hers, the other resting on her back, they began dancing together to the music, his thoughts returning to the night of the party …

He'd waited under the oak tree for what seemed like hours, listening to the music and laughter floating through the night air. When the party drew to a close, the music stopped and the voices faded as the guests began to head home. Only a few remained. A small group had gathered on the main lawn and were playing croquet.

He never found out why it had taken her so long to join him. At the time, he assumed her parents were keeping a close eye on her and she was finding it difficult to slip away unnoticed. He was about to give up and head home when, through the gap in the yew hedge, he caught a glimpse of her making her way across the lawn. When she saw the guests playing croquet, she'd given them a wide berth, her pace quickening with every step she took.

Once in the orchard, she removed her heels and flung them behind her, moving carefully to avoid the apples that lay on the ground. His heart beating fast, he went to meet her. She stretched out her arm, took his hand and without saying a word, pulled him into the wood. Only when they were far from view of the house and gardens did she come to a stop. She turned to him breathlessly, her face patterned in the moonlight that filtered through the foliage of the trees. He'd gone to speak, but she took his face in her hands, her soft lips meeting his, silencing him. Keeping a firm grip on his hand, she led him further into the depths of the wood, only releasing him when they came to the river.

Will wondered if being in his arms again brought back memories of that night to her too. When they reached the river's edge, she'd loosened her hair until it hung free and full round her shoulders, before unfastening her gown, pulling it down over the curves of her hips until it tumbled to the ground. Without turning to look at him, she stepped out of the dress that lay at her feet and hurried down the grassy bank and began wading out into the river. Will watched her as she lowered herself into the water and swam a few strokes before turning to face him.

'Aren't you going to join me?' she asked, a smile playing on her lips.

Nodding, he fumbled with the buttons on his shirt, his breath becoming laboured as he undressed. Finally, after what seemed like an age, he ran down the bank to join her, wading through the cold water before swimming out to meet her. Tentatively, they'd drawn closer, her lips meeting his, the strong currents swirling round them as he pulled her close, threatening to drag them under. Drawing back her hair, he'd kissed her again, his mouth leaving hers and finding her neck, his kisses lingering over her bare shoulders, her wet skin glistening in the moonlight.

The lips he'd longed to kiss ever since were now so near; her neck that he'd trailed kisses down a breath away. He longed to pull her close until he could feel the rapid beating of her heart as he had then. Glancing up, his eyes met hers, and he instinctively knew she was thinking of that night too, remembering every kiss, every touch, reliving every moment, just as he was.

Voices echoed round the great hall.

Upon hearing them, they automatically stepped back from each other. The music had stopped but they hadn't noticed, the needle continuing to scratch round the record, only stopping when the gramophone unwound itself. Isobel suggested hiding, and taking Will by the elbow, steered him towards the French window. Together they slipped behind the curtains, opened the doors and stepped onto the terrace.

'Do you think they saw us?' whispered Isobel.

'I do hope not,' said Will.

They stood in silence for a moment so as not to be overheard. A full moon broke through between banks of drifting clouds and moonlight shone down upon them.

Isobel gazed up at the stars shimmering in the night sky. 'What a beautiful night,' she said.

Will noticed she was shivering. 'You're freezing,' he said. 'We should go back inside.'

'Not yet,' she whispered.

Will removed his jacket and placed it round her shoulders. He wanted to pull her close and hold her as he had on that summer's night. They'd stayed together, lying in each other's arms, talking through the night. In the early hours of the morning, when it became too cold for them to remain outside any longer, they returned to the house. Will had wanted to leave her then, worried they'd be discovered together, but she invited him into her bed, where they remained together until morning, the dawn coming too quickly, the glimmering stars fading one by one.

Before leaving her, he'd removed the bronze triskele pendant that hung round his neck. 'I want you to have this.'

'But it's yours, you've had it for years. Your mother - your birth mother - gave it to you.'

'And now I'm giving it to you,' he said, holding the pendant up before her. 'The triple spiral symbolises different things to different people. In Neolithic times the triskele was thought to be a symbol of eternity, connecting the past, present and the future.' Isobel lowered her head and he hung the pendant round her neck. 'For some, the strands represent the realms of the earth, the underworld, and the heavens: others believe they represent the forces of nature: earth, water and fire.'

He remembered Isobel tracing the triple spiral symbol on the front of the disc with her finger. 'What does it symbolise to you?'

'The binding together of three spirits …'

'… with no beginning and no end,' Isobel finished.

When she raised her head, Will saw her eyes were filled with tears.

'You'll come back and see me before I go?' she asked him.

'Of course,' he replied, pulling the covers over her.

'You promise?'

Smoothing her hair from her face, he kissed her. 'I promise.'

He wondered if she still had the pendant but thought it unlikely. She'd probably forgotten he'd even given it to her.

The light waned as a dark cloud passed over the moon, plunging them into darkness. Isobel turned to face him, glancing up at him through her darkened lashes. She opened her mouth to speak but hesitated. Will reached forward and lifted her face, her lips parting as he leant forward, but she pulled away quickly.

'No, Will - don't.'

Without saying another word, she darted past him, not daring to look at him, hurrying across the terrace and disappearing into the house.

*

Later, as she lay in her bath, she had no recollection of making her way upstairs. She lay listening to the tap dripping, wiping away the tears that welled up in her eyes. Realising the water was almost cold, she pulled up her legs and wrapped her arms round them. She blamed herself for what had happened. She shouldn't have led Will onto the terrace. Alone together, the moon and the stars above, what had she thought was going to happen? But then she hadn't been thinking. She'd desperately wanted to relive their night together, a night she had clung to the memory of for too long, romanticising it, making it out to be more than it was, she hadn't given any thought to the repercussions should they have been discovered together.

Rising from the tepid water, she stepped down on the cold tile floor, took a towel from a shelf and began to rub herself down. Once dry, she wrapped the towel round her and moved towards the sink where she found the mirror had steamed up. Wiping away the condensation, she glanced at her reflection. She'd forgotten to remove her mascara. It had left dark smudges under her swollen eyes.

Emerging from the bathroom, she heard the wind howling round the house with renewed strength. Inside the house was silent - everyone else was probably asleep. She glanced at the carriage clock on the mantelpiece. It was almost midnight, though it felt later than that. Crossing the room, her feet cushioned by the soft, heavy carpet, she noticed the fire that she'd lit earlier that day had long burnt itself out. Shivering, she removed her towel, slipped on her nightgown and hurried into the deep four-poster bed.

After switching off the lamp on her bedside table, she lay her head down on her pillow. Although exhausted, she couldn't sleep. The incessant howling of the wind irritated her nerves, and she fidgeted restlessly in her cold bed, her mind racing. Closing her eyes, an image of James's ashen face and sunken eyes preyed upon her mind.

After about ten minutes, just as she had begun to drift off to sleep, a faint voice calling from somewhere in the darkness quickly brought her back to consciousness.

Somebody, please help me …

Sitting up, she reached for the lamp. Her fingers found the switch and the light flicked on. She glanced anxiously about the room, but saw there was no one there, and heard only the wind howling down the chimney. Was it the wind, or was someone in the house calling out for help? She knew she wouldn't be able to sleep until she was certain everyone in the house was safe.

After readjusting a strap that had fallen over her shoulder, she pulled back the covers, threw her legs over the edge of the bed and stood up. Rising to her feet, she caught a glimpse of herself in the cheval glass. Although very flattering, her nightgown was not going to keep her warm, so she slipped on her silk robe that lay at the foot of the bed.

Once in the corridor, she listened intently for a few moments before continuing.

Somebody, please help me …

The voice sounded strange but familiar and appeared to be coming from downstairs. Tiptoeing down the corridor, she slipped along the gallery without a sound, the portraits of James's ancestors staring down at her from the walls.

'Is anybody there?' she said, descending the staircase.

There was no sound or movement in the hall below and she received no reply to her enquiry.

Although Hodgson had yet to extinguish the candles of the tabletop and floor standing candelabras, many had burnt out. Advancing across the old medieval hall, her bare feet making no sound on the stone floor, she kept out of the dark shadows that surrounded her.

Ahead, on a small oak table, stood a three-branched candelabra, its candles alight. Reaching forward, her hand trembling, she grasped the stem.

Somebody, please help me …

She ran round the staircase to where the voice seemed to be calling from. Below the staircase, she found a door, which she presumed led to an understairs cupboard. Was somebody locked inside, unable to get out? Moving slowly towards the door, the candelabra held high above her head, she knelt forward and peered through the keyhole.

She could see only darkness.

She realised she was being ridiculous. Of course, there wasn't anybody there. Straightening herself up, she heard the voice again and gasped, clasping her hand to her mouth.

She hadn't imagined it that time.

Pressing her ear to the door, she listened with bated breath. There was somebody in there, and it sounded as though they were making their way up a flight of stairs. It was a woman; she could almost visualise her crawling up the stone steps …

This wasn't an understairs cupboard - the door led to a cellar.

'Is anybody there?' she said uncertainly.

Again, there was no reply, but this time she heard what sounded like faint muffled sobbing. Gingerly, she reached forward, her hand closing round the door handle. She turned it slowly but found the door locked. She needed the key - but where would she find it? She had to fetch Hodgson.

'Who's there?' she said, this time with more conviction. 'I know there's somebody there.'

Anybody, please!

The door began to shake as though being struck violently from the other side.

'I'll go and get help,' said Isobel, her voice barely audible above the rattling of the door.

Then, as suddenly as it had started, the door stopped shaking. Why had no one else in the house heard anything and come to investigate?

As she stood staring into the darkness, the house grew noticeably quiet. Even the ticking of the grandfather clock was silenced. She knew she had to get help, but found herself unable to move, and suddenly became aware that there was someone in the room with her. She could feel eyes upon her, sending a chill down her spine, and she was seized by a feeling of utter dread.

The hall seemed to be growing darker by the second, the candles of the candelabra growing dimmer as though slowly being starved of oxygen. She had to get out of the shadows. She had to get upstairs and back to her bedroom …

Run …

They were almost upon her.

For God's sake, run …

Out of the corner of her eye, she saw the handle of the cellar door turning slowly. Moments later the flames of the candelabra were extinguished, plunging her into darkness.

CHAPTER TEN

Thirteen Months Earlier

At the end of their first summer together, shortly before she resumed her studies at university, Tessa convinced James to let her see Wychwood House for herself. He drove her there on a Saturday in mid-September, and they arrived late in the afternoon, having stopped for lunch at a pub in Galashiels on the way down. James had their day all planned out. He'd had Emily's room cleaned and there were fresh sheets on the bed. The larder was stocked with bread, cheese, and cold meats for him - Tessa being a vegetarian. There was even a bottle of champagne chilling down in the cellar for them to open in the evening, preferably in front of a roaring fire.

He wasted no time showing her the house, keen to get the tour over and done with as quickly as possible so they could start enjoying the rest of their day together. As he led her through the great hall and up the staircase, she told him she thought it far grander than she imagined. 'I was expecting something much smaller,' she said.

He began by showing her the bedrooms on the third floor that had been ravaged by damp and rot. Afterwards, they made their way downstairs to Emily's bedroom.

To his disappointment, she didn't seem as impressed with the room as he'd hoped. She didn't even seem to notice the four-poster bed.

'Wait till you see the view,' he said undeterred, leading her over to the bay window.

They stood together at the window, staring out across the lawn to the river below. A black crowd of crows dispersing amongst the trees along the riverbank caught Tessa's attention.

'Someone's down there,' she said.

Glancing towards the river, James saw the white-haired man standing underneath a tree, staring up at the house. He hadn't seen him for months, and in that time, he'd completely slipped from his mind. He briefly considered opening a window and calling out to him but thought better of it.

'Do you know him?' asked Tessa.

'I've seen him in the village. He lives in one of the cottages opposite the kirk. I think he might be Tom Rutherford.'

'One of the brothers who broke into the house?'

James nodded.

Tessa didn't seem convinced. 'You think he'd come back to live in the village after what happened?'

'Where else would he go?'

The white-haired man, realising he was being watched, turned and walked away, following the river downstream, disappearing from view in the dark shade of the trees.

James culminated his tour in the drawing room, showing her the sofa and armchairs that he now knew to be an Epstein Cloudback suite. Together they began looking through the trunks and suitcases that had been brought down from the attic.

When Tessa went to open Emily's steamer trunk, James told her not to bother.

'All of Emily's clothes are in her bedroom.'

Tessa opened the trunk anyway, curious to see inside, to find its interior lined with old newspaper.

'It's not completely empty,' she said. 'There's an old statement of account from Jenners Department Store in here.' She held up the document for James to see. 'It's dated August 1936 and is addressed to the Countess of Leithen …'

James approached Tessa. 'They must have made a mistake,' he said, taking the statement from her. 'Henry wasn't an earl. The title wasn't his, or Emily's, to use.'

'Well, it appears they were using it. Have you come across any other correspondence addressed to either Henry or Emily?'

'No, but I found some documents belonging to his grandfather William Roxburgh. If the title hadn't become extinct, he would have been the first to inherit the earldom.'

'Was he referred to as an earl in these documents?'

'To tell you the truth I paid them little attention.'

'Where did you find them?'

James stared at the boxes and trunks spread out across the floor of the library.

'I'm not sure,' he said, after a pause.

'There's bound to be something in the office.'

'All the cabinets are locked, and I've yet to find the keys to open them.'

'If you haven't found them by now, it's unlikely you will. Couldn't you just force them open?'

'They're made of solid mahogany. Even with a hammer and chisel, it would take us all night.'

'What about the desk in the study? It wouldn't take much effort to prise open one of the drawers.'

'I might damage the woodwork …'

'Do you want to know if Henry was an earl or not?'

James went to fetch a knife from the kitchen, returning to find Tessa waiting for him in the study. He sat down and began prising open the top drawer as carefully as he could to prevent damaging the desk. Inside he found only stationary, but in the larger second drawer, alongside photograph albums and old film canisters, he found letters, bills, receipts and bank statements belonging to Henry,

All were addressed to the Earl of Leithen.

Hidden away at the bottom of the drawer was a ledger. The last entry, made in September 1938, revealed debts of over three thousand pounds.

'That's about a hundred thousand pounds in today's money,' he said.

'And I thought my student loans were bad,' replied Tessa.

Tucked between the pages of the ledger were estimates from carpenters, glazers and decorators.

'It appears Henry had plans to redecorate the rest of the house, though these were never realised.'

'I'm not surprised. Do you think Henry adopted the title to get credit to pay off his debts?'

'It's possible. Though it's more likely he really was the Earl of Leithen, and the title didn't become extinct as I was told. If I could find a reference to his father or grandfather as an earl I'd know for certain.'

'Do you know where they are laid to rest?'

'My great-grandfather's buried in the churchyard at home. Granted his tomb is very old and worn, but I don't believe he's referred to as the twelfth Earl of Leithen on the inscription – I think I'd have noticed if he was. I'm certain his father wasn't buried there. He wouldn't have been. My great-grandfather didn't buy the Manor until after he died. He's probably buried down in the village.'

'Well, if he did inherit the title, his gravestone will be a testament to the fact.'

*

After locking up, James drove Tessa down to the village. The sun had set by the time they pulled up outside the kirkyard. Worn, crumbling gravestones, covered in nettles and brambles, glimmered faintly in the dusk. Many had broken into pieces that now lay buried in the long unkempt grass.

'This could take us all night,' said James. 'Half the names on these gravestones are illegible.'

Together they made their way up a gravel path towards the gabled porch of the kirk. A warped door hung on rusted wrought-iron hinges. They continued round the kirk, following a flagstone path covered in rubble, moving slowly, avoiding the fallen buttresses that lay hidden in the grass and weeds that grew up against the side of the building.

'This wasn't quite what I had in mind for this evening,' said James.

'What did you have in mind?' asked Tessa, a smile playing on her lips.

Before he could tell her, he noticed a burial vault with a carved Romanesque doorway directly behind the kirk.

'If my ancestors are buried anywhere,' he said, 'it's in there.'

Drawing nearer, they saw the entrance to the vault in more detail and noticed the intricate patterns of chevrons and crenellated mouldings on the arch above the doorway. Grotesque heads with branches sprouting from their mouths had been carved on top of the shafts supporting the sides of the arch. Three steps led down to the doorway. Another two steps, separated by heavy grilled doors, led into the vault. James pushed against the doors, but they held fast. Leaving Tessa, he returned to the Land Rover, collecting his keys and a torch before making his way back through the kirkyard.

Selecting one of the smaller keys, one he had yet to find a use for at the house, he inserted it into the lock. The key turned and he pushed open the doors. With Tessa at his side, he descended the steps into the darkness. Once in the vault, he switched on his torch, the light revealing the stone coffins that filled the gloomy chamber. Stopping before the first coffin he came to, he shone his torch onto the engraved breastplate and read the inscription.

To the Glory of God
and
In Loving Memory of
Major General William Henry Roxburgh KCB
10th Earl of Leithen
Who died at Wychwood House June 15th 1884
Aged 63 Years

'Why was I told the title had become extinct?' he said, his eyes fixed on the engraving. 'Why didn't my father just tell me the truth?'

'Maybe he doesn't know the truth,' said Tessa.

James turned to face her. 'No, he knows all right,' he said. 'He never wanted me to come here. Now I know why.'

Taking centre stage in the vault was an elaborately carved stone coffin engraved with Egyptian characters and hieroglyphs that looked more like a sarcophagus than a coffin. Inside lay the body of Lord Patrick Roxburgh, who, according to the inscription on the lid, lived between the years 1555 to 1609. The coffin, however, did not look four hundred years old. It looked like it had been put there more recently than that.

A voice called out to them from the darkness.

'What are you doing down there?'

Startled, James turned suddenly, shining his torch toward the entrance of the vault. The beam revealed the white-haired man standing in the doorway, dressed in old shabby clothes, his face gaunt and pale.

'You're the young man who's renovating Wychwood House,' he said, shielding his eyes from the light.

James lowered his torch. 'I'm James Roxburgh.'

The white-haired man's eyes widened. 'You're a Roxburgh …'

'Henry Roxburgh was my great-uncle.'

'You're planning on living at Wychwood House?'

James nodded. 'Yes, I am.'

'Both of you?'

'I don't see how that is any of your business.'

The white-haired man stepped into the vault and turned to face Tessa. 'I wouldn't go back to the house if I were you, miss,' he said. 'It's not safe for you there.'

'You're Tom Rutherford, aren't you? You broke into my house with your brother and those two girls.'

'How do you know who I am?'

'I found the transistor radio at the foot of the staircase. I assume it belonged to you.'

The white-haired man looked away, his grey, haggard eyes falling to the floor. 'It belonged to my brother Andy.'

'Why did you take the girls up to the house in the first place?' asked Tessa.

'Andy had a girlfriend. He didn't want to be seen out and about with another girl.'

'And you were okay with that?'

'I didn't have much of a say in the matter.'

'You could have mentioned he had a girlfriend.'

'Andy wouldn't have liked that.' Tom pulled out a tobacco pouch and a pack of Rizla papers from the pocket of his jacket. 'Anyway,' he continued, 'I don't think telling them would have made any difference. Hazel was so eager to spend the afternoon with Andy, she didn't even go and see her grandmother before setting off.' Sifting some shag tobacco into a paper, he began shaping a cigarette with his hands. 'Why are you asking me these questions?' he asked. 'Surely, if you know who I am, you know what happened to us in the house.'

'I know the police found your fingerprints on the axe and assumed you killed your brother and the two girls,' said James, 'but that's not the whole story, is it?'

'You've seen it, haven't you?' asked Tom, his eyes lighting up. 'You've seen the hellhound. The one that attacked us.'

'I encountered a large black dog, but it wasn't a hellhound. I'm guessing it came from the village and was put in the house to scare me away.'

'For what purpose?'

'To prevent me from finding the magic circle that you and your brother drew on the floor of the great hall.'

'I don't know what you're talking about,' said Tom. 'I didn't see anything drawn on the floor of the hall. That was our first and only visit to Wychwood House.'

'Why don't you tell us your side of events,' suggested Tessa, eager to defuse the growing tension between the two men.

Tom struck a match, his eyes fixed on James as he lit the cigarette held between his lips.

'We decided,' he began, 'or rather Andy did, to take the girls up to the house because we knew the caretaker wouldn't be there that day. We'd seen him get on the bus Ronnie and Hazel arrived on. We broke into the house by smashing a pane of glass in the French window. For some reason, the key was still in the lock, so it wasn't difficult to get in. Once inside we stayed in the drawing room where it was light, helping ourselves to some drinks while listening to some records on the gramophone.'

'Then what happened?' asked Tessa.

'Andy told me he was going to explore the rest of the house with Hazel. She didn't seem too keen on the idea but went anyway. I stayed in the drawing room with Ronnie, remaining by the French window. I didn't like being in the house. I was worried the caretaker would return and set his dog on us.'

'The caretaker had a dog?'

Tom nodded. 'He was often seen patrolling the grounds with it as a warning to trespassers. I don't know what breed it was. It could have been a mastiff, probably a Cane Corso, I'm not sure. I never got close enough to find out. Really, he needn't have bothered. The locals always feared the house, always have, and probably always will. Anyway, after about five minutes or so I heard Hazel cry out from the hall. When Ronnie and I went to investigate, we found Hazel and Andy sitting on the stairs together listening to the transistor radio. They'd lit a candelabra on a table nearby. Hazel's face looked pale in the candlelight, and I noticed she was trembling. Evidently, Andy had come on a bit strong, and she hadn't liked it. When I asked her if she was okay, Andy told me to get lost. I invited Hazel to return to the drawing room with us, but Andy rose to his feet, blocking her way. I think he'd have hit me if -' He paused abruptly.

'What?' asked Tessa.

Tom drew on his cigarette, inhaling deeply. 'That was when we realised there was something in the room with us.'

'The dog …' suggested James.

'It was no dog. It appeared from the shadows, prowling towards us, its eyes glowing red in the darkness. No one dared move, no one except Ronnie. She was standing in the doorway and probably thought she could get out of the house before it attacked her. She was wrong. When she backed away the creature pounced on her, dragging her kicking and screaming into the darkness. That was when Hazel let out an ear-piercing scream that echoed through the house, bringing us to our senses. Andy was the first to move. He picked up the candelabra and advanced across the hall, calling to Ronnie, but she was nowhere to be found.

'Seeing the creature had gone, he told me to get Hazel out of the house. I reached for her, but she remained seated on the stairs clutching the banisters for protection, too terrified to move. I told her to keep her eyes on me and I promised I'd get her out of there. It wasn't far to the drawing room. We'd be outside and safe before she knew it … She took my hand and I led her across the hall, our pace quickening with every step we took. By the time we reached the drawing room we were running, the bright sunshine hurting our eyes as we made for the French window. Realising Andy wasn't behind us I called out to him, but he didn't reply. I wanted to go back to check if he was all right, but I'd promised Hazel I'd get her out of the house.'

'What happened to her?'

'When I stepped out onto the terrace, I felt her hand slip from mine as she was wrenched from my grip. I spun round to find her gone. The drawing room was empty.'

'Why didn't you just go to the village and get help?'

'It would have taken too long. By the time I got help, it would have been too late. I doubt I could have convinced anyone in the village to return to the house anyway. The only option open to me was to take on the hellhound myself, even if that meant losing my life in the process. I knew I'd never be able to rest until that creature had been destroyed. I wasted no time searching the grounds for a weapon, and it didn't take me long to find the axe in the old stables. I couldn't have been more than ten, fifteen minutes before I returned to the house …'

'What did you find?' asked Tessa.

'Once again the hall appeared to be empty. There was no trace of either Hazel or my brother. The creature appeared to have gone too. Only when I searched the library did I see it again. It appeared suddenly from out of nowhere, blocking my exit. When I saw the beast, I hurled my axe at it, but it was no use. The creature hardly flinched when the weapon struck it. I thought I too was done for when I noticed an open doorway ahead of me and ran for my life, locking myself in the study. I attempted to escape through the window, but the shutters were locked. If I hadn't thrown my axe, I could have gotten out sooner …

'I tried to leave by the study door, only to glimpse the creature pacing the hall. Realising I was trapped, the awfulness of the situation dawned on me, and I broke down and wept. I remained there for hours, too terrified to move, not knowing what to do - praying for someone to come and rescue me. Eventually, I pulled myself together and managed to force apart the shutters, open the window and slip away. By the time I escaped it was pitch black outside. I headed down to the village, but somehow lost my way - I don't know how. I was only able to find my way home the following morning when it became light enough for me to see my way through the wood.'

'Could it have been the caretaker's dog that attacked you?' asked Tessa. 'He could have left it guarding the house whilst he was away for the day …'

'I tell you, it wasn't a dog that attacked us,' said Tom. 'If it was, the animal would have been killed when I hit it with the axe. Also, the police would have discovered the bodies and found traces of blood in the house, wouldn't they? But there was no blood, and the bodies were gone. Taken … I knew once they found the axe with my fingerprints on they'd think I did it. I had no choice but to tell them what happened, even though I knew they wouldn't believe me.'

'Why didn't this hellhound attack the police when they searched the house?' asked Tessa.

'I wondered that too. I'd hoped once they'd seen the hound for themselves, they'd believe my story, but it didn't appear during their search of the house. For ages, I wondered why that was. Then I realised they were let in by the caretaker. We broke in. That's why. And that's why it hasn't attacked you or any of your builders either. Not yet anyway.'

'I'll tell you why it didn't appear,' said James quickly, the words bursting out of him. 'It didn't appear because this hellhound is nothing more than a product of your deluded imagination. If, as you say, that was your only visit to Wychwood House, when did you draw the magic circle on the floor of the great hall? A design that intricate could not have been completed in a hurry. It would have taken over an hour at least. I doubt Ronnie and Hazel would have stood by while you and your brother finished it. It could only have been put there before you lured them to the house -'

'James, don't,' said Tessa, interrupting him.

'The presence of the magic circle proves Ronnie and Hazel's murders were premeditated.'

'I don't know what you're talking about,' said Tom. 'I would never have hurt Hazel - or Ronnie.'

'Which is why you had second thoughts, going to their aid when it was too late,' said James. 'When you tried to intervene your brother attacked you, didn't he? That's the real reason you searched the grounds for a weapon. Your brother was the one you struck with the axe.'

'You think Andy killed Ronnie and Hazel?'

'No, we don't,' said Tessa.

'And you buried the bodies in the wood to cover up his crime,' said James.

'James, stop this!' cried Tessa, reprimanding him suddenly. 'It's all too horrible.'

'He set a rabid dog on me.'

'We don't know for certain it was him.'

'Who else would it be?'

'Andy was no saint,' said Tom, 'but he wouldn't have hurt anyone.' He dropped his cigarette onto the floor, grinding it out with the sole of his shoe. 'And if I'd buried the bodies in the wood, the police would have found them, wouldn't they?'

'Not necessarily,' said James.

'You want to know who's responsible? I'll tell you. It was Henry

Roxburgh. He was the one with the interest in the occult! He was the one that summoned that hound from Hell!'

James glared at Tom threateningly. He was about to say something when Tessa took him by the hand.

'I think it's time we were going,' she said. She led him out of the vault, round the kirk and across the kirkyard.

When they were out of earshot, James said, 'He's nothing but a crazy old man.'

'Nevertheless, you were too hard on him. Don't you think he's been through enough?'

When they reached the Land Rover, they heard Tom call out to them.

'For God's sake,' he cried, 'stay out of the shadows!'

*

James decided against returning to Wychwood House that evening. He thought it unlikely, under the circumstances, Tessa would be able to relax at the house, and she certainly wouldn't want to spend the night there. He had another reason for returning to Moray Place. He was eager to speak to his father and find out why his grandfather hadn't inherited the title following Henry's death. Although it was almost ten o'clock by the time they reached the apartment, he rang home from the landline in the hall, whilst Tessa fixed them something to eat in the kitchen.

Upon answering, his father told him he'd been expecting his call.

'I'm surprised it's taken you this long to discover the truth.' He sounded slightly disappointed. 'Really, all you had to do was pick up a copy of Debrett's …'

'I had no reason to look because I was told the title became extinct in the nineteenth-century following the death of Lady Roxburgh.'

'A narrative adopted by the family to avoid awkward questions being asked about Henry. Questions I assume you are about to ask me …'

'So you've known all along Henry was an earl?'

'For a long time now,' his father said. 'Your grandfather told me all about his brother and what became of him when I was still at school.'

'What did become of him?'

'In the final years of his life, Henry Roxburgh brought great shame upon his family. When his estate failed to provide the income required to fund his extravagant lifestyle, he ended up owing a lot of people a lot of money. To avoid his debtors he went to Europe, spending time in Monte Carlo, Biarritz and Cannes, before losing himself in North Africa when some of those he owed money to went looking for him. While on active service, my father tracked him to Cairo where he was told his brother had died from pneumonia or malaria - I can't remember which, it could have been both - but he was unable to find where he had been buried or procure a death certificate. Eventually, he was granted probate over Henry's estate, but as there was no death certificate, he was refused permission to take his brother's title and his seat in the House of Lords.'

'A death certificate must have been produced at the time.'

'Not necessarily,' said his father thoughtfully. 'There must have been hundreds of thousands of unaccounted for civilian deaths during the Second World War.'

'But Henry wasn't just anybody. He was a member of the British aristocracy.'

'A disgraced member.'

'Nevertheless, he deserves to be buried in the family vault alongside the other Earls of Leithen.'

'If my father couldn't find a death certificate at the time it's unlikely you will now.'

'But if we could find a copy, you could become the fourteenth Earl of Leithen.'

'Even if, by some miracle, we were able to procure the death certificate, I doubt it would be possible for me to reclaim the title after all this time. Anyway, what would be the point? When Henry inherited the earldom, the aristocracy had been in decline for decades. Your great grandfather, who sat on the board of directors of a finance company, knew the days of the aristocracy were coming to an end, which was why he encouraged his sons to work in business and finance. Your grandfather took his advice, becoming the chairman of a company that operated in the City. Henry didn't. Whereas your grandmother was the daughter of a wealthy banker, Emily was the daughter of a viscount. Henry refused to marry outside the aristocracy; he was too proud to accept being an earl no longer afforded him a privileged position in life. Your grandfather tried to encourage him to sell up and invest the money in shares, but his advice fell on deaf ears. In clinging to a world that no longer existed, Henry lost everything.'

'A world that still exists for some,' said James. 'There are still over eight hundred hereditary titles in Britain. If you inherited the title you could sit in the House of Lords.'

'Since the reforms in the late nineties, only about ninety of those pears can sit in the Lords. It is highly unlikely I would ever get elected.'

Tessa appeared from the kitchen and signalled to James that dinner was ready.

'Don't you think it all sounds a little bit too convenient?' he said after she'd returned to the kitchen. 'Grandfather had nothing to gain from finding Henry's body. He had no interest in inheriting the title.'

'Careful, James …'

'Had he found him he would have been forced to pay death duties -'

'My father had no interest in inheriting the title, or Wychwood House for that matter, because he wanted to sever all ties with the past. He turned his back on that world and advised me to do the same because he didn't want me making the same mistakes as Henry did.'

'You think what I am doing here is a mistake?'

'Have you given any thought to how you are going to live in the house once it's finished? Of course, you could rear pheasants and partridges and turn the place into a shooting estate, which given time could become a viable business … But then you were never one for shooting, were you? The estate is not grand enough to charge the public to look round the house and gardens. Now if someone of note had lived there, a famous artist or writer, you might have been able to arouse some interest in the place, but as it is, I think it unlikely.'

'Our ancestors were important men,' insisted James. 'They lived lives written about in history books. They rubbed shoulders with kings, fought in battles that changed the course of history. Lord Roxburgh was one of the most powerful men in Scotland -'

'That was a long time ago now …' His father paused before proceeding, as though contemplating what to say next. 'According to legend,' he said thoughtfully, 'there can only be one living phoenix in existence at any time. At the end of its life, it combusts and is consumed by flames. Only then can a new phoenix emerge from the ashes, stronger and more powerful than its predecessor.'

*

That night, unable to sleep, James drove back to Wychwood House. Arriving just before sunrise, he headed straight to the library to find dawn's faint light filtering in through the windows. Switching on his torch, he began scouring the shelves for books devoted to the study of magic, spiritualism - even astrology - anything that would suggest Henry or any of his ancestors held an interest in the occult.

Numerous history books filled the shelves. Some were well known: Holinshed's *Chronicles of England, Scotland, and Ireland,* Plutarch's *Lives of the Noble Greeks and Romans*, Gibbon's *The History of the Decline and Fall of the Roman Empire.* Others, like *The Illustrated History of the British Empire in India and the East* by E. H. Nolan, and Ward and Lock's *Illustrated History of the World*, were less familiar. There were two biographies of James I. The first, Lucy Aikin's *Memoirs of the Court of James I.* The second, by William Harris, stood on the shelf below alongside biographies of Cromwell and Charles I by the same author. There was also a biography of Sir Walter Scott by John Gibson Lockhart, the son-in-law of the famous author.

His attention was drawn to eight volumes of Charles Knight's *Pictorial Shakspere* beautifully bound in red Morocco leather. On the same bookshelf, bound in dark green Morocco, were numerous volumes of *The Works of Charles Dickens*, a three-volume set of Trollope's *Barchester Towers* and a four-volume set of *The Prime Minister.* Both sets were bound in cloth. The bottom two shelves of the bookcase were filled with the *Edinburgh Edition of the Waverley Novels* by Sir Walter Scott. Alongside these works were novels by authors James wasn't as familiar with. Two names, Oliver Goldsmith, the author of *The Vicar of Wakefield*, and Charles Reade, author of *The Cloister and the Hearth*, rang a bell, but there were many he hadn't heard of. Books by Margaret Oliphant, Charlotte M. Yonge and S. R. Crockett filled the shelves. There were over twenty volumes of the works of G. J. Whyte-Melville, a writer of fox-hunting stories and historical novels.

To his disappointment, there were no Gothic novels, not even an Ann Radcliffe. He was about to give up on his search when he came across three books on the supernatural. Two, *Glimpses of the Supernatural* and *Glimpses in the Twilight*, were by the Rev. Frederick George Lee; the third, Elliot O'Donnell's *Byways of Ghost-Land.* On the shelf above were two books by Arthur Conan Doyle he didn't recognise, their titles *The New Revelation* and *The Vital Message.* Opening the first, he saw it was devoted to the study of spiritualism and psychical research.

There were other books on the same subject, including one by Elliot O'Donnell, called *Spiritualism Explained. Raymond or Life and Death* by Sir Oliver J. Lodge claimed to include examples of the evidence for survival of memory and affection after death. All were written during or shortly after the First World War, leading James to wonder if his great grandfather George Roxburgh had sought solace in spiritualism following the death of his eldest son Edward, hoping to find proof of existence beyond the grave. It seemed highly likely, but that meant he had yet to find any evidence to suggest Henry held an interest in the occult.

Undaunted, he continued his search, and after about a further ten minutes he discovered a large tome bound in vellum. Written on the wide spine was, *Henrici Cornelii Agrippae ab Nettesheym armatae militiae equitis aurati, et iuris vtriusque ac Medicinae Doctoris Opera I & II.* At the bottom of the spine, he saw it was printed in Lugduni, which he knew was the Latin name for Lyon, and had been published in France in 1550. Next to it was a smaller work, bound in calfskin, its title, *C. Agrippa Opera Tom I.* Opening the book, he saw it was also printed in Lyon by 'Per Beringos Fratres', though this time no date of publication was given.

The spine of the third book, also bound in vellum, was faded and he couldn't read the title. The book next to it had a small red Morocco label that read, *Petit Albert.* Slowly and carefully, so as not to damage the spine, he slipped the small calfskin bound book off the shelf. Inside he read the title page, *Secrets merveilleux de la magie naturelle et cabalistique du petit Albert.* The book was translated from the original Latin by Alberti Parvi Lucii in Lyon in 1752 and had been published by the heirs of the Beringos Fratres, who were, according to the title page, the choice of Agrippa.

Returning it to the shelf, he read the title of another book,

Clavicules de Salomon. Opening the book, he skimmed the title page: *Les veritables clavicules de Salomon, suivies du fameux secret du papillon vert.* He couldn't see a date of publication, but the book, written in French, claimed to be printed in Memphis, Egypt. On the shelf below stood a set of four books with beautiful gilt spines, their titles printed on black Morocco labels: *Le Dragon Rouge, Tresor du Vieillard des Pyramides, Secrets du Petit Albert*, and *Secrets D'Albert le Grand.* On the same shelf was J. Collin de Plancy's *Dictionnaire Infernal.* Flicking through the yellowing pages, he saw the book was illustrated with fantastical drawings of demons. According to the title page, the book was a print of its sixth edition, published in Paris in 1863. One of the books, *Buch Abramelin*, written by Abraham von Worms, was in German. He picked up a tiny volume, handwritten in Latin, called *Arbatel de magia veterum*, and saw it had been published in Basilea, which he assumed was Basel in Switzerland, in 1575. He remembered reading somewhere that, at the time, Basel had been the European capital of books.

Except for Collin de Plancy's *Dictionnaire Infernal,* the names of the books were unfamiliar to him, and apart from Agrippa, he hadn't heard of any of the named authors. He searched the rest of the bookcase but could not find a copy of Aleister Crowley's *The Book of the Goetia of Solomon the King* the Magical Circle of King Solomon had appeared in. He thought it possible an illustration of the circle appeared in another book - but which one? Picking up *Clavicules de Salomon,* he began thumbing through the book's pages. There were many illustrations in the book - there was even one of the Grand Pentacle of Solomon - but it bore little resemblance to the Magical Circle of King Solomon.

He was about to climb the ladder to the balcony when he felt his phone vibrate in his breast pocket. Seeing the call was from Tessa, he promptly left the library and made his way to the drawing room, answering the call when he stepped out onto the terrace.

Tessa asked him where he was.

He told her he was at the house, explaining he hadn't been able to sleep. 'I had to find out for myself if there was any truth in what Tom said about Henry.'

'Is there?'

'I've found several books on the occult in the library, but no evidence to suggest they belonged to Henry. Their dates of publication range from the sixteenth to the nineteenth-century and could have been purchased at any time over that period. The most recent publication dates from 1863 when William Roxburgh lived at the house.'

'Do you think a man with his military background would be interested in books on magic?'

'Probably not,' admitted James. 'I always imagined him to be a practical, level-headed man, more interested in hunting and shooting than the supernatural. They could have belonged to his son, Albert ...'

'Wasn't William's wife a practising Catholic?'

'Yes, she was.'

'I doubt she would have approved of her husband, or son, buying books on the occult.'

James agreed. 'And she certainly wouldn't have allowed a book on demonology to be displayed in the library.'

'You've found books on demonology?'

'Just the one. There are about two shelves devoted to books on spiritualism and the occult, which in a library that contains over a thousand books on a wide range of subjects, doesn't amount to much.'

'But it does suggest an interest, nonetheless.'

'A collection like this could only have been built up over many years. Many, if not all, would have been difficult to find and expensive to buy, especially at the time. Henry had neither the time nor the money to have purchased them all himself.'

'Have you found the book the magic circle was copied from?'

'Not so far,' said James. 'I just wish I could find out its purpose. Even if Henry had been the one responsible for drawing it, I doubt his aim was to raise a hound from Hell. There has to be another reason, just as there has to be a reason other members of my family held an interest in the occult, however fleeting that interest may have been for some.'

'There's a shop in Edinburgh which sells books on magic and spiritualism,' said Tessa. 'You could ask there. They may have heard of the Magic Circle of King Solomon and the books you've discovered.' She gave him directions to the shop. 'You can't miss it,' she said. 'There's a sphere of brass rings like you have in the study, displayed in the window.'

James thought it was as good a place to start as any.

*

The skies above Edinburgh were grey and overcast the following day, a thick, drizzling rain falling from the leaden sky. Zipping up his trench coat, pulling up the collar, James made his way through the city. By the time he reached the old town, the rain began falling heavily. Following Tessa's directions, he saw the sphere of brass rings displayed in the window of the bookshop as he approached. Behind the sphere, antique books filled the shelves of an old bookcase.

Ducking out of the rain, he pushed open the door, a bell above his head ringing as he stepped into the dimly lit bookshop. His eyes wandered over the tall bookcases stacked with books from floor to ceiling. Prints and etchings hung from the walls; others were propped against the bookcases. Squeezing past a customer who stood browsing a shelf of Penguin classics, he made his way into the dark recesses of the old building. Behind a carved oak counter, leafing through a book that lay open before him, stood a man with a well-trimmed Van Dyke beard dressed in what looked like a purple smoking jacket.

'Excuse me,' said James, approaching the counter. 'What do you call that model of brass rings you have displayed in the window of your shop?'

'It's a replica of an armillary sphere made by Caspar Vopel, a sixteenth-century cartographer from Cologne.' Seeing he'd aroused James's interest he continued. 'The original dates from 1543, the year Copernicus printed his *On the Revolutions of the Heavenly Spheres,* though it is based on Ptolemy's geocentric model of the solar system. The order of the spheres from the Earth in Ptolemy's model began with the Moon and was followed by Mercury, Venus, the Sun, Mars, Jupiter, Saturn, the Fixed Stars, and finally the Primum Mobile. Later on, medieval philosophers added the Empyrean Heaven, the dwelling-place of God. Many replicas have been made over the years prized by those who clung to the belief that the Earth is at the centre of the universe.'

'The one I have is very similar,' said James.

'You already own one?'

'Yes.'

'Would you be interested in purchasing another?'

'Not at the moment,' said James.

He told the bookseller he'd come into the possession of several old books that had been in his family for generations and was hoping to find out more about them.

'Do you have any of them with you?'

'No, but I wrote down a few of their names.' He reached into his breast pocket and pulled out a notebook. 'Have you ever heard of *Clavicules de Salomon, Le Petit Albert, Arbatel De Magia Veterum, Buch Abramelin, Le Dragon Rouge* or the *Dictionnaire Infernal*?'

The bookseller stroked his beard. 'I sold an early edition of *Le Dragon Rouge* only last week,' he said, a smile curving his thin, straight lips. 'They are grimoires - books of magic. All are collectors' items and like the armillary sphere are highly prized. I make it my business to know as much as I can about them. A *Dragon Rouge*, depending on the condition, can fetch anywhere between two to three thousand pounds. The *Dictionnaire Infernal* is quite common, however, though the coveted 1863 edition illustrated by Louis Breton is worth more. Which version of the *Clavicle of Solomon* do you have?'

'It's a French edition,' said James, 'printed in Memphis, Egypt. There wasn't a date of publication.'

'Sounds like one of the first editions printed in France in the eighteenth-century. Depending on the state it's in, it could fetch up to five thousand pounds.'

'I'm not particularly interested in their value. I just want to find out more about them.'

'Well,' the bookseller began, teetering on his heels, '*Le Petit Albert* and *Le Dragon Rouge*, along with other grimoires such as *Le Grand Albert*, the *Grimorium Verum*, and *La Poule Noire*, were printed in France in the late eighteenth and early nineteenth-century. A bookseller from Troyes began publishing cheaply produced books covered in blue sugar paper in the early seventeenth-century. The books, known as *Bibliothèque Bleue de Troyes*, sold well, especially in the nineteenth-century, littering Parisian bookstores before spreading like a plague across Europe. The books themselves are popular, sensational texts and of little real value. The cheap paper they were printed on hasn't aged well. The ones that have survived exist in various states of decay today.

'Many, with the notable exception of *La Poule Noire*, claim to date from the Middle Ages. *Le Dragon Rouge*, known in English as the *Grand Grimoire*, purports to have been written in the early sixteenth-century - though it was actually written in the nineteenth. The most notorious of all grimoires is *The Great Book of Saint Cyprian*, which claims to date from antiquity, was written in the 1840s. It is attributed to the Faustian figure of St Cyprian of Antioch, a pagan magician who summoned demons before being saved through his conversion to Christianity. It remains popular to this day, especially in South America. Many believe reading the book backwards summons the Devil. Just touching it is considered a sin by many Catholics.'

'Do all grimoires contain rituals for invoking demons?'

'Apparently, the *Grand Grimoire* contains instructions for summoning the Devil - though I've never read it myself. The *Sixth and Seventh Books of Moses* comprise magical incantations and seals for the reader to recreate the miracles depicted in the Bible. But they are exceptions. That so many do include rituals for invoking spirits is due, in part, to a magic papyrus known as the *Testament of Solomon,* that originated in Babylonia or Egypt sometime before the fifth-century, during the decline of the Roman Empire. The *Testament* tells how, during the construction of the Temple of Jerusalem, King Solomon was given a magical signet ring, later known as the Seal of Solomon, by the archangel Michael to combat a demon who was harassing one of his workers. Through the power of the Seal, the king learnt how to evoke and constrain the demons, sealing them in a brass vessel. He even made some assist with the construction of the Temple of Jerusalem. The list of demons, their powers and how to command them, would, alongside various depictions of the Sacred Seal of King Solomon, go on to be reprinted, and later illustrated, in many subsequent grimoires.

'Soon after, other works in what we now call the Solomonic cycle, including the *Ars Notoria,* the *Almandel*, and the *Sworn Book of Honorius*, began to appear. The most influential of all was undoubtedly the *Clavicula Salomonis*, the *Key of Solomon*. Its origins lie with the *Testament of Solomon*, which formed the basis of a textbook of magic from the Byzantine Empire known as the *Magical Treatise of Solomon*. The name *Clavicula* wasn't adopted until the text was translated from Greek into Latin in Renaissance Italy the following century. Over the years that followed the book became available in Italian, French, English and German. Unlike the *Testament of Solomon*, the *Key of Solomon* provides instructions for invoking spirits.'

'For what purpose?'

'To find stolen items, gain favour and influence, and make someone fall in love with you. You could even call on the spirits to make you invisible. The edition of the *Clavicle of Solomon* that you own includes an additional ritual to make a girl dance naked. It all sounds harmless enough now, not to mention ridiculous, but at the time the Church confiscated and burnt medieval grimoires; those found in possession of magical texts were arrested and charged with heresy. By the sixteenth-century, the *Clavicle of Solomon* had made its way onto the Catholic Church's list of prohibited books, which only helped to increase its popularity, especially in Italy.'

The bookseller caught James's eye. 'That which is forbidden is always more alluring, don't you think?'

'I've always thought so,' replied James.

The bookseller smiled, revealing a row of sharp white teeth. 'The year the first edition of the Index Librorum Prohibitorum appeared,' he continued, 'one of the most notorious of all grimoires, the *Fourth Book of Occult Philosophy* was published. Falsely attributed to Heinrich Cornelius Agrippa, it first reared its ugly head in Germany in 1559, with another edition popping up in Basel six years later. The *Opera* that you own is a later edition that comprises the *Fourth Book* along with some of Agrippa's real works, as well as the *Heptameron*, the *Ars Notoria* and the *Arbatel De magia veterum*. The *Heptameron* and the *Arbatel* share a similarity with the *Fourth Book* in that all three were credited to men who didn't write them. The *Arbatel* was falsely attributed to Paracelsus, who in his time was accused of consorting with demons. The *Heptameron* was said to be authored by the Italian philosopher Peter de Abano, who was put on trial by the inquisition accused of being a sorcerer. Accrediting the *Fourth Book of Occult Philosophy* to Agrippa helped seal his reputation as a necromancer and black magician.

'The *Heptameron* included in the *Opera* is a little book of great interest as many believe it to be the basis of goetic rituals used in the *Lemegeton Clavicula Salomonis*, otherwise known as the *Lesser Key of Solomon,* a work more notorious than even the *Fourth Book of Occult Philosophy*. Unlike the *Fourth Book*, the *Lesser Key of Solomon* did not appear in print until the twentieth-century, existing only in manuscript form, which only added to its appeal. The *Lesser Key of Solomon* is made up of five books. The first is the *Ars Goetia*, I can't remember the names of the second and third books off the top of my head. I believe the last two are made up of texts from the Solomonic cycle, *Ars Almadel* and *Ars Notoria.* In addition to the goetic rituals taken from the *Heptameron,* within its pages is the list of demons King Solomon evoked alongside illustrations of their seals. Although the number and order differ, this catalogue of demons is taken from Johann Weyer's *Pseudomonarchia daemonum,* which first appeared as an appendix to his *De praestigiis daemonum* published in the 1570s. There are other illustrations, including the Magical Circle of King Solomon, the Triangle of Conjuration, the Ring of Solomon, the Secret Seal, and the brass vessel for containing spirits.'

'Do you have a copy of the *Lesser Key of Solomon?'*

'I may have a copy of *The Book of the Goetia of Solomon the King,* which is the first section of the *Lesser Key* translated by S. L. MacGregor Mathers.'

'I thought Aleister Crowley wrote the *Goetia of Solomon.'*

'Crowley published the translation without crediting his fellow Golden Dawn member in 1904.' Appearing from behind the counter, the bookseller led James towards a dim corner at the far end of the shop. 'I believe I have some books by members of the Golden Dawn in the back somewhere,' he said. 'It is rather dark down here, I'm afraid. Very few of my customers venture down this far.'

Kneeling before a bookcase, he began browsing the shelves.

'I know I have a copy of Waite's *Book of Ceremonial Magic* here somewhere.' His eyes fell on the spine of a paperback tucked between two larger hard-backed books. 'Here we are.' He tugged at the spine of the book, pulling it from the shelf. He opened the book, his eyes struggling to read the text. 'There are sections on the *Arbatel of Magic, Grimorium Verum, Grand Grimoire, Black Pullet,* the *Key of Solomon* and the *Lesser Key of Solomon* - I can't see one on *Le Petit Albert,* but there are chapters devoted to *Abramelin the Mage,* the *Fourth Book of Cornelius Agrippa* and the *Heptameron.* In an attempt to prove the futility of ceremonial magic, Waite attempted to combine the texts into the ultimate grimoire.'

'He didn't believe in ceremonial magic?'

'No, but other members of the order, including Mathers and Crowley, weren't so sceptical. I have Mathers' version of the *Book of the Sacred Magic of Abra-Melin* - your *Buch Abramelin* - here. For

Mathers, it was a key text as it emphasised the spiritual development of the magician. You're in luck. I also have Joseph Petersons' version of the *Lesser Key of Solomon.* It is by far the best translation of the seventeenth-century grimoire. Unlike Mathers' *Goetia*, the complete text is included.'

'Why even after the Age of Enlightenment did people continue to believe in magic?' asked James.

The bookseller shrugged. 'I don't know - but they did. The 1849 edition of the *Books of Moses* sold particularly well. Soon after there was a renewed interest in the occult led by Éliphas Lévi. In the 1860s a Rosicrucian Society devoted to the study of magic was formed. This was the first of many orders that arose in the latter half of the nineteenth-century that would combine Masonic ritual with the study of occultism. Inspired by the occult fiction of Edward Bulwer-Lytton, the aim of Madame Blavatsky's Theosophical Society was 'to investigate the hidden mysteries of Nature and the physical powers latent in man.' If you want to learn more, I recommend Waite's translations of Éliphas Lévi's treatises on magic, *Transcendental Magic: Its Doctrine and Ritual.* I also have a copy of Blavatsky's *Isis Unveiled* and her *Secret Doctrine* in stock if you're interested. Should you want to know more about Renaissance magic a good place to start would be Frances Yates' *Giordano Bruno and the Hermetic Tradition* and D. P. Walker's, *Spiritual and Demonic Magic from Ficino to Campanella.* I'm afraid to say I didn't get very far with either - both are rather scholarly and complex works. But you seem an intelligent young man - you may fare better than I did.'

The bookseller led James back through the shop. 'It is easy to dismiss the study of magic now,' he continued, 'but its influence should not be underestimated. The fall of Constantinople in 1453 to the Ottoman Empire is often regarded as marking the end of the Middle Ages, just as the reintroduction to the west of the works of Plato and the Neoplatonists by Greek scholars fleeing the lost Byzantine Empire is seen as the beginning of the Renaissance. However, fifteen years earlier, a Neoplatonic philosopher, Gemistus Pletho, had accompanied the Byzantine Emperor John VIII to the Council of Florence. Whilst there, the Greek scholar had lectured on Plato and Aristotle, to an audience that included Cosimo de' Medici, the Duke of Florence.

'Inspired by Pletho, Cosimo sent out agents to scour the

libraries of monasteries in Constantinople and its surrounding regions, in search of ancient magical texts. Legend has it, in 1460, one of Cosimo's agents, an Italian monk Leonardo da Pistoia, discovered fourteen of seventeen treatises collected by a Byzantine monk Michael Psellos in the eleventh-century. The work, known as the *Corpus Hermeticum*, was attributed to Hermes Trismegistus, an ancient Egyptian sage. Cosimo selected Marsilio Ficino, an Italian humanist and philosopher who he'd encouraged to learn Greek as a boy, to translate the text. They were deemed of such importance, Cosimo had Ficino interrupt his translation of Plato to work on the *Corpus Hermeticum* so he could read it before he died.'

'Why?' asked James. 'What did the work contain?'

'Hermes Trismegistus was believed to be a contemporary of Moses. Some claimed he was the son of Prometheus, others that he was the grandson of Abraham. For Ficino, he was one in a long line of ancient theologians that included Zoroaster, who the ancient Greeks and Romans saw as the inventor of magic, Orpheus, Aglaophemus, Pythagoras, before culminating in Plato. To his initiates, Hermes Trismegistus promised the secret knowledge of the ancient world, revealed to him by God. In his dialogue *Asclepius,* he describes how the Egyptians attracted celestial influences to animate statues, bringing them to life, and in *Pimander*, a chapter in his *Corpus Hermeticum*, he describes how God created the world.

'Although occasionally reminiscent of the Book of Genesis, the text differs significantly in several ways. It was these differences that appealed to the Renaissance mind. Hermes taught that man is divine in origin. Human souls were created in the astral region, not made of dust as they had been in the Bible. The Hermetic Texts, in elevating man to the position of a magus, played an important part in the development of Renaissance humanism. The church had taught man should be obedient to God. The only book worthy of study was the Bible. Science and magic were viewed with suspicion. Renaissance humanism, with its emphasis on the potential of the human mind and personal spiritual development, shifted the focus from God to man, heralding a new era in art, philosophy and the sciences.'

James smiled. 'Man was reborn,' he said. 'Renaissance …'

The bookseller nodded.

James took the books on Renaissance magic by Yates and

Walker but knew he was never going to get round to reading all of them. He had neither the time nor the inclination, but the bookseller had proved so helpful he thought he should compensate him in some way for his time.

Upon his return to Moray Place, he stacked them on the desk in his study, where they remained unread for months.

CHAPTER ELEVEN

Isobel dropped the candelabra, ran across the great hall and sprinted up the stairs. Once in her bedroom, she wedged a chair underneath the door handle, switched on all the lights and jumped into bed. Settling herself down, she lay listening for any sounds coming from inside the house. More than once she thought she heard footsteps outside her room but didn't dare investigate for fear of what she might find if she did.

She didn't fall asleep until the early hours of the morning. Even then she slept restlessly, her dreams haunted by a vision of a decaying, living corpse, with dry, flaking skin drawn tightly across a face contorted by terror and fear, crawling up steep stone steps - a nightmarish vision that woke her suddenly from her sleep.

Upon waking she thought the whole experience had been nothing more than a nightmare - that was until she noticed all the lights were on in the room and saw the chair wedged under the door handle. According to the carriage clock on the mantelpiece, it was almost half-past nine. The others would be having breakfast and were probably wondering where she was.

After switching off the lamp on her bedside table she pulled back the padded eiderdown and crossed the room. Her jeans lay folded on a chair. As she slipped them on underneath her nightgown, she contemplated what she would tell the others. It was unlikely they'd believe her - she wasn't sure she believed it herself. After all, she hadn't seen anything, had she? But then she couldn't think of a rational explanation for what had happened.

Could someone have been locked down in the cellar? Had it just been Miriam or Jemima locked down there whilst looking for more champagne, a victim of a practical joke played on them by Alexander. It was possible, though unlikely. And it didn't explain who or what had been watching her from the shadows. Whoever, or whatever it was, hadn't been human - of that she was certain.

If she suggested the supernatural, they'd laugh at her. Alexander would, no doubt, take great delight in her story and would spend the rest of the weekend ridiculing her. No, she wouldn't mention it - she couldn't confide in them. Not even Will? It was going to be awkward enough seeing him without throwing that into the mix. Memories of the previous night flashed through her mind. She sank back onto the bed, her heart racing when she recalled what had happened.

After removing her nightgown, she slipped on a wool-knit sweater and hurried across the bedroom, deciding to wash after breakfast. She switched off the bedroom light, removed the door wedged under the handle and slipped out into the passage. She listened for the murmur of voices as she descended the staircase but heard nothing. The house seemed silent and empty. Where was everybody?

Moving round the staircase, she saw the cellar door was shut. The three-branched candelabra she'd dropped the night before had been picked up off the floor and returned to the oak table.

Hodgson, having spied her out in the hall, appeared from the drawing room and bid her a good morning. Isobel asked him if she'd missed breakfast.

'No, in fact, you are the first one down.'

She glanced at the grandfather clock next to her.

'It's only half-past eight?'

Hodgson nodded. 'The clocks went back last night,' he said.

'Of course they did …' Isobel hesitated before continuing. 'Hodgson, did you hear anything odd, or out of the ordinary last night?'

'I can't say I did, miss.'

'I thought I heard strange sounds coming from downstairs.'

'I'm afraid the house is very old. It often creaks and groans … especially at night.'

She wanted to say more but found she couldn't. Instead, she asked him if he needed any help with breakfast.

'Everything is done, thank you. There's just the coffee to bring through.'

Isobel asked after James as she followed Hodgson down the stone passage to the servants' quarters.

'He tells me he's feeling much better.'

'Will he be joining us for breakfast?'

'He hopes to.'

When they reached the hallway, Isobel noticed bells of different sizes hanging on a board attached to the wall. Each bell was labelled with the room to which it had been wired. Once this part of the house would have been alive with activity as tradesmen and delivery men came and went, passing maids as they hurried upstairs to clean rooms and make beds. She could almost hear the bells ringing, summoning the staff to duty.

She asked Hodgson if they still worked.

'Yes, they do,' he replied. 'But I'd rather you didn't pull them. Ms Crenshaw insists on using them even after I told her not to and simply refuse to respond when summoned. She really is quite impossible.'

Once in the kitchen, he filled a kettle and placed it on the blackened range. Isobel perched herself on the edge of the table and glanced round the room. There didn't appear to be any modern appliances in the kitchen, not even a kettle or toaster, let alone a fridge or washing machine. She wondered how, if they weren't somewhere else in the house, Hodgson coped without them. Did he have to take their clothes to a laundrette? She smiled to herself. It was funny how in the cold light of day she found her thoughts turning from uncovering the dark secrets of the house to the practicalities of living there.

'If I wanted to find out more about the history of the house,' she asked, turning to look at Hodgson, 'where do you think I should start?'

He was staring absently into space and didn't appear to have heard her.

'I blame myself for the way he is,' he said. 'I could never discipline him effectively - I was always far too soft on him. Maybe if I'd had children of my own, I'd have been better suited to the task.'

'Raising James wasn't your responsibility.'

'When he moved to the Manor, he knew no one and could not

make friends at school. He was alone and scared and looked to me for advice and guidance.' He paused before continuing. 'I'm trying to install some sense of personal responsibility into him now, but I fear I am too late.'

'It's not your fault James is like he is.'

'I just wish I could have done more to help him.'

The kettle came to the boil, and Hodgson began pouring the hot water into the large chrome cafetière.

'There are some books on the desk in the study,' he said. 'The house and James's ancestors are mentioned in a few of them.'

'Thank you. I think I'll take a look.' She lifted the cafetière and carried it out of the kitchen, making her way back through the house.

Once in the drawing room, she poured herself a cup of black coffee, before heading out into the great hall.

*

No one spoke at breakfast. Miriam sat quietly sipping a cup of black coffee. A soft-boiled egg lay untouched on a plate in front of her. Even Alexander, normally so boisterous and loud, seemed unusually reserved. For some reason, he was still wearing his Highland dress, though he did not explain why he hadn't changed into fresh clothes. Both Isobel and Jemima were absent. Will wasn't surprised Isobel hadn't joined them after what had happened. She'd probably spend the rest of the weekend trying to avoid him.

'Would you pass the marmalade, please?'

Will glanced down at the pots of jams and marmalades on the table in front of him. 'Whisky or Seville orange?'

Alexander pondered the question. 'This morning I think I'll opt for Seville orange.'

Will passed him a pot of marmalade, drank down his coffee and rose to his feet. Maybe it would be advisable to stay away from Isobel from now on, he told himself as he crossed to the sideboard.

He sighed. If only it were that easy.

'Where did you disappear to last night?' asked Alexander.

Will helped himself to a portion of scrambled eggs from a chafing dish. 'Me - I never left this room.'

'When we retired for the evening, we came to get you. You

weren't in here then.'

'I may have slipped out for a breath of fresh air.'

Miriam looked at Will with disapproval. 'This house is cold enough as it is without you insisting on filling it with fresh air.'

Will sat back down at the table. 'I wouldn't have to if he didn't keep polluting the house with his awful cigar smoke.'

Alexander regarded him with a calculating eye. 'Did Isobel step out onto the terrace with you?'

Will stared absently at his scrambled eggs. 'Hmm?'

'Isobel. You remember her, I'm sure.'

'She may have joined me briefly. But it was too cold for her, so she went back inside.'

Miriam buttered two slices of toast and cut them into soldiers. 'Too cold for me too,' she muttered under her breath.

'I couldn't have been far behind you.'

'Was Isobel with you?' asked Alexander.

'No. I was alone,' said Will. When he returned to their bedroom, he'd found Jemima sitting beside a sleeping Miriam, who informed him she'd had a little bit too much to drink and had passed out.

After finishing his toast, Alexander discreetly pushed back his chair and stood up. After crossing to the sideboard, he poured coffee into a cup, and said, 'I'd better take this up to Jemima to see if I can wake her.'

With the steaming cup of coffee in hand, Alexander promptly left the room, leaving Will alone with Miriam. Out in the great hall, the grandfather clock struck the hour, the chimes echoing throughout the house.

Miriam sighed heavily. 'There really are some appalling manners being exhibited this weekend,' she said, decapitating her soft-boiled egg. 'But then when your host sets such a bad example, it's not surprising.'

'James can't help being unwell, Miriam.'

'If he wasn't up to receiving guests, he should have postponed our visit.'

'I'm sure he would have happily postponed our visit. He probably asked Hodgson to ring and let us know he wasn't well on several occasions. I'm afraid to say we are only here at Hodgson's insistence. It was either us or his father, and, as the lesser of two evils, he settled on us.'

Miriam dipped a soldier into the runny egg yolk. 'Why would Hodgson want us here? Surely our being here is just more work for him?'

Because some people think about others and not just themselves, he thought. 'He's worried about James. He's probably hoping we'll convince him to leave this house - at least until he's well again.'

'Well, surely you can do that. It wouldn't take much to convince me to leave this place.'

'I've tried, but he won't listen to me. He's spent a considerable amount of time and effort on this house - he's not ready to leave just yet.'

Miriam grimaced and rubbed her temples. 'Well, you'll just have to keep trying,' she said. 'The sooner we leave this house the better.'

*

Alexander made his way upstairs, stepping tentatively up the staircase, slowing when he came to the gallery. He'd left Jemima sleeping in their bed, sneaking out of the room before she woke, not even stopping to change his clothes, unable to face her before breakfast. He wasn't quite sure what she'd witnessed the night before but was certain she'd seen enough to warrant an argument. Her sudden, unexpected appearance had been a regrettable end to an evening that had started out so promisingly.

Miriam, who'd been her usual reserved self at first, had relaxed after enjoying a couple of glasses of champagne, revealing a side of herself Alexander had never known before. To his great surprise, she'd seemed comfortable in his arms as they'd waltzed round the drawing room and hadn't even protested when he'd pulled her close.

Exhausted from dancing, they'd withdrawn to a corner of the room together, ignoring the others. During their intimate conversation that followed, he'd found her charming and playful, flirtatious even, greeting his jokes with a captivating, coquettish laugh, drawing him to her. He'd always suspected if he chipped away at her thick veneer of modesty and respectability for long enough, eventually he'd lay bare a fiery, hot-blooded woman - and it finally looked like his long-held suspicions were about to be proved true.

Eager to continue their little tête-à-tête, he'd gone to pour her out another glass of champagne, only to find they'd finished their last bottle, which gave them the perfect excuse to slip out of the room together. Their search for Hodgson led them to the servants' quarters. Thankfully, he wasn't in the kitchen so they continued looking for him in the other rooms, both secretly hoping they wouldn't find him, eager to be alone together.

Alexander had felt the adrenaline pumping through his veins at the thought of stealing a kiss or two from her. After all, he told himself, an opportunity like this didn't come along very often. By the morning, she'd have reverted to her old, haughty, distant self, repressing any feelings she had for him deep down inside her. He had to strike while the iron was hot, so to speak.

After passing the servants' staircase, they came to the office, and he stuck his head round the door to find the room empty. Seeing moonlight flooding in through the windows, he realised it wouldn't be long before they were discovered there, so they continued searching for somewhere a little more private. Across the entrance hall, set in the far wall, he noticed a door made of ancient oak studded with iron nails. The door had yielded to his touch and swung open, admitting them to a darkened room. Tall narrow mullioned windows set in the thick stone walls let in very little light, leaving the room in darkness.

'Well,' Miriam said, 'I think we can safely say Hodgson's not in here.'

Before their eyes could grow accustomed to the darkness, Alexander swung the old wooden door shut behind them.

'We should go back …' Miriam spoke breathlessly, her voice trembling.

Stepping towards her, Alexander took her hand to prevent her from leaving, drawing her closer to him.

'Not just yet,' he whispered.

Moonlight shining through the high windows illuminated her pale face and he noticed her step towards him, their lips almost touching when the door swung open flooding the room with light. They both turned to see Jemima standing in the doorway.

She asked them what they were doing in the dark.

When Alexander told her they couldn't find the light switch she turned on the lights. 'It's here,' she said.

When he saw they were in the chapel, standing at the foot of the aisle, Alexander instantly stepped back away from Miriam. A visibly furious Jemima then suggested rejoining the others. Both Alexander and Miriam nodded meekly in agreement and promptly followed her back through the house.

When they returned to find the drawing room empty, they decided to call it a night, much to Alexander's disappointment. Miriam, after climbing the stairs, had felt a little worse for wear and had to be helped to bed by Jemima. She'd fallen asleep before her head had hit the pillow.

Alexander knew then Jemima was going to be - understandably - furious with him. He'd expected her to burst into the room soon afterwards and start hurling accusations at him, but thankfully he'd fallen asleep before she'd put in an appearance. Whether she still harboured any ill feeling towards him remained to be seen. Oh well, he told himself, knocking gently on the door, there's only one way to find out. When he received no reply, he pushed against the door and stepped inside the room …

He found Jemima sat up in bed, her eyes meeting his as he closed the door behind him.

'I brought you some coffee,' he said.

She glared at him as he made his way round the bed.

'Did you sleep well?' he asked, placing the cup down on the bedside table next to her.

'Did you?'

'Very well, thank you.'

'I thought your guilty conscience might have kept you awake.'

'Why should I have a guilty conscience?'

'You know perfectly well why!' she cried, her voice loud and harsh. 'You should be ashamed of yourself taking advantage of Miriam in that state.'

'What state? So, she had a few drinks …'

'She was drunk.'

'Nevertheless, I was not trying to take advantage of her.'

'It didn't look like that to me. If I hadn't walked in when I did, you'd have been smooching like a couple of teenagers at a disco.'

'I do not smooch!' Alexander exclaimed. He decided to adopt the deny everything approach. 'I wouldn't dream of kissing Miriam.'

'You spent the whole of the night dancing and talking to her - rather intimately I might add.'

'I danced with you too.'

'Until Miriam stepped into the room.'

'I wanted to make sure she had a good time. You know how much she was dreading the party.'

'How far were you willing to go to ensure she had a good time?'

'Miriam and I are friends,' Alexander insisted, 'that's all.'

'Really? I've seen the way she fawns over you.'

'You're imagining things.'

'Am I? She makes no secret of her dislike of me.'

'She dislikes everyone. I wouldn't take it personally.'

Jemima rose from the bed, took a sip of coffee before placing the cup back down on the bedside table. 'Everyone except you, it would seem.'

'I can assure you I only had eyes for one person last night. Did I tell you how ravishing you looked?'

'No, you did not.'

'Well, you didn't compliment me on my outfit either.'

He stepped back to allow her to look him over. He knew only too well he looked damned good in a kilt. Many a fair young lass had surrendered to his charms in the past upon seeing him in his highland dress.

'You look ridiculous,' said Jemima, crossing to the dressing table. She grabbed her wash bag before storming out of the room, slamming the door behind her as she went.

*

After breakfast, Will decided to check on James. He hadn't joined them for breakfast, and no one had seen him since the party. The previous evening Isobel had mentioned his bedroom was next to hers, so he headed to the other wing of the house in search of his friend. She'd mentioned hers was the first door along the corridor, so he continued until he reached the next one. Finding the door closed, he knocked before entering. When there was no reply, he pushed the door ajar and saw the room was in darkness. Calling out to James, he stepped across the threshold and entered the darkened room. The curtains were drawn, and the lights were off. As his eyes grew accustomed to the darkness, he saw the room was empty.

Flicking on the lights, he noticed the bed had been made. The suit James had worn the night before hung on the wardrobe door. So, he was out of bed, but where was he - and why hadn't he joined them for breakfast? Leaving the bedroom, he decided to explore the rest of the house. He was curious to see what the servants' bedrooms were like. He imagined cramped dingy rooms with sloping ceilings and small windows.

Returning to the gallery, he continued down the corridor, passing his bedroom, then the bathroom and came to a green baize door that communicated with the back staircase and the servants' quarters. At the top of the staircase, blocking his way, stood a wooden door. He turned the handle but found it locked. Disappointed, he retraced his steps, continuing past the first floor to the ground floor, where he made his way through the servants' quarters to the great hall. Once in the hall, he found himself drawn to the library. Books had always been a great comfort to James; he was often to be found in the library at the Manor reading Lord Dunsany, his mind lost in another world.

Upon entering the room, he noticed Isobel sitting on a window seat, looking out onto the garden, deep in thought and unaware of his presence. A book lay open on her lap. He found he wanted to sneak out before she noticed him but stopped himself. After all, he couldn't spend the day avoiding her. The sooner he apologised for his behaviour the better.

He stepped forward, a floorboard creaking under his foot. Isobel, twisting in her seat, gave a little gasp.

'Sorry, I didn't mean to scare you,' he said.

She breathed a faint sigh of relief. 'The house is making me a little jumpy.'

'I was looking for James.'

'He's not in his room?'

'No, he's not.'

Silence fell between them.

Will turned his attention to the books on the shelves. The spines of many were too damaged to make out their titles. The ones he could read were obscure books he'd never heard of before, countless volumes of encyclopedias, and biographies of Scottish Kings and Queens.

He glanced at the book that lay on Isobel's lap. 'What are you reading?'

Isobel held up the book and Will read the title: *The Otherworld: Glimpses of the Supernatural* by Frederick G. Lee.

'I found it amongst a pile of books on a desk in the study. I was hoping to uncover the mystery of Wychwood House.'

'From a book about the supernatural?'

'There are books on the history of the area too. This just happened to be on the top of the pile.'

She rose to her feet and led him across the room.

'I've learnt all about the Black Lady of Broomhill House and the Drummer of Cortachy. He was murdered at Airlie Castle; the sound of his drums in the night is thought to be an omen foretelling the death of the Earl of Airlie or a member of his close family. There are also many tales of a Major Weir, who was said to carry with him a staff given to him by the Devil. In later life he confessed to witchcraft and Satanism, amongst other things, and was burnt alive at the stake - his ghost was said to haunt his house in Edinburgh for centuries. I've yet to find a reference to Wychwood House.'

She opened the door to the study and stepped into the low-ceilinged room.

'Most are very old and stuffy, I'm afraid,' she said, leading him to the books. Some were stacked in piles; others lay strewn across the desk.

Sitting down on a swivel chair, she switched on a desk lamp as Will began looking through the books. Most were devoted to the history of the Scottish Borders, but at the bottom of the pile, he came to a further book by Frederick G. Lee called, *Glimpses in the Twilight.* Stacked on top of another pile was a book by Elliott O'Donnell, its title, *Scottish Ghost Stories.*

'I also found a book by William Godwin called *The Lives of the Necromancers*, Margaret Murray's *The Witch-Cult in Western Europe,* and *Daemonologie* by King James I.'

'King James wrote a book on demonology?'

Isobel nodded. 'He wrote it when he was still King of Scotland. It's a treatise on witches, necromancy, demons, werewolves, fairies and ghosts. Even Sir Walter Scott wrote letters on the subject. There's a collection of them in here somewhere …'

Will glanced down at the floor, his eyes avoiding Isobel's. 'I want to apologise for last night. I acted inappropriately.'

Isobel shifted uneasily in her chair. 'There's no need for you to apologise. I was just as much to blame.' After a pause, she said, 'Will, that summer we spent together was wonderful and I'll never forget it -'

'Neither will I,' he interrupted.

'But it was a long time ago now, and we've both moved on. Can't we just go back to being friends?'

'Do you think we can,' he asked, his eyes meeting hers, 'after what happened?' He held her gaze. 'You made it quite clear at the time you didn't want to see me again.'

'I'm sorry for the way things ended between us, I really am.'

'So am I,' he said. 'You never told me why you didn't want to see me …'

Isobel sighed regretfully. 'What purpose will discussing this serve now, other than to bring back painful memories for us both? We were young - too young. If we'd have been older maybe things would have been different.'

'If as you say, you want us to be friends, you owe me an explanation, one you denied me at the time.'

When Isobel hesitated, Will said, 'Did your parents find out about us?'

'Yes.'

'How?'

'I don't know.'

'Did they forbid you from seeing me?'

'Not as such. Ultimately, the decision was my own.'

Will wondered how true that was. He'd always hoped the decision had been forced upon her.

'Then why didn't you want to see me again?'

After a pause, Isobel said, 'Because you broke your promise.'

'What promise? What are you talking about?'

'You told me you'd come and see me the morning after the party.'

'I did. When I returned to the Manor, I encountered your father in the parlour. He told me you were asleep and wouldn't let me up to your room to see you. I asked him to tell you I'd been to see you to say goodbye - I'm guessing he didn't pass on my message.'

Isobel shook her head. 'No, he didn't.'

'I'd have hung about, but I promised I'd take my mum to the hospital to see my dad. I tried ringing your house later that day.

Your mother answered and told me you'd gone out - though she wouldn't tell me where.'

'I was in all that day.'

'I had a feeling you were. I should have driven to your house to speak to you, but by then I'd figured they'd found out about us, and I didn't want to make a bad situation worse.'

He wasn't surprised to learn her parents had found out they were seeing each other. They hadn't been very discreet at the party, spending the whole night together, neither caring at the time, both determined to be with the other regardless of the consequences.

'I wrote to you at your school a couple of times.'

'I didn't receive any of your letters.'

'I even tried ringing you there. I left a message for you to contact me.'

'I didn't get the message either.'

'Your parents appear to have done a very thorough job.'

Isobel nodded slowly and murmured, 'It would appear so.' She glanced up at Will, her eyes meeting his, her face full of regret.

'Why didn't you try and contact me?' he asked.

'I was too worried I'd find out what they'd led me to believe was true.'

Crossing to room, Will glanced out of the window, his attention drawn to the fountain.

'I needed you and James after my dad died,' he said, 'and neither of you were there for me.'

'I wasn't aware he'd passed away when you came to see me. I wish you'd have told me at the time.'

Both thought back to that afternoon, remembering what was said, or rather what wasn't said. He'd gone to see her the day she returned from school. It had only been three weeks since his father's funeral and he was still numb with grief. A strange stillness hung in the air that day, his echoing footsteps the only sounds he could hear, almost as if the world was holding its breath. Her father had answered the door and this time allowed him to see Isobel. He went to fetch her, leaving Will standing out in the cold. He'd instinctively known then something was wrong and had braced himself for the worst. When Isobel appeared, she didn't smile at him or even meet his eye. Instead, she'd glanced at the floor, her face expressionless. She'd told him she couldn't see him or James that holiday, having important exams to study for.

When he asked if she was going to visit the Manor, she told him she wouldn't be. Choosing his words carefully, he'd asked her if she wanted to see him - and James - again. She'd told him she didn't. He'd tried to convince her to change her mind, but his words fell on deaf ears. Eventually, her father told her to say goodbye, and after she'd obeyed him, he promptly closed the door on him.

Will turned to face Isobel. 'When I returned home, I'd told my mother what had happened. She told me to try calling you.'

'Did you?'

'No. I knew you wouldn't be able to answer the phone before your parents did.'

Later that day he'd suggested spending Christmas at his aunt's, remembering she'd suggested it herself at the funeral. His mother had agreed it would be for the best and made the necessary arrangements. He didn't go to the Manor to see James - he didn't even know if he'd returned for the holidays - nor did he make any further attempts to contact Isobel.

Two days later he left the village for what would be the last time. They didn't return home after Christmas, his mother remaining with her sister, Will resuming his studies at Oxford in the New Year.

'I'm sorry, Will. If I'd known …'

'Would it have made any difference?'

'Of course it would.'

Will turned to leave, pulling open the door.

'Please don't go …'

'I should rejoin the others. They'll be wondering where I am.'

'I really want us to be friends again - for all three of us to be friends again.'

Pausing momentarily in the doorway, Will said, 'I'll check on you in a bit, to see how you're getting on.'

Isobel forced a smile. 'Thank you.'

*

When Will returned to the study he found Isobel slouched over the desk, her head resting in her hand, staring down at a book with half-closed eyes.

'I thought you might like some tea.'

Isobel glanced up to see he'd entered the room carrying a silver tray, on which stood a teapot, a blue china cup, a jug of milk and a plate of well-buttered muffins.

'Thank you,' she said, stifling a yawn.

She took the tray from him, setting it down amongst the books and papers on the cluttered desk. Will asked her how she was getting on.

Isobel lifted the teapot and began to pour out. 'I haven't found anything out about the house, though I think I've figured out where it gets its name from. Apparently, Patrick Roxburgh, later Lord Roxburgh, witnessed first-hand the witch trials being held less than fifty miles away in North Berwick. The trials were the first major prosecution of witches in Scotland after the Witchcraft Act was implemented. Torture was used to extract confessions from the accused, their relatives and neighbours threatened with persecution themselves if they did not condemn them. Appalled by what he'd seen, Patrick Roxburgh prohibited any persecution of those accused of witchcraft on his estate, which at the time included the village; the surrounding woodland becoming a haven for those fleeing persecution from the witch-hunts.

'He was soon advised to change his position, for in Scotland those who refused to accept that witches and witchcraft existed, and those who consulted, aided or abetted a person suspected of witchcraft, were thought equally guilty of the crime. Many accusations were rallied at Patrick Roxburgh in an attempt to discredit him - including consorting with witches on the Sabbath. To salvage his reputation, he was forced to allow trials to be held in the village. The bodies of those convicted and executed were hung in the wood as a deterrent to those seeking shelter there.'

Will perched himself on the edge of the desk. 'And this place became known as the House in the Witches' Wood.'

Isobel nodded. 'Lord Roxburgh was, by all accounts, a rather fascinating figure,' she continued. 'Born in 1555 he was the eldest son of Duncan Roxburgh, Baron of Leithen, a Warden of the Middle Marches.' She began to read from the book lying open on the desk before her. '"At an early age, he betrayed a passion for mathematics. His father, perceiving this, and acting on the advice of his mother and sisters who were keen on social distinction, sent the young man to Christchurch, Oxford. There he met the acquaintance of Sir Philip Sidney, the nephew of the Earl of

Leicester, a favourite of Queen Elizabeth." It goes on to mention he completed his education, according to the fashion of his day, by travelling for some time on the continent. "His studies were interrupted upon receiving word his father had been mortally wounded whilst performing his duties as March Warden." Although reluctant to take up his father's post, he set his sights on bringing those who had murdered his father to justice. "But justice was not easily served in the Borderland. With no military background, he found he was no match for the Elliots, Armstrongs and Grahams who terrorised the region and was forced to employ the services of a band of cutthroats and villains, many of whom had been reivers themselves, who became his deputies, captains, and troopers."

'Years later, having united the kingdoms, King James immediately set about restoring order to the Marches, and in 1605 he established a commission to bring law and order to the region. "Patrick Roxburgh hunted down men with ruthless efficiency. In the first year of the commission's existence, he executed over thirty men. Many were hung, but if a rope could not be found they were drowned in a deep pool in a river. Reiver families were disposed of their lands, many were exiled, others were deported …" For his part in bringing law and order to the Borderland, Patrick Roxburgh was created a Lord of Parliament under the title of Lord Roxburgh. In the matter of a few years, he had become one of the most important and influential men in Scotland. His aim was to become the first Lord High Commissioner to the Parliament of Scotland, which would have made him the head of the government in Scotland at the time. His life, however, came to a tragic end before he was able to achieve his ambition.'

'Why, what happened to him?'

'He perished in the fire that destroyed the peel tower that once stood here.' Isobel rubbed her tired eyes and closed the book in front of her. 'It's a bit of a slog getting through these books, I'm afraid. Most date from the late nineteenth-century, the most recent dating from the nineteen twenties -' She paused, then rose suddenly from her seat.

'Of course!' she cried. 'That's it! I can't believe I didn't think of it sooner.' She turned to leave.

'Aren't you going to tell me what you've figured out?'

Isobel glanced back at him over her shoulder. 'There's no time to explain now.' Lowering her voice, she whispered, 'meet me in my bedroom after lunch.'

'I'm not going to do that.'

'You have to.'

'Why?'

'Because I think I've solved the mystery of Wychwood House.'

CHAPTER TWELVE

Lunch was taken in the dining room. Neither Isobel nor James were present. Their chairs sat empty at the table. Considering how tired she'd looked, Will assumed Isobel had gone back to bed. James's whereabouts remained a mystery.

Jemima didn't appear to be talking to Alexander, despite his best attempts to engage her in conversation, an ill-feeling growing between them. Will did not know what had caused the altercation and didn't care, assuming Alexander had made an inappropriate remark or two Jemima had found offensive, as was his custom.

When lunch drew to a close, Jemima announced, to no one in particular, she was heading upstairs to soak herself in a hot bath. When Alexander and Miriam migrated to the drawing room, Will held back, waiting until they were out of sight before starting across the hall.

'Where do you think you're going?'

Turning, Will saw Alexander stood in the doorway of the drawing room, a whisky and soda in his hand.

'I was just going upstairs for a bit …'

Alexander's eyes narrowed. 'I'd like to go upstairs for a bit too, but I promised Miriam a rubber of bridge.'

'Well, I don't know how to play.'

'I don't see why I should be the one keeping her company again.'

'She seemed quite content reading her book this morning. You're the one that seems to need the company.'

Alexander took Will by the arm and steered him into the drawing room. Miriam had sat herself back down on one of the armchairs. Releasing Will, Alexander crossed the room, glanced out of the French window, and made some comment about not going for a walk that afternoon as it was raining.

'What do you want to go for a walk for?' asked Miriam. 'I thought we were going to play bridge.'

Alexander stretched himself out on the sofa. 'Will doesn't know how to play.'

Miriam looked horrified. 'Didn't they have a bridge club at your school?'

Will shook his head apologetically.

'You know, the state of the education system in this country is deplorable.' She let out a long-drawn-out sigh. 'We'll just have to play rummy instead.' She glanced at Alexander. 'Where are those cards you borrowed from Hodgson?'

'Right next to you.' Alexander gestured to the coffee table. 'There are only so many games of rummy one can play, Miriam.'

'What about cribbage?'

'No one's played cribbage in over fifty years. How about a game of poker? Would make things a bit more interesting …'

Miriam leant over to the coffee table and picked up a pack of cards. 'I am not gambling with you.'

Alexander drank down his whisky and soda. 'Isobel's bound to know how to play bridge. She'll be down soon …'

Will thought that unlikely. 'Even with Isobel you need a fourth,' he said. 'I know James can play …'

'James isn't here,' said Alexander.

'He's not exactly the most hospitable of hosts, is he?' sniffed Miriam.

'I could go and see if I can find him for you,' said Will.

Alexander glared at him. 'You're not going anywhere.'

Through the open door, Will saw Hodgson cross the great hall and enter the dining room.

'Why don't you ask Hodgson?' he said. 'I know he can play - he taught James.'

'We are not playing cards with the staff,' said Miriam, shuffling the deck.

'Hodgson is hardly staff, Miriam.'

'Don't be ridiculous, William. What would I do if I wanted

someone to fetch me a drink?'

Will sighed. 'Rummy it is then.'

Miriam soon grew tired of playing cards, and it wasn't long before she returned to her book. When Alexander, after finishing off two generous whisky and sodas, fell asleep on the sofa, Will left the drawing room and made his way upstairs to Isobel's bedroom. He knocked gently on the door and heard Isobel call to him from within. Hurrying inside, shutting the door after him, he found her sitting in front of the dressing table wearing a robe, her hair wet.

'You missed lunch,' he said.

Isobel glanced at him in the reflection of the mirror, and told him, as he suspected, she'd fallen asleep upon returning to her room.

'I didn't get a wink of sleep last night,' she said, but didn't explain why.

Will told her that had she joined them for lunch, she'd only have found herself being roped into playing cards with Alexander and Miriam afterwards.

Isobel, turning in her seat, faced him. 'The reason I couldn't find a reference to anything happening in the house earlier today,' she said, curling her legs underneath her, 'is because the books I looked through are too old.'

'They are?'

'Which means something must have happened to Henry and Emily Roxburgh.'

Will regarded her thoughtfully. 'Why do you think that?'

'Because not one member of James's family has visited the house since.'

'So, what do you think happened here?'

Uncurling her legs, Isobel sprang to her feet, took his hand and dragged him over to the wardrobe. 'Open it,' she said.

Will eyed her suspiciously. 'No one's going to jump out on me, are they?' he asked.

'No, of course not.'

Opening the wardrobe, he looked at the gowns and dresses hanging on the rail. 'What is it I'm supposed to be looking at?'

'The gowns and dresses of course.' She led him over to the dressing table. 'In here I found nightdresses and lingerie.' Pulling open a drawer, she held up a transparent negligee. 'Do you really not see where I am going with this?'

Will glanced nervously over his shoulder at the door. 'I think you should put that away.'

Isobel rolled her eyes and placed the nightgown back in the drawer. 'And then there's all the jewellery.' Opening a trinket box, she lifted out a diamond necklace.

Will's eyes narrowed. 'They belonged to Emily Roxburgh …'

'Do you really think any woman would leave all these beautiful things behind? The dresses possibly - they weren't in fashion when she left - but not the jewellery. Which can only mean one thing …' She turned to face Will, pausing for dramatic effect before continuing. 'Emily Roxburgh never left this house.'

'Why, what happened to her?'

'I assume Henry murdered her.'

Will studied her curiously for a moment. He wasn't sure if she was making fun of him.

'What possible reason would Henry have for murdering his wife?'

Isobel shrugged regretfully. 'I haven't the faintest idea,' she sighed. 'You're not convinced, are you?'

Will shook his head. 'Your evidence is circumspect at best. You're going to need more than a dozen dresses and some jewellery to support your claim. Maybe if we had something more substantial to go on …'

Isobel slumped herself down on the four-poster bed. 'Oh, you sound like a lawyer,' she said despairingly.

'How on earth did you reach such a conclusion?'

'Because …' She left her sentence unfinished, unsure whether to continue. After a pause, she said, 'Will, there's something I need to tell you … I know this is going to sound incredible, but last night as I lay in bed I …' She hesitated.

'Don't tell me you heard voices in the night, too? Apparently, Jemima keeps hearing all sorts of things.'

'When was this?'

'Since she arrived, I'd say. Imaginations are bound to run wild in an old place like this. It won't be long before the rest of us start glimpsing all sorts of things hidden away in the shadows.'

Isobel sighed. 'I didn't imagine this, Will.'

'Well, what did you hear?'

'A woman. She was calling out for help.'

'How do you know it wasn't the wind you heard?'

'Because I could hear her as clearly as I can hear you now. At first, her voice was so clear I thought she was in my room - but when I switched on the light there was no one there. Then, when I stepped out into the corridor, I heard her voice again - this time calling to me from downstairs. Fortunately, a few of the candles were still alight in the hall - I don't think I'd have continued if they hadn't been. I found the door to the cellar below the staircase. The door was locked, and I couldn't see anything when I peered through the keyhole - it was too dark - but I could hear something. There was someone down there, Will. They were dragging themselves across the floor and up the steps. I tried to open the door, but it was locked.'

'Where was Hodgson?'

'I intended to go and find him, but as I turned to leave the door began to shake violently as though there was somebody on the other side trying to force it open. I was surprised no one else in the house heard anything.'

'I couldn't hear anything over Miriam's snoring. I doubt anyone else could either.'

'Well, it didn't last for long and stopped as suddenly as it had started.'

'What did you do?'

'I was about to go and get help when I realised someone else was in the room watching me.'

'Who was it?'

Isobel shrugged. 'I don't know. Moments later the flames of the candelabra I was holding blew out and I ran for my life.'

'Did you mention hearing strange noises in the night to Hodgson?'

'He told me it was probably just the wind.'

'I'm sure that's exactly what it was.'

A floorboard creaked in the corridor outside the bedroom. Isobel glanced over Will's shoulder and gestured to the door. 'Somebody's out there.'

Slowly crossing the room, Will flung open the door to find Alexander stood in the corridor. 'Were you eavesdropping on us?'

'Yes, terribly sorry,' said Alexander. 'Awfully bad habit of mine.' Entering the room, he glanced at Isobel sitting on the four-poster bed. Her robe had parted slightly, revealing her long, shapely legs. 'This is all very cosy. What are you two up to?'

Isobel, closing her robe, eyed him with suspicion. 'I could ask you the same question.'

'Miriam insists on playing bridge. Can you play?'

Isobel shook her head. 'My grandmother tried to teach me once, but I never paid much attention.'

'Thank God for that. We'll just have to do something else instead.'

An ear-piercing scream rang throughout the house. Momentarily they stood frozen to the spot, stunned into silence.

Alexander recovered his wits first.

'What was that?' he said.

Isobel led the way out of her bedroom. 'It sounded like Jemima.'

Once in the corridor, they called out to her but there was no reply. Alexander ran across the gallery and hurried down the corridor to his bedroom, Will and Isobel following on closely behind him. The room was empty - Jemima was nowhere to be found.

'Where is she?' cried Alexander, his eyes darting round the room.

From the corridor, Will noticed the bathroom door at the end of the corridor was shut.

'She must be in there,' he said.

Alexander darted past Isobel and Will bounded down the corridor and hammered on the door.

'Go away, leave me alone!' she cried, before letting out another scream.

Her scream was suddenly silenced.

Turning the handle, Alexander found the door was unlocked but wouldn't open. He knelt forward and looked through the keyhole. Jemima lay slumped against the door.

'She must have fainted,' he said.

Slowly they pushed against the door. When there was enough room, Isobel slipped inside. She found Jemima lying unconscious on the floor, wrapped in a towel.

'She's okay,' said Isobel, dragging her away from the door. 'You can come in.'

The door swung open, and Alexander stepped into the bathroom. He bent down, picked Jemima up in his arms and carried her to their bedroom. When he laid her down gently on the bed, she began to come round.

'It's all right,' said Alexander, brushing her tangled hair away from her face. He spoke to her soothingly. 'You're okay. What happened?'

Slowly, her eyes opened. 'When I left the bathroom,' she gasped, 'I came face to face with a man in the corridor.'

'Who was it?'

'I don't know,' she said. 'The lights were off, and I couldn't see his face in the darkness. When I asked him who he was he didn't answer …' She tightened the towel round her that had come loose. 'Instead, he tried to grab me, but I darted back into the bathroom before he could. I tried to lock the door, but he kept banging and pushing against it - I had to use all my strength to keep him out.'

Alexander took her hands and tried to soothe her. 'It's all right, you're safe now.'

Noticing a bottle of brandy on the dressing table, Will filled a tumbler.

'That was when I screamed.' Her face turned pale, and she began to tremble. She looked like a frightened child. 'I thought he'd gone away but he started hammering on the door again.'

Tears welled up in her eyes and she broke down and cried.

'That was me,' explained Alexander.

'What did you do that for?'

Alexander shrugged apologetically.

Will pressed the tumbler into Jemima's shaking hands. The glass clattered against her teeth. She drank the brandy down and shivered.

'What is going on?' asked Miriam, hurrying into the room. She looked genuinely concerned. Following closely behind her was Hodgson. 'We heard a scream.'

'Jemima's had a bit of a fright, that's all,' said Will.

Miriam glanced anxiously round the room. 'Please tell me she hasn't seen a rat!' she cried. 'That really would be the last straw …'

*

That evening they didn't dress for dinner. Heavy argyle sweaters, wool jumpers and cardigans were worn instead of dinner suits and evening gowns. Even Alexander had opted to wear a V-neck shooting sweater with suede shoulder and elbow patches over his shirt and tie. Comments were made about Hodgson's cooking, but as the meal drew on, conversations became awkward and stilted. There were long pauses where no one spoke.

Gradually, one by one, they lapsed into silence. Furtive looks were passed round the table. They sat expectantly, waiting for someone to say something. But no one did.

After dinner, Hodgson brought out the port. He placed a heavy cut-glass decanter down on the table in front of James. He offered a glass to Jemima, but she declined with a timid shake of her head. Outside the wind howled and screamed round the house, rattling and shaking the latticed windows. The chandelier blown by a draught swung precariously above their heads.

'Looks like we're in for another stormy night,' said Isobel, breaking the silence.

'Lord Lytton would've had a field day,' added Alexander. When his host passed him the port, he cleared his throat and said, 'James, something happened this afternoon -'

Isobel gave him a disapproving look. 'Now is not the time, Alexander.' She gestured to Jemima sitting opposite him.

Once again, the wind howled against the side of the house.

'Now seems a perfect time …'

James looked across the table at his guests and asked what had happened.

Alexander poured himself out a glass of port. 'Jemima had a bit of a scare earlier.'

'You did?' asked James, looking at Jemima with concern.

'It was nothing,' she said dismissively. She was visibly trembling as she spoke. 'I'd rather not talk about it.'

'Are you all right?'

'She's fine.' Alexander passed the decanter to Miriam. 'She encountered a man in the corridor upstairs as she was leaving the bathroom.'

'Who was he?'

'We don't know. The bounder didn't introduce himself before making a grab for her.'

James looked at Jemima. 'Someone grabbed you?' he asked.

'No,' explained Alexander. 'She ducked back into the bathroom before he could get his filthy mitts on her. That wasn't the end of it though, he gave chase and tried to force open the bathroom door. Fortunately, she was able to hold him at bay. By the time we arrived, he'd turned tail and scarpered.'

'Did you recognise him?' asked James.

'No,' said Jemima. 'I couldn't see his face in the darkness.'

'How tall was he?'

'Slightly under six foot.'

'Is there anything else you can tell me about him?'

Jemima shook her head.

'Who do you think it was?' asked Alexander.

'I'm afraid I've no idea,' said James.

'Could he have been one of the men we've seen round the grounds?' asked Will.

'What men?'

'The gardener and the man who unlocked the gates for us when we arrived.'

'Oh, them. They work for a local firm of landscape gardeners.'

'Could it have been one of them?'

'They never come into the house,' said James. 'I've seen them in the servants' quarters from time to time - they sometimes have lunch in the kitchen - but they've never ventured into the rest of the house. Anyway, they don't work weekends. I'll speak to Hodgson about the intruder and ask him to conduct a thorough search of the house.'

'If you ask me,' said Alexander, 'I think you've imagined the whole thing. There wasn't anyone in the corridor. What you saw was nothing more than a trick of the light - a shadow.'

'Shadows don't try and force open doors,' said Jemima.

'Did you open a window in the bathroom before leaving?'

'I think so.'

'There you are then. It was the wind that caused the door to rattle. No one was trying to force it open.'

'There was someone on the other side of the door.'

Alexander suggested it could have been a ghost and looked expectantly across the table at their host. 'What about it, James?' he asked. 'Is Wychwood House haunted?'

'Don't say such things!' cried Jemima.

'Of course not,' said James, scoffing at the idea. He sat back in his chair before continuing. 'I've seen doors open and shut for seemingly no reason, had windows blow open on me and heard floorboards creaking in the night. All could be attributed to the supernatural - but in truth were probably just caused by the wind.'

He placed his hand reassuringly on Jemima's. 'You'll be pleased to know in the time I have lived here I have never seen a ghost and do not believe Wychwood House to be haunted.'

'I never thought for one moment that it was,' she replied.

Will poured himself a glass of port. 'You know,' he said to her, pushing the decanter away from him. 'If you want to visit a real haunted house you should visit the Manor. The ghost there has haunted the house for centuries.'

'My parents discouraged us from talking about the spectre,' said James, 'and forbid others from telling us anything about it either. But at one of the Christmas parties held at the Manor every year, one of my relatives had too much to drink, gathered us round the fire and told us all about it.

'He claimed there had been numerous sightings of a woman dressed in white with a veil over her face. She was believed to have died of a broken heart following the death of her fiancé during the Civil War. Ever since, she'd walked the corridors of the Manor searching for her lost love, appearing to bearded men in the night.'

'I was thought too young to be told the story at the time,' said Isobel. 'But that didn't stop James telling me all about him later that night. I was terrified for months.'

'You got your own back when we were older, didn't you?' replied James. 'Isobel often claimed to have seen the ghost and would convince us to go searching for her in the middle of the night.'

'I never really saw anything,' insisted Isobel, casting an anxious glance at Will. 'I was only trying to scare you.'

'Fortunately for us, the real ghost never made an appearance during our time there,' said Will.

'When he was a young man,' said James, 'my grandfather claimed to have seen her in the servants' quarters once - though what he was doing sneaking round that part of the house in the middle of the night, he wouldn't say.'

Alexander was about to say something when Miriam cut him off. 'I'm sure we can figure that out for ourselves without your help, thank you.'

They heard the solemn chiming of the grandfather clock in the hall. The curtains stirred and the candles flickered; some were blown out. Half of the room was now in darkness.

Miriam shivered and pulled her cardigan round her. 'I think

that's enough talk of ghosts for one night.'

James nodded in agreement. 'Tomorrow you should all go to Edinburgh,' he said. 'You look like you could do with getting out of the house.'

'You want us to go without you?' asked Isobel.

'I wouldn't be up for a trip at the moment. Really, you should go. You must be close to tearing your hair out with boredom by now.'

'We came here to see you,' said Isobel, 'not to have fun.' Everyone laughed and she added apologetically, 'I'm sorry, that didn't come out right.'

Alexander suppressed a smile. 'Maybe you're right,' he said. 'We can't come to Scotland and not hear bagpipes being played.'

'I'm sure we'll cope,' said Miriam.

'There's a whisky museum,' said James.

Alexander's eyebrows rose. 'In that case, what are we waiting for?'

James pushed back his chair and rose to his feet. 'I know a wonderful restaurant you'd love. Afterwards, rather than drive back here in the dark, you could spend the night at my apartment in Moray Place.'

Isobel shook her head. 'We couldn't.'

'We could,' said Jemima.

'How about you sleep on the idea?' James led them out of the room. 'Shall we retire to the drawing room before the rest of the candles are blown out?'

Miriam took Alexander's arm and hurried him out of the room. 'Quickly, before they regale us with another tale from their childhoods.'

*

Isobel was not ready to leave. She didn't want to go anywhere until she'd uncovered the mystery of Wychwood House - and she couldn't do that in Edinburgh. She also wanted to know why James wanted them out of the house. Was it because of what happened to Jemima? Maybe she should tell him about her own experiences and the voice she'd heard calling out from the cellar. Would he believe her, or would he just tell her it was nothing more than the wind blowing through the house?

Stepping into the great hall, she turned to James. 'We couldn't possibly leave you here on your own.'

'Since we last spoke, I've been considering your advice. I've decided to spend Christmas at the Manor, after all.'

'You have?' said Isobel with surprise, her voice echoing round the great hall. 'That's wonderful.' She paused, then added, 'You're not just saying that to get rid of us, are you?'

'No, of course not. We'll all be together again before you know it.'

'But I don't want to leave just yet. There's still so much I want to know about the house and your ancestors.'

James turned to look at her. 'I'm afraid there's not much else to tell. There's only so much you can learn from bits of paper and photographs. You can never really know the kind of people they were or what their everyday lives were like.'

'You haven't told us anything about Henry and Emily. I'd like to know more about the woman whose room I've been staying in and whose clothes I've been wearing. By the amount of jewellery she'd been given, Jemima thinks she must have been very beautiful.'

'She was.'

Isobel's eyes widened. 'You have a photograph of her?'

'I have a few. There are even some old films of her and Henry.'

'I'd love to see them.'

'I'll show them to you now if you like.'

Isobel followed her host across the hall.

'I can never decide if I prefer this room or the library,' he said upon entering the study. He sat down on the swivel chair, switched on the lamp, and looked at the books scattered across the desk. 'Hello, looks like someone's been in here …'

'Oh, I was in here earlier with Will,' said Isobel. 'We wanted to learn more about the house. I hope you don't mind.'

'Not at all' he said, but seemed somewhat taken aback.

Isobel felt as though they'd been caught out and shouldn't have been there.

Taking out a small set of barrel keys from his pocket, James unlocked the top drawer of the desk. 'So, did you find out anything?'

'Not about the house, I'm afraid. We learnt that this part of the Ettrick Forest was once known as the Witches' Wood. We wondered if that's where the house gets its name from.'

'I believe it is,' said James. 'For centuries it was known as Calidon House, only the locals ever referred to it as the House in the Witches' Wood. The name Wychwood House wasn't officially adopted until the nineteenth-century when William Roxburgh lived here.' He lifted a photograph album and some film canisters from the drawer. 'The photographs were taken not long after Henry and Emily moved here.' He leant across the desk and passed the album to Isobel.

She opened the album and glanced down at the first photograph. Emily, dappled with sunshine, was standing in the sunken garden wearing a light summer gown.

'She must have been about your age when that photograph was taken,' said James.

'She looks happy,' said Isobel thoughtfully.

'You seem surprised.'

She was, but she couldn't tell him why.

In the second photograph, Emily was in the drawing room, dressed in the gown Isobel had worn the night before.

'Is there one of Henry?'

James nodded. 'On the next page.'

Isobel turned the page, her eyes falling on a photograph of Henry. He was standing on the terrace steps frowning as he squinted into the sun. The photograph was not very flattering. 'Are there any others of him?'

'Not many,' said James, rummaging through the drawer. 'He appears to have been a little camera shy. There's one of him when he was at Oxford … it's in here somewhere …' He pulled out a photograph and handed it to Isobel.

The picture showed Henry standing under the Bridge of Sighs, alongside some fellow students. He looked younger than he did in the first photograph and seemed happier and more relaxed. Isobel turned her attention back to the album and began flicking through its pages as James set up the projector screen so they could view the films he'd found. In one photograph, Emily was standing on the terrace surrounded by a group of about a dozen people. Many were considerably older than their hosts. One, a portly, red-faced man, seemed to be sweating profusely. In another photograph, a tall, gaunt grey-haired man with a pair of thick gold-rimmed pince-nez perched on the end of his nose, stood next to a short woman with a round face and plump cheeks.

Lifting the projector off a shelf, James carried it over to the desk and removed it from his case. Isobel noticed it still had a round three-pin plug. She was about to say something when she noticed the room still had round pin sockets.

'Does it still work?' she asked, watching James plug the machine in.

'It did the last time I tried it.'

To her surprise, when he flicked a switch a low hum filled the room and the bulb inside the machine came on. James removed one of the reels of film from its canister, placed it on the front mount and threaded it carefully into the projector, inserting the end of the film into a slot on the take-up reel. Isobel watched him closely, interested to know how the machine worked.

'Most of the films are of various parties held at the house,' said James, setting the control switch to forward projection.

Both spools began to turn, and an image appeared on the screen. James adjusted the knob round the lens, bringing the picture into focus. The film was silent and showed a garden party being held on a warm summer's day. It appeared to be the same party the photographs were taken at.

Isobel recognised many of the guests: the red face man with sweat pouring down his face; the short plump woman with the round face and plump cheeks; the tall gaunt man, his thick gold-rimmed pince-nez glasses remained perched on the end of his long, thin nose.

'What an odd assortment of people,' she said. 'Do you know who they are?'

James brushed aside a dark lock of his hair. 'No idea, I'm afraid. I've often wondered that myself.' He pointed to a photograph of a stern-faced woman with thin lips, wearing a mink coat. 'I've always thought she could have been a Russian Countess who fled here after the revolution. The woman standing next to her looks a lot like Elizabeth Ponsonby.'

'Who?'

'One of the Bright Young Things.'

The camera panned left, coming to rest on Emily. She was wearing a summer dress and sat talking to the short plump woman. When Emily looked up suddenly, the camera panned back to the tall, gaunt man who appeared to be making a toast. Henry, looking embarrassed, stepped into the frame, and he was quickly joined by Emily, who stood by his side.

'Although too young to be a member of the Bright Young Things herself,' continued James, '- she wasn't presented at court until 1934 - she spent a few years on the party scene before marrying Henry in the summer of 1936. Cecil Beaton once photographed her, and she was deemed glamorous enough to warrant a mention in the pages of *Tatler*, the *Bystander* and the *Sketch*. I've found scrapbooks and albums she kept, containing press cuttings and photographs of herself and her friends alongside celebrities they partied with, most of whom are forgotten now, though I did find one picture of her on the arm of Stephen Tennant at his brother David's Gargoyle Club. She can also be glimpsed in the background of a photograph of Noël Coward that appeared in the Daily Mail.'

The film came to an end, and Isobel, feeling disappointed she hadn't learnt anything from it, turned her attention back to the album whilst James put the projector and screen away. Turning the page, she came to some photographs taken at a fancy-dress party held in the great hall. Men and women dressed in fanciful costumes posed together. Many were wearing tunics and togas of Ancient Greece and Rome; others were dressed in medieval costumes. Knights of the Round Table stood alongside fair damsels, and a young man dressed as a faun, wearing pointed ears, his legs clad in fur, stood amongst a gaggle of young women in thin sheer dresses and long flowing translucent robes. Isobel assumed they were supposed to be nymphs. Other women were wearing ethereal faerie outfits, complete with wings and crowns of foliage and flowers.

Guests she recognised from the previous photographs stood amongst them. The red face man, dressed as Emperor Nero, sat strumming a lyre. The Russian Countess had a bow in her hand and wore a knee-length toga, hunting boots and had a quiver filled with arrows strapped to her back. Isobel couldn't see the tall gaunt man, but noticed a man dressed as a monk, his face hidden by the hood of his long monastic habit, and assumed it was him. In the final photograph, Emily was pictured wearing a flowing silk dress embroidered with lions on the hem. Again, there was no picture of Henry.

Isobel closed the album. 'Why did they leave Wychwood House?'

'According to a ledger I found, they were in a lot of debt. Partying like the Bright Young Things took its toll on their finances. When they could no longer afford to live here, they left Britain for Europe, unaware of the storm gathering there.'

'Well, they certainly left in a hurry.'

James glanced up at Isobel, his dark eyes fixing on hers. 'Why do you say that?'

'Because Emily left all her clothes and jewellery behind.'

'Maybe she only intended to leave here for a short while.'

'But she never came back for them …'

'I doubt she could face coming back here after Henry's death.'

'She could have arranged for someone to collect them for her …'

James took the album from Isobel. 'The whole world had been turned on its head - they probably didn't seem that important.'

Isobel raised herself up on her toes and caught a brief glimpse of some journals and ledgers in the top drawer before James placed the album on top of them.

'Shall we rejoin the others?' he said, locking the drawer. He rose wearily from his chair. 'I fear I have been neglecting them far too much this weekend. I'm afraid I've been a terrible host.'

'You're not well. Everybody understands that.'

Once in the library, Isobel asked James if he'd met anyone whilst living in Edinburgh.

He told her he had. 'She was studying at Edinburgh University, or rather still is. We were together for about a year, but she's spending this year studying abroad. I'm afraid I haven't seen her since I moved here in March.'

'What was her name?'

'Tessa,' said James. 'I'm afraid she wasn't too keen on this house. She preferred living in the city and never expressed any desire to live here with me. I suppose, deep down, we both knew once I moved to Wychwood House our relationship would be over.' He paused at the doorway to the great hall. 'Do you think you could leave London and live somewhere so far away from your friends and family?'

'And give up my hopes of a career?' said Isobel. 'No, I don't think I could.'

'Not even if you loved the person you were going to live with?'

'A man who truly loved me would not ask me to give up on my

dreams.'

'No,' said James thoughtfully, 'I don't suppose he would.'

CHAPTER THIRTEEN

Will returned to the drawing room from the kitchen, where he'd been helping Hodgson wash up and put away, to find Alexander pacing back and forth in front of the fireplace, a whisky and soda in one hand, an unlit cigar in the other.

'Many now bemoan the glory days of the aristocracy,' he said, 'days when a noble elite dominated political, economic and social life. But they forget these well-educated men of breeding - men ordained by God - presided over the largest and greatest empire in history. Theirs was a better time, a time when each knew his place.' Seeing Will had joined them, he added, 'A time when only the right sort of people went to university.'

'And chorus girls were visited in secret,' added Miriam, 'and weren't invited into the home.'

Will glanced at Jemima sitting on the sofa, an empty drink in her hand. She wasn't listening to Alexander and didn't appear to have heard Miriam's snide remark.

'When the world of the aristocracy vanished,' continued Alexander, 'the rich social fabric of our country was rent asunder. Gone was the carefully layered hierarchical society loyal to the monarchy and Empire, a hierarchy that existed just as much for the lower, inferior classes, as it did for the nobility.'

'By refusing the majority of men,' interrupted Will, 'and all women, the vote.'

'Their subordinates were content with their lot and only too happy to serve their masters.'

'Tell that to the Chartists and Luddites.'

'In any society, there will always be troublemakers. However, by the Victorian era, there was a general acceptance of the station in life to which one was born. Social inequality was regarded as necessary.'

'Necessary for the rich to stay rich.'

'"Take but degree away, untune that string, And, hark, what discord follows!"' said Alexander. He paused thoughtfully before continuing. 'Thankfully, the wealthiest in society still wield the greatest political power. Social mobility is stagnating and once again the privately educated are inhabiting the highest echelons of British society.'

'Rather than a world for the few,' said Will, 'a world of green baize doors and separate entrances and staircases, isn't it better to live in a society where all people, regardless of their upbringing, race and sexuality are given equal opportunities and rights?'

'"It is useless to pretend all men are equal,"' said Alexander. He turned to look at Miriam. 'Dubious views?' he said despairingly. 'The man's a bloody Bolshie!'

Miriam promptly cleared her throat. 'Over the course of this weekend,' she said, quickly changing the subject, 'we've played every card game known to man and managed to exhaust every possible topic of conversation.' She sipped silently from a glass of water. 'I really don't think I could spend another day sitting here doing nothing.'

Jemima set her empty glass down on the coffee table in front of her. 'I wouldn't mind seeing Edinburgh while I'm here,' she said.

Will knew she couldn't care less whether she saw the city or not, she just wanted to get out of the house.

'We can't just leave James,' he insisted.

Alexander poured himself another glass of whisky. 'How about a compromise?' he said, topping his drink off with soda. 'We'll go to Edinburgh for the day and come back here for dinner. I doubt any restaurant in Edinburgh could compete with Hodgson's cooking.'

'Besides, James is never around during the day,' added Miriam.

Jemima rose to her feet. 'Well, I think I'll head up to bed.' She glanced back at Alexander. 'Are you coming?'

'You go on up. I want to have a word with Will.'

'I think I'll head up too,' said Miriam, following Jemima out of the room.

Alexander leant his arm on the mantelpiece. 'What were you doing in Isobel's bedroom this afternoon?'

Will perched himself on the arm of the sofa. 'We were just talking.'

'A man who, when found in a woman's bedroom, claims to have been talking to her is either a fool or a liar. Which one are you?'

Will stared into Alexander's mocking eyes. Another glass of whisky and he'd be drunk.

'Don't you think you've had enough to drink tonight?'

'No, I don't.' He knocked back his whisky defiantly. 'I can't say I blame you. If a woman like Isobel had invited me to her bedroom, I wouldn't have refused the invitation either. After all, life affords few such opportunities - especially for someone like you. However, if you want to be a member of polite society you should know there's a certain code of behaviour a gentleman should adhere to.'

'What would you know about being a gentleman?'

'Just because I don't behave like one doesn't mean I don't know how one should act. But then, I've never claimed to be anything other than what I am. You, on the other hand, have always given the impression you were a decent chap - and I for one have always thought you were.' He paused, draining his glass. 'When you first started seeing Miriam, Bill had his suspicions about you, but I put his mind to rest by vouching for you - against my better judgement. Don't prove me wrong, Will. I'd hate to be the one to tell him what you've been up to this weekend.'

'I'm sure you'd be delighted to be the one to tell him. And I don't believe for one moment you vouched for me.'

Alexander placed his empty glass on the coffee table and slunk back into one of the armchairs. 'It wasn't the first time either. When you applied to work at the firm, I put in a good word for you then too.'

'You're not seriously suggesting I'm working at the firm because of your recommendation?'

'No, of course not. You were employed because James's father asked Bill to take you on. And he only did that so he could keep an eye on his son.'

Will sighed heavily. Alexander's cynical attitude was beginning to annoy him.

'Did it ever occur to you that I might have been employed at the firm on my own merit?'

Alexander laughed. 'Oh, don't be naïve, Will,' he said. 'But then you're not, are you? You've known all along that was why you were taken on by Bill - at Robert's request. That's why whenever he comes into the office to ask about James, you feel obliged to tell him if you've heard from his son because you know you wouldn't be working there if it wasn't for him.'

Will scoffed. 'What rubbish,' he said.

'Is it? Then why did you promise him you'd bring James back with you?'

'I did no such thing!'

'It's going to be a bit awkward if you don't, isn't it?'

Out of the corner of his eye, Will caught sight of two figures looming in the doorway. Turning, he saw James staring at him with accusing eyes, a look of betrayal on his face. His friend disappeared back into the hall, fading from the room like a shadow.

Will followed after him, passing Isobel who gave Alexander an angry look.

'You did that on purpose, didn't you?' she said.

Alexander put his hands behind his head and relaxed back into the armchair, a smug smile of satisfaction creeping across his face. 'Of course not,' he said.

*

Will was angry with Alexander but angrier with himself for letting him speak to him like that. If he'd shut him up earlier James wouldn't have overheard them. He found his friend in the library walking restlessly about the room.

'I heard what Alexander said -'

'You heard what Alexander wanted you to hear,' said Will, raising his voice assertively, interrupting his friend. 'He's just trying to stir things up, that's all. Your father often comes into the office to see Bill - he is his friend as well as his lawyer, you know. Occasionally, whilst he's there, he pops in to see me and asks after you. If I've heard from you, I tell him - there's no reason why I shouldn't, is there? If you'd call him occasionally, he wouldn't have to.'

'Why are you taking his side?'

Will lowered his voice. 'I'm not taking anyone's side.'

James moved towards the fireplace. 'Did he ask you to come to the house and convince me to return home? I want the truth, Will.'

'When Hodgson left and you were alone in the house, he came to see me. He was worried about you - we both were. He asked me if I'd been to the house. I told him I hadn't but would check on you - not because he asked me - because I wanted to.'

'So why didn't you visit me then?'

'I was about to when I received your invitation.'

James turned his dark eyes on Will. 'Hodgson left in the middle of August, yet you waited until you were invited to visit - why?'

'I told you why,' said Will. 'Trainees, if they know what's good for them, don't take time off in their first year.'

'So you say.'

'Well, you weren't there for me when my father died. You didn't even attend his funeral. Your father did. He told me he'd notified you of his death and even apologised for your absence.'

'Whose fault is that?'

'You were the one who became distant. I hardly ever saw you when we were at Oxford, and when I did you weren't very friendly towards me.'

'Can you blame me?' asked James. 'I haven't been able to trust you in a long time, have I, Will?'

Will felt his stomach tighten. Was this about Isobel? Had he known about them all along? Dropping James's gaze, he looked down at the floor.

'I didn't think so,' said James.

Seeing his friend head for the door, Will called after him. When he ignored him and walked on, Will asked him where he'd been when Jemima screamed.

James stopped dead in his tracks. 'I didn't hear her,' he said without turning round.

Behind them, the fire roared, sending sparks shooting up the chimney.

'Everyone else did,' said Will. 'Even Hodgson and he was in the kitchen.'

James shrugged his shoulders. 'I must have been asleep in my room.'

The dark shadows under his eyes suggested otherwise. 'You

don't look like you've slept in days.'

'What exactly are you accusing me of, Will?'

'I'm not accusing you of anything,' he said quietly. 'I'm just worried about you, that's all. Why do you insist on remaining in this house, James? Have you seen yourself recently? You look terrible.'

'Nothing you say will ever convince me to leave Wychwood House.'

'Why? Is there a reason you don't want to leave? Is there something holding you here?'

'I don't know what you're talking about.'

'Don't you? Where exactly have you been spending your days? Neither Isobel nor I have been able to find you when we've gone looking for you. You asked me for the truth, it's time you were honest with me -'

Before he'd even finished his sentence, the wind whistled down the chimney, filling the room with ash and smoke. Coughing and spluttering, Will crossed the room and opened a window. Gravel, swept up by the wind, flew into his face. Shielding his eyes, he turned to see James staring about the room with unfocused eyes, his face white and bloodless. He looked terrified, as though he'd seen someone or something in the room.

Will looked about him but couldn't see anyone else in the library with them. When he glanced back at James, he saw his friend stumbled forward and collapse onto the floor. Seeing him fall, Will ran across the room, grabbed his friend's arm and helped him to his feet.

James insisted he was all right.

'No, you're not,' said Will, sitting him down on the Chesterfield. He called for help.

Almost immediately, Hodgson appeared. 'Is everything all right?' he asked.

'He almost passed out. Help me take him upstairs.'

Hodgson took James's arm and together they helped him off the Chesterfield.

'I'll be fine … I don't need help,' he said, trying to shake Hodgson off.

But Hodgson kept a firm grip on him, and they led him out of the library. Once in the great hall, Hodgson told Will he could manage by himself from there. Releasing his hold on James, he watched as Hodgson led him up the staircase. Moments later, Isobel appeared from the drawing room and asked what was going on. Will told her what had happened.

'Do you think we ought to fetch a doctor?' she asked.

'I don't think a local doctor is going to be of much help. He wasn't last time.' He led Isobel across the great hall. They stopped at the foot of the stairs. 'We'll see how he is in the morning.'

As he stepped onto the staircase, Isobel barred his way.

'Will, wait,' she said, lowering her voice. 'I have to know what's in that cellar.'

'We're not kids anymore, Isobel. I can't go sneaking about the house with you in the middle of the night.'

'Well, I'm going to find out what's down there whether you come with me or not.'

'And how are you going to do that? I thought you said the door's locked.'

'It is,' said Isobel.

'Then how are you going to open it?'

'With this …'

She held a key up in front of him.

*

That night, as he lay in bed listening to the melancholy sound of the rain pattering on the window, Will deliberated whether to join Isobel on her little excursion down to the cellar. He knew if they were discovered together there'd be hell to pay, but he couldn't let her go down there by herself. Without someone looking out for her she could hurt herself. After all, would it really be any different to when they were kids sneaking round the Manor in the middle of the night?

Leaning over to switch off his lamp, he glanced at his phone on the bedside table. Seeing it was ten minutes to twelve, he assumed Isobel had thought better of it too. She's probably fast asleep, he told himself before switching off the lamp and rolling over onto his side. He'd almost fallen asleep when he heard the floorboards creaking in the corridor outside his room.

Without a moment's hesitation, he slipped out from under the covers and hurried barefoot across the room, grabbing his dressing gown before pulling open the door. Struck by the awful thought that he'd find Jemima, or worse Alexander, making their way down to the bathroom, he breathed a sigh of relief when he saw Isobel creeping down the corridor towards him, a three-branched candelabra in her hand, her eyes twinkling with excitement.

Wrapping his dressing gown round him, he was about to say something when Isobel held a silencing finger up to her lips. Handing him the candelabra, she tightened her robe round her, affording him a quick look at the black slip she was wearing. The thin silk georgette fabric stretched tightly across her upper thighs, providing him with a brief, tantalising glimpse of her long slender legs.

They certainly weren't kids anymore …

Slipping her arm into his, Isobel led him down the corridor. They walked slowly, treading carefully to avoid loose floorboards. Only when they reached the gallery did she speak.

'I knew you wouldn't let me down.'

'I could hardly let you go down into the cellar by yourself.'

'If it turns out I was imagining it all you won't laugh at me, will you?'

'Of course not.'

Slowly and silently, they descended the staircase, their dark quivering shadows following behind them. They reached the bottom of the stairs and Isobel led Will round the staircase, his bare feet cold on the stone floor. All the candles had been extinguished leaving only the dim light from the candelabra to guide them. As their eyes grew accustomed to the darkness, vague objects took shape in the gloom that surrounded them.

From across the hall, they heard the solemn chiming of the grandfather clock.

'It's midnight,' said Isobel.

A chill ran down Will's spine. He noticed Isobel peering nervously about her as though expecting someone to jump out on them at any moment. When they came to the cellar door, she placed the candelabra on the floor, knelt forward and listened at the keyhole.

Will asked her if she could hear anything.

She shook her head. 'Not a thing.' Her eyes widened suddenly. She'd heard something. Reaching for Will, she pulled him towards the door.

Will leant forward. He strained his ears but without success.

Isobel turned to look at him, her hair falling across her face.

'Can you hear her now?' she asked.

Will shrugged apologetically. 'I can't hear a thing, I'm afraid.'

Isobel pulled her hair back, tucking it behind her ear. 'Listen at the keyhole.'

Will lowered his head until, once again, their lips were just breaths apart. Feeling his heart beating rapidly, he began raising his eyes to hers when, once again, her eyes widened, and she jumped back abruptly.

'You must have heard her that time.'

Will shook his head.

Without a second thought, Isobel produced the key from the pocket of her robe and fitted it into the lock. 'I'm going down there,' she said, turning the key.

She pulled the heavy door open, her nose wrinkling at the musty damp smell that came from the cellar, and reached for the candelabra, holding it up before her as she peered down into the darkness. Someone or something was dragging themselves across the floor of the cellar. The sound was so faint it was barely audible but seemed to be growing louder with every passing moment.

Will stood up, placed his hand on Isobel's arm, and said, 'You wait here.' He removed one of the dripping candles from the candelabra and ducked through the doorway. 'I'll go.'

'Why do you get to go?'

'I want to see whatever's down there for myself.'

Descending the precipitous flight of stone steps, he felt for a handrail but saw there wasn't one, and continued down the steps, peering ahead into the vaulted room. Was there something down there?

A cold draught blew through the great hall and swept down into the cellar, extinguishing the flames of the candles, plunging him into darkness.

'Quick, light the candles!' he cried.

'I can't find the matches.'

'Why didn't you bring a torch?'

'I couldn't find one!'

Will heard Isobel fumbling with what sounded like a little box of matches. She dropped one, broke another. The third match ignited, and she lit the candles on the candelabra.

Will held out his hand. 'Throw me the matches.'

'I'll pass them to you.' Isobel ducked into the cellar. 'We don't want to lose them.' She handed him the small box.

Will took out a match and struck it against the side of the box. Lighting his candle, he heard Isobel whisper his name. Glancing up, he saw the blood had drained from her face. Her eyes were wide with terror, her mouth open.

'What is it?'

She stared past him, her eyes fixed on the bottom of the steps. 'Get out of there,' she said, retracing her steps. There was genuine fear in her voice. 'Now!'

Will froze, unable to move, the hairs rising on the back of his neck.

Someone was behind him. Just a few steps away …

Reaching the top step, Isobel stepped back into the hall, the cellar door swinging shut behind her, knocking her to the floor. Will darted up the stairs, his candle extinguishing as he went, slamming his shoulder against the door with all his strength. The door frame cracked but held.

Isobel sprang to her feet and grabbed the doorknob, pulling at it with all her strength, but the door wouldn't budge.

'It won't open!' she cried.

No sound came from within the cellar.

'Will, are you all right?'

Again, he didn't reply. What had happened to him?

Her whole body trembling, she stepped back away from the door. 'I'll go and get help …'

She glanced round the room in desperation, in the vain hope that someone would appear and come to their aid, but no one did. Then, once again, she became aware there was someone or something in the room with her - she could feel eyes upon her - and again found herself unable to move.

Glancing furtively about the room, she caught sight of a vague, indistinct figure of a man standing in the shadows.

'Who's there?' she said. 'I know someone's there -'

Hearing a great crash, she jumped and turned to see the cellar door fly open. Will stumbled out, falling headlong out of the cellar onto the great hall's cold stone floor. Scrambling to his feet, he slammed the door shut.

Isobel ran to his side and turned the key in the lock. Stepping back away from the door, they watched as it began to shake, slowly at first and then with great force, as though it was going to be ripped from its hinges and flung across the hall.

Isobel reached for Will's hand. They stood together trembling, neither knowing what to do or say. Moments later, the door stopped moving as suddenly as it started, and the house fell silent once more.

Will let go of Isobel's hand and dusted himself down. 'I really think we should go back to bed,' he said. 'I've had rather enough excitement for one night.'

Isobel seized his arm, causing him to jump.

'Please don't do that again.'

'Can't you feel it?' She held him tightly. 'Something's watching us!'

Will shivered. Eyes were upon them.

Hearing the staircase creak, they glanced up to see a ghostly pale face gazing down on them. Isobel let out an ear-piercing scream that Will stopped by placing his hand over her mouth.

When Isobel saw it was none other than Miriam staring down at them, she regained her composure.

Miriam fixed her gaze upon them. 'What on earth are you two doing?' she cried.

'We thought we heard someone in the cellar,' said Isobel rashly.

Will shot her a stern look.

Isobel shrugged apologetically. 'Sorry, I panicked,' she whispered.

Hodgson appeared behind them. 'Is everything all right?' he said. 'I thought I heard a scream.'

'Apparently, someone's been locked in the cellar,' said Miriam.

'They have? Oh dear, I'll go and get the key.'

'Don't bother,' said Isobel awkwardly. 'I have it.'

She turned the key in the lock and pulled the heavy door open. Will held up the candelabra and they peered down into the cellar.

Above them, Miriam said, 'Well …?'

There was, of course, no one there.

'You must have heard the wind whistling through the coal chute down there,' said Hodgson, taking the key from Isobel. 'Here, let me close that for you.' He locked the cellar door and pocketed the key.

To Will's horror, he saw Alexander appear on the staircase next to Miriam.

'What on earth is going on?' he asked.

Seeing him, Miriam's face turned crimson, and she ran up the stairs. Will followed after her but heard their bedroom door slam shut before he reached the gallery.

'I don't know what's going on here,' said Alexander, 'but I can guess.'

Passing Will, Isobel whispered an apology before sheepishly making her way back to her bedroom.

Alexander clapped Will on the back. 'Well done, old man,' he said, laughing.

He walked back to his room, leaving Will alone on the staircase.

CHAPTER FOURTEEN

Twelve Months Earlier

James's research into his ancestors came to an abrupt end when he discovered, to his horror, the fourth and fifth Earls of Leithen had been stockholders of the Royal African Company. Established by King Charles II and his brother, the Duke of York, later James II, in the 1660s, the company held a monopoly on trading those unfortunate souls bound into slavery along the West Coast of Africa, shipping them across the Atlantic to the sugar plantations in the Caribbean and the colonies in North America.

Fearful of what else he might unearth about his ancestors, he lost interest in his family's history and genealogy, realising, to his detriment, his ancestors weren't the men he'd hoped they'd be. They were not the chivalrous knights he'd dreamt of as a boy; their kings were not noble.

In the autumn, when the nights began to draw in and his visits to Wychwood House became less frequent, he decided to turn his attention to the books on Renaissance magic he'd purchased and soon came to realise the bookseller hadn't been exaggerating when he'd said they were scholarly, complex works. Both Yates and Walker's books would take some time to digest.

From Yates's book, he learnt, to his disappointment, that Hermetism, rather than being based on the writings of an Egyptian sage Hermes Trismegistus who lived in antiquity, actually developed in the second to third centuries AD, around the same time as Neoplatonism, Gnosticism and Christianity. In the third chapter of Yates's book, he came across the name Picatrix, a celebrated book of magic, and wondered if it was the Liber Piccatrix he'd found in the study. Written in Arabic in the eleventh-century, its original title was Ghayat al-Hakim, 'The Goal of the Sage'. Norab the Arab had been credited by some as being the author of the book, others believed it was Picatrix himself, though both were mysterious figures, and little was known about either. The text was translated under the patronage of Alfonso X of Castile, known as Alfonso the Wise, at the Toledo School of Translators in 1256.

Eager to learn more, he headed to the Central Library on George IV Bridge, where, from an encyclopedia, he learnt the school was actually a group of scholars who came together in Toledo during the twelfth and thirteenth centuries to translate philosophical works from Arabic, Greek and Hebrew. Scholars from all over Europe travelled to study in the Moorish kingdom as early as the end of the tenth-century, but it wasn't until after the mostly peaceful conquest of the fortified city by the Kingdom of Leon that the school was set up. Alfonso the Wise employed Jewish, Christian and Muslim scholars at his court and personally supervised the translation of the books.

He then turned his attention to the Picatrix, which he learnt had been translated by Alfonso the Wise's personal physician, one of the most prominent translators at the Toledo School, the Jewish scholar Yehuda ben Moshe. Through deciphering the cryptic messages held in the books of the ancient sages, Plato, Aristotle and Hermes Trismegistus, Picatrix aimed to unlock their ancient mysteries and discover their secret knowledge. For Picatrix, astrology, the science of the stars was the root of magic, and within the pages of his book, astrological images, talismans, and the invocations of spirits and demons were discussed - there was even a whole chapter devoted to necromancy. The book would go on to influence Renaissance philosophers, becoming, for many, as indispensable as the Corpus Hermeticum.

Alfonso also had Jewish sacred writings translated at his school, including kabbalistic texts. The mysteries of the Kabbala had been revealed to Adam by God through his angels in the form of a map of the cosmos following his expulsion from the Garden of Eden, so that one day he may return to his lost paradise. This map, known as the Tree of Life, revealed how everything in the universe is connected and structured around the ten names of God. The Kabbala would later be incorporated into Agrippa's Occult Philosophy and would become an important component of Western esotericism, while the Tree of Life provided the structure of many magical organisations including the Hermetic Order of the Golden Dawn and Crowley's Order of the A∴A∴.

In the weeks that followed James found himself returning to the library almost every day. One day, towards the end of October, he began reading about the Theosophical Society and the Hermetic Order of the Golden Dawn. The headquarters of the Theosophical Society had originally been in New York but had moved to India after Madame Blavatsky and Colonel Henry Steel Olcott converted to Buddhism. The Golden Dawn's first temple was founded in London, but others followed, including one in Scotland.

Upon reading this, he was hit with a sudden thought his ancestors might have been members of a magical organisation, so continued his research, spending the whole day reading, paying little attention to anyone else. It was only when a librarian appeared through the double doors and politely informed him that the library closed at five on a Thursday did he realise the time. Glancing round, he saw all the other tables were empty. There was no one else in the reading room. After returning the books he was reading to the shelves, he left the library and hurried towards the Geography building on Drummond Street where he was due to meet Tessa at five.

He found her standing waiting for him outside carved stone gateposts. Realising he hadn't eaten anything all day, he offered to buy her dinner at their favourite restaurant on Victoria Street. They made their way back down Drummond Street, passing Rutherford Bar, which Tessa informed him had been Robert Louis Stevenson's favourite saloon.

Once inside the restaurant, they were greeted by a waiter who showed them to a table by a window with views overlooking the street below.

'I'm beginning to think my ancestors believed in astrological magic, that invoking angels and demons was possible. I also think some of them may have been members of the Hermetic Order of the Golden Dawn.'

'Why do you think that?'

'There was a Golden Dawn temple in Edinburgh - the Amen-Ra Temple I believe it was called.'

'Your ancestors were members of a secret magical organisation?'

'If they were, they would have been in good company,' said James. 'They'd have rubbed shoulders with poets and writers such as Arthur Machen, Edith Nesbit, Bram Stoker, W.B. Yeats, Sax Rohmer, and Algernon Blackwood. Charles Dodgson - Lewis Carroll - was a member of Madame Blavatsky's Theosophical Society, and Arthur Conan Doyle was a famous proponent of spiritualism. Even Churchill was a member of the Ancient Order of Druids.'

'Winston Churchill?'

James nodded. 'By the mid-nineties,' he continued, 'several magical orders had sprung up. There was the Ordo Templi Orientis that claimed its occult heritage from the Knights Templar, The Brotherhood of Amun-Ra - which should not be confused with the Golden Dawn's Temple of Amen-Ra - and the Ordo Aurum.'

'Why Amun-Ra?'

'He was the Egyptian Sun God - the King of the Gods. His name means hidden light. Magic has always been associated with ancient Egypt; many believe it's where its origins lie. The magicians of ancient Egypt wielded magic wands and cast spells to control ghosts and demons - even the gods themselves. They believed it was through magic - not religion or science - that man could become equal to the gods. That for them - and for many since - was the appeal of magic.'

Seeing Tessa glance at a young man and woman sitting at the table opposite theirs, her hand in his, whispering to one another as they stared into each other's eyes, he decided to change the subject. Despite his best efforts to convince her otherwise, she clearly regarded the study of magic as superstitious nonsense. She thought he should be spending his time more productively by going back to university, telling him he could finish his degree in Edinburgh, but he told her he was too busy.

'When would I find the time?' he said.

'It seems to me,' she replied, 'you have nothing but time.'

*

James continued his visits to the library throughout the rest of October and didn't visit Wychwood House for weeks. So consumed by his task did he become, he didn't even notice when the snow began to fall. In November he thought it unlikely he'd get to the house that month either - that was until he received a call from Mr Turnball summoning him to his ancestral home.

Detecting a note of concern in his builder's voice, he asked him if something was wrong, but he wouldn't say. After sending Tessa a message to let her know where he was going, he pulled on his long black, double-breasted greatcoat, knotted a cashmere scarf round his neck, and stepped out of his apartment. The wind whistled through Moray Place, shrieking and roaring round corners and up over roofs, sending the falling snow whirling in the frosty air.

The short flight of stone steps leading from his building down to the street was icy and he slipped as he stepped onto the snow-covered pavement, stumbling into the path of an elderly man. As he helped James steady himself, he muttered something about the weather before walking on.

The snow had begun to fall the night before and had continued ever since, dropping silently until all of Edinburgh was covered in a thick white veil, giving the city an almost fairy-tale feel. He drove slowly out of the city, down icy roads edged with dirty, grey slush. At Galashiels, the snow turned to slushy rain and the roads cleared. Only patches of snow remained on the fields and hillsides.

He arrived at the house to find Mr Turnball's men loading their tools onto the van, their pale drawn faces caught in his headlights. Greeting them as he stepped out of his Land Rover, he realised he didn't recognise any of the men. The ones he knew - who'd begun working on the house in the summer - appeared to have left Mr Turnball's employment. Wrapping his overcoat tightly round him, he crossed the courtyard, to find Mr Turnball standing waiting for him by the front door, a torch in his hand.

When James greeted him, he saw his breath fog in the cold air. Without saying a word, his builder led him through the entrance hall into the house. Inspection lamps and floodlights filled the great hall with light, illuminating every part of the cavernous room.

'You have a lot of lights on in here,' said James. 'I could see the house from the valley road.'

'It gets very dark in here once the sun sets,' explained Mr

Turnball. He stepped over extension cables that lay draped across the stone floor. 'I don't want any of my men getting … hurt.' The tone of his voice was short, businesslike, and no longer as warm as it once had been.

James blew into his hands to warm them up. 'I didn't recognise any of your men. What happened to Kenny and Graham?'

'They left.'

'When?'

'About a month or so ago. I've had a lot of lads walk out on me and refuse to come back. They won't give a reason, but I know why.'

James realised Mr Turnball was leading him to the library. The door to the room had been closed. Usually, it stood open.

'What's happened here?'

'Someone was attacked in the library.'

'One of your men?'

'No, they're all accounted for.'

Behind them Mr Turnball's men began removing the lamps and floodlights from the hall, hurrying from the house as they went.

'Then who was he?'

Mr Turnball shrugged his shoulders. 'I don't know,' he said. 'Whoever he was, he's gone now.'

'Gone where?'

'Your guess is as good as mine.'

Confused, James asked Mr Turnball who attacked the intruder.

'It wasn't a person, it was a -' He left his sentence unfinished.

'The dog is back? I thought I'd scared it off. You don't need to worry about that mangy mutt. It's just a stray looking for food and shelter. It attacked me when I stayed here late one night.'

'That's all I thought it was until …'

'Until what?'

'Until I heard the man it attacked cry out. A dog couldn't have elicited screams like that from a grown man.'

'Did you see the dog attack the man yourself?'

'No, but one of my men did. The creature pulled the poor soul down from the balcony and dragged him across the floor into the darkness. Although we only glanced in briefly before closing the door, we could see neither hide nor hair of either. Both had vanished.'

'I have to see for myself.'

Mr Turnball barred his way. 'Don't go in there,' he said, raising a hand. 'Leave with us and don't come back.'

'I can't do that.'

'Then at least wait until all my men have left the house.'

James agreed he would and asked for the keys to the house.

'They're missing,' explained Mr Turnball. 'They were in my coat earlier on today but appear to have been removed.'

James gestured to the library. 'You think *he* took them?'

'He must have. We've looked for them everywhere - except in there of course.' After a pause, he said, 'I'm not a superstitious man, Mr Roxburgh. I don't believe in ghosts or the supernatural. But that creature in there is not from this world.'

With that he handed James the torch he was holding, turned and made his way back across the hall, leaving the house through the entrance hall. Moments later James heard his van driving away.

Once again, he was alone in the house.

If the man who'd been attacked wasn't one of Mr Turnball's men, who was he? Why had he snuck into the house and what could he have been after? There was nothing of worth in there - except perhaps for some of the books and paintings, but he could hardly have smuggled them out of the house without being noticed. The most valuable objects in the house were the Sevres, Meissen and Dresden porcelains, but they were on display in the glass cabinets in the dining room.

Unsure whether or not he should enter the library alone, afraid the creature might attack him, he briefly considered leaving the house, before remembering Tom's words when he'd asked him why the hellhound hadn't attacked the police when they searched the house: '… they were let in by the caretaker. We broke in.'

Of course - the man had snuck into the house - he hadn't been let in. Certain the creature wouldn't attack him, he took a deep breath and opened the library door. Remaining in the doorway, the door's handle within reach, he switched on the torch, shining its beam into the library, only proceeding when he saw the room appeared to be empty. Moving slowly, cautiously, he came to the staircase that led up to the gallery where the attack had supposedly taken place. He raised his torch, the beam moving up the steps, following the gallery to the far wall where it passed over the entrance to the study.

There he saw one of the bookshelves had swung open and

stood away from the wall. Behind the bookcase, partially hidden in shadow, he could just make out an old featureless metal door. He assumed the door led to a secret, hidden room above the study, a room he had, until then, been unaware of. His intruder must have been after something in that room before he was attacked. But what? There was only one way to find out …

Peering nervously round the library, listening intently for the slightest sound, he climbed the staircase and made his way along the gallery, the torchlight illuminating the books that filled the shelves of the bookcases, stopping before the door. The door was featureless except for a small keyhole. The keys to the house lay before the door, dropped, he assumed, by the intruder as he'd been dragged from the gallery. He picked up the keys, examining them in the torchlight. He knew which key to use, the brass key which he had yet to find a use for, the key he'd always assumed was for a safe hidden away somewhere in the house. After selecting the key, he inserted it in the keyhole.

Hearing a click, he pushed against the door, grimacing as the old worn hinges squeaked as the door opened, the agonizing sound echoing throughout the library. A foul musty smell of decay and death that almost made him wretch overcame him. The door had only opened a fraction when it stuck, refusing to budge, the gap too small for him to fit through. He sank back against the railings, pausing for breath, only to feel the hairs on the back of his neck rising.

The creature had returned - of that he was certain.

Turning suddenly, his torch in hand, he saw the hellhound creeping across the floor of the library below him, its glowing eyes fixed on him. James froze, too terrified to move. Then, recovering his wits, he turned, sank against the railings and pushed against the door with all his strength until finally, the door yielded, opening enough for him to pass through. Pausing briefly to glance over his shoulder, he watched in horror as the creature sprang up suddenly, rising off the floor. With one gigantic leap, the hound was almost upon him, landing only a few feet from where he sat.

Only when he beheld the creature up close did he notice the gash on its side, its ribcage visible through the wound - a wound inflicted by Tom when he had struck the hound with an axe … Seeing the hellhound snarl at him, baring its fangs, he scrambled to his feet and threw himself through the opening, tumbling into the hidden room, kicking the door shut behind him before jumping up and locking it from the inside just as the creature rushed against it.

The steel door appeared strong and secure; he was sure it would keep the creature out. It looked like it had been brought there from a bank vault or strongroom. On closer inspection, he saw it wasn't just the door, the whole room appeared to be encased in steel. A sudden, horrible thought then came to him. If the hound could seemingly disappear at will and reappear without warning, what was stopping it from materialising on the other side of the door? He stood rooted to the spot for a few minutes, too terrified to move, his back against the door, listening intently for the slightest sound, expecting the creature to appear, but it never did.

Locked doors seem to hold it at bay … But why?

Many of the heavy wooden doors in the house, particularly the ones leading from the great hall, were embellished with iron studs, hinges and handles. He remembered reading somewhere that, in the past, iron was used to ward off evil spirits, ghosts, witches and other supernatural creatures, which was why people nailed horseshoes to their doors, something he once considered superstitious nonsense …

Holding his coat sleeve over his nose and mouth to defuse the awful smell in the room, he raised his torch, the beam falling on a faded Ottoman carpet. Lying on the carpet, a few paces from the door, was a revolver. Kneeling forward, he picked up the gun and saw it was a standard service revolver like one his grandfather had once owned. Ahead he could just make out the vague outline of a desk. Rising to his feet, the revolver still in his hand, he shone his torch across the room, the beam coming to rest on a human skull. Skeletal remains held in place by a dusty faded grey herringbone tweed jacket lay slumped back in a chair behind the desk.

James clasped his hand over his mouth, his eyes widening with horror. He knew instantly he was looking at the remains of his great-uncle Henry Roxburgh. Stepping forward to examine the skeleton up close, he saw there was a bullet wound in the frontal cranium. He opened the revolver. There were five bullets in the six-chambered cylinder. A shot from a few metres away would undoubtedly have killed Henry instantly. But who had killed him and why?

He made his way round the desk, kicking a small metal object across the room as he went, catching a brief glimpse of it before it slid under a bookcase. Realising it was the bullet that had once been lodged in Henry's brain, he shuddered.

Behind the desk, on a table in the corner of the room, stood a gold sphere consisting of a spherical framework of rings with a model of the Earth at the centre. Astronomical instruments, including a beautiful gold-plated astrolabe, jostled for space on the shelf of a bookcase. A crystal globe was acting as a bookend to hold a pile of rolled-up scrolls in place. On the shelves below were rotten, decaying books of varying ages and sizes covered in dust an inch thick in places.

Turning his attention back to the desk, he discovered a set of small brass barrel keys ranging in size from about one to three inches long. They looked like keys to furniture and cabinet locks, and he assumed they were for the desk in the study and the cabinets and bureau in the office. Pocketing the keys, he noticed an ancient manuscript bound in tanned animal hide lying on the desk. Opening the heavy tome, he saw the thick pages of yellowing parchment were handwritten in a script he didn't recognise. Next to the manuscript lay a journal. Inside the journal were notes, written in Latin, which seemed to be attempts to decipher the text.

Many pages had been ripped out towards the end of the journal, and he found a folded A4 piece of paper held within the pages. The Magical Circle of King Solomon had been drawn on the paper. It was the version without the coiled serpent that had appeared on the floor of the great hall. At the top of the page was written Sloane 3648. He assumed the circle had been copied, either by Henry or someone he knew, from a manuscript held in the British Library.

The only other book on the desk was a copy of Trithemius' *Polygraphia.* Opening the book, he saw it was a 1561 edition printed in Paris. Henry appeared to have been using the work to decipher the ancient manuscript. He couldn't help but wonder why his great-uncle had ripped so many pages out of the journal. Had he deciphered rituals he did not want others to know, or see? If that was the case, why not just destroy the manuscript itself? Why leave it out on display for others to find?

He assumed the man who had sneaked into the house was after the manuscript. There was little else of value in the room. Was he working alone or with others? And how did he, or they, know of the existence of the manuscript? He thought it unlikely anyone who'd visited the house during the time Henry and Emily lived there would still be alive today. Even if they were, would they really be able to remember the document after so many years? He was sure no further attempts would be made to retrieve the manuscript, not while the hellhound remained in the house at least.

Continuing his search, he pulled open the drawers of the desk. Inside the top drawer, he found a rusty film canister and an irreparably damaged Paillard-Bolex cine camera. Remembering he'd seen a projector in the study he left the canister on top of the desk to view later. Except for some stationary, there was little else in the bottom drawer. When he closed both drawers, he noticed a gold signet ring on the third finger of his great-uncle's left hand.

Lifting the hand carefully to inspect the ring, the finger crumbled and broke, the ring rolling across the desk. Moving quickly, he caught the ring before it fell onto the floor, and holding it up to the light, examined it carefully and saw it was engraved with what he assumed was the Eye of Horus. He was sure he'd seen the ring before, but for now, at least, he couldn't remember where, though he was sure it would come to him in time.

When the smell in the room became too much for him to bear, he decided to leave the room. Only upon reaching the door did he remember the hellhound. Even if it had retreated from the gallery, it would still be somewhere in the library. He thought it unlikely he'd be able to sneak out of the house without being spotted. His only option was to wait until the morning, in the hope the rising sun would drive the creature away.

He couldn't remember if the curtains were open or closed in the library. He thought it unlikely the builders would have shut them. If he did remain in the room, could he face spending the night there? He'd never suffered from claustrophobia before, but then he'd never had to spend the night in such a small, enclosed space with a corpse before. He wasn't even sure if there would be enough air in the room. If the chamber was hermetically sealed, he could run out of oxygen before morning.

He realised then the room couldn't be airtight - if it was the body would have mummified. He shone his torch round the room, finding a small air vent covered in dust and dirt in the far wall. Crossing the room, he held his hand up to the vent and wiped away the grime that had amassed over the years. Only then did he feel a faint draught of cold air blow onto his fingers.

Retracing his steps, his eyes fell on the books spread out across the desk. So far, he hadn't found a reference to hellhounds in any of the grimoires he'd looked through, leading him to believe the ritual for summoning one had been taken from the manuscript. Hopefully, these instructions were still to be found in the journal and hadn't been on one of the many pages that had been ripped out of the book.

Opening the journal, he scanned the pages, eventually happening on instructions for summoning the demonic creature and, under the heading 'License to depart', how to exorcise the beast. Unfortunately, Henry had translated the rituals into Latin, which meant it would take him slightly longer to read than if it had been translated into English. There didn't appear to be a reference to the Magical Circle of King Solomon being used in the ritual, leading him to believe Henry had added it as an extra precaution to protect himself - which meant he didn't need to use the Magical Circle of King Solomon to banish the creature, the words alone would be enough. They had to be enough. They were all he had. Those and the five remaining bullets in the revolver …

He decided to wait until morning before venturing out, in the hope the hellhound would be gone by then, believing it better to spend the night locked in a room with a corpse than the rest of eternity in Hell. He almost called Tessa to let her know what had happened, but thought against it, worried what would happen if she came to the house, deciding instead to send her a message to let her know he'd be staying the night at the house. He briefly considered adding a few lines to tell her how he felt about her just in case he didn't make it out of there alive, but he wasn't one for sharing his feelings. If he started now, she'd only suspect something was wrong and start worrying about him. Glancing at his phone he saw he had no signal anyway. The reception in the house was patchy at best. He wasn't surprised to find it non-existent in the enclosed room.

After switching off his phone to save power, he sat himself down in a corner of the room. Only then did he realise how quiet the room was. He couldn't even hear the grandfather clock ticking in the great hall. He wondered how long the room had been there. Had his ancestors used it as a safe room to provide somewhere to hide in the event of a break-in, somewhere to put valuables when they were away from the house?

He tried his best to stay awake but fell asleep shortly after midnight, waking with a start the following morning cold and disorientated, his body aching. The torch had switched off, the batteries drained. He had no idea what the time was or how long he'd been asleep, it was far too dark in the room for him to see his watch. He reached for his phone, switched it on and saw it was a quarter past eight. The sun would be up and shining through the library windows - assuming, of course, it wasn't overcast that day. He rose to his feet, his legs stiff and cold, crossed to the door and turned the key in the lock. He pulled the door open as slowly as he could to avoid making a sound, stopping as soon as the opening was wide enough for him to slip through. Light flooded into the room, hurting his eyes, and he breathed in the fresh clear air.

When he saw the hellhound wasn't on the gallery, he sighed with relief. Before leaving, he decided to take the manuscript, Henry's journal and Trithemius' *Polygraphia* with him, holding them close to him with one hand, the revolver clasped in the other. Leaving the hidden room, he stepped onto the gallery. Sunlight streamed in through the windows illuminating every corner of the room, the sight lifting his spirits. There was nowhere for the creature to hide. After closing and locking the door behind him, he promptly left the house.

Once in the village he pulled his Land Rover over to the side of the road and saw he had received missed calls and texts from Tessa asking where he was. He immediately called her, telling her he'd decided to stay at the house overnight due to the weather. He'd tried to call her but hadn't been able to get a signal. That part, at least, was true.

On the journey back to Edinburgh he contemplated what to do about Henry's body. He wondered whether he should call the police and report his discovery but wasn't sure that was such a good idea. After all, they wouldn't be able to investigate his death. Whoever had killed Henry was probably dead now too. Even if by some miracle they were still alive they'd be far too old to stand trial. Also, he didn't want to show the room in which he'd made his gruesome discovery to anyone. They'd see the collection of books, many of which were devoted to demonology and black arts, as well as all the occult paraphernalia. He remembered the librarian telling him many in Selkirk would be interested in learning what had happened at Wychwood House. The story of Henry's discovery would inevitably reach the local press, causing his family a great deal of embarrassment.

But if he didn't call the police, what would he do with Henry's remains? He couldn't simply bury his bones in the wood. Henry deserved a proper burial, one denied to him for the last seventy years. There had to be a way of interning him in the family vault without getting the police involved.

Such questions were, however, irrelevant until he'd banished the hellhound from the house - if such a thing were possible. He thought it unlikely he'd be able to sneak back inside the hidden room while the creature was still in there, let alone remove Henry's body undetected.

For now, it would just have to remain where it was.

*

James didn't tell Tessa what happened at the house, keeping the discovery of his great-uncle's body to himself. The following week he began reading his journal, eager to learn more about the ancient manuscript. Drawn from ancient Zoroastrian texts, Jewish mysticism, Hermetic literature, Egyptian magic, Hindu scriptures, and greatly influenced by the Arabic study of astral magic, the manuscript appeared to be a comprehensive textbook of magic. Clearly, it had been a labour of love that had taken years, if not a lifetime, for its unknown author to compile. Many of the texts alluded to would have been very difficult to obtain at the time of its composition. How it came to be in Henry's possession remained a mystery.

The first section of the manuscript covered elemental or natural magic, which involved harnessing the occult forces of gemstones, plants and animals, and making use of their healing and protective properties, which sounded too much like crystal healing and other New Age nonsense for him to take seriously. The next section, talismanic and celestial magic, was heavily influenced by *Picatrix* and taught how to create talismans and amulets into which the influences of the sun, moon, planets and stars could be drawn, imbuing the object with magical powers. The third section concerned ceremonial magic, which was where the ritual for summoning a hellhound was to be found. Also included was the obligatory list of demons alongside their powers that was a staple of grimoires before and since, though there were no corresponding illustrations like those found in the later *Dictionnaire Infernal.*

There was a fourth part devoted to astral and transcendental magic, but it was here the pages had been ripped out of the journal, which surprised him. He thought it would have been the section on ceremonial magic Henry would have destroyed. If he wanted to know what rituals were contained in this section that his great-uncle deemed so awful he had to exorcise them from his book, he was going to have to decipher it himself.

Over the weeks that followed he attempted to do just that, keeping both the journal and manuscript out of sight, only working on the text when Tessa was at university or working in the pub. The task proved a laborious, time-consuming job he soon grew tired of. Eventually, he gave up and locked the manuscript away in the drawer of the desk in his study, alongside the journal, Trithemius' *Polygraphia* and the Webley.

*

During the winter months that followed, James was at a loss to know what to do with himself as he waited for what seemed like an eternity for the days to lengthen so he could return to Wychwood House and face the hellhound. Feeling his life was on hold until then, his restlessness and boredom put a strain on his relationship with Tessa. He desperately wanted to tell her about the hound but knew he couldn't. She wouldn't believe him anyway and the only way he could convince her of its existence would be to take her to the house to see the creature for herself. But that was not something he was prepared to do, for fear of the consequences.

During December, the hours she worked at the pub increased and he saw less of her, and as he was spending all of his time at his apartment in Moray Place, he came to know his neighbours. Since living there he'd often been invited to dinner, but he'd always made excuses. But now, with nothing to do but wait, he agreed to attend a party on Christmas Eve held by Sir John Murston and his wife Cecilia, who lived next door to him. There he met a number of his other neighbours, many of whom related the history of the estate, keen to point out the Moray Feu was built in the nineteenth-century for Scotland's upper classes, an exclusive development for the country's elite. He spent most of the evening with Sir John

Murston's granddaughter, Sophie, who seemed glad to find someone her own age at the party.

Later, when she had returned from work, Tessa asked him if he'd enjoyed himself. He told her he had, and she asked him who had been there.

'A couple of baronets, a retired architect, and a Lord something or other. There was also a Scottish Advocate, judge and one-time member of the privy council. I made the mistake of telling him one of my ancestors had been a member of the privy council. He told me he'd never heard of him, and I replied he was a little before his time.'

Amongst their ranks were fund managers and bankers working for private equity firms, along with their sons and daughters back from Fettes for the holiday, who referred to themselves as 'new' money.

'People I thought you left London to avoid.'

'It was only one party,' said James. 'You can't expect me to spend Christmas Eve on my own.'

'Was there anyone your age there?'

'Just Sophie,' he said.

'Sophie?'

'Sir John's granddaughter. She's studying International Relations at St Andrews. Apparently, working in the diplomatic services is something of a tradition in their family.'

'Is she pretty?'

'Who Sophie?' he said. 'Yes, I suppose so.' He thought she possessed a refined elegance rare nowadays, though he didn't tell Tessa that.

'Will you be seeing her again?'

He assured her if he did it would only be in passing. However, he did see her again, shortly before she returned to university. They had lunch together.

'I would have preferred to have spent the evening with you,' he said.

'Well, I have no choice but to work.'

'No, you don't,' said James. 'I could support you through university.'

'On the condition I moved to Wychwood House with you once I'd finished?'

'Well, that would be entirely up to you at the time.'

'What would we do there?'

'I don't know,' said James. 'I haven't thought that far in advance. I suppose we could rear pheasants and partridges and turn the place into a shooting estate … which given time could become a viable business,' he added, remembering his father's words.

'Please tell me you're joking,' said Tessa.

'Well, we could always turn it into a hotel or self-catering accommodation.'

'If I'd wanted to run a hotel I'd have stayed at home and not bothered going to university!'

They had frequent arguments about their future over the following weeks, both knowing their relationship was coming to an end, but neither wanting to be the one to admit it was over. The following September Tessa was going to study abroad for the academic year. By the time she returned James hoped to be living in Wychwood House.

In the New Year, her visits to Moray Place became less frequent. Then in February, when James told her he'd be returning to Wychwood House in March and didn't know when he'd be back, they decided to call it a day. There were no arguments, no tears, just a mutual agreement that splitting up was the best thing to do, which only seemed to make matters worse. He'd have preferred a fight or two, the end of their relationship appearing anticlimactic without them.

Once she'd gone the apartment felt empty without her and he was glad to be leaving it. Thankfully, he didn't associate Wychwood House with her, her one and only visit there having been brief. His planned return to his ancestral home was, however, postponed by the weather. Heavy rain fell from dark leaden skies for the first two weeks of the month.

Whilst waiting, finding himself with nothing better to do, he contacted a local firm of stonemasons and asked them to provide him with a stone coffin, a replacement for one that had been damaged beyond repair, to be delivered to the Roxburgh family vault in the village. When asked what he wanted inscribed on the coffin he hesitated. While he knew his great-uncle's date of birth, he wasn't certain on what day he'd died. The year had to be 1938, the month most probably October, but the day? He was about to pick a day at random when he remembered the desk calendar in the study. The date shown on the calendar was the 31st of October which seemed the most likely day Henry had met his sudden, untimely demise.

At the end of the two weeks when the rain began to ease, Sophie, who was visiting her grandparents for a couple of days, came to see him. When he told her he was no longer seeing Tessa, she convinced him to take her to dinner that evening at a restaurant. Although reluctant at first, he agreed. By then he hadn't left his apartment in weeks and thought an evening out would do him good.

After leaving the restaurant he walked her back to her grandparents' house, and she made him promise to visit her at St Andrews.

'I think we could have fun together,' she said.

'I'm sure we could.'

She kissed him goodnight and disappeared inside the townhouse. Although he'd enjoyed their evening together, he knew he'd never visit her at her university.

For once he'd set foot back inside Wychwood House, he knew there'd be no return to normal life for him …

*

The following morning, he woke to clear skies. According to the forecast the weather was set to stay that way for the rest of the week so there was no reason for him to postpone his return to Wychwood House for any longer. After breakfast, he packed a bag with a week's worth of clothes and filled another with food and provisions, and the materials - tins of paint, brushes - he needed to replicate the magic circle on the floor of the great hall. He expected the generator to have run down or just packed up, so he also took two torches, some matches and candles with him. Before leaving he grabbed Henry's journal, the manuscript and the book he'd taken from the hidden room, and finally, and most importantly, his great-uncle's Webley.

He arrived at the house around midday, entering the building through the tradesman's entrance. As far as he was aware the hellhound had never been seen in this part of the house before. Nevertheless, he kept a tight grip on the revolver as he unpacked the Land Rover, setting himself up in the kitchen. The sun set just after six that evening, giving him plenty of time to complete the magic circle before the shadows deepened and night fell.

Once in the kitchen, he flicked a switch, and the lights came on. The diesel generator was still working, though for how long remained to be seen. He decided to keep the lights off as much as possible, relying instead on torches and candlelight. He didn't want to go down into the coal cellar to fill the fuel tank, not even during the day.

After unpacking, the first thing he did was unlock and open all exterior doors in the house, even the ones leading into the small, enclosed courtyard. He wanted there to be plenty of ways for him to get out of the house should he need to, the more exits the better. When he finished, he walked round to the terrace and unlocked the doors of the French window, leaving them wide open. He could have walked into the great hall from there, but didn't, preferring to enter through the front door.

When he re-entered the house, he saw the library door remained shut. Other doors were closed too, and he decided to leave them that way. Without further delay, he dipped a brush into a tin of black paint and began drawing the two concentric circles on the floor close to where they'd been originally. He worked slowly, methodically, keeping his shaking hand as steady as he could as he applied the paint to the floor. He didn't want there to be any mistakes.

He finished the design by placing a candle in the centre of each of the four hexagrams. When he was satisfied the circle was correct and in order, he crossed the hall, the revolver grasped in his hand and opened the door to the library. He didn't look inside the room before returning to the circle.

His heart racing, he stood in the red square at the centre of the circle, his feet covering the words written there, breathing slowly to relax, unsure whether he could go through with it. It all seemed somehow ridiculous and terrifying at the same time. He'd memorised the words he had to say. He didn't want to have to read them out from the journal, so he'd committed them to heart.

But as he waited doubts began to fill his mind. He kept having to check the magic circle to make sure he hadn't made a mistake by getting a letter or symbol wrong. If he'd made a mistake, he wouldn't get a second shot at this. Unsure whether the circle would protect him, he kept the gun at his side. If the hound stepped into the circle, he could shoot it numerous times before running out of there. It wasn't far to the front door - wounded would the creature be able to catch him?

As the evening drew on the temperature dropped and the house became cold, so cold he could see his breath. The only sound he could hear was the grandfather clock ticking away the seconds, the Westminster quarters echoing throughout the hall every fifteen minutes. The thought of the hellhound appearing suddenly began preying on his nerves until he became startled by every sound and began mistaking the flickering shadows cast on the walls for the demonic creature. After about an hour he began wondering whether he should enter the library to tempt the hellhound out but knowing its habit of appearing unexpectedly decided against it, worried the creature would catch him before he'd made it back to the circle. But the longer he waited the more impatient he grew. Where the hell was it? Why wouldn't it come out?

Shortly before midnight, when he began to feel tired, he sat himself down, laying the revolver by his side, keeping it within reach. Moments later, his eyes began to close. The grandfather clock chimed the hour, waking him suddenly. Rising to his feet, he realised he had to get some sleep, so decided to call it a night. He needed to be alert and ready for the creature should it appear. If he drifted off asleep again, he'd be out for the night. After some consideration, he decided his best option was to sleep in his Land Rover. It would be warmer there than anywhere in the house. He could drive down to the old stables, far away from the house. He'd be safe there.

The following day he decided that he was going to have to draw a circle on the floor of the library and confront the hellhound there. For whatever reason, whether it was to protect the manuscript or Henry himself, the hound appeared to be guarding the hidden room, and James knew it wouldn't appear until he approached that room as he had before. He could drop down from the gallery onto the circle once it appeared, keeping the door to the great hall behind him should the circle not work.

The decision made, he grabbed the tins of paint and brushes he needed and was making his way through the house when he heard a car approaching. For a moment he wondered if it was friends of the intruder who'd come to an unfortunate end in the library, but upon reaching the office, he saw, to his horror, Tessa stepping out of a taxi.

Hurrying out of the house, he heard her ask the taxi driver to wait for her. When she turned to face him, James saw she wasn't wearing any make-up and had her hair pulled back away from her face. She looked pale and tired. Evidently, she too had struggled with their break-up.

'Tessa,' he said, 'what on earth are you doing here?'

'I had to see you.'

James led her through the crenellated gateway, out of earshot of the driver.

'Why?' he asked anxiously. 'What for? You always seemed so thoroughly opposed to this place. Why come here now?'

'I was worried about you,' she replied. 'I haven't heard from you in a while. You haven't replied to any of my messages.'

'There's no need for you to be worried about me.'

'You look terrible. When did you last eat?'

'Earlier today. I'm fine. Really I am.'

'Aren't you going to invite me inside?'

'I can't. Not at the moment.'

'Why, what's going on here?' she asked, glancing round the courtyard. 'Where are your builders? Are you here alone?'

'At the moment.'

She glanced towards the house, clearly wondering why he was so keen to get rid of her.

'Once you said we came from different backgrounds,' began James, drawing her attention away from the house, 'and have lived very different lives. At the time I didn't see why we couldn't be together. Now I do. Seeing you here now makes me realise how out of place you'd look living in a house like this.'

Instead of being angered by his words, she looked at him with concern, clearly knowing something was wrong. Although his tone had been harsh, she didn't seem convinced by his little speech and knew it was just designed to get rid of her.

'It wasn't our background that caused our breakup,' she said. 'It was this house.' After a pause, she added, 'Look at what living here is doing to you. Look at what you've become.'

For a moment he thought he'd have to force her to leave, but, to his great relief, he heard the taxi driver calling to her. He appeared in the gateway but didn't cross the threshold.

'I need to get back to Selkirk, miss,' he said, glancing anxiously up at the house.

Tessa took James's hand in hers. 'Come back with me, James,' she pleaded with him. 'Leave this place.'

'I can't.'

'Why not?'

James gestured to the taxi driver. 'You'd better not keep him waiting any longer.'

'All right,' she said. 'I'll go. If that's what you want.'

'That's what I want.'

After kissing him gently on the cheek, she stepped away from him before finally letting go of his hand. Turning, she walked away, disappearing through the gateway.

As he watched her go, James had to stop himself from calling out to her. Since their break-up, he'd often considered doing as she suggested and turning his back on his ancestral home and its demonic resident once and for all so they could be together. Why not just leave with her as she'd suggested, return to Edinburgh and forget about the house once and for all? It wouldn't take him long to lock the doors and secure the windows to ensure no one could get in …

But he knew he couldn't - not until he'd laid the beast to rest at least. Only then could he be free of the place.

When he heard the taxi drive away, he returned to the house and wondered what to do next. Should he continue as planned or wait until he was sure Tessa had gone? He decided to wait until after lunch, just to be on the safe side. The day remained fine, and the sun was still shining - he'd have plenty of time to complete his task - so he made his way to the kitchen where he had something to eat before collecting the paints and brushes that he'd left in the office and made his way back through the house to complete his task.

Before entering the library, he stopped to light the candles of the magic circle in the great hall, just in case the hound appeared before he had a chance to complete the second circle. He then proceeded to the library where he began applying the acrylic paint to the floor, marking out the Solomonic circle. He worked faster than before, focusing all his attention on completing his task, only noticing the room had grown darker when he'd finished. Glancing out of the window, he saw heavy leaden clouds had appeared on the horizon, blanketing the once blue skies.

A storm was approaching …

Strong winds and sleet battered the house, rattling the windows. Doors slammed shut as the wind swept through the house. Even the door of the library closed, baring his exit, trapping him inside the room. Across the room, he saw a shadow seemingly rise from the ground and slowly take shape before his eyes. Instantly, he darted to the stairs, climbing the ladder, the hound giving chase, leaping up onto the gallery just as he climbed over the railings and dropped down onto the floor below.

There was not enough room on the gallery for the hound to manoeuvre, giving him time to reach the circle. Momentarily distracted as he watched the hound leap down from the gallery, he slipped on the wet paint, smudging the design, breaking the circle, the gun slipping from his hand, sliding across the floor. Scrambling to his feet, he pulled open the door and darted out of the room.

Had he thought he could have made it to the front door he would have kept on running, but seeing the hound appear from the library, he ran into the circle. Turning he saw the creature stalk towards him slowly, its eyes fixed on the flickering flames of the candles. Did it recognise the circle of Solomon and realise his intentions? He wondered how intelligent the creature was. Did it act on instinct alone or was it capable of problem-solving?

'In nomine patris et filii et spiritus sancti, inquam, discedant: ire propriis loco tuo …' he cried, his voice cracking, his whole body shaking with fear.

The hellhound stepped forward, approaching the circle, its hideous gaze meeting his. Worried his pronunciation was wrong he reverted to English.

'Withdraw. Let there be peace between us …' he began, but the words seemed to have no effect on the creature.

It continued its approach, placing a paw over the outer circle. James stepped back in terror. The circle was supposed to protect him from the beast! Why wasn't it working? He realised then he had to get out of there, the magic circle appearing to be useless against the creature. But rather than retreat, he found himself stepping forward. Fuelled by rage and anger he screamed at the creature, the words spewing out of him with incredible venom.

Seeing the hellhound cower before him he continued.

'You will obey me!' he cried. 'Depart I say! Leave this place and return only when summoned!'

The flames of the candles flared up and were suddenly

extinguished and he saw the hound had vanished, disappearing from sight. Unable to believe his eyes, he scanned the room for the creature. When he was sure it had gone, he fell to his knees, crying out in joy.

Finally, the house was his.

CHAPTER FIFTEEN

Will spent the night in the drawing room, pulling the sofa closer to the fireplace to keep warm. Unable to sleep, he lay on his back watching the patterns cast by the fire's flames dancing on the walls and ceiling above him. Shaken by his experiences in the cellar, he found himself unnerved by how eerily quiet it was in the house. The only sounds to break the silence came from the cracking of the fire and the ticking of the grandfather clock in the great hall. Outside, the wind had eased. A gentle breeze blew softly against the ivy that covered the walls of the house, the calming rustling sound soothing his nerves. His eyes began to feel heavy. Moments later, they were closed.

Hearing footsteps echo off the stone floor of the great hall, he tried to rouse himself but found his eyes wouldn't open. They felt too heavy. His body wouldn't move either. He lay on the sofa paralysed. The drawing room door creaked open. Someone was in the room. He could hear muffled footsteps on the carpet.

They were getting closer …

With a great effort, he sat bolt upright and stared round the room. There was no one there. The room was empty. He listened intently but heard nothing. Once again, the house was silent. Had someone entered the room, or had he simply been dreaming?

He saw the door to the great hall was ajar – he was sure he'd closed it. So, he hadn't been dreaming. Someone had been in the room. But who? And what were they doing sneaking in and out of the house in the middle of the night? Seeing the fire was almost out, he crouched before the fireplace and placed a log on the dying embers. Then, when he made his way across the room to close the open door, he caught a fleeting glimpse of a figure entering the library - a glimpse so brief he couldn't make out who it was. For a moment he hesitated, then hurried across the hall in pursuit.

Stepping into the library, he saw darkness hid the room from view.

'Is anybody in here?' he asked quietly, seemingly unable to raise his voice above a whisper.

When there was no reply, he wondered if someone was hiding from him in the darkness just metres away from where he stood. It seemed unlikely. If they were, they would have said something - wouldn't they? Reaching out in the darkness, he found the light switch. He flicked the switch, but the lights didn't come on.

Remembering the box of matches Isobel had handed him in the cellar, he reached into his dressing gown pocket to retrieved them. After striking one, he began to search the room, moving slowly across the polished oak floor, glancing nervously about him, afraid of what the flickering flame might reveal.

Finding the library empty, he made his way towards the study. Opening the door, he peered into the room. Again, there was no one there. The study, like the library, was empty. The books lay on the desk where they'd left them earlier that day. Hearing floorboards creak above his head, he glanced up at the low ceiling. Someone was moving about in the room above. As he stood listening, cold air crept into the room - air so cold he could see his breath.

After lighting another match, he hurried out into the hall. Shielding the flame with his hand, he moved slowly across the stone floor. Behind him, in the shadows, he thought he heard someone whispering. Turning suddenly, again he saw there was no one there. He found himself backing across the hall, his eyes fixed on the dark shadows. Ducking inside the drawing room, he shut the door firmly behind him, wedging a chair underneath the handle before making his way over to the drinks cabinet where he poured a small amount of brandy into a glass. Lifting the glass to his lips, he noticed his hand was trembling.

'Now who's imagining things?' he said quietly to himself, before making his way back across the room to the sofa.

*

The following morning, he woke up shivering. The room was cold, the fire having died out in the early hours of the morning. Sitting up, he stretched himself out and yawned, then crossed to the French window, pulled back the curtains and looked out onto the garden. The strong winds had stripped many of the trees of their leaves, their long, spindly branches reaching out across the lawn. He could feel the cold penetrating through the glass. Winter was creeping up on them. It wouldn't be long before the first frosts.

Feeling ridiculous in just his pyjamas and dressing gown, he decided to leave the drawing room before anyone came downstairs and discovered him there. After pushing the sofa back to its original position, he crossed the room, removed the chair he'd wedged under the handle, opened the door and stepped out into the great hall. The house was still very quiet. So quiet in fact, he could hear the pendulum swaying inside the grandfather clock. He couldn't hear anyone else stirring in the house. According to the clock, it was still only half-past seven - still early. The others wouldn't be up for a while yet.

Once upstairs, he crept down the corridor, passing Miriam's bedroom as he went. He thought better of sneaking in to grab some clothes, deciding instead to wait until she'd gone down to breakfast. Stepping into the bathroom, he shivered. A window had been left open overnight, leaving the room cold. After pulling it shut, he ran a bath, the steaming water flowing from the taps soon warming up the room.

Rubbing the stubble on his chin, he glanced in the fogged-up mirror, fixing his gaze on his reflection.

'You've made a right old mess of things, haven't you?' he said to himself. 'What on earth were you thinking? Why didn't you just stay in bed last night and fall quietly off to sleep?'

Not only had he jeopardised his relationship with Miriam he'd put his career at risk too. Bill was hardly going to be impressed with him when he found out what he'd been up to. He wouldn't be surprised if he threw him out on his ear - which was exactly what he deserved. When the bath was three-quarters full, he lowered himself into the soapy water. He hadn't made up his mind about what to tell Miriam. Telling the truth would only make matters worse. She'd never believe him anyway. If he tried lying to her, she'd see straight through him. Either way, he was stuffed.

Hearing floorboards creak and doors open, he reluctantly dragged himself out of the bath. After slipping his dressing gown back on, he hurried out of the bathroom and saw Miriam's bedroom door was ajar. Assuming she'd gone down to breakfast, he poked his head into the room. To his dismay, she was still there, sat bolt upright in bed, peering down at an open book resting in her lap. Before he could withdraw from the room she glanced up, staring at him over the glasses perched on the end of her nose, her face veiled in frozen inscrutability like a schoolteacher who was about to scold one of her unruly pupils.

But the more she stared the less he knew what to say or do.

'If you've come in here to apologise you can save your breath,' she said.

Shuffling sheepishly into the room, Will faced her cold gaze. 'I feel I owe you an explanation …'

The glasses on the end of her nose quivered with indignation. 'I do not wish to know the sordid details.'

'There is a perfectly innocent explanation for what happened last night.'

Removing her glasses, Miriam placed them on her bedside table. 'Well, it did not look innocent,' she said. 'Why were you down in the cellar together in the first place?'

'We were …' He didn't know what to say. Dropping his eyes, he glanced down at the floor.

'Were you after a bottle of wine or some champagne perhaps? What did you plan to do next? Find an empty room to enjoy a nightcap together?'

'No, of course not.' He had no choice - he had to tell her the truth no matter how ridiculous it sounded. 'Isobel thinks the house is haunted.'

Miriam's eyes fixed upon his. 'Does she indeed …'

'On Friday night she thought she heard a woman calling out for help.'

'That still doesn't explain your little jaunt down into the cellar.'

'She thought the woman was down there.'

'What on earth would she be doing down there of all places?'

Will gave a slight shrug. 'I don't know.'

Miriam closed her eyes sanctimoniously. 'Why don't you admit you were trying to seduce Isobel instead of concocting a ridiculous story about ghosts in cellars?'

'I wasn't trying to seduce Isobel.'

'Are you sure about that? Both you and Alexander have been fawning over her like a couple of lovesick schoolboys ever since we arrived.'

'You're imagining things …'

'Whatever plans you had for me this weekend were forgotten the moment you laid eyes on that Hamilton woman -'

'Hamilton-Jones,' said Will, correcting her, though he immediately wished he hadn't.

'From now on, if you know what's good for you, you'll stay away from her.'

Will dropped his head. 'Yes, of course.'

After a pause, Miriam said, 'Now will you please leave …?'

'I need some clothes,' he said apologetically.

'Your bag is behind the door. I packed it for you. Now take it and get out!'

Picking up his duffle bag, Will promptly left the room, making his way down the corridor. Opposite the bathroom was another bedroom. Finding it empty, he slipped inside, closing the door behind him. The room was similar to the one he'd shared with Miriam. The wallpaper was the same, though there was just a single, unmade bed. There was no wardrobe, just a chest of drawers. To his great embarrassment, he realised he was going to have to ask Hodgson to make up the room for him. He couldn't sleep on a bare mattress.

After dressing, he made his way downstairs where the smell of food cooking drew him down the long stone passage to the servants' quarters. Once in the kitchen, he found Hodgson standing at the range, frying kidneys in a pan.

'Alexander has asked me to make him devilled kidneys for breakfast,' said Hodgson. 'Would you care for some?'

Will had no idea what devilled kidneys were but thought they sounded disgusting. He declined Hodgson's offer. 'I'll just have some eggs this morning, thank you.'

'Very good, sir.'

He was about to ask Hodgson to make up the bedroom for him when Isobel entered the kitchen. She bid them both a good morning and asked Hodgson if there was anything else to take through to the drawing room.

'Just Alexander's kidneys,' he said, handing Will a plate.

Will followed Isobel out of the kitchen. Once out of earshot she apologised to him for what had happened the previous night and he told her there was no need for her to apologise.

'Where did you sleep?' she asked.

'On the sofa in the drawing room.'

'Have you spoken to Miriam this morning?'

Will frowned. 'I'm afraid so.'

'Did you tell her what we were doing?'

'I tried, but she didn't believe me.'

'Then we're just going to have to convince her otherwise.'

'I think we've done enough damage,' said Will. 'Anyway, I'm not convinced we saw anything last night.'

'Well, I certainly did.'

Will's eyebrows rose. 'Did you?'

'Yes,' said Isobel firmly. 'And I know you did too.'

'I didn't see – or hear, for that matter – anything last night.'

'You saw the cellar door rattling for no apparent reason.'

'That could easily have been caused by a draught coming from the coal chute.'

'That could not have been caused by a draught! Anyway, the coal cellar is under the servants' quarters. The cellar under the great hall is used to store wine.'

After a pause, Will said, 'Well, what did you see?'

'A woman. She looked like she was wearing one of Emily's dresses.'

'Was it Emily?'

Isobel shook her head. 'If it was, she was unrecognisable,' she said. 'Her face was contorted by terror and fear…' Just like in her nightmare. What the hell was going on? When they drew closer to the drawing room door, she added, 'There has to be an explanation for what happened last night.'

'Oh, there is,' said Will with a sigh. 'That's the problem.'

Isobel hesitated before entering the drawing room. Glancing through the open door, she saw Alexander and Miriam sitting at the table in silence.

'I think I'll give breakfast a miss this morning,' she said.

Will thought it for the best but didn't say anything. He watched her make her way back to the kitchen. Once she was out of sight, he entered the room, placing the kidneys down on the table in front of Alexander. Neither Miriam nor Alexander acknowledged his presence and Alexander didn't even thank him for bringing his breakfast through from the kitchen.

Despite his efforts to engage Miriam in conversation, she continued to ignore him, until the awkwardness of the lengthening silence became quite unbearable. Across the table, Alexander chewed noisily, grinning at Will between mouthfuls, clearly relishing the bad feelings that had grown up between them. Unable to suppress his laughter any longer, let out a large cackle that echoed round the house.

Miriam turned bright scarlet, stood up abruptly and stormed out of the room.

Will glanced across the table at Alexander. 'You're not helping.'

'Cuiusvis hominis est errare; nullius nisi insipientis in errore perseverare.'

'What does that mean?'

'It means you're a damn fool.'

'I know I am, but you don't have to look so happy about it.'

'I warned you this would happen if you didn't stay away from Isobel.'

Will suppressed his anger. 'Is that what you were doing?' he said through clenched teeth. 'It sounded to me as though you were trying to put me in my place.'

'I was. You see, Will, that's always been your problem. You've never known your place, have you? You're not one of us and you never will be. Your behaviour this weekend has made that abundantly clear. You had such a promising career ahead of you, it's a shame it had to end so soon. Of course, you were bound to get caught out eventually. To be accepted in this world, first and foremost you need money, which of course you don't have. You need to have gone to the right school, which again, you didn't. You need to know how to hunt, shoot, even fish, and at the very least you need to know to pass the port to the right.'

'No, you pass the port to the right,' said Will. 'I can pass it any damn way I please. That's the difference between us. I'm not bound by ridiculous rituals and rules. I can think for myself, form my own opinions, not have others tell me how I must act to be accepted. Do you know what your problem is, Alexander? You can't, or rather won't, imagine a world unlike the one you've been born into, even when it's crumbling down around you. You ridicule anyone who thinks differently than you, or dares dream of a better world for all, and not just for people like you.' He rose from his seat. He wasn't going to sit there and listen to Alexander speak to him like that again. 'And I have never asked,' he added, before leaving, 'nor have I ever wanted to be accepted into your so-called world. No one capable of thinking for themselves would.'

'If you didn't you wouldn't be here.'

'I am here,' said Will, 'because, unlike you, I was invited by James.' Turning, he left the room.

'You're still trespassing, Will … and you always will be.'

*

Although furious, Will kept walking. He wasn't going to let Alexander provoke him into doing something rash, so he made his way to the library, where he decided to stay until things cooled down. Settling himself down on the Chesterfield, he propped his head upon a cushion, the warmth of the roaring fire soon warming him through. It wasn't long before his eyes grew heavy. Moments later, he was asleep.

'Will …'

He woke suddenly. Someone was calling out to him in a hushed voice. Sitting up, he glanced round the room, his gaze finding Isobel at the entrance to the study.

'I need you to keep a lookout for me.'

'Why, what are you going to do?'

Isobel glanced at the open door and beckoned him closer. Sighing, Will rose from the Chesterfield and crossed the library.

'What are you up to?' he said, ducking into the study.

He found Isobel sitting at the rosewood desk.

'This is where James keeps the photographs he has of Henry and Emily,' she said. Picking up a silver letter opener, she began prising open the top drawer of the desk. 'There might be something in here that will tell us what happened to them.'

Will closed the study door. 'You can't go rooting through his desk,' he whispered.

The drawer sprang open, and Isobel lifted out the photograph album James had shown her the night before. Underneath she found a journal, ledgers, and the film canisters.

Will perched himself on the side of the desk and began looking through the photographs in the album. 'Is this Emily?' he asked. Holding up the album, he pointed to the picture of her standing on the terrace steps.

Isobel nodded. 'James seemed to think it was taken when she'd just moved here.'

'She's pretty.' He turned the page. 'Is this Henry?'

Nodding, Isobel lifted the ledgers and the journal out of the drawer.

'He doesn't look very well in this picture,' said Will.

'I thought that too,' agreed Isobel. 'He seems rather run-down.'

Opening the journal, she noticed an envelope fall out onto the desk. Inside the envelope, she found some newspaper cuttings and a small piece of paper. The paper was blank except for a hieroglyphic symbol. Placing the piece of paper back inside the envelope, she examined the cuttings. They were taken from the *Henley and Oxford Standard, Hertfordshire Pictorial* and the *Henley and South Oxford Gazette.*

'Will, read this,' she said, offering him her seat. Will sat down on the swivel chair and looked down at the front page of the *Hertfordshire Pictorial.*

'"Stomach acidity is one of the penalties of modern life."'

'Above that.'

Hitchin man charged with murder

This morning at Oxford Crown Court, Guy Easton, aged 24, was brought before the magistrates charged with the murder of Charles Appleby, aged 29, of Oak House, Chipping Norton.

The body was discovered with revolver shot wounds lying face down in the grounds of Oak House on Saturday morning.

Appleby, a scholar at Magdalen College, Oxford was the son of Dr and Mrs Charles Appleby, of Oak House, Chipping Norton.

'Read it to me,' said Isobel, pulling up a chair from the corner of the room.

Will cleared his throat. '"It is understood that on Friday evening, a party was held by Mrs Appleby, the victim's mother, a well-known hostess renowned for entertaining lavishly. Guy Easton was amongst the weekend guests who included …" I think they were more interested in who was as at the party than the murder itself. Here we go … "The Housekeeper, Mrs Hill, said she was woken in the early hours of the morning, around four-thirty, by raised voices in the drawing room. Hearing the front door slam shut, she looked out of the window and saw a young man, who she later identified as the accused, walking away from the house … she did not hear any revolver shots. The body was discovered by the Head Gardener the following morning in the rose garden." It goes on to give a detailed description of the trial.'

Six Wounds Found By Doctor.

Dr John Robertson, who performed the autopsy on the body of Charles Appleby, described the wounds he found, 6 in all.
The cause of death, said the doctor, was due to head and brain injury from a gunshot wound to the right temple, and to a lesser extent other parts of the body.

'So, Easton must have led Appleby out into the rose garden and shot him.'

Will put down the paper. 'Six shots fired and no one heard anything. Rose gardens aren't usually far from the house.'

'He could have used a silencer or muffled the sound of the shots with a cushion.'

'Still, someone would have heard something - at the very least a cry for help.'

'And then Easton was seen walking away from the house. If you'd just shot someone, would you leave casually by the front door?'

Will leant forward, the leather chair creaking underneath him. 'Maybe he didn't want to draw attention to himself.'

'He did that when he slammed the front door shut. Why not just sneak round the house unseen?'

Will steepled his fingers. 'Appleby must have been alive when Easton left.'

'Maybe after their argument, Appleby was so angry he found the gun and went after Easton, catching up with him some distance from the house. He pulled the gun on him, they got into a fight and the gun went off accidentally, killing Appleby.'

'That would explain why the shots weren't heard. However, it couldn't have been an accident. The whole barrel was emptied into him. Also, Easton would have had to drag the body back to the rose garden.'

'And if he'd dragged a body that had been shot six times he'd have been covered in blood.'

'Precisely.'

'I've got it,' said Isobel, rising to her feet. 'Easton made sure he was heard and then seen walking away from the house because Appleby was still alive when he left.' She began pacing up and down the room. 'After a little while, Easton returned to the house where he found Appleby in the rose garden cooling off after their argument. He snuck up on him from behind, knocked him unconscious and filled him full of lead.'

Will suppressed a smile. 'I think you might be onto something there,' he said. 'However, whether it was Easton who killed Appleby remains to be seen. The question now is did Easton have time to sneak back and kill Appleby?' Will glanced back at the newspaper cutting.

Accused Tells His Story

'"When he left the house, Mr Easton claimed Mr Appleby was alive but refused to discuss the nature of their argument or why he was seen running away from the house. He also denied owning a pistol. After leaving Oak House, he walked to Chipping Norton station and caught the first train back to London. Both the station master and ticket collector witnessed Easton buying a ticket and getting on the train."'

'Does it say what time the train left Chipping Norton station?'

'No, it doesn't,' replied Will. He leant back in his chair. 'If only I had a Bradshaw … Let's assume the first train left at six o'clock. Depending on how far the house is from the station that still gives Easton an hour to an hour and a half …'

'Plenty of time to return to Oak House and kill Appleby.'

'"Easton was next seen when he visited his friend Edward Seaton, a reporter for the Daily Post, at his home in St John's Wood. By this time, Seaton had heard Appleby had been killed. He tried to persuade Easton to turn himself in, but he fled the house.

Seaton immediately contacted the police and Easton was arrested on the Euston Road outside St. Pancras Station a little after nine o'clock."'

Isobel pulled her feet up onto the chair. 'I wonder where he was going.'

'And what does all this have to do with Emily and Henry?' Will and Isobel glanced down at the photograph of Guy Easton. A young, handsome face stared back at them.

'Apparently,' said Will, 'Easton was a graduate of Christ Church College, Oxford and had just been recruited into the Royal Air Force Volunteer Reserve.'

'Of course,' said Isobel, springing to her feet, 'that's where I know him from.' Rummaging through the open drawer, she found the picture of Henry under the Bridge of Sighs. Amongst his fellow students was Easton. 'He was at Oxford with Henry.'

'That would explain why Henry has the cuttings. If someone I went to university with was accused of murder, I'd want to know what happened to him.'

Isobel perched herself on the edge of the desk. 'What did happen to him?'

'Apparently, during his cross-examination, Mr Easton was heard to cry out, "She's in danger. You must get her out of there."'

Isobel leant forward and glanced down at the clipping. 'You made that up.'

'No, I didn't,' replied Will. 'Here, see for yourself.' Turning the page round, he pointed to the relevant section in the article.

'Does it go on to say who he's referring to?'

After studying the page for a few moments, Will shook his head.

'It must have been Emily,' said Isobel. 'When Easton was picked up outside St. Pancras Station, he must have been on his way here.'

'Why would Emily have been in danger?'

'I don't know. But if Easton was coming here, he must have been in love with Emily. Maybe Henry learnt they were once lovers and were planning to run away together ...'

Will laid the clipping down on the desk. 'So instead of just letting her go, he killed her ...'

'Maybe he was very possessive and couldn't bear the thought of her being with another man. When Emily tried to run away, he locked her in the cellar and kept her there for days. Then one night her cries for help became too much for him. In a drunken rage, he flung open the door and marched down into the cellar. There, quivering in fear, was Emily.' She held up her hands as though strangling someone. 'He placed his hands round her delicate neck and squeezed until -'

Will lowered her hands. 'I get the picture.' He remained doubtful. 'I just don't think Henry would have killed Emily simply because she wanted to leave him. There has to be more to it than that.'

Footsteps echoed throughout the great hall.

'Quickly,' whispered Will, picking up the photo album. 'Someone's coming …'

'Will, I've been thinking,' said Isobel, gathering up the articles and stuffing them back inside the envelope. 'There must be someone in the village who knows what happened here.'

'Hurry up …'

They heard a knock on the door. Slipping the envelope back inside the journal, Will placed it back in the drawer, laying the photograph album carefully down on top of it.

'Come in,' said Isobel, seeing Will shut the drawer.

The door swung open, and Hodgson stepped into the room. 'Ah, there you are,' he said. 'I was just wondering if anyone cared for some tea.'

'No, thank you, Hodgson,' replied Isobel. 'We were just about to go for a walk.'

'It is quite lovely out there now, though I would wrap up warm if I were you. The wind up here can be very cold.'

Isobel glanced over her shoulder at Will. 'Aren't you coming?'

He shook his head regretfully. 'No, not this time, Isobel.'

'But we're so close to finding out what happened -' Glancing at Hodgson, she left her sentence unfinished.

'I'm sorry. I can't.'

'Then, I'll go alone.' Passing Hodgson, she disappeared into the great hall.

Hodgson glanced at Will, a look of concern on his face. 'Is something the matter, sir?' he asked.

'It's nothing, Hodgson.'

'Is Miss Isobel going down to the village?'

Will nodded. 'She's hoping to learn more about the house.'

'What is it she wants to know? I may be able to help. It would save her the walk.'

'She wants to know what happened to Emily Roxburgh.'

Hodgson stood thinking for a few moments. 'The last time I saw her,' he said slowly, 'was at James's grandfather's funeral. I'm afraid to say she passed away herself a few months later. Such a shame - she was a very lovely woman.'

Isobel appeared in the doorway. 'You've met Emily Roxburgh?'

'Only that once. She attended the funeral with her second husband.'

'Do you remember his name?'

'I'm afraid not. I don't believe I was introduced.'

Disappointment surged up inside Isobel. She felt terribly disappointed and knew it was showing on her face. Turning quickly, avoiding Will's gaze, she crept slowly out of the room.

CHAPTER SIXTEEN

Isobel did not join them for lunch. The others probably thought she was trying to avoid Miriam, but Will knew better. He was beginning to regret refusing to go down to the village with her. After lunch, he would find her, and if she still wanted to go, they would. Let the others think what they like …

Seeing Miriam's cold disapproving gaze meet his, almost as if she knew was reading his thoughts, his confidence waned. Maybe it would be better to stay where he was for now. After all, there was nothing to be gained from making a bad situation worse.

It was almost two o'clock when he made his way upstairs to find Isobel. Stepping onto the gallery, he saw a figure hidden by the shadows emerge from James's bedroom.

He called after his friend, but he continued on without answering, before disappearing round a corner. Will hurried down the bookcase-lined corridor in pursuit, passing Isobel then James's bedroom before turning a corner himself and making his way up a short flight of steps that led to a narrow passage. Shortly he came to the gallery and saw James disappear down the corridor that led to the bedrooms on the other side of the house, though again he only saw him briefly and still wasn't certain it was him. He assumed he was heading down to the servants' staircase through the green baize door at the end of the corridor.

Quickening his pace, he continued after his friend, passing the guest bedrooms. Once through the baize door, he caught a brief, momentary glimpse of shoes on the staircase above before they disappeared from view, and climbing the steps in pursuit, came to the baize door on the second floor. Pushing it open he stepped into another corridor half-hidden in the darkness. There was no sign of James or anyone else anywhere ahead of him.

Floorboards creaked faintly above his head. Whoever he was following was now on the third floor. Retracing his steps, he returned to the staircase and reached the sturdy wooden door he'd found locked the day before. To his surprise, when he turned the handle, the door yielded, and he stepped through the narrow doorway onto bare wooden floorboards that creaked and groaned underfoot. Glancing ahead, he saw there were five doors, two at each side, and one directly ahead of him. Had James slipped into one of the rooms? He listened at the first door. No sound came from within. Tapping softly upon the door, he pushed it ajar.

The room was in darkness. Dust motes danced in a thin beam of light that came in through a gap in the shutters. Just to the left of the door, lengthways along the wall, an iron bedstead stood on a brown linoleum floor. The sloping ceiling only allowed space for the bed, a wardrobe and a bedside table. A well-worn Bulldog Drummond novel lay on the table. Passing the open door of the wardrobe, he breathed in the smell of mothballs. Inside, clothes hung on a rail.

The melancholy aura that pervaded the house seemed more prevalent in this dingy little room. He wondered how many servants had resided there since the early nineteenth-century when the house was built, returning tired and exhausted to their cramped quarters after a long day's work.

The next room he came to was empty except for a rusty bedstead that stood upended against a wall. Returning to the corridor, treading carefully over the bare floorboards, he made his way from door to door, listening carefully at each one he passed. Upon opening the fifth and final door, he discovered another staircase leading up to another small doorway. How many floors were there in this house? With one hand on the banister, he climbed the steps, ducking through the doorway when he reached the top of the staircase.

Straightening himself up, he saw he was in an attic. The air was musty and damp, the room dark. The only light came from a dirty, cobwebbed window. Outside the wind whistled and moaned as it swept round the house. From the depths of the house, he heard the grandfather clock chime the hour. As his eyes became accustomed to the darkness, he saw the attic was filled with old steamer trunks and suitcases. He moved through the attic passing boxes overflowing with children's toys. Behind glass display cabinets filled with wildfowl, owls and hawks, paintings had been stacked against a wall, their frames damaged and broken. A stained, dirty mattress lay on the floor, and there was a sleeping bag rolled up beside it - a modern one - not one from the past.

Lying in a dark corner of the room, his face to the floor, was a man. He appeared to be unconscious and had brown crew cut hair. Will stepped forward, drawing closer to the prostrate figure, the loose floorboards creaking underneath his feet. Kneeling before him, he rolled him over onto his back and saw he had a scar running down the side of his face.

A floorboard creaked behind him, but before he had a chance to turn round, he felt a sharp blow on the back of his head and fell forward, losing consciousness before he hit the floor.

*

When Isobel woke, she saw a cup of tea and a sandwich had been left on her bedside table. Hodgson must have brought it in for her when she didn't join the others for lunch. Sitting up, she reached for the cup. The tea was cold, so she grabbed the sandwich instead.

A gentle knock at her door almost made her jump out of her skin.

'Come in,' she said, placing her sandwich back down on the bedside table.

The door opened and Jemima stepped into the room.

'Morning,' said Isobel, stretching out her body.

'Afternoon,' said Jemima, correcting her.

Isobel looked round for her Blackberry. 'What time is it?'

'It's about twenty past two.'

'I thought we were going to Edinburgh today.'

'No one's mentioned anything.' Jemima sat herself down at the dressing table, turning to face Isobel. 'We missed you at lunch.'

'I wasn't hungry.'

'You can't avoid Miriam for the rest of the weekend. You're going to have to face her at some point.'

'It's Will I'm trying to avoid.'

'Why are you trying to avoid him, of all people?'

'Because I've made a total fool of myself, that's why.'

Jemima caught Isobel's eye. 'You two were more than friends once, weren't you?'

'Is it that obvious?'

Jemima nodded. 'And not just to me.'

Isobel told her all about their summer together and how she'd been led to believe Will had broken the promise he'd made to her.

'But he had come to see me - my father had turned him away. He'd even rung my house and spoken to my mother - but she didn't pass his message on either.'

Instead, she'd said, 'What did you expect from a boy like that?'

Remembering Will's words, she wondered if she'd known the truth whether it would have made a difference. At the time, she'd been too willing to believe their lies. She'd wanted the life they had, to go to the parties they went to, and take the holidays they did. But she soon learnt it was an empty life, the relationships and marriages of the people she met were, for the most part, unhappy, their lives unfulfilled. What she'd had with Will was real, and she'd thrown it all away for what? What made it worse was that in allowing her parents to influence her decision she'd set a bad precedent. They'd been meddling in her life ever since.

No, it wasn't a world she'd wanted to leave then, but it was now.

She told Jemima she'd ended their relationship the following Christmas, telling her she'd instantly regretted her decision.

'The following day, I went to the cottage to see him, but neither he nor his mother was home. Their neighbour told me they were spending the holiday with his aunt and didn't know when they'd be back. I asked her if she had either his aunt's address or telephone number, but she didn't.'

'Why didn't you just call Will on his mobile?'

'He didn't have one - and neither did I. At the time my parents forbid me from owning one. Now I know why.' Unable to face the journey home, she'd called one of my friends from a phone box to collect her. 'I was close to tears when she arrived and convinced her to drive me to the beach Will had taken me to in the summer. I thought it unlikely he'd be there but had to try.'

'Did you find him?'

Isobel shook her head.

She remembered being beaten by a painfully cold bitter wind blowing in from the Bristol Channel as she searched the beach, unable to leave, knowing if she did, he would be lost to her. Eventually, her friend came looking for her, finding her sitting on the wet sand, numb with cold, staring at the waves hammering and pounding the timbers of the Barque.

'The following day, I returned to school. I never heard from Will or saw him again until a couple of days ago.'

'Well, you're together again now. Can't you pick up where you left off?'

Isobel shook her head slowly. 'He's not the same person he was back then.'

She couldn't help but feel that was partly her fault. The awful realisation then hit her that the boy she'd known was lost to her forever.

'I still don't understand why you think you've made a fool of yourself,' said Jemima.

'On Friday night I heard something,' began Isobel before stopping herself, unsure whether to confide in Jemima.

'What did you hear?'

Deciding she could, she continued. 'A woman's voice, calling out for help,' she said. 'I traced the voice to the cellar, but when I tried to open the door, I found it locked.'

'So last night you returned with the key, taking Will with you …'

Isobel nodded.

'So that's what you two were up to. I have to say I'm a little disappointed. Well, what did you see?'

'A woman, a young woman, but she was little more than a decaying corpse come to life.'

'Please, you'll give me nightmares,' said Jemima.

'She certainly gave me nightmares.' Two nights before she'd even glimpsed the creature, the image having stayed with her since.

Maybe that's all it was. Maybe she'd just projected her nightmare onto whatever it was she'd glimpsed down in the cellar - a trick of the light, or a shadow on the wall - her imagination filling in the gaps. Maybe she hadn't seen anything after all. Maybe …

'Who do you think she is, or rather, was?'

'I thought she might have been Emily Roxburgh.'

Jemima picked up a trinket box. 'Because all her jewellery and clothes are still here.'

'Obvious, isn't it? It took Will ages to realise that. But according to Hodgson, Emily lived for many years after leaving Wychwood House, and even remarried.'

'Then if it's not her, who is it?'

Isobel sighed despondently. 'I've no idea.'

Opening the trinket box, Jemima looked at the jewellery inside. 'And why did she leave all these beautiful things behind?'

'I was going to go to the village with Will. I thought someone there might know more.'

Lifting a gold locket out of the box, Jemima glanced at Isobel in the reflection of the mirror. 'So why haven't you?'

'He refused to go.'

'Why?'

'I assume he doesn't want to be seen with me anymore this weekend. He never believed my theory about Emily anyway.'

'Didn't he see the woman in the cellar?'

'He told me he didn't. Part of me wonders if I didn't imagine the whole thing.'

'Well,' said Jemima, 'I certainly didn't imagine the man who tried to grab me when I came out of the bathroom yesterday. Something strange is going on in this house, and it has something to do with that man and why he's in the house.'

Isobel couldn't help but agree.

Jemima suggested they go down to the village together. 'There's still time before it gets dark.'

'I don't think so. I've made enough of a mess of things as it is.'

Jemima opened the locket. 'Is this Henry?' she asked, glancing at a photograph inside. 'He's rather dashing.'

'He is?' said Isobel with surprise. Crossing to Jemima's side, she peered at the photograph that showed a young man with dark wavy hair and high cheekbones. 'That's not Henry … That's Guy Easton.'

'Who?'

'I think I'd like to take that walk down to the village after all.' She took the locket from Jemima and placed it back in the trinket box. 'Is it still raining?'

Rising to her feet, Jemima crossed the room and glanced out of the bay window. 'Looks like Will's beaten us to it.'

Isobel joined her at the window. Below them, making his way down the garden, was Will.

Opening a window, Jemima called out to him, but he didn't hear her. 'He seems to be in quite a hurry. Do you think something's happened?'

When Isobel didn't reply, Jemima turned to find her pulling on her knee-length boots.

'I'm going after him,' she said, hurrying out of her room, her footsteps fading away as she made her way down the corridor.

*

When Alexander woke from his customary post-lunch nap, he found Miriam sitting in an armchair, engrossed in her book, her glasses perched on her nose. Where the others were, he didn't know, or care, for that matter. Jemima's absence, in particular, didn't surprise him. He'd certainly come a cropper where she was concerned. Oh well, he told himself, they'd be back in London soon and, thankfully, he wouldn't have to see her again.

'Strange saying that,' he said out loud, not meaning to. 'Come a cropper.'

Miriam glanced up from her book. 'Did you say something?' she asked.

'I was just wondering where the saying 'comes a cropper' originates from.'

'What on earth for?'

'I don't know,' said Alexander. 'I just was.' Sitting up, he rose to his feet. 'Care for a drink, Miriam? I could make you one of those Pina Coladas you like.'

'No, thank you.'

'How about a drop of whisky? It's quite excellent.'

'There won't be a bottle left in Scotland at the rate you're getting through them.'

'I haven't had that much to drink.'

'Yes, you have. You drink far too much, you smoke far too much, you eat far too much. You do everything too much.'

'Not as much as I'd like, believe me.'

'It's about time you acted more responsibly and started looking after yourself a bit better.'

'I didn't realise you cared so much for my welfare.'

'Someone should,' said Miriam. 'Clearly, you don't. You've been living beyond your means for some time now, in more ways than one.'

'I don't know what you mean,' said Alexander, feigning ignorance.

'You've been gambling your life away in that club of yours,' she began. When Alexander tried to interrupt, she held up a protesting hand. 'No, don't try and deny it. I know you have.'

'I'll bounce back. I've lost money before, and I'll lose it again. But I'll be all right. I always have been and always will be.'

'You won't if you don't reign in your spending.'

'The "age of austerity" is not for me.'

'It is if you know what's good for you.'

'That's my problem, Miriam, I've never known what's good for me. I need a firm hand to guide me, to steer me through these troubled waters I've found myself in.'

'Please stop. You're making me seasick.'

Alexander thought she seemed capable of administering a firm hand when required. He realised then, for the first time since they'd almost kissed, they were alone. He decided, against his better judgement, to broach the subject.

'Don't you think it's time we talked about what happened the other night?'

'There's nothing to talk about because nothing happened.'

'But something *almost* happened.'

'But nothing *did* happen.'

'It *would* have if Jemima hadn't walked in on us when she did.'

'But it *didn't* because Jemima walked in on us when she did.'

Alexander sighed. 'We could go on like this all day.'

'And nothing will ever happen between us.'

'Not even if I change my wicked ways?'

'You'll never change, Alexander Mortimer de Villeneuve. You wouldn't know how to.'

Hearing someone cough discreetly behind them, they both turned to see Hodgson had entered the room.

'Yes, what is it?' asked Alexander.

'Miss Powell has asked me to tell you she will be taking a nap this afternoon, and under no circumstances does she wish to be disturbed.'

'Who?'

'Jemima … the young lady you brought with you, sir.'

'I know who Jemima is.'

'Well, now you know her surname too.'

'Yes, thank you, Hodgson. That will be all.'

'Very good, sir.'

Alexander glanced back at Miriam to see she had risen from her armchair.

'Where are you going?' he asked.

'I think I'll follow suit and take a nap,' she said. Before Alexander could say anything, she added, 'And under no circumstances do I wish to be disturbed either.'

Realising he was alone, Alexander picked up his empty glass and made his way over to the drinks cabinet, pausing momentarily before pouring out more whisky into his glass. Maybe he should heed Miriam's words. He had been overdoing it lately. Oh, to hell with it, he thought. You only live once. May as well make the most of your brief time on this earth. After all, you never knew what tomorrow might bring.

But then, it wasn't tomorrow he had to worry about …

*

Isobel didn't catch up with Will until he was making his way along a path through the Witches' Wood. Falling into step beside him, she asked him where he was going, but he didn't reply.

'What's happened, Will? Tell me …'

Again, he said nothing.

'Tell me!' she repeated, impatiently.

He halted so abruptly she found herself ahead of him.

'I can't get a signal on my phone. Do you have yours with you?'

'Why, who are you -' She stopped herself. 'You're going to call James's father, aren't you?'

When Will didn't reply, Isobel said, 'Alexander was telling the truth about you, wasn't he? You really did promise Robert you'd bring James back with you.'

Will turned to face her, his eyes fixed on hers. 'I didn't promise anything to anyone,' he said. He noticed she'd left the house without her cape and was wearing just her boots, jeans and a flannel shirt.

'You promised me you wouldn't give up on James.'

'I didn't know how serious the situation was then.'

The path they were following levelled out and they came to a wooden stile straddling a drystone wall.

Isobel barred Will's way. 'You know what will happen if Robert comes here and sees James like this,' she said. 'You know where he'll end up, don't you?'

Drawing her gently to one side, Will climbed the stile, and made his way across a field, increasing his steps until Isobel practically had to run to keep up with him. 'Something's going on here,' he said, 'and I don't think either you or I are going to get to the bottom of it.'

'But you think his father will?'

'His father and the police.'

'You want to get the police involved?'

Will nodded and said, 'Men are guarding the gates and keeping watch on the house from the gardens. For all we know,' he added, glancing over his shoulder, 'they're following us now.'

'There was no one guarding the gates when I arrived. Hodgson opened them himself and left them open for you.'

'Well, they were closed when we got there. We were let in by a man who appeared from the lodge.'

'Who was he?'

'I don't know, he kept his face well hidden under the hood of his raincoat.'

'He must have been one of the gardeners James has employed to work on the grounds.'

'Landscape gardeners don't go sneaking about houses during the middle of the night, or during the day for that matter. Jemima encountered one yesterday, and I heard them in the house last night.'

'Well, what do you think they're up to?'

'I believe they're holding James in the house against his will.'

'What on earth for?'

Will shrugged his shoulders. 'I've no idea,' he said.

'If you want to get the police to investigate, you're going to have to be a lot less vague.'

'I haven't finished yet,' said Will. 'This afternoon -' He stopped himself.

'What happened this afternoon?' asked Isobel. 'For God's sake, Will, tell me!'

'After lunch, when I was on my way to see you, I glimpsed someone I assumed was James leaving his bedroom. I followed after him and he led me up to the attic.'

'What was he going up to the attic for?'

'I don't know. I don't even know if it was James I was following. I only ever caught brief glimpses of him, and when I called out to him, he ignored me. It could have been one of his captors.'

'What happened when you reached the attic?'

'I'm not sure, my memories are a little hazy, to say the least. There was someone in the room, lying unconscious on the floor. When I turned him over, I saw he had a scar running down the side of his face. After that everything went black. I woke up on the floor with a splitting headache and a bump the size of a golf ball on the back of my head.'

'Was the man with the scar still in the attic with you when you woke?'

'No, he'd gone.'

'So whoever knocked him out must have knocked you out too. Do you think it was James?'

'James has no reason to attack me.'

'He will if you call his father.'

Will ignored her remark and continued. 'If it was James, he must have mistaken me for one of the men holding him here.'

'Now you come to mention it, I did hear sounds coming from James's bedroom on my first day here.'

'What kind of sounds?'

'There was a smash and I heard James cry out,' said Isobel. 'When I asked him about it, he told me he'd knocked over an expensive vase, though I got the impression there was more to it than that.' She paused, then asked, 'But if James is being held prisoner, why hasn't he told us?'

'Because he doesn't want us getting involved. He's probably worried what will happen to us if we do.'

'Why, if he doesn't want us getting involved, did he invite us to the house?'

'He must have invited us before the men arrived.'

Isobel did not look convinced. 'Why don't we just go back to the house and speak to James before doing something rash like calling the police?' she said.

'Do you think we'll be able to find him?' asked Will. 'We have to act now before it's too late.'

Without saying anything, Isobel walked ahead of him.

As he continued his descent of the hill Will began to doubt himself. Until then he'd been sure he was right, but now, after voicing his suspicions, he realised he sounded a little ridiculous. He thought it unlikely the police would believe his story. Maybe they should return to the house, find James and figure out what exactly was going on at the house, before involving anyone else. After all, he'd look pretty foolish if the men he suspected of holding James in the house turned out to be nothing more than landscape gardeners. They weren't due to leave until the following morning - a lot could happen in that time.

No, he told himself, his resolve strengthening, he'd never be able to get through to James when he was in one of his dark moods. Whereas Isobel had often tried to 'snap him out of it', which only ever seemed to make matters worse, Will had always known when to keep his distance from his friend. After further consideration, he concluded that, while he was being a little premature in contacting the police, he would inform Robert of his suspicions - regardless of how ridiculous they sounded - leaving the decision to call the police up to him. After all, James's father commanded an air of authority he lacked and was more likely to be taken seriously than he was.

A faint pillar of smoke rising from a chimney came into view and he hurried after Isobel, quickening his pace. Hearing him approach, she turned to face him, her body seething with silent rage.

'The Will I knew wouldn't have turned his back on his friend!' she cried out venomously. 'He used to tell me there was nothing he couldn't do or achieve, and I used to believe him. What happened to him, Will?'

'He grew up, Isobel,' he replied bitterly. 'It's time you did too.'

Seeing her face turn scarlet, Will instantly regretted the harshness of his words. He watched her walk ahead of him, and let himself fall behind, the distance between them lengthening with every step she took.

When she reached the village, he called out to her to slow down, but she continued and no matter how fast he walked, he didn't seem to be able to catch up with her. An overgrown path led the way past an old crumbling stone cottage, its roof covered in moss and lichen. Drawing nearer, he saw the cottage was empty. No curtains hung at the windows and the floorboards were bare. In the garden, just visible amongst the brambles and weeds, lay an overturned wheelbarrow.

The path led to a nineteenth-century single-roomed school building surrounded by iron railings. He couldn't see Isobel on the path ahead of him. But just as he called out, he glimpsed her standing in the schoolyard and hurried after her, the gate squeaking as he pushed it open.

'It doesn't look like it's been used in years,' she said.

Will approached the building, and shielding his eyes with his hands, peered through a window. Rows of desks with inkwells set upon bare wooden boards filled the classroom. Metal coat pegs hung on the wall by the door, above which were the names of pupils. A piano stood in the far corner of the room, and on the blackboard, the seven times table had been written out in chalk.

Retracing their steps, they left the schoolyard, returning to the main street. They crossed the road, passing a house that had once been a shop. A sign with the name of the proprietor still hung above the doorway. They stopped momentarily before proceeding, standing in silence, looking down the deserted street.

'Where is everybody, Will?'

Will shrugged his shoulders. If anyone still lived there, they were hidden inside their houses. He pulled his mobile phone out of his pocket.

'I still can't get a signal,' he said. 'Have you got your phone on you?'

'For the last time,' cried Isobel, 'you are not using my phone to call James's father!'

At the end of the street, just past the inn, stood a red telephone box.

Will led the way and they walked in silence, their footsteps echoing down the street the only sounds they could hear. Both felt they were being watched by unseen eyes peering at them through the windows of the terraced cottages.

They came to the inn, passing under the squeaking sign that swung gently in the wind. Glancing up, Will saw it was called *The Wychwood Inn.*

'I'll be right back,' he said, hurrying inside the telephone box.

He picked up the receiver and began dialling the Manor's number. It was only when held the receiver to his ear did he realise there was no dial tone.

'It's out of order,' he said, stepping out of the telephone box. 'I'll try in the pub.'

He returned to the inn and pushed against the door. To his surprise, it opened.

CHAPTER SEVENTEEN

Will held open the door for Isobel, who reluctantly entered the building, her nose wrinkling as she stepped into a stuffy, smoke-filled room. Heavy curtains hung at the windows. No pictures were hanging on the bare, whitewashed walls, the low ceiling supported by great oak beams blackened with age. Three grave elderly men, grotesque figures with old, worn-out faces that seemed to belong to another age, turned towards them. The first, a white-haired man, stood warming himself by a roaring fire that crackled and hissed in the fireplace. The other two sat hunched over a table playing dominoes.

Pewter tankards hung in rows above a long mahogany bar that ran across the rear of the inn. Behind the bar, the dim lights reflecting off his bald head, stood a stocky, heavy built man they judged to be the landlord. He seemed friendly enough and smiled when he saw them.

'Lost your way, have you?' he said, polishing a glass.

'Why do you say that?' asked Will.

'This place isn't exactly a haven for tourists.'

One of the men playing dominoes laughed, whilst the other covertly watched the young couple make their way to the bar.

'We were surprised to find you open,' said Will, sitting himself down on a barstool. 'We thought the village was deserted.'

'I'm afraid there's not many of us left,' replied the landlord. 'Though that wasn't always the case. In its halcyon days, the village boasted a school, shops and a post office. It was a small close-knit community where everyone knew everyone else. The local children would play happily in the streets and fields after school.'

'What happened to change all that?'

'Work grew scarce. The young people left and headed to the city. Houses were left empty and fell into disrepair.'

'Just like Wychwood House.'

'Yes, I suppose,' said the landlord. 'So, you're visiting our new laird?'

'Is there a telephone here I can use?' asked Will. 'The one outside appears to be out of order.'

'It's in the back.' The landlord gestured towards a dim corner of the pub.

Will noticed Isobel was trembling slightly. When he glanced at her, she avoided his gaze. She was disappointed with him, and he knew it.

'You look cold, miss,' said the landlord. 'How about something to warm you up?'

'Do you serve coffee here?'

'I'm afraid not. We serve whisky here, Scotch whisky.'

'I'll have a small Scotch then.'

'Make it two,' said Will.

The white-haired man thrust tobacco into the bowl of his pipe. 'If you want my advice -'

'They don't want your advice, Tom,' said the landlord, somewhat threateningly.

'- you'll leave Wychwood House the first chance you get.'

'Pay no attention to him. He's not quite the full ticket.'

Isobel asked him why he thought they should leave Wychwood House.

The landlord poured out two glasses of whisky. 'Please don't encourage him, miss.'

'It's all right. I'd like to hear what he has to say.'

Noticing Tom licking his lips upon seeing the glasses on the bar, Isobel pulled out a stool and gestured for him to join them.

'Here, let me buy you another drink,' she said.

Tom hitched himself up onto the stool and the landlord shot Isobel a disapproving look before reluctantly pouring out another glass of whisky. Isobel then asked Tom what happened to Henry and Emily Roxburgh whilst they were living at Wychwood House.

Striking a match, Tom lit his pipe. 'Until they arrived in 1931,' he began, 'Wychwood House stood empty for most of the year. After his eldest son died in the First World War, Charles Roxburgh rarely visited the property. No hunt balls or shooting parties were ever held there again. The house was shut up and the staff that remained during the war were let go, not that there were many of them left by then. Henry's arrival with his young bride heralded a new age for the village. With her good looks, expensive clothes and jewellery, Emily was thought very glamorous. Many would go to church on Sunday just to see what she was wearing. Although at times Henry's temperament could appear sullen, in her presence he brightened, his eyes never leaving her. Their marriage seemed a happy one and they were often seen picnicking on the banks of the Yarrow on warm summer afternoons. At Christmas, they hosted a dinner for their tenants and servants, and in the summer the local children were invited to a party on the grounds. There was a lot of talk about when they would start their own family.

'Not long after moving to Wychwood House, Henry became interested in learning about his family's history, and became particularly fascinated with his sixteenth-century ancestor Patrick Roxburgh, a former Warden of the Middle Marches and later Lord of Parliament. Through his friendship with the local minister, Reverend Curran, he searched through the parish records for details of his ancestor and learnt that the records of his birth and death had been stricken from the parish records and town annuls. The local minister at the time had even refused to have him buried in the family vault.'

'Why' said Isobel, 'because he wouldn't allow those accused of witchcraft to be prosecuted on his estate?'

'You know about Lord Roxburgh then?'

'A little. I know he was forced into allowing trials to be held in the village after being accused of consorting with witches himself.'

'Many accusations were made against Lord Roxburgh during his lifetime,' continued Tom, 'and even more after his death. Some claimed his sympathy for witches stemmed from the belief that his mother, who had disappeared not long after his birth, had been a witch. Others suggested his sudden rise to power was achieved with the aid of the witches he harboured.'

'What was it about him that fascinated Henry?'

'Lord Roxburgh was a profound scholar and patron of the arts, with a respectable situation in society; but he was also a devotee of the occult arts, a subject which interested Henry. Eager to salvage the reputation of his prestigious ancestor, Henry began searching for his remains, eventually discovering he'd been buried amongst the ruins of Dryburgh Abbey in an unmarked grave. His decision to have his body removed from the Abbey and placed in the Roxburgh's vault caused a great stir in our little community. No one could understand why this man and his studies fascinated Henry. They thought he was unearthing secrets that should have stayed lost.

'The story of Lord Roxburgh's downfall was often told on long winter evenings as a warning to all deluded wretches who dared meddle in the occult, his fall from grace beginning when he fell for Eleanor Lowther, the young and beautiful daughter of a local minister. At fifty-four, thirty-seven years her senior, he was no longer the handsome young man of court he had once been, and Eleanor, who was already engaged to one of Sir Robert Carey's men, declined his proposal. Infuriated, Roxburgh refused to rest until she became his, his obsession with her growing uncontrollably, consuming him.

'One night, when Eleanor's father, Reverend Lowther and his wife were making their way home, something spooked their horses as they crossed a bridge. Their carriage went tumbling down into the river below and they were both drowned. Many, including Eleanor, believed witchcraft was to blame, instigated by Lord Roxburgh. She fled for fear of her life, heading south to England to be with her fiancé, but Roxburgh intercepted her before she reached the border, returning her to the Black Tower of Calidon where he kept her imprisoned for weeks. Word of Eleanor's imprisonment soon reached her fiancé. Arriving at the village, he called on the bravest and strongest men from miles around to join him in confronting their laird to demand Eleanor's release. Many rallied to the call to arms, but upon entering the Witches' Wood, they were set upon by a demonic creature drawn from the pit of Hell. A horrible scene ensued. Many were killed. The ones who lived to tell the tale were never the same again. Eleanor's fiancé was amongst the survivors, though he was gravely wounded, remaining in a critical condition for days.

'No one dared enter the Witches' Wood after that. Lord Roxburgh was not seen again until a few weeks later when he appeared with Eleanor at the parish kirk. He demanded the minister marry them there and then. When his demands were refused, Roxburgh threatened the minister's life and the life of the villagers. After the ceremony took place, Roxburgh promptly returned to Calidon Tower with his young bride. Although he had yet to recover from his wounds, when Eleanor's fiancé heard of the wedding, he set off once again to rescue her from the clutches of the evil laird. Under the cover of night, bravely facing the dangers that awaited him in the Witches' Wood, he headed up to the tower, where he found Roxburgh celebrating his nuptials with his men.

'Sneaking into the tower when the celebrations were over, treading carefully over the bodies of Roxburgh's men lying drunk on the floor, he freed Eleanor from her imprisonment, and together they set off into the night, following the river upstream to Selkirk. When Roxburgh found her gone, he roused his men and they set off in pursuit, catching up with the young couple as they fled along the riverbank, surrounding them at the stone circle, where Roxburgh ran Eleanor's fiancé through with his blade, killing him instantly, before turning his rage on his young bride.

'Following the discovery of the young man's body, Roxburgh was called to account by the local magistrate. The charges levied against him included murder, necromancy and consorting with witches. The date of the trial was set but Roxburgh refused to attend when summoned. A few days later, the villagers discovered Eleanor's fiancé's death had not been in vain, for it appeared he had vanquished the creature that lurked in the Witches' Wood. Surrounding the tower, the villagers demanded Roxburgh surrender himself and face justice. When he failed to appear, the villagers set the tower alight to smoke him out, but their efforts were in vain.

'Roxburgh was heard uttering his evil incantations as Calidon Tower burnt down around him. Overhead, the heavens grew dark, lightning flashed and thunder roared, the earth trembling with fear under their feet. Those present believed their laird was summoning a demon in order to make a pact with Satan, offering him his soul in exchange for sparing his life. All fled the scene fearing the demon would appear, not even those with the bravest of souls daring to remain. But neither a demon nor Roxburgh appeared. By the following evening, the fire had died down and the villagers were able to enter the tower. Only when they found his charred, smouldering remains were they satisfied that justice had been finally served.'

'What happened to Eleanor Lowther?' asked Isobel.

'No one knows. Her body was never found.' Tom drank down his whisky before continuing. 'Not long after Henry had his ancestors' remains moved to the village,' he began, 'he was seen at the family vault at all hours. Curious chants and invocations were heard that resounded over the village in the night. Children woke up screaming, suffering from terrible nightmares. Worse was to come. Cattle died, crops failed, even the birds seemed to vanish from the wood. Only the corvids remained, drawn there in great numbers.

'Henry's unholy work was thought to be to blame. It was even said he'd drawn witches back to the wood. These strange events were soon brought to the attention of the police. After their investigation, no sounds were ever heard from the kirkyard at night again. Shortly after, more and more guests began arriving at the house. They were thought to be very strange and odd individuals. Many seemed to be staying at Wychwood House permanently.

'Henry was never seen during the day. The only sighting of him was by a group of children who later reported he looked haggard and drawn, his appearance terrifying them. When Emily stopped attending church, the villagers began to grow concerned for her and turned to the local minister, Reverend Curran for help. One day in September he made his way up to the house, where he was informed by one of the servants that both Emily and Henry were recovering from a long illness and unable to see him. A few weeks later, he returned to the house to check on their recovery. Whether he saw them or not will never be known, for as he made his way back down through the wood, he was attacked, his screams reaching the village. The villagers hastened to the scene where they found their minister had been torn to shreds, his body ripped apart as though he had been attacked by a savage beast.

'After that terrible event, no one dared venture out after dark. If cries were heard in the night, no one went to investigate - the unfortunate victims were left to their hideous fate. Families took their children to stay with relatives. Those who had no choice but to remain lived in fear, too terrified to sleep at night. This continued for months until some of the villagers began to notice that on winter days no smoke rose from the chimneys. Others realised there hadn't been any visitors or deliveries to the house for weeks. The following spring - I believe this was in 1939 - a group of men went up to the house. They found the doors locked and the windows shuttered. The house had been deserted.'

'Did the police investigate?'

'The villagers never reported the sudden disappearance of their laird and his wife. They didn't want there to be an investigation, preferring not to know what had happened to them. No one in the village ever spoke their names again - well almost no one - and until recently the fate of Henry Roxburgh remained a mystery.'

'How recently?'

The landlord removed Tom's empty glass from the bar. 'I think we've had enough stories for one day. Time you went home, isn't it, Tom?'

Tom thought better of defying the landlord a second time. Tapping out his pipe, he rose ponderously to his feet and turned to leave, gesturing to Isobel to follow him out.

Will took out his wallet and paid for the drinks. 'I'll make that call and we'll head back to the house,' he said to Isobel. 'The others are probably wondering where we are.' Glancing at his watch, he saw it was almost three.

The landlord wiped his cloth slowly across the bar. 'Bring our new laird with you next time you pay us a visit.'

'James hasn't been down to introduce himself?'

'No, he hasn't.'

Slipping off her stool, Isobel headed for the door in pursuit of Tom. Will called after her, but she ignored him and left the inn.

'I'd go after her if I was you, son,' said the landlord.

*

When Will stepped out onto the street, he noticed the wind had picked up. Isobel was making her way towards the kirkyard where Tom stood waiting for her. He called after her, but she continued to ignore him, following Tom into the kirkyard, catching up with him outside the burial vault.

'Is this the Roxburgh's family vault?'

Tom nodded. 'You'll find the answers you're looking for in there,' he said, stepping back, allowing Isobel to pass him.

Pulling open the grilled doors, she paused at the entrance of the vault and peered down into the darkness. Descending the stone steps, she read the inscription on the first coffin she came to.

Here Lyes Buried y Body of Charles Joseph Roxburgh
7th Earl of Leithen
Who Departed this life Octob r. 6 th 1751
in y 45 th Year of His Age

Glancing back over her shoulder, Isobel saw Tom hurrying out of the churchyard. Seeing Will appear at the entrance to the vault, she asked him if he still had the box of matches on him. Retrieving them from his trouser pocket, he passed them to her.

'Isobel, we need to get back to the house.'

Opening the box, Isobel struck a match, the flame illuminating the burial chamber, her attention drawn to an ornately carved stone coffin at the far end of the chamber. Above it, abutting the far wall, were slate gravestones. Isobel drew nearer to the coffin, the flame of the match revealing the engraving cut into the stone.

In Memory of
James Roxburgh

Will heard her gasp and asked her what she'd found. The match Isobel was holding burnt down to her fingers. Dropping it onto the floor, she struck another, and leaning closer to the coffin, wiped away the dust to reveal the full inscription.

In Memory of
Henry James Roxburgh
13th Earl of Leithen
Born 7th June 1913. Died 31st October 1938.

'Henry was the thirteenth Earl of Leithen? That has to be a mistake.'

Glancing down at the coffin of William Roxburgh near to where he stood, Will could just make out the words engraved into the stone.

'No, it's not,' he said. 'It would appear the title didn't become extinct after all.'

Straightening herself up, Isobel turned to look at Will. 'According to Tom, the fate of Henry remained a mystery until recently, which means James must have been the one who discovered his body in the house.' A cold shudder ran through her.

'How can you be so sure?'

'Look at the coffin, Will. It's only just been placed here.'

'Why hasn't James told us any of this?'

'Makes you wonder what else he's not telling us.' Isobel glanced back at the coffin. 'Will, Henry died on the thirty-first of October. It's the thirty-first today.'

Will found himself consumed by a feeling of dread. They had to get back to the house. Instinctively, he reached his hand out to Isobel.

'Come on,' he said, struggling to keep the tremor of fear out of his voice, 'we have to go.' Taking her hand, he led her out of the vault.

They climbed the stone steps, the wind howling through the kirkyard, the grilled door slamming shut behind them.

'What is it, Will?' asked Isobel, her voice barely audible above the sound of the wind, 'what's wrong?'

Will kept a tight grip on her hand as they left the churchyard. 'I have a terrible feeling that whatever they have planned for James is going to take place tonight.'

'What do you think they have planned for him?'

'We'll figure that out later.'

Hurrying down the street they passed the pub.

'Aren't you going to call the police?'

'I'll call them once James is safely out of Wychwood House.'

They ran back down through the village to the path and reached the deserted cottage. A slate fell from the roof of the cottage, crashing onto the path in front of them, stopping them dead in their tracks.

Isobel, pausing for breath, said, 'They're hardly going to let us just walk out of there with him.'

'There's only two or three of them at most,' said Will. 'We more than outnumber them.'

'They might be armed.'

'That's a chance we'll have to take.'

Neither spoke as they made their way back across the field towards the Witches' Wood. Overhead, wisps of clouds drifted across the darkening sky. Stumbling over the stile, they started up the hill, following a bramble-crossed path, the slope growing steeper once they were in the wood. The path narrowed, the tall ferns crowding round them. They scrambled on through the bracken, making their way round jutting shelves of grey rock, continuing until their legs felt they could go no further.

Through the trees ahead of them, Will caught sight of Wychwood House. He increased his pace, Isobel stumbling at his side.

'We're almost there,' he cried, helping her to her feet. 'Just a little further …'

Only when they reached the top of the hill did they stop, panting and breathless, throwing themselves down upon the long grass.

Will recovered first.

'Go,' said Isobel, her breath coming in choking gasps. 'Don't wait for me …'

Reluctantly, Will continued without her. There was no time to climb the wall. He kicked at the wooden door with all his strength until it swung open, falling from its hinges. He ran up the lawn, only stopping when he reached the terrace steps, glancing over his shoulder to check Isobel was still behind him. Seeing her pass through the open doorway he ran on, flinging open the doors of the French window, stepping into the drawing room.

Miriam was sitting on her armchair by the fire reading her book, while Jemima lay dozing on the sofa. Upon seeing Will enter the room, Alexander, who was propping up the drinks cabinet, asked him where he'd been. After regaining his breath, he told them he'd been down in the village and asked them if they'd seen James.

'We thought he was with you,' said Alexander, sipping a whisky and soda.

Yawning, Jemima sat up. 'Is Isobel with you?'

Will removed his coat, flinging it over the back of a chair. 'Yes. She's right behind me.' He noticed Miriam glare venomously at him as he made for the door.

Stepping into the great hall, he made his way into the library. The large room was empty. He tried the study, but still nothing. When he returned to the hall, Isobel appeared from the drawing room, followed by Alexander and Jemima.

'Have you found him?' she said, breathing hard.

Will shook his head regretfully. He turned to Alexander. 'Where's Hodgson?'

'How on earth should we know?' he replied.

'He said something about afternoon tea,' said Jemima. 'He's probably in the kitchen.' She glanced anxiously at Isobel. 'What's going on?'

'I'll explain later,' replied Isobel. She followed Will down the corridor to the servants' quarters. When they were out of earshot she said, 'James couldn't have found Henry's body in any of the rooms. It must have been concealed or hidden somewhere.'

They found Hodgson in the butler's pantry.

'Ah, Master William, Miss Isobel,' he said, seeing them approach. 'There you are. I was just about to make tea …'

Will asked him if he'd seen James.

'Not since this morning.'

'Have you any idea where he might be?' asked Isobel.

'Have you tried his bedroom?'

Isobel noticed the set of cast iron keys hanging on the wall next to her. 'There are only fourteen keys,' she said, lifting them off a hook. 'There used to be fifteen. What happened to the fifteenth key, Hodgson?'

'I've only known there to be fourteen keys, miss.'

'No, there were fifteen,' said Will. 'When we were kids, we used to try and work out what each of the keys was for. One was different from the others and made of brass.'

Isobel's eyes fixed on Hodgson. 'There's another room in this house, isn't there?'

Of course, Will thought, that must be where James has been hiding. Why hadn't he thought of that before? Isobel always seemed to be one step ahead of him.

Hodgson dropped Isobel's gaze. 'Another room, miss?'

Isobel placed her hand on his arm. 'Hodgson, please. We think James is in terrible danger.'

Hodgson fell silent. Why wouldn't he help them? Didn't he realise the seriousness of the situation?

'I know where it is,' said Will. For once, he was one step ahead of Isobel …

He raced back down the corridor to the great hall, Isobel and Hodgson hurrying after him. They found him standing in the doorway of the library looking up at its ceiling.

'All the rooms on this floor have high ceilings,' he said, leading them into the study. 'All except this one.'

Their eyes jerked upwards to the study's low ceiling. He was right.

'And if there is a room up there,' he said, retracing his steps, 'there has to be a door to that room - which also has to be concealed.'

They glanced up at the gallery to the shelves of books that filled the walls.

'And where better to conceal a room than behind a bookcase?' said Isobel.

'But which one?' Will followed Hodgson's gaze to the furthest bookcase. That one.

Without a moment's hesitation, he climbed the steep flight of wooden steps up to the balcony, Isobel and Hodgson following behind him. Stopping before the bookcase, he began pulling books from the shelf, eventually discovering a hidden catch behind the bookcase which, once released, swung out to reveal a steel door.

Isobel turned to look at Hodgson. 'What's in there?'

Hodgson shook his head. 'I don't know,' he said gravely. 'I've never been inside myself. Master James kept it a secret from me, though I saw him enter it once.'

The door of the hidden room groaned and creaked as Will pushed it open. He felt his heart thumping as he stepped inside the darkened room and called out to James.

There was no reply.

The air inside the room was stale. He felt for a light switch but there didn't appear to be one. Stepping forward, he knocked a pile of books onto the floor. As his eyes grew accustomed to the darkness, he saw a desk across the room. Isobel handed him the box of matches. Scraping one against the side of the box, he held it in front of him and gasped at the sight that met his eyes.

James lay slumped over the desk. In his hand was a revolver.

CHAPTER EIGHTEEN

Six Months Earlier

The burial of Henry Roxburgh took place without ceremony. No prayers were said, there were no readings. The kirk in the village no longer appeared to have a minister attached to it. Only James attended his great-uncle's internment, placing his remains in the stone coffin he'd had made for him. He felt there should have been more to it than that, believing Henry deserved better, but in keeping his discovery of his great-uncle's body a secret, he'd avoided an investigation and the potential embarrassment to his family of the story appearing in the local papers.

When he returned to the house, he decided to honour Henry and Emily's memory by viewing the films he'd found in the study that showed them in happier times. Only when he'd begun watching them did he remember the other reel he'd discovered in the hidden room, the day he'd found his great-uncle's body. Bringing the film he was watching to an abrupt stop, he left the study and went to fetch it.

Upon his return, he threaded the film into the projector, flicked the switch on the side of the machine and watched as an image appeared on the projector screen. Two men, one of whom he soon recognised as Henry, were standing within a magic circle. They appeared to be in a graveyard standing amongst headstones, illuminated by the light of a full moon. The ruins of a church or abbey were just visible in the background.

The man he didn't recognise stood holding a burning torch, illuminating an old book Henry was reading from. There was no sound, the film being silent like the others, but he could see Henry's lips moving as he spoke, though he couldn't make out what he was saying. Studying the film intently, he wondered what they were up to when he saw a faint shadowy figure slowly materialised before Henry and the other man.

He was sure if he looked closely at the reel, he'd find the film had been spliced just before the spirit appeared. Henry probably made the film to entertain his guests, telling them how on one night, under the light of a full moon, he'd contacted a spirit from beyond the grave. He'd probably copied the design of the circle from one of the grimoires he'd found to make it look authentic.

The figure remained standing in front of Henry for some time before fading from view. The film came to an end and James switched off the projector. It had to be a trick, he told himself.

But he didn't dare examine the film to see if it had been spliced for fear he'd find it hadn't.

*

The following morning, he was woken from a deep sleep by a car horn honking from the drive. Once outside he hurried through the gateway to find his racing green Triumph Stag parked outside the chapel with Hodgson sitting behind the wheel. Seeing James approach, he stepped out of the car and greeted him warmly.

'I was beginning to think there was no one here,' he said.

'What time is it?' asked James, looking a little bewildered and confused.

'It's just after eleven. Have you just woken up?'

James nodded and asked him why he was there.

'No one's heard from you in weeks. We were beginning to worry.'

'Well, as you can see, I'm perfectly well.'

'Pardon me for saying so,' said Hodgson. 'You don't look it.'

Although it was a bright, sunny day, a cold north-easterly wind blew on them causing James to shiver, so he suggested going inside the house. The door by the chapel being locked, he retraced his steps, leading the way back through the gateway.

Hodgson took a moment to admire the house. 'You haven't been answering your phone,' he said.

James explained it had run out of power and he'd neglected to bring a charger with him.

Hodgson then asked him how long he'd been living in the house.

'Not long. A few weeks now. How did you find me?'

'I drove to your apartment in Edinburgh.'

James gestured to his sports car. 'In that old thing?' he said.

'I thought you might be missing it.'

'I have.'

James led Hodgson through the entrance porch and into the great hall.

'I spoke to one of your neighbours, I believe his name was Murston -'

'Sir John Murston.'

'He told me he'd seen you packing up your Land Rover and assumed you were heading here. He mentioned you'd been seeing a young woman who worked at a pub in the city, *The Bride of Lammermoor,* I believe it was called, so I went in search of her. Luckily for me, she was working last night.'

'She always works on Friday nights.'

'It was Saturday yesterday,' said Hodgson. 'It's Sunday today.'

'It is?' said James, surprised. 'I must have lost track of time.'

He realised then he didn't even know the date. He showed Hodgson into the drawing room, leading him over to the French window to show him the view of the river below.

'It's a good thing I didn't decide to visit you earlier in the week,' said Hodgson, 'or I'd have never found you. Fortunately, the young lady knew who I was when I introduced myself.' He explained she'd provided him with directions to the house and given him her key to the apartment. 'I stayed there last night before driving down this morning.'

The trunks, storage boxes and suitcase were still in the room and Hodgson noticed the wallpaper peeling from the walls.

'There still appears to be a lot of work to do on the house,' he said.

'I had problems with the firm of builders I hired,' explained James. They left the drawing room through the far, green baize door, making their way through the servants' quarters to the kitchen. 'I doubt I'll have any problems from now on though,' he added thoughtfully.

'Why do you say that?'

'Hmm … oh because I dismissed them.'

Once in the kitchen, they'd had lunch together, eating what remained of the food James had brought with him. He asked after his parents and was told they were well.

When they had finished eating, Hodgson asked him how long he'd known Tessa.

'Ever since I first arrived in Scotland.'

'She seemed worried about you,' said Hodgson. 'Apparently, when she came to see you, you turned her away.'

'I know,' said James regretfully. 'I wish I hadn't, but -'

'What?'

'We have no future together. She's going to study abroad in October.'

'October is months away yet.'

'If I left now the house will never get finished.'

Later that day, shortly before they retired for the evening, Hodgson raised the subject again.

'I've overseen many building projects carried out on the Manor over the years,' he said, 'and have experience dealing with builders and other workmen. Why don't you let me oversee the restoration of the house for you?'

'You'd do that for me?'

'Of course.'

James, feeling a weight lift from his shoulders at the thought, considered it a very kind offer and thanked him. Contacting another firm of builders, not to mention the painters and decorators, plumbers and electricians required to finish the house had filled him with dread.

Work soon restarted on Wychwood House, which under Hodgson's watchful eye, proceeded considerably faster than it had done before. Mr Turnball and his men had finished the majority of the repairs and building work required on the house, leaving only a few minor jobs to do, including replacing the gates beside the lodge. Both James and Hodgson now had separate keys to open them, though there was still only one set of keys for the house.

Painters, decorators, joiners and plasterers were hired to redecorate the rooms where necessary, whilst James and Hodgson sorted through the boxes, trunks and everything else that had been brought down from the attic, throwing out anything that was damaged beyond repair. James decided to hang the portrait of the elderly lady in the austere Victorian dress, who he now believed to be Lady Roxburgh, in Emily's bedroom, a room that may have once been hers - though he imagined, if it was her room, the decor would have been considerably different during her time in the house.

In the evenings, because the reception wasn't good enough to make lengthy calls, James began writing to both his mother and Will regularly, posting the letters in a postbox in the village the following day. Whenever the weather was fine, he would join Hodgson in the flower garden to tidy up the overgrown beds, removing unwanted saplings and weeds, trimming back the roses and shrubs. Both realised it was going to take more than their combined efforts to clear the walled kitchen garden that had become a tangled mess of brambles and weeds.

It was while they were working in the garden together one day that Hodgson asked James if he would be inviting anyone to see the house for themselves now it was almost finished.

'No,' he said, 'I don't think I will. My father was right when he told me I should stop living in the past. The sooner I'm rid of this place the better.'

Hodgson seemed surprised by his words and looked a little relieved to hear them.

'So, you'll be putting the house up for sale then?'

James told him he would. While he had no intention of turning the house into a shooting estate or hotel that didn't mean no one else would. 'I'm sure I'll find a buyer for the place.'

In August, when the last of the workmen had finished their labours, Hodgson and James found themselves alone in the house once again. At breakfast one morning James caught sight of a figure lurking outside the house and asked Hodgson if he'd employed gardeners to work on the grounds.

'I've been meaning to,' said Hodgson, 'but I haven't got round to it yet.'

'Then who was that I just saw on the terrace?'

Hodgson rose to his feet. 'There's someone out there?' he said, hurrying over to the French window.

'I saw them just now.'

Hodgson pulled open the doors and briefly stepped out onto the terrace before returning to the drawing room.

'Well,' he said, closing the doors and locking them, 'if there was someone there, they've gone now.'

'Who do you think it was?'

'I don't know, but I've seen others watching the house. I caught one peering in through the office window. They're probably just locals coming to see what the house looks like now. I wouldn't worry about them.'

'Maybe we should open the house to visitors and charge an entrance fee,' suggested James.

Hodgson smiled. 'That's not a bad idea.'

Although he tried to make light of the situation, James could tell he was concerned by their presence, though neither spoke of the incident again that day.

'Now that work on the house is finished,' said Hodgson, 'why don't you go and visit that young lady of yours?'

'Tessa? She'll be leaving Scotland soon.'

'Not until October. That's still weeks away. You'll have plenty of time together before she leaves.'

That night, shortly before heading up to bed, James decided he would return to Edinburgh to see Tessa after all. The house was finished and would soon be put up for sale. There was no reason for him to stay there. Only then did he realise the Webley, manuscript, journal and reel of film showing Henry performing the ceremony in the grounds of the ruined abbey, were in the drawer of the desk in the study. Although the drawer could be locked it could also be forced open easily enough, so he decided to return them to the hidden room where they wouldn't be found.

Upon entering the study, he came to the decision he would burn the film rather than keep it, and after carrying it into the library he threw it onto the fire that blazed away in the hearth. He briefly contemplated throwing the manuscript and journal on the flames too but couldn't quite bring himself to do so.

Once inside the hidden room, he lit a candelabra and sat himself down at the desk. He decided then to remove the brass key to the room from the key ring and take it back to Edinburgh with him. That way, even if Hodgson, or one of the builders, found the door behind the bookcase, they wouldn't be able to open it. He didn't want Hodgson, or anyone else for that matter, finding out about the room.

When he pulled open the bottom drawer of the desk, he heard a voice speak to him.

You cannot leave now.

Unable to tell where the voice was coming from, he glanced round the room.

You have come far, but you must finish your journey. Only once you become an adept at magic will you reach your true potential.

The voice sounded like an echo, the origin of which he couldn't hear.

'My journey?' he asked, reaching for the revolver lying on the desk in front of him. 'Who are you? Where are you speaking from?'

He wondered if someone was outside the house, their voice travelling through the air vent. Although possible, deep down he knew it wasn't the case.

Study the manuscript, unlock the secrets of nature, learn how to draw on the forces of the universe, and in time you too could become a magus capable not only of creating storms and raging tempests that can sink even the largest and sturdiest of ships at sea, but of tearing asunder the earth, causing earthquakes of staggering destructive power! Then, one day, you too could transcend your earthly bounds as I have, and leave the confines of your petty, narrow-minded world behind.

'Such things aren't possible.'

Then how am I speaking to you now?

*

That night, shaken by his experience in the hidden room, James slept restlessly, his sleep plagued by strange dreams, dreams he forgot as soon as he woke, though one image, of a dark-robed figure wearing a ram's skull mask, remained.

The following morning, he was woken by the sound of raised voices drifting through his open window. Rising from his bed, he looked out to see Hodgson arguing with someone in the courtyard below. So heated did their argument become, the trespasser took a swing at Hodgson who dodged the blow before striking back, hitting the man hard in the stomach, winding him. Seeing this, James ran from his room. By the time he reached the courtyard, Hodgson was alone.

He asked him if he was all right. 'I saw what happened,' he said.

'I'm fine,' said Hodgson. 'But I really shouldn't have struck him.'

'Where's he gone?'

'He headed in the direction of the stables.'

They agreed to keep all the exterior gates and doors locked from then on.

'I've spoken to the police about our little problem,' said Hodgson, when they returned to the house.

'What did they say?' asked James.

'That they're probably just teenagers from the village.'

'I don't think there are any teenagers living in the village. Not anymore.'

'And that man I just encountered was no kid,' said Hodgson. 'He had a scar running down the right side of his face and seemed a rather unpleasant individual. I've also noticed another, stockier man with a shaved head. Neither are very young, and judging by their demeanour both appear to have had military backgrounds. They're definitely working together.'

'What makes you say that?'

'Because they're both wearing the same signet ring.'

'They were?' James felt for the signet ring in his pocket but hesitated before taking it out, worried Hodgson would want to know where he'd found it. At that moment he remembered where he'd seen the ring before and led Hodgson up the stairs to the gallery to show him a portrait of one of his ancestors, pointing out the ring on the third finger of his left hand.

'Did it look anything like that?'

'It looked exactly like that. Who are they, James? What the hell is going on here?'

'I don't know,' he replied, though he had a feeling he'd find out soon enough.

Hodgson took his phone out of his pocket. 'I'd better report this latest incident to the police,' he said. 'It would help if I could get photographs of the men. Both are bound to have criminal records. The police may be able to identify them. I'm afraid a camera phone isn't going to do it. I'll need a proper camera, one with a zoom lens.'

'Do you have one?'

'Not with me. I'm sure I could pick one up in either Selkirk or one of the other towns nearby.'

When Hodgson had left him to make his phone call, James studied the other portraits on the gallery. All the earls had the same ring on their fingers, all except the first. There was no portrait of William Roxburgh, or his son Albert, and he was certain Lady Roxburgh wasn't wearing the ring when she'd had her portrait painted. He returned to the great hall and saw his great-grandfather George was also wearing the ring, though neither his first wife nor their young son was in their portraits. There was no portrait of Henry, just photographs. He headed to the study, unlocked the drawer in the desk, and lifted out the photo album. In one of the photographs, he could clearly see the signet ring on Henry's finger, and turning the pages, saw many of his guests were wearing the ring too.

When he replaced the album in the drawer, he remembered seeing the Eye of Horus carved into the stone below the inscription on Lord Roxburgh's sarcophagus, though he'd paid it very little attention at the time. Although he'd only glimpsed it briefly, he was certain it matched the symbol on the signet rings. There was, of course, no portrait of his illustrious ancestor. If there ever was one it perished in the fire that destroyed the Tower of Calidon alongside Lord Roxburgh.

Why had so many of his ancestors worn the ring? Was it a family emblem? If it was, why choose an Egyptian symbol? But then it couldn't have just been for his family, Henry's guests had all worn the signet rings too. Evidently, his ancestors had been members of a magical order that studied the occult, an organisation similar to the Hermetic Order of the Golden Dawn, though it appeared to have been founded much earlier than its famous counterpart.

He wondered what the name of this society was. Except for the signet ring, he'd found no reference to the order anywhere in the house. Clearly, it had something to do with the Eye of Horus, the Egyptian symbol of protection, but during his research into the occult, he hadn't come across a magical organisation with Horus in its name.

*

After breakfast, when Hodgson drove to Selkirk, he decided to walk down to the village to see if anyone had seen the man with the scar or any of his compatriots. He was certain they'd accessed the grounds from the riverside of the house, following the track that led from the stable block. The riverside could be reached from the village by following a path that led through the Witches' Wood. There was no wall or gate to prevent people from reaching the house that way, leaving it vulnerable to trespassers. So few people ever visited the village, he was sure one of the men would have been noticed. Tom was bound to have seen something - not much escaped his notice.

Although he'd walked along the river's edge and followed a path up the hill to the ridge, he'd never ventured into that part of the Witches' Wood before. He didn't know how long it would take for him to reach the village through the wood, estimating the walk would take about fifteen, twenty minutes at most. Following the track down the hill, he checked the stable block before proceeding further. There was no indication anyone had been there. The gate remained open as it always was, and he saw his Triumph parked next to the old Daimler that was still covered by the canvas tarpaulin.

Continuing on, he wandered along the river's edge before heading back up the hill, traversing the steep ridge and following the path into the Witches' Wood. Crows cawed in the trees ahead. He entered the wood and had not gone far when the shadows around him began growing darker. Feeling a little disoriented, he didn't recognise where he was and began to feel a little lost. The crows were now circling him overhead. Glancing down he saw he was no longer following the path. When he tried to retrace his steps, he found his way barred by trees crowding round him in all directions. Many of the trees appeared to have been stripped of their leaves. Stirred by the wind their bare branches clawed at him like spindly skeletal hands.

Dark shadows loomed before, and he heard approaching footsteps. Terror gripped his heart. He suddenly felt faint and realised he was losing consciousness as if starved of oxygen. Moments later he stumbled forward and fell to his knees.

A voice - a woman's voice - spoke to him from somewhere in the darkness.

'Are you all right?'

Wearily, James glanced up to see an indistinct figure approach.

'Here, let me help you.'

James felt himself being lifted to his feet.

'Thank you,' he said, straightening himself up. 'I don't know what came over me.'

When he'd regained his composure, he saw he was addressing a woman with smooth, silky jet-black hair, her eyes hidden behind a pair of dark Gucci sunglasses.

'Where have you come from?' she asked.

'From Wychwood House. It's not far from here.'

The dark-haired woman led him from the wood, supporting him as they went.

When they'd left the wood, James told her he could manage by himself and thanked her for her assistance. Stepping back, he saw she was wearing a well-tailored V-neck white summer dress that emphasised the curves of her body.

'I should introduce myself,' he said. 'My name's James Roxburgh.'

'Mine's Cordelia … Cordelia Raven.'

'We don't usually get many tourists through here. What brings you to the area?'

'What makes you think I'm a tourist?'

'Well, you don't look like a local.'

A smile played on her sensual, full-lipped mouth. 'You're right,' she said. 'I'm not. I've been invited to celebrate the start of the shooting season with friends.'

'Are we past the twelfth already?'

'We are,' said Cordelia. 'I thought I'd do a bit of sightseeing while I was in the area.'

She insisted on seeing him safely home, so he led the way, following the ridge along the hillside.

'When you're not visiting friends, where do you live?'

'Pont Street, Belgravia.'

'What a coincidence,' said James. They joined the river and wandered along its bank. 'I was born in Belgravia.'

'That is a coincidence, though I wasn't born there.'

'I guessed as much from your accent.'

'I grew up in Northern Italy, in the Emilia-Romagna region, not far from Bologna.'

James told her he'd travelled all over Italy but had never visited that part of the country.

'I haven't been back there for a long time now.'

He detected a note of sadness in her voice.

When they came to the river's edge, he pointed out Wychwood House. A grey heron, seeing them approach, flew off and disappeared downstream.

Cordelia removed her sunglasses to reveal her large black eyes and long lashes. 'This is where you're staying?'

'This is where I live. It's my ancestral home.'

'Who were your ancestors?'

'The Earls of Leithen. Before I came here the house had stood empty for over seventy years.'

Cordelia's eyes stared into his, mesmerising him. 'Do you live here alone?'

'I do,' he murmured, feeling a little dazed. She had a fascinating, beguiling beauty.

'I'd love to see inside,' she said, 'but I really should be getting back. My hosts will be wondering where I am.'

'Another time, perhaps.'

'Well, it was nice meeting you, Mr Roxburgh. I hope you are feeling better.'

The thought he should invite her to have dinner came to him, a thought he quickly dismissed. However, before he could stop himself, he found the words had already left his mouth.

'How about having dinner with me tonight?'

'As long as you don't serve grouse,' she replied. 'I've had more than my fill this week.'

James smiled. 'I won't.'

She offered him her left hand. As he kissed it gently, he noticed her ring finger was bare.

'Until tonight,' she said. 'Shall we say eight?'

'I look forward to seeing you then.'

Before she left, he told her how to reach the house from the village. 'I'll leave the gate open for you.'

James remained where he was as he watched her wander back down along the river's edge before disappearing from sight. He felt totally bewitched by her and only once she'd gone did he feel the spell had been broken. At that moment he questioned whether inviting her to have dinner with him had been such a good idea.

What had he been thinking? He knew exactly what he'd been thinking. He hadn't spoken to a woman - except for his mother - in months.

He couldn't help but wonder what a woman like her was doing there of all places. Did she have something to do with the men they'd spotted lurking about the ground, or was he being unduly suspicious, and she was who she claimed to be? Either way, she was the only one he was going to admit to the house and Hodgson would be there to keep an eye on them. And if she was working with the men? Well, then he'd finally find out who they were and what they wanted with him.

When he returned to the house, he made his way to the drawing room where he fixed himself a drink to steady his nerves. As he sat himself down on one of the armchairs, he wondered what had made him almost lose consciousness. He hadn't slept well the night before, but then he hadn't been feeling unwell. It had all been a very strange and unsettling experience …

Before he had a chance to finish his drink, he heard Hodgson calling to him from the great hall. He appeared moments later, his face pale and ashen.

James asked him what was wrong.

'It's my sister,' he said. 'She's been involved in a car accident.'

James instantly felt a sinking feeling in the pit of his stomach. 'Is she all right?'

'She's in intensive care.'

James insisted he leave immediately.

'I wouldn't like to leave you under these circumstances,' said Hodgson.

'I'll be fine.'

'I'll leave you the number of the police officer I spoke to so you can contact him should either of the men return.'

James thanked him and assured him he would call them if he needed to. He then went to get the Land Rover for Hodgson while he packed his bags. When he appeared from the house with a suitcase in his hand, James told him to remain down south for as long as he needed to and not to rush back on his account.

'And keep me updated on your sister,' he added, placing Hodgson's suitcase in the back of the four-wheel drive.

'I will,' said Hodgson. He reminded James to charge his phone every now and again.

James told him he would.

'Are you sure you're going to be all right without me?'

'I'll be fine,' repeated James. 'Now go.'

Hodgson mentioned he'd left the keys to the house in the butler's pantry before driving off, leaving James alone.

As he watched him go, James wondered if he should have told him about his encounter with the dark-haired woman in the Witches' Wood, coming to the decision it was best he didn't know. He'd only worry if he did. When he returned to the house through the entrance hall the thought struck him that Cordelia's visit to the house and Hodgson's sister's accident were somehow related, but he quickly dismissed the idea from his mind. After all, how could they be? It just wasn't possible. He was being ridiculous, and he knew it, though he continued to feel uneasy about the whole situation.

Another thought then struck him. Without Hodgson, they wouldn't have anything to eat at dinner - nothing fresh anyway. Oh well, he thought, there was nothing he could do about it now. There was no way of contacting his guest to cancel dinner - he didn't have her number.

Before making his way back through the house, he retrieved his phone from the office where he'd left it charging. Pausing momentarily before leaving the room, he glanced into the courtyard and saw a spider had spun its silky threads across a window.

*

That afternoon he fell asleep. He hadn't intended to - he'd wanted to keep a watch over the house - but had been so exhausted he couldn't help himself. When he woke, he felt refreshed, and, as he drew himself a bath, he did his best to make himself look presentable for his guest. His hair was in dire need of a trim - he hadn't had a haircut in over five months - and his stubble was bordering on a beard. He looked healthy though. Working in the garden had given him a nice tan.

Whilst bathing, he decided what to wear at dinner, opting for a glen plaid three-piece suit to make up for his slightly dishevelled appearance. His derby shoes would need a quick polish too. Once he felt clean and refreshed, he stepped out of the bath and dried himself off with a towel. After slipping on a bathrobe, he walked barefoot back to his bedroom where he dressed, folding a white linen handkerchief into his breast pocket and dabbing on some

Clive Christian cologne before leaving the room.

He wandered down to the lodge shortly before eight o'clock to unlock the gates, pulling them open for his guest. He was making his way back to the house when he heard a car approach and glanced over his shoulder to see a black Rolls Royce Phantom coming down the drive towards him. It was one of the earlier models, though he didn't know which one.

The Rolls pulled up outside the chapel and the driver, a distinguished-looking gentleman with white hair, stepped out of the vehicle. As he made his way round the car James saw he was wearing a chauffeur's uniform complete with cap and gloves. He opened the rear passenger door and helped Cordelia out of the car, his hand taking hers. She appeared wearing a long, flowing off-the-shoulder red silk gown, and her hair was up revealing her long, elegant neck. Evening gloves covered her hands and most of her arms. She held a clutch purse in her left hand, and what looked like a very expensive diamond necklace hung round her neck.

After she thanked the driver, he returned to the Rolls. To James's great relief he reversed the car before heading back down the drive. He wondered if the car and driver were hers or she'd just borrowed both for the evening, though thought it improper to ask. She greeted him warmly, offering him her hand. He kissed it gently and after complimenting her on her appearance, and she on his, he led her to the entrance gate.

The gate was locked, he explained, because he'd had some trouble with people trespassing on the grounds.

'They appeared to have gone now,' he assured her, holding open the gate.

She walked through the gateway into the courtyard and James followed after her, locking the gate behind him. He told her how Hodgson had been called away unexpectedly and - being unable to cook himself - he hadn't prepared them anything for dinner.

'I'm afraid I'm a bit of a loss without him.'

'Is Hodgson your butler?' asked Cordelia. The diamond earrings she was wearing glistened in the twilight.

'Not exactly. He looked after me when I was younger -'

'And has been ever since …'

James smiled, a little embarrassed. 'Yes, I suppose so,' he said. 'I am sorry. If I'd had your number, I'd have called you to cancel. There's an Indian restaurant in Selkirk we could go to …'

'You want me to go to a restaurant in Selkirk dressed like this?'

'I suppose not. I'm sure we'll find something to eat in the kitchen.'

'That's all right. I've eaten far too much over the past few days. I'm not that hungry.'

James led the way through the entrance porch, unlocked the front door and opened it, allowing Cordelia into the house. After James locked the door behind them, they crossed the great hall together.

'The restoration of the house was only completed last week.'

'Will you continue to live here now it's finished?'

'No, I'm looking to put it on the market. I'm keen to return to Edinburgh.'

He noticed his guest did not seem the least bit frightened as he led her across the hall. Her eyes did not search the shadows. Instead, she glanced at the portraits and paintings hanging on the walls.

'Your ancestors?' she asked, her gaze drifting up to the gallery.

'The Earls of Leithen.' Seeing her attention was drawn to the portrait hanging above the fireplace, he added, 'All except him of course. He's -'

'James IV of Scotland.'

'You know your Kings of Scotland.'

'The Duke and Duchess have a similar painting hanging in their house,' said Cordelia.

'The Duke and Duchess …?'

'… of Dalkeith. My hosts. Do you know them?'

'No, I can't say I do.'

When James led Cordelia down the passageway to the servants' quarters, she asked him if he was the heir apparent to the earldom.

'No, my grandfather never inherited the title following his older brother - my great-uncle's - death.'

'Why not?'

'No death certificate could be procured at the time. I was told he left Britain shortly before the start of the Second World War, travelling to Europe before heading to North Africa when the war began. He died soon after in Morocco from either pneumonia or malaria. That was the story I was told anyway. The truth is he died in this house under mysterious circumstances.'

'Please, you'll give me nightmares.'

They descended the short flight of stairs and entered the kitchen.

'I'm sorry,' said James, casually dropping the house keys on the table. 'Would you prefer I change the subject?'

'Not at all.'

He could only offer her cold chicken and a salad, but she didn't seem to mind. As he prepared their meals, she asked him how he knew his great-uncle had died in the house when he was told otherwise.

'Because I found his body.'

'Where?'

James paused before proceeding. 'Hidden down in the cellar,' he said tentatively.

'How awful for you.'

James noticed her shiver slightly. He didn't know if it was because she was cold or because his story had frightened her. Assuming the former he suggested they eat in the drawing room. 'I lit a fire for us in there earlier,' he explained.

He led the way out of the kitchen and back through the servants' quarters, entering the room through the green baize door at the far end of the room. Although the sun had set it was still light. The trees across the Yarrow were silhouetted against a beautiful pink sky. He decided to leave the curtains so his guest could admire the view while he went to fetch them some wine from the cellar, grabbing a bottle of Chablis Grand Cru before rejoining Cordelia in the drawing room, sitting himself down on the sofa next to her.

When he poured out the wine, she asked him how his great-uncle had ended up in the cellar.

'He was murdered,' he replied, handing her a glass. 'Someone - I don't know who - shot him. I believe he became involved with a secret society devoted to the study of the occult.'

He said this to see if he could elicit a reaction from her, but she didn't flinch or look surprised by his words, her expression remaining the same.

'Now I know you're joking,' she said.

'I'm afraid I'm being serious. The name of the order had something to do with Horus.'

'The Egyptian god?'

James nodded, his dark eyes meeting hers.

'And you think this order had something to do with his death?'

'I do, though I suppose there's no way of proving that now, not seventy years after the fact.'

Cordelia sipped at her wine. 'Why would they kill him?' she asked, before stretching herself out languidly on the sofa.

'I'm still trying to work that out.'

'Well, it all sounds very mysterious.' She sounded a little drowsy.

'Doesn't it?' said James. He started feeling a little drowsy himself. 'Members of the order can be identified by a signet ring they wear on the third finger of their left hand.'

'On their ring finger?' Cordelia fixed her eyes on his once more, mesmerising him, just as she'd done earlier that day. 'How odd.'

'Isn't it?'

Dropping her gaze, he noticed his guest had eaten very little of her meal.

'Why were you really walking through the wood today?' he asked, regarding her with suspicion. 'And why did you come here this evening?'

'Because you invited me to have dinner with you,' she said, her voice remaining calm and casual.

'Why did you accept my invitation?'

'Why do you think?'

'I've been trying to figure that out all evening.'

'You have? Surely it's obvious.'

'Not to me,' said James impatiently.

'You're a very handsome young man,' she said innocently. 'Since arriving in Scotland, I've been terribly bored. The Duke and Duchess's guests were dreadfully dull and I'm not very fond of shooting birds. Until I met you, I didn't think there was anyone of interest in the area.'

'You flatter me.'

Cordelia placed her empty wine glass down on the table. 'All right, you've caught me out. The truth is your name was mentioned by the Duchess the other night at dinner. Apparently, you're well known in the area, and I was told all about the trouble you had with your builders and how the work on the house was abandoned for a while before you returned earlier in the year to finish what you'd started. They painted such a mysterious picture of you in my mind, I felt compelled to see you in the flesh.'

James's eyes narrowed. 'Did you indeed?' he said. 'Well, have I lived up to your expectations?'

'You have,' she murmured, slowly brushing her fingers over his face, turning it towards her, 'so far …'

She edged closer to him; her body warm against his, her eyes drawing him to her. He tried to resist, unwilling to let his guard down, preferring to stay alert, but found he couldn't. Once again, he was under her spell. Her lips met his, her kiss passionate, intense and deep, leaving him wanting more. Suddenly overcome with tiredness, he could feel himself losing consciousness, his surroundings melting away, and it took him a great deal of effort to break free from her embrace.

He moved away from her suddenly and sat upright in his seat, regaining his composure. Cordelia's eyes remained fixed on his, but he avoided her gaze. Seeing him glance momentarily across the room towards the French window, she drew his attention back to her

'You haven't given me a tour of the rest of the house,' she said. 'How about showing me the bedrooms?'

'What's wrong with staying here?'

Once again, James glanced back out onto the terrace, and once again Cordelia drew his attention back to her. Although he couldn't see anyone, he was sure there was someone out there.

'Which one is it?' he asked his guest. 'The one with the scar or the one with the shaved head? Or are they both out there this evening?'

'I don't know what you're talking about.'

'Then why do you keep drawing my attention away from the window?'

'You really are a most infuriating young man,' said Cordelia. Leaning forward she kissed him again, her lips lingering on his before pulling away, leaving him momentarily stunned and disorientated.

Before he knew what was happening, she was on her feet and crossing to the French window. Seeing the key was in the lock, she turned it and pulled open the doors. 'Well,' she said impatiently, addressing someone outside on the terrace, 'what are you waiting for?'

Realising his worst fears had come true, James felt his heart skip a beat. At the same moment, he remembered he'd left his keys in the kitchen on the table where he'd dropped them. There couldn't be anyone out there, not unless ...

The man with the scar stepped forward, entering into his line of sight. 'Ask him to invite me in,' he said, gesturing to James.

'That would defeat the purpose of your entering the house,' said Cordelia.

'Is it safe for me to enter?'

'Of course.'

'That's what your comrade thought,' said James. 'Have you heard from him lately?'

'Don't listen to him,' said Cordelia. 'He's bluffing.'

'Is he?' asked the man with the scar.

'I've had an awfully long and tiresome day, and would like to go to bed, which I won't be able to do if you remain out there all night.'

Reluctantly the man stepped into the house. He remained riveted to the spot, his eyes fixed on the door that led to the great hall as if expecting the hellhound to burst in at any moment. When it didn't appear, he relaxed and made his way over to the drinks cabinet where he fixed himself a drink.

'Please,' said James, 'help yourself.'

Although terrified he knew he had to remain calm. If he panicked, he anticipated things turning ugly, and he didn't want that. Only then did he notice the man with the scar was holding the keys to the house in his hand. Cordelia must have returned to the kitchen when he was down in the cellar, passing them out to her accomplice waiting outside the back door.

He glanced at his guest and said, 'Who are you and what do you want with me?'

'You know what I'm after,' she said. 'You'd save us all a lot of time if you just handed it over.'

James glanced at the French window. Seeing the man with the scar had left the doors wide open, he briefly considered running from the house before catching a glimpse of the shaven-headed man smoking a cigarette out on the terrace.

'Hand what over?'

'You seemed to have all the answers earlier,' said Cordelia. 'Why feign ignorance now?' She fixed her dark eyes on his. 'I'm here for the Sacred Seal of King Solomon.'

'The what?'

'Don't pretend you haven't heard of it.'

'Of course I've heard of it. I just don't understand why you think I have it.'

'You couldn't have exorcised the hellhound from this house without it.'

A grin crept across James's face. 'Couldn't I?' he said, his eyes remaining fixed on hers. This time he could tell she wasn't sure if he was bluffing or not.

'Do you want me to break his arm?' asked the man with the scar.

'No, that won't be necessary,' said Cordelia. 'It's too late and I'm too tired to start looking for the Seal tonight anyway. We'll begin our search first thing tomorrow morning.'

Which gave him time to escape. The key for the gates by the lodge was on the same key ring as his car keys which were still in his pocket. They couldn't lock the gates without them, not unless they'd brought a chain and padlock with them anyway, which seemed unlikely. Upon realising this, he decided to hide his keys down the back of the sofa so they couldn't be taken from him. That way he could retrieve them later.

'I think it's time we retired for the evening, don't you?' said Cordelia.

James agreed. 'I've certainly had more than enough excitement for one day.'

'Would you mind showing me to a room?'

'Certainly.' James rose from his seat. 'What about Scarface? Will he require a room too?'

'No, he'll be standing guard outside yours.'

'I feared as much.'

Before leaving, Cordelia turned to the shaven-headed man out on the terrace and said, 'Have Lionel bring my bag up to my room.'

As he led her across the great hall, the man with the scar following after them, James asked her who Lionel was.

'My chauffeur. He's been with me for years.'

'The Rolls is yours? I'd assumed you'd borrowed it for the evening.'

'No, it's mine.'

They made their way up the staircase and James asked her if the jewels were hers too. She told him they were.

'You must be a very rich woman.'

A smile played on her lips, but she didn't say anything.

Clearly, she wasn't after the Seal of Solomon in order to sell it - unless of course, that was how she made her living. If a grimoire sold for thousands of pounds, how much would an ancient artefact like the Seal of Solomon sell for? Hundreds of thousands, millions even?

He showed her into Emily's bedroom. 'My room's next door.'

She noticed the door connecting the rooms. 'Is that door locked?'

'At the moment.'

'Where's the key?'

'In my room.'

She told the man with the scar to bring her the key and he dutifully escorted James to his bedroom. He opened the door and the man followed him inside, his eyes scanning the room, he assumed, for anything that could be used as a weapon. After taking the keys out of the locks of both the main door and connecting door, he checked James's pockets, removing his phone, placing it in his own pocket. He didn't speak to James or make eye contact with him the whole time. When he left the room, he shut the door and turned the key in the lock.

James breathed a sigh of relief when he'd gone. Evidently, his captors didn't know about the secret staircase leading down to the study, which wasn't surprising, the door being seamlessly disguised in the wall panelling. He decided to wait until later when everyone would be asleep before leaving the room and making his way down to the study just in case they came to check on him. He'd have to change out of his suit into darker clothes anyway so he wouldn't be seen as easily, selecting a pair of black trousers and a navy shirt that hung in his wardrobe.

He soon realised he'd been wise to wait, for not long afterwards, whilst he was undressing, he heard a key turn in a lock and turned to see the door connecting his room to Emily's swing open. Cordelia appeared in the doorway dressed for bed in a red satin slip. Fortunately, he'd only taken off his jacket and waistcoat when she appeared and had yet to change into his other clothes.

'I hope you're not going to try and escape tonight,' she said. She'd removed her diamond necklace and now wore a silver pentagram necklace in its place.

James began unbuttoning his shirt. 'You can't hold me prisoner in my own house,' he said.

'The sooner you tell me where the Seal is, the sooner I'll leave it.'

'If I knew where it was, I would give it to you - but as I don't, I'm afraid I can't.'

'That's as maybe,' said Cordelia, 'but there's something you're not telling me. You didn't find your great-uncle down in the cellar, did you? If you had you'd have interned him in your family vault about a year before you did.'

'He was buried down there.'

'No, he wasn't. You found him somewhere else in the house, didn't you?'

Fixing his eyes on hers, James took a step towards her.

'Why don't we continue this conversation in your room?' he said. 'It's much more comfortable there.'

'You're staying in here tonight,' she replied, placing her hand on his bare chest to stop him from taking another step closer.

'Alone?'

'I insist.'

She pushed him away from her and he stumbled back. Before he could regain his balance, she closed the door on him. Certain that was the last he'd see of her for the evening - she'd seemed genuinely tired - he slipped on his dark trousers and navy shirt before switching off the light and lying down on the bed. He'd decided to leave the curtains open. The moon, high in the sky, cast its pale light through his window and across his bedroom. He was sure it wouldn't be long before the man with the scar fell asleep too. The hypnotic sound of the grandfather clock in the great hall would see to that.

As he lay in bed, he noticed to his dismay it was a quiet, still night with no wind - not the best conditions for him to attempt his escape. Every door that squeaked when opened and every floorboard that creaked would be heard throughout the house. He wondered where old Lionel and the shaven-headed man were keeping themselves. Lionel was probably asleep in one of the bedrooms - but the other man? Like his compatriot he too would be standing guard somewhere - but where? He was probably in the great hall keeping an eye on the staircase in case he managed to sneak past the man outside his room. He thought it highly unlikely he'd be in either the study or the library, which meant he'd be able to reach the hidden room undetected.

He decided to retrieve the Webley from the room. His Triumph wasn't the quietest car; if they heard him driving up from the stable block, he might need it. Somehow, he also had to retrieve his keys from the drawing room too. If the shaven-headed man was in the great hall he might see him - though he would be watching the staircase, not the doors leading from the hall. If he kept to the shadows, he might be able to pass through the room unnoticed. All he really needed was the gun. There were five bullets in the Webley and his captors appeared to be unarmed.

He waited until he heard the grandfather clock in the great hall chime midnight before proceeding. He found the brass key that he kept folded up in a pair of socks in his chest of drawers, before moving slowly across to the room, treading carefully to avoid any loose floorboards. As he slid the panel in the corner of the room back to reveal the secret stone spiral staircase on the other side, he noticed a large black bird perched on his windowsill, its inquisitive black eyes watching him intently. When it realised it had been spotted, the bird flew away suddenly, disappearing into the night.

After sliding the panel back into place, James began descending the stairs in darkness, feeling his way along the wall as he went. Once in the study, he saw the curtains had been left open. Moonlight streamed in through the window, illuminating the desk, but leaving the rest of the room in darkness. A letter opener lying on the desk caught his eye. Although it wasn't very sharp, he still took it just in case he encountered anyone in the library, slipping it into his sock. In the darkness, it might be mistaken for a knife.

Seeing the door leading from the study to the library stood open, he hurried from the room and wasted no time climbing the ladder to the gallery, only hesitating when he pulled back the bookcase to reveal the steel door. This would be the first time he'd stepped inside the room in months. He hadn't dared return to the room since for fear of what would happen if he did. But now he had no choice but to enter. If he wanted to get out of there, he'd need the gun.

Taking the key out of his pocket, he placed it in the lock, turned it slowly and pushed the door open just enough for him to slip through. The room was in complete darkness, but he remembered he'd left a box of matches on the desk the last time he was there. He found the box, lit a match and made his way round the desk.

Sitting himself down on the chair, he opened the bottom drawer and pulled out the Webley. He felt happier with it in his hand. They couldn't stop him from leaving now …

He hurried out of the room, slipping through the gap between the door and its metal frame. Before leaving, he decided to keep the room hidden and was in the process of swinging the bookcase back against the door when someone approached him.

He heard footsteps on the gallery too late, receiving a blow on the back of his neck before he had a chance to turn round.

*

He woke to find himself sitting in a chair, his arms bound behind the back with a thick rope, his feet tied to the legs. Dazed, he looked about him to find he was still in the library. The curtains were open - they'd never been shut - and the sun had yet to rise. Only a very faint light came in through the windows. Feeling warmth on the left side of his face, he turned to see a fire roaring away in the hearth.

'I'm really quite disappointed in you,' said Cordelia, appearing from the shadows. 'That was far too easy.'

James glanced up to see the bookcase had been pulled back and the steel door was open. Someone - he guessed it was the shaven-headed man - was in there searching the room. He glanced back at Cordelia and saw she had her hair tied back away from her face. To his disappointment, he saw she'd changed out of her slip and was now dressed completely in black, wearing leather leggings, a long sleeve tunic top and sharp stiletto heels.

'How?' he asked, a little bewildered. He noticed the silver pentagram necklace still hung round her neck.

'I was keeping a close eye on you.'

He wondered how that was possible. There was a cover over the keyholes of both doors, and they couldn't have installed a surveillance camera in his room - he'd have noticed it.

'You should have shut your curtains,' she added, by way of explanation - though James didn't really understand how she could have been watching him from outside his window.

'You're the reason I passed out in the wood, aren't you?' he asked. 'If I didn't know better, I'd say you were a wit -'

Cordelia quickly interrupted him. 'I don't appreciate being

called names,' she said.

'I imagine you've been called plenty in the past.'

'As you can see, we've discovered the room you found your great-uncle in,' she said, ignoring his remark. 'We found your keys too. Slipping them down the back of the sofa when we weren't looking was a smart move - you almost impressed me with your quick thinking.'

'Almost? I'll try harder next time.'

'Make sure you do,' she replied. 'I am however impressed you managed to resist me. Not many do.'

'Resist you?' said James. After a pause, he added, 'You were trying to hypnotise me, weren't you?'

Cordelia nodded. 'I wanted to find out where the Seal is,' she said. 'I thought it unlikely you'd hand it over willingly. It would have been better for you if you'd just given in to me.'

'Why?'

Raising her leg, she placed her shod foot on his chair in the space between his legs. 'Because,' she said, 'we've yet to recover it.'

'That's because it's not in the house.'

'It must be!' she cried, losing patience with him. 'It has to be!'

She leant forward and for a moment James thought she was going to kiss him, but instead she grabbed his hair and yanked his head back.

'And you,' she said, seething with anger, 'are going to tell me where it is.'

'How can I convince you I'm telling the truth?'

'Not lying about where you found your great-uncle would have helped.'

'I didn't want you finding the room.'

'Why not?'

'Because …' A shiver ran down his spine.

'You're scared.'

'Of course I'm scared,' said James. 'I'm not used to people breaking into my house and holding me against my will.'

'But we're not the ones you're scared of,' said Cordelia, her eyes fixed on his. 'You're terrified of something, or rather someone, in this house.' Dropping his gaze, she glanced about the room. 'A presence …'

She then released him from her grip. When James lowered his head, she slapped him across the face, splitting his lip, drawing blood. James didn't flinch, his eyes remaining fixed on hers. He knew if he showed weakness, she'd exploit it.

'You appear to have a high threshold for pain,' she said. 'I like that in a man.'

At that moment he remembered the letter opener he'd tucked into his sock. If he could just loosen the ropes tied round his right hand, he could reach it …

'Is that the best you can do?'

'I'm only just getting started.' There was a dark, malevolent look in her eyes as she gestured across the room.

Out of the corner of his eye, James saw the man with the scar pull an iron poker from the fire, its tip glowing red. Having loosened the ropes that bound his right hand, he extended his arm, the tips of his fingers touching the letter opener. A little further and it would be within his reach …

'Do you know how they used to torture people with red-hot pokers during the Spanish Inquisition?' Cordelia asked him.

'No,' he replied, 'but I can guess.'

Shifting in his chair, he felt a cold sweat break out on his forehead. Underneath the chair he grasped the opener in his hand, pausing momentarily as the man with the scar approached, only continuing when he saw his eyes were fixed on Cordelia. He lowered the poker towards James's face.

'He really doesn't want to have to use this on you,' said Cordelia.

'I bet he does really.'

'Maybe, but not on that pretty face of yours. That would be too cruel.' Removing her foot from the chair, she violently ripped open James's shirt to reveal his bare chest. 'Last chance. Where's the Seal?'

'Raven!' a voice cried out. 'Stop this immediately!'

Cordelia stood bolt upright and spun round to see an elderly gentleman standing in the doorway.

'Untie him,' he said.

While not a tall man, he had an imposing presence. His voice was assertive and commanding, and the man with the scar obeyed him without question. Clearly, he outranked Cordelia in their little organisation.

When the man with the scar began untying James, he noticed the letter opener James had slipped back into his sock. Removing the paper knife, he handed it to Cordelia who smiled briefly at her prisoner.

'When I heard you were here,' said the elderly man, 'I feared the worst - though I never could have imagined anything as awful as this. What on earth are you doing?'

'I came here for the Seal and I'm not leaving without it,' said Cordelia.

'The Sacred Seal of King Solomon does not exist. It's a myth - like the Holy Grail and the Staff of Moses.'

'If it doesn't exist, how did he exorcise the hellhound from this house?'

'He's a Roxburgh.'

'So was Henry,' said Cordelia. She glanced up at the shaven-headed man who had appeared on the gallery. 'Well?'

He held up the Paillard-Bolex cine camera. 'I've found it,' he said.

'What on earth do you want with that?' asked the older man.

'The film in the camera will prove the existence of the Seal.'

'You may see something that looks like the Seal, but it will only be a reproduction, not the real thing.'

Cordelia addressed the shaven-headed man. 'Have the film developed,' she said.

The shaven-headed man nodded obediently.

'My dear boy, I do apologise,' said the older man, seeing James rise to his feet. 'I'm afraid Cordelia can be a very naughty girl when left unsupervised for any length of time.' He shook James's hand. 'Allow me to introduce myself. We have met before, but it was a long time ago now when you were still a young boy. I doubt very much you remember me. I'm Joseph Wrayburn. I was a friend of your grandfather's.'

'You're one of the trustees …'

'Yes, I had that honour.'

'My father told me you must be at least a hundred years old by now.'

'Not quite.'

While he looked considerably younger, he couldn't have been far off.

'How did you get in?' asked Cordelia. 'I thought I ordered all the doors to be locked.' She stared accusingly at the man with the scar.

'They were,' said Wrayburn. 'I let myself in.' He held up a set of black skeleton keys. 'They belonged to the caretaker.'

'I thought they were lost,' said James.

'I've kept them safe these past seven or eight years since he retired.'

'You employed the caretaker?'

'Caretaker*s*,' explained Wrayburn. 'There were three in all over the years. All were local men. Two were from Selkirk. I can't remember where the other one came from. We could never convince any of them to enter the house, though I can't say I blame them.' He glanced out of the window. 'I've spent all night driving and am beginning to feel quite tired. It's still early. Why don't we all get some rest before morning?'

Cordelia agreed. 'Lock him in his room,' she said, gesturing to James.

'There's no need for that,' said Wrayburn.

'He might try and escape again.'

'He won't want to leave until he's heard all I have to say.'

James considered this and agreed he wouldn't. He was far too tired to attempt another escape that night. However, despite Wrayburn's words, he wasn't given the option. The man with the scar locked him in one of the rooms in the attic, quarters previously occupied by servants, only letting him out in the morning to wash and change in the bathroom.

*

They reconvened at midday. One of the men - he assumed it had been Cordelia's chauffeur Lionel - had prepared lunch for them. Wrayburn asked James to select the wine to accompany the meal and appeared impressed by his choice.

'I expect you have a lot of questions,' he said.

James told him he did and began by asking him why his grandfather had left Wychwood House to him.

'I'm afraid to say,' said Wrayburn, 'when he was persuaded to sign the codicil his mind was failing him, and he didn't know what he was doing.'

'Just as my father suspected …'

'Your father's a very shrewd man.'

'Why trick my grandfather into leaving the house to me?'

'We've been hoping a Roxburgh would return to Wychwood House for years now.'

'Why do you care who lives here?'

'Your ancestor, the second Earl of Leithen, helped found our organisation, and all the subsequent earls were members - granted, some were more involved than others - but they were all involved to some extent.'

'But not my father or my grandfather.'

'No, your grandfather didn't want anything to do with us.'

'That's not surprising after what happened to his brother, is it?'

'You appear to be labouring under the misapprehension that our organisation had something to do with your great-uncle's death.'

'Who else would have killed him?'

'I always assumed he took his own life.'

'He couldn't have. I found his gun on the other side of his desk six feet from his body.'

'Well, I suppose that does rule out suicide.'

'It certainly does.'

'Ours is a society devoted to the study of magic and the occult. Our members do not go about murdering people.'

'You just involve them in near-fatal car crashes …'

'I'm afraid I don't follow you.'

'Hodgson - you know him I'm sure - has a sister who was involved in an accident that left her in a critical condition, the purpose of which was to lure him away from this house. You're not going to deny your involvement in that, I hope.'

Wrayburn glared furiously at Cordelia who shrugged innocently.

'There are black sheep in every family,' he seethed through clenched teeth. 'Upon my return to London, I will ensure she gets the best care available.'

'You do that.'

'I can assure you none of our members would have harmed your great-uncle,' continued Wrayburn. 'They had no reason to. He was like a brother to them - which leads me to believe it was either his wife who killed him or her lover.'

'What an utterly preposterous suggestion. Emily Roxburgh could not have been responsible for the murder of her husband, and I find it equally unlikely her supposed lover would have either. Who was he anyway?'

'His name was Guy Easton.'

James's eyes narrowed. 'I know that name …'

'He was standing trial for murder.'

'Of course,' said James. 'The newspaper clippings I found in the desk in the study. Was Easton found guilty?'

'No, he was exonerated - eventually.'

'This is the man you think murdered my great-uncle?' said James. 'And not some member of a sinister secret society?'

'The Brotherhood of Amun-Ra is not a sinister secret society!'

'Is that its name? I thought it had something to do with the Egyptian God Horus.'

'Horus?' Wrayburn looked a little confused. 'Oh, the ring. This is the Eye of Ra, not Horus. Although similar there are differences. You've seen this ring before I take it?'

'In the portraits of my ancestors, and on the lid of Lord Roxburgh's coffin.'

'Henry Roxburgh had that made for him following the recovery of his ancestor's remains from Dryburgh Abbey.'

'I assumed as much.'

'I expect you've found his manuscript amongst your great-uncle's belongings …'

'I did,' said James, 'but I didn't realise Lord Roxburgh was the author.'

'Fortunately for us, it survived the fire that destroyed the Tower of Calidon.'

Wrayburn then asked James what he knew about the second Earl of Leithen.

'Only what I pieced together from biographies of Montrose and Charles I, amongst others,' he said. 'I know he was the eldest of the first earl's three children - two of whom survived to adulthood. I believe he joined the Covenanters during the First Bishops' War, marching with Montrose and nine thousand men to seize Aberdeen. When Montrose was sent to prison for trying to unseat the Earl of Argyll, who wanted to dispose Charles I, my ancestor became the king's agent in Europe where he was tasked with raising forces and money for the English Civil War. He briefly took up a command in the Royalist army and fought against the Scottish Covenanters and the English Parliamentarians at the Battle of Marston Moor.'

'I'm impressed,' said Wrayburn. 'You have done your research.

As a young boy - he could have only been about five or six at the time - he discovered the manuscript amongst the ruins of the Tower of Calidon, shortly before his father had Calidon House built in its place. Years later, after the Scottish Civil War, he fled to Norway with Montrose, before travelling with his family through Europe, taking the manuscript with him wherever he went. Riding the wave of interest in Rosicrucianism, the work drew great interest from Europe's notables and elite, and by the middle of the century, along with others, he'd founded what would later become the Brotherhood of Amun-Ra.

'By the mid nineteenth-century the Brotherhood had founded temples in London, Edinburgh and Paris and continued to expand well into the twentieth-century, when other smaller temples began appearing throughout the county, including one in Oxford. Today only the Osiris Temple in London remains, the majority having closed in the late thirties, early forties, though a few remained open until the seventies. Unlike the Hermetic Order of the Golden Dawn, the Brotherhood's secrets have never been revealed and its members have remained anonymous. Even now the society itself is not known to the public, which is one of the reasons we've continued to remain popular to this day. Our membership - while not a high as it was in its heyday - has remained consistent over the years since.'

'Why tell me this now?' asked James. 'Why didn't you tell me this when I inherited the house?'

'We wanted you to discover Wychwood House for yourself.'

'I discovered the hellhound for myself too.'

'How were we to know it was still in the house after all these years?'

'You could have checked.'

'We've lost too many of our members to that beast in the past. We weren't willing to lose anymore.'

'Well, you lost one more last November.'

'His entry into the house was not sanctioned by me.'

'I could have been killed.'

'But you weren't,' said Wrayburn. 'If we'd approached you when you'd returned from Italy and brought you here it would not have been the same as you finding the house for yourself. It is the difference between being taken to the summit of a mountain or climbing to the top yourself. The view is the same, but the sense of accomplishment is greater. You have made sacrifices and endured hardships to reach this point but look at what you have accomplished. In exorcising the hellhound, you've more than proved your potential. There are not many – if any – who would have dared faced that beast, the stakes being too high even for Cordelia here. Isn't that so, my dear?'

Cordelia did not reply to Wrayburn. Instead, she caught James's eye and raised her glass to him, her eyes remaining fixed on his as she took a sip of wine. James could tell she was not entirely convinced, as Wrayburn appeared to be, that he had exorcised the hound himself, believing he'd used the Seal of Solomon to rid the house of the creature.

'Over time,' continued Wrayburn, addressing James, 'with our help, you too could become an adept at magic.'

'You want me to join the Brotherhood of Amun-Ra?'

'We do,' said Wrayburn. 'And one day, like so many of you ancestors before you, you could rise to the highest grades of our order. The second Earl of Leithen is one of our Secret Chiefs.'

'You mean, he was.'

'No, he still holds the position.'

'Even after death?'

'Yes, even after death,' said Wrayburn. '"If we could only realise that we are immortal beings, how differently we should live ..."'

James leant forward in his chair and placed his elbows on the table. 'Where exactly in London is this Osiris Temple of yours?' he asked, fixing his eyes on the older man.

'When you are ready you will be taken there.'

'I'm ready now –'

'No, you're not. Not yet anyway.' Wrayburn paused briefly before proceeding. 'Had I known when I was initiated into the Oxford Temple in my second year at university – I read Classics at Exeter – I was about to embark upon a journey that would take a lifetime to complete, I doubt I would have joined the order. At the time, I did not appreciate quite how much study and practice would be expected of me. When I proceeded to the Second Order a few years later and became an adept I thought that would be the end of my studies. I was wrong. I have now reached the grade of Magus, a position only a few others have ever achieved in the order's long history. There is only one more grade, the state of Ipsissimus, the highest mode of attainment, left for me now. Only when I have reached this grade will my studies be complete, and my journey finally come to an end.

'You see, the study of magic, particularly Transcendental Magic, is not a task one should undertake lightly. The French occultist Éliphas Lévi once wrote, "Once started, we must reach our end or perish. To doubt is to become a fool; to pause is to fall; to recoil is to cast one's self into an abyss. If you persevere with it to the close and understand it, it will make you either a monarch or a madman."'

After lunch, Wrayburn announced his intention to return to London. James showed him out and they walked across the courtyard together, stopping when they came to the entrance gate.

'I'm leaving too,' said James. 'I'm putting the house up for sale and returning to Edinburgh.'

'I'm afraid it's not that simple,' said Wrayburn, unlocking the gate with his set of keys. 'I don't think Cordelia wishes to part with your company just yet. I would prefer it if she came back with me, but I'm afraid I can't force her to leave. Unfortunately, I'm no match for her anymore. She's not that bad really, just a little old-fashioned in her methods. Let her look for the Seal. She won't find it and eventually, she'll give up and disappear as suddenly as she arrived.'

He passed through the gateway before closing and locking the gate behind him. He then turned to face James, his eyes fixing on his.

'Initiates into our order are taught rituals through which they learn how to manipulate the elements. In order to do this, they must be sensitive to celestial influences. All possess these senses, though they lie dormant in most. To bring these celestial influences under control requires extensive study and training, not to mention perseverance. While it is not something a person can teach themselves, you have your ancestor's manuscript to guide you, so you may fare better than most. You never know,' he continued, lowering his voice, 'you may even find a way to extricate yourself from your current predicament.'

He seemed to want to say more but stopped himself. It was only when he drove away that James became aware someone had been watching them. Glancing over his shoulder, he saw the man with the scar waiting for him outside the entrance porch. He gestured to James who followed him back inside the house.

CHAPTER NINETEEN

'Oh God, James!' Isobel rushed past Will to his side.

Lifting him slowly, she saw, to her relief, there was no blood on the desk. When she eased him back into his chair, his head fell back, and he exhaled slightly.

'He's still breathing.' She prised the revolver from his hand and tucked it discreetly into the back of her jeans. 'James, can you hear me?' she asked gently.

Seeing a wrought iron candelabra stood on the desk, Will struck a match and applied the spluttering flame to the candles. James's eyes opened slowly, and he glanced up at Isobel, then across the desk at Will. He tried to speak, but his words were too faint to hear.

'We're going to get you to a hospital,' said Will. He glanced over his shoulder at Hodgson standing in the doorway. 'Help me get him out of here.' Throwing James's left arm round his shoulders, he lifted him from his seat as Hodgson hurried across the room. Together they carried him out onto the gallery.

Following after them, Isobel glanced briefly about the room. There were books everywhere. They filled the shelves of the bookcases and stood piled in tottering heaps in shadowy corners of the room. Many lay spread out on the desk alongside papers and notebooks. Only when she stepped out of the room did she remember the missing key. She returned to the room, rummaging through the books and papers piled on the desk, finding the key hidden beneath an old manuscript. After blowing out the flames of the candelabra, she hurried onto the gallery, closing the door gently behind her. When she'd locked the door, she pushed the bookcase back against the wall and quickly replaced the books Will had removed from the shelves. She didn't want anyone else finding the room.

Hearing footsteps echo throughout the hall, she hurried down the balcony and slid down the staircase handrail just as Alexander and Jemima stepped into the library. Seeing Will and Hodgson carry James over to the Chesterfield, Alexander asked what was going on.

Isobel noticed Will exchange a look with Hodgson as they eased James down onto the sofa, settling him back on the cushions.

'We found him passed out in the study,' she said before they had a chance to speak.

Alexander's eyes narrowed. 'I thought Will had looked in the study …'

'I … didn't see him,' said Will tentatively.

'He'd fallen behind the desk,' added Isobel.

Straightening himself up, Will regained his composure. 'I'll drive down to the village and call for an ambulance,' he said.

'Why not just call one from here?' asked Alexander.

'I can't get a signal.'

Isobel took her Blackberry out of her back pocket. 'Me neither.'

Will was beginning to think there was a reason for that but didn't say anything.

'I think it would be better if I go in the Land Rover, sir,' said Hodgson.

Will agreed. 'Be as quick as you can.'

When Hodgson had left the room, he turned to Alexander and Jemima. 'When the ambulance gets here, we'll all go with it,' he said. 'You'd better go and pack. Where's Miriam?'

'I think I saw her go upstairs,' said Jemima, making for the door. 'I'll tell her we're leaving.'

Alexander followed her out of the room. 'She won't need telling twice,' he said.

Will removed his coat and shivered. 'It's cold in here,' he said. After hanging his coat on the back of a chair, he crossed to the fireplace and threw a log on the dying embers of the fire. From across the room, he heard Isobel say, 'I'll get James some water,' and turning, he saw she'd gone.

She returned a few minutes later, carrying a glass of water. Kneeling before the sofa, she held the glass to James's lips. He took a sip and rested his head back down on a cushion, his eyelids drooping heavily over his tired eyes.

'Don't return to the room,' he whispered, his words barely audible. 'Lock the door. For God's sake, don't go in there …'

His eyes closed and moments later he was asleep.

Isobel rose to her feet, turned to Will, and drew him across the room. 'Has James ever tried anything like this before?' she whispered.

'No, of course not,' he replied. 'Well, not that I know of anyway.'

Isobel removed the revolver she'd tucked into the back of her jeans and started examining the weapon. 'Where did he find this?'

'Looks like a standard service revolver - probably a Webley.'

Isobel flipped it open and saw there were five bullets in the six-chambered cylinder. 'Looks like it's been fired.'

Will felt the barrel was cold. 'Not recently. I doubt it even works.'

Isobel spilled the cartridges into her hand, and after squinting down the barrel, spun the cylinder with her fingers, pulling the trigger to test the hammer. 'It still works.' After reloading the revolver, she said, 'If James didn't fire it then who did? Do you think Henry used it to …?' She left her sentence unfinished.

Will nodded gravely. 'James must have found it in that room alongside Henry's corpse.'

Isobel shivered. 'What a gruesome discovery,' she said. 'Why was Henry's body left to rot in there for the last seventy years? They must have searched the house when he went missing. Even if he hadn't told anyone about the room, it wouldn't have taken them long to discover it. It didn't take us long to find it.'

'Maybe they couldn't get into the room because Henry had locked himself inside.'

'The key to the room was with the rest of the keys to the house,' said Isobel. After a pause, she added, 'Someone must have shot Henry and locked his body in the room shortly before locking up the house and leaving.'

'Who would have done such a thing?'

'It must have been Emily.'

'Do you think she would have been capable of killing her

husband?'

'Maybe she had a good reason. Maybe she found out Henry had Easton framed for Appleby's murder.'

'You think Henry killed Appleby?'

'Either he did, or someone close to him. Probably the same person that sent him those newspaper cuttings.'

Will did not look convinced. 'The question we should be asking is why James didn't tell us he'd found Henry's body.'

'Because we'd want to see the room where he discovered his corpse. And he couldn't do that because he doesn't want us to see what's in there.'

'Why? What's in there?'

'I don't know,' said Isobel, pulling the brass key out of her pocket, 'but I'm going to find out.'

'James told you to stay out of there. Why don't you go and pack instead?'

'There's plenty of time for that.' After handing him the revolver, she asked if he still had the matches.

Will passed them to her and watched as she hurried back to the hidden room. As the bookcase swung open, she glanced over her shoulder to find Will watching her from below.

'Don't be too long,' he said.

Nodding, she unlocked the door and slipped inside the room. After crossing the worn oriental carpet, she struck a match and relit the candles held in the candelabra. She realised then she was going to have to close the door behind her. She couldn't leave it open for the others to see. She was going to have to shut herself in the room.

The thought sent a shiver down her spine.

After closing the door, she returned to the desk, and kneeling forward, began rummaging through the drawers. In one, she found a reel of film. Lifting it out, she unwound the reel and held the film up to the candlelight. Unable to make out an image in the frame, she lay the reel down on the desk. She would have to view it through the projector in the study later - if she had time. She then sat herself down on the chair and began sorting through the books and scraps of paper that lay strewn across the desk. Most of the scraps of paper were covered in almost illegible notes scribbled down by James.

A large, worm-eaten, leather-bound book slid off the desk and fell with a thud onto the floor. She picked it up, and when she couldn't make out the title on the cracked leather binding, flipped it open. She could just make out the words on the title page in the darkness.

Mysteriorum Libri Quinque
or, Five Books of Mystical Exercises of Dr. John Dee
An Angelic Revelation of Kabbalistic Magic
and other Mysteries Occult and Divine
revealed to Dr. John Dee and Edward Kelly

'Looks like Henry really was dabbling in the occult,' she said, closing the book.

Continuing her search, she stumbled upon the ancient manuscript and Henry's journal. She opened the journal and saw where the pages had been ripped out. On subsequent pages, she recognised James's handwriting. Although neat at first, his writing soon became an illegible scrawl across the remaining pages of the journal. She wondered how many hours he'd spent hidden away in the room deciphering this ancient text. It wasn't surprising he looked so pale and drawn. She'd only been in there for a few minutes and already found the musty smell of the room unbearable.

Her mind swimming, she closed her eyes and began rubbing her temples. Did the manuscript have something to do with Henry's death? Had he, as the villagers feared, unearthed secrets that should have stayed lost, secrets that had driven him to madness and despair? She couldn't read the journal, the handwriting, both James and Henry's, was far too unruly for her to make out what was written. She would have to take both the manuscript and journal with her and look at them later when she had more time to study them.

Once again, her search led her to more questions, and once again, she found herself running out of time. The ambulance would be there soon, and they would be leaving. She was beginning to feel she would never solve the mystery of Wychwood House.

Maybe that was for the best …

*

Pulling up a chair, Will glanced down at his friend lying on the Chesterfield. His eyes remained closed, and he appeared to be sleeping.

'This is what you struck me with, wasn't it?' he said, examining the revolver he held in his hand. He kept his voice low so he wouldn't be overheard. 'You recovered it from the attic, didn't you? Did you hide it up there, or was it taken from you and hidden there by the man with the scar?'

He remembered the mattress in the attic and wondered if, when the men weren't guarding the house or watching their prisoner, they were sleeping up there. After all, it was unlikely they'd ever be discovered in such a remote part of the house. He regretted not having the opportunity to question Hodgson, eager to find out what he knew about the men holding James in the house. He thought it unlikely he'd get much out of him. Neither he nor James seemed to want to involve their guests - understandably so. Clearly the less they knew the better. He couldn't help wondering why, if Hodgson was able to come and go as he pleased, he hadn't gone to the police. Had the men threatened James's life? Hodgson must have thought them capable of murder or he would have contacted the authorities.

After slipping the revolver into the inside pocket of his coat, he sat back in his chair and contemplated his friend, watching him as he rested.

'I should have told you I was seeing Isobel,' he said. He wasn't sure if James could hear him, but he wanted to tell him anyway, not knowing when he'd have another opportunity. 'But she was worried about her parents finding out about us, so we kept our relationship a secret from everyone - even you.'

James's eyes opened slightly but soon closed.

'I meant to tell you when we were at university, but never found the right time, our relationship being a little strained by then. I understand why now. You'd found out we were together by then, hadn't you? You were angry with me for not telling you. I'd probably have felt the same if you'd started seeing Isobel and hadn't told me. Then when I returned at Christmas, she told me she didn't want to see me again.'

'Why didn't you tell James once it was over?'

Will turned to see Jemima had entered the room. He wondered how much she'd overheard.

'I don't know,' he said. 'Maybe because talking about it would have been too painful.'

'She regretted breaking up with you.'

'She did?'

Jemima told him how she'd gone to his village the following day to see him, and how, when she'd found out he was spending Christmas with his aunt, had one of her friends drive her to the beach he'd once taken her to.

'She really did that?' asked Will.

Jemima nodded.

Will didn't say anything. Instead, he asked her if she'd packed.

'I never really unpacked,' she said. 'I've come to tell you Miriam's locked herself in her room and refuses to come out.'

'Why?'

'I don't know. She wouldn't say.'

*

When Isobel slipped out of the hidden room, she saw Will had left the library leaving James alone. As she made her way along the gallery, she glanced out of the window and saw the sun was low in the sky. According to her watch, it was a little after half-past three - the sun would set in less than an hour.

Although there was a fire roaring away in the fireplace, the room still felt cold. She noticed a blanket box stood against the far wall. After placing the reel of film, the manuscript and journal down on a side table, she retrieved a woollen throw from inside the box. Unfolding the throw, she lay it carefully over James. His face looked thin and drawn and there were heavy shadows under his eyes. Isobel wondered when he'd last slept.

The setting sun streaming in through the windows fell upon him. He stirred, his eyes opening momentarily. Seeing the light was hurting his eyes, Isobel crossed the room and pulled one of the curtains too, before returning to James's side, sitting herself down on the chair that Will had pulled up next to the Chesterfield.

*

Upon reaching her bedroom, Will called out to Miriam to open the door. When there was no reply, he turned the handle to find the door locked. He listened intently for a few moments and heard what he thought sounded like someone crying inside the room.

He knocked rapidly and loudly on the door. 'I know you're in there, Miriam,' he said. 'I can hear you.'

'Go away!' she cried.

'We're leaving. If you don't open the door, we'll go without you.'

He heard footsteps and moments later the key turned in the lock. The door opened and Miriam stepped back allowing him to enter.

'Well, it's about time,' she said, avoiding his gaze. 'I don't think I could spend another night in this awful place.'

Will grabbed her suitcase from the bottom of the wardrobe and threw it open on her bed. After opening the chest of drawers, he pulled out a handful of clothes and flung them into the suitcase.

'Don't just throw them in,' sniffed Miriam, 'you'll ruin them!'

'I'm afraid I don't have time to pack them neatly,' said Will. 'We need to leave now. Something's going on here. We need to get out of here before …'

'Before what?'

'Before they try to stop us.' He glanced up at Miriam and saw her eyes were red and swollen. 'Have you been crying?'

Once more, she turned away, avoiding his gaze. 'No, I have not.'

'Look, I'm sorry for what happened. I really am -'

'You think that is why I am upset?'

'Isn't it?'

'I am upset because when we get back home, I'm going to be the laughing stock of London.'

Will removed her evening dress from the wardrobe. 'No, you're not.' He carefully folded the gown and placed it gently into the suitcase. 'No one's going to say anything.'

'Alexander is. When have you ever known him to keep his big mouth shut?'

'He wouldn't do that to you.'

'Yes, he would.' She wiped her eyes with a handkerchief. 'And I can't say I blame him. Right now, I couldn't be lower in his estimation. Oh, I wish I hadn't let you talk me into coming here in the first place.'

Will stopped what he was doing and turned to look at her. 'Why do you care what Alexander thinks about you?'

'I don't.'

'Yes, you do,' said Will. 'And you always have.' A sudden realisation hit him. He paused, then added, 'You're in -'

'If you finish that sentence, I'll throw you headfirst out that window.'

'You are though, aren't you?' She didn't have to admit it; he could see in her eyes he was right. 'That's why you insisted Alexander join us this weekend …'

'I asked him along because I am not in the habit of spending the weekend away with men I've just met.'

'It's been three months now, Miriam.'

'So you keep reminding me.'

'And in that time, nothing has happened between us because you are in love with Alexander.'

'Nothing has happened between us because I know you only agreed to go out with me to ensure your future at the firm once your training is complete.'

'Did Alexander put that idea into your head?'

'He didn't have to,' replied Miriam. 'I worked that out for myself.'

'If you believe that,' said Will, 'why have you continued with this little charade? Was it to make Alexander jealous?'

'Of course not. Do you really think I could be interested in a man like him?'

'If you don't have feelings for him, why are you crying?'

'I think I've had about enough of these insinuations, William!' cried Miriam. 'If you think you can excuse your behaviour this weekend by claiming impropriety on my part you've got another thing coming,' she continued without pausing for breath. 'I can assure you my father is going to be less than impressed with you once I tell him what you've been up to. When he's done with you, no reputable law firm in London will hire you. You'll be finished!'

Fixing his eyes upon her, Will stared at Miriam in silence for a few moments, before saying, 'You might want to sort your face out before you come downstairs - you look a mess.'

With that he left, taking Miriam's suitcase with him and his suit that still hung in the wardrobe, leaving the door open as he went.

*

Isobel sat with James for some time, watching him as he slept, before deciding to view the reel of film she'd recovered from the hidden room, eager to know what was on it. James was going to be asleep for a while. She was sure she could keep an eye on him from the study. Carefully, so as not to wake him, she rose to her feet, and after retrieving the reel of film, journal and manuscript from the side table, crossed the library and stepped into the study.

After setting up the screen, she lifted the projector off its shelf and carried it over to the desk. Once she'd unpacked the projector from it's the carrying case, she found a socket and plugged it in, a low hum filling the room.

She removed the film from its metal canister and placed it on the front mount, threading it carefully into the projector just as she'd watched James do. Positioning herself on the edge of the desk so she could see him lying on the Chesterfield, she switched the projector on and set the control switch to forward projection. The spools began to turn, projecting an image onto the screen.

The scratched film showed a man dressed in a long white robe that covered his entire body. The reel James had shown her had been in a better condition. Although the hood of the robe hid his face from view, she was sure the robed figure was Henry. He appeared to be standing within a large circle that had been painted onto the floor of the great hall, surrounded by four flickering candles.

The poor condition of the film made it difficult for Isobel to make out the design of the circle, or anything else for that matter, however, just discernible in the background were other robed figures, though she couldn't see them clearly enough to recognise any of them.

*

After collecting his duffle bag from the room he'd temporarily occupied, Will returned to the gallery and charged down the staircase, two steps at a time.

'I wouldn't be in such a hurry to get back to London if I were you.'

Ahead of him, sitting on a chair by the front door, a glass of whisky in his hand, was Alexander. 'Bill's not going to be very happy when he learns what you've been up to here.'

'And I'm sure you're going to be the one to tell him.'

'I'd be delighted to.'

'You know,' said Will, pausing momentarily at the bottom of the staircase, 'if you worked harder, and didn't take so many of those three-martini lunches you love so much, you wouldn't have to feel so threatened by me.' He continued to the door.

'How on earth could I ever be threatened by someone like you?' Alexander sniffed. He placed his glass down on the stone floor. 'I'm not the one who went to a third rate comprehensive and whose father was a mechanic.'

Will stopped suddenly, turning to face Alexander. 'Don't you dare speak about my father!' he cried furiously, his voice shaking with rage. 'He was a better man than you'll ever be.'

Alexander sat up in his seat - he'd gone too far, and he knew it.

'You take that back, Alexander.' Will placed Miriam's suitcase, his suit and his duffle bag down on the floor before stepping towards him. 'Or I swear I'll …'

Alexander rose to his feet. 'You'll what?'

Will smelt the whisky on his breath. They glared savagely at one another; their eyes fixed on the others. Alexander blinked first.

'You know,' said Will, noticing beads of sweat dripping down Alexander's forehead, 'you're a nasty drunk, and you're not very pleasant when you're sober. Sit down before you fall down.' He pushed Alexander back down onto his chair.

Alexander reached for his drink, but Will kicked it over.

'I wouldn't be so keen to see the back of me if I were you,' he said. 'Once I'm gone, you're going to have to start seeing Miriam.'

Alexander mopped his brow with his pocket square. 'Why on earth would I do that?'

'Because, old man,' said Will, picking up Miriam's suitcase, 'she's in love with you.'

Alexander's face fell and Will thrust the suitcase at him.

'You can carry her bags from now on.'

Will picked up his suit and duffle bag, pulled open the front door and hurried through the entrance porch, disappearing from view.

*

The robed figure remained standing within the magic circle; the candles flickering round him. Isobel, perched on the edge of the desk, stared at the film transfixed, waiting for something to happen, her attention momentarily diverted away from the film when she heard raised voices in the great hall.

Slipping off the desk, leaving the film playing, she hurried across the study, glancing at James as she went, before pulling open the door. She couldn't see anyone in the great hall and was about to return to the desk when she heard the staircase creak. Someone was making their way downstairs. Moments later she saw Jemima step off the staircase and hurry across the hall towards her.

Isobel asked her what was going on.

'You could hear them down here?'

'Of course,' said Isobel, 'they were arguing in the hall.'

'Who were?'

'Will and Alexander I think.'

Jemima led her into the study. 'Well, I heard Will and Miriam having a very heated argument in their bedroom.' She explained how Miriam had locked herself in the room and refused to come out.

Isobel frowned, embarrassed. 'They weren't arguing about me, I hope.'

'No, not about you,' said Jemima. 'They were arguing about Alexander.'

'I don't understand. Why Alexander of all people?'

'Apparently, Miriam has feelings for him.'

'For Alexander,' said Isobel incredulously. 'Really?' Then realising who she was addressing, she apologised. 'Does he feel the same way about her?'

'I didn't think so until the night of the party.'

'Why, what happened on the night of the party?'

'I walked in on them as they were about to kiss.'

'You did? Why haven't you told me this before now?'

'You've been a bit preoccupied,' replied Jemima. 'And then I had my encounter outside the bathroom and forgot all about it. If it wasn't over between Will and Miriam before, it is now.'

'Where's Will?'

'I saw him storm out of the house,' said Jemima. 'He's probably gone to get his car.' She noticed the projector standing on the desk and glanced at the film playing on the screen. 'What are you watching?'

'I found an old reel of film.'

She noticed Henry was still standing in the magic circle.

'Who is that?' asked Jemima.

'I believe it's Henry Roxburgh, James's great-uncle.'

'What on earth is he doing?'

'I've no idea,' said Isobel. She switched off the projector, fearful of what might happen next.

'I should go and check on Will,' she said, eager to show him the film. 'Will you keep an eye on James for me?'

'Of course,' said Jemima, making her way into the library.

Isobel waited until she'd seen her sit down before turning to leave. She hurried across the study and pulled open the door to find Will making his way towards her, his sudden appearance startling her.

Instinctively, she stepped back, allowing him into the room.

'My car's out front,' he said, his eyes avoiding hers. 'You'd better go and pack.'

Isobel felt she ought to say something about his argument with Miriam but couldn't think of anything. Once again, she couldn't help but feel more than a little responsible for what had happened.

'Will,' she said, 'I have something to show you.' She crossed the room and closed the door to the library.

Will glanced at the projector and the empty canister lying on the desk beside it. 'We don't have time to watch home movies now -'

Isobel switched the projector back on. 'You'll want to see this one. I found it in the room we discovered James in.'

Twisting round, she turned her attention back to the film. Will was about to say something when he noticed the robed figure raise his hands high above his head. At the same moment, something appeared before the circle, materialising seemingly from out of nowhere.

Neither Isobel nor Will could make out what it was, but both agreed it appeared to be some sort of animal, its eyes appearing to glow in the darkness, reflecting the light from the candles.

Then, as quickly as it appeared, it vanished.

The camera moved, panning across the room as though searching the shadows for the creature. There appeared to be about a dozen or so people in the great hall, all dressed in robes like Henry, though it was hard to determine the exact number in the darkness. At times, the poor condition of the film made it difficult to make out anything at all.

A couple of men were standing outside the library, but most of the guests were crowded round the door to the drawing room. All appeared to be searching for something, and all stopped moving suddenly, turning in unison to look at a distraught woman standing by the staircase. Seeing all eyes were upon her, she pointed to a shadowy corner of the room.

The camera swung across the great hall, focusing on the darkened corner by the library, but there didn't appear to be anything there. Isobel noticed one of the men who'd been standing outside the library had vanished. The cameraman then swung round to reveal the other man who'd been standing next to him running for the front door. Isobel immediately recognised him from the fancy dress party where he'd been photographed dressed as a faun.

He pulled at the heavy oak door, but when it wouldn't open panic ensued. The other guests in the room began pushing and shoving their way into the drawing room. Isobel and Will looked on in horror as the scene unfolded before their eyes, watching as the guests ran frantically round the great hall. Some headed down to the servants' quarters. Others ran into the dining room, closing the door after them. Henry was nowhere to be seen in the ensuing chaos.

The cameraman turned the camera, focusing his lens on the red-faced man who appeared to be appealing for calm. Behind him, the young man, who'd been unable to open the front door, could be seen running across the hall, the camera following him as he went. Momentarily distracted by something, he ran into what looked like a heavy dish and fell to the floor, scattering flaming embers across the room. Before he had a chance to stand, he was pulled into the shadows, his face contorting with terror as he disappeared into the darkness.

The film then became a blur of movement as the cameraman ran for his life. Eventually, the image came back into focus to reveal the view from the landing of the staircase looking down into the hall below. The image blurred once more as the cameraman turned to reveal the red-faced man standing next to him, sweat pouring down his face. He pointed down into the hall before running up the rest of the stairs to the gallery, the camera leaving him as the cameraman returned to filming the great hall.

Isobel leant forward, scrutinising the flickering image on the screen.

'There's something down there,' she said.

Will glanced at her. 'What can you see?'

Isobel strained her eyes. 'I can't quite make it out …'

A large black dog appeared suddenly from the shadows and leapt up the staircase, causing Isobel to jolt back in her seat. The camera began to shake violently as the cameraman, alone on the staircase, remained rooted to the spot, too terrified to move as he awaited his fate. Moments later, the image fractured, and the reel bumped to an end.

Isobel switched off the projector. 'What the hell was that?' she said.

'It looked like a dog to me,' said Will, 'but a dog couldn't have caused all those people to panic like that.'

'Dog's eyes don't glow in the dark,' said Isobel. 'And they can't leap up staircases in a single bound.' She looked at Will. 'The reel of film wasn't all I found in the room.' She showed Will the manuscript and Henry's journal. 'Henry must have copied the circle from this manuscript.'

'And you think this manuscript belonged to Lord Roxburgh?'

Isobel nodded. 'I do,' she said. 'This journal contains Henry's attempt to translate the ciphered text and I believe it contains instructions on how to summon that creature.'

Will noticed many of the pages had been ripped out of the journal.

'I guess Henry didn't want to see what was written on those pages,' said Isobel.

'Why didn't he just destroy the whole thing?'

Isobel shrugged. 'Maybe he needed the rest for something else.'

Will continued to flick through the journal and noticed subsequent pages had been written on. 'This is James's handwriting. He's deciphered the text Henry destroyed. So this is how he's been spending his days - or knowing James - nights. No wonder he looks so awful.' He glanced at Isobel. 'Do you think this manuscript has something to do with Henry's death and why James attempted to take his own life?'

'I do.'

'What on earth could be so awful that would lead both men to take such desperate measures?'

'I haven't had a chance to look yet. There wasn't sufficient light in the room for me to make out what's written on the pages.'

'Well,' said Will, 'there's enough light in here and I still can't make out what he's written. It's all a bit of an incomprehensible mess.'

'It's probably for the best we don't know.'

'Go and see if you can find Alexander and Miriam, and I'll -' His words were interrupted by Jemima calling to them from the library.

Sensing panic in her voice, Will sprang to his feet, pulled open the door and hurried into the library, Isobel following after him.

Seeing them approach, Jemima glanced up. 'It's James,' she said, 'he's not breathing ...'

Drawing nearer, they saw James's arm slip from under the blanket and fall limply to the floor. His eyes looked hollow, his cheeks sunken, his lips bloodless.

It wasn't possible, thought Isobel, he couldn't be ...

CHAPTER TWENTY

Clasping her hand to her mouth, Isobel rushed to Jemima's side, falling to her knees before the Chesterfield. James remained motionless as she lifted his arm. She felt for a pulse on his thin wrist but couldn't find one, his skin cold to the touch. At the same time, Jemima leant forward, moving her face close to his to see if she could feel his breath on her cheek.

James's eyes flicked open suddenly, and wrenching his hand from Isobel, he lunged at Jemima, grabbing her arm. He stared at her absently, his eyes unable to focus.

'You're in danger!' he cried, his voice cracking. 'You have to leave this house!'

'It's all right,' said Jemima, anxiously trying to release her arm from his grip. 'Isobel and Will are here.' She felt his grip tighten as he pulled her closer.

'Go now, before it's too late!'

Jemima yanked her arm away, but James immediately took hold of her wrist.

'Let go of me!' she cried.

Isobel helped Jemima release herself from James's grasp, taking his hand in hers.

Once free, Jemima rose to her feet and moved away from the sofa. Will asked her to find Miriam and Alexander and wait for them by his car. Agreeing, Jemima hurried from the room, telling Isobel she'd grab her suitcase from her room as she went.

Only then did Will realise they'd need another vehicle. He

wouldn't be able to fit six in his Mini Cooper and he wasn't prepared to leave anyone behind - not even Alexander.

'We're going to need the keys to James's car,' he whispered to Isobel.

She nodded discreetly and lifted the glass of water from the side table and handed it to James.

'Where are the keys to your car, James?' she asked as he sipped the water. She spoke to him with a soothing soft voice in an attempt to keep him calm.

James glanced up at his friends with tortured eyes. 'We can't leave here in cars,' he said. 'They'll be waiting for us at the lodge.'

Will asked him how many men there were guarding the house.

'Three, sometimes four. One of them will have gone with Hodgson. They always do.'

'Well,' said Will, 'we outnumber them.'

'And we have your great-uncles' revolver,' added Isobel.

'If they try to stop us, we'll force our way out.'

James sighed. 'I wish it were that easy,' he said.

He beckoned Will to his side. When he moved forward, Isobel stood up and moved aside allowing Will to kneel before the sofa.

James drew him closer. 'Leave me here,' he whispered. 'Take Isobel and get out of the house. Get far away and don't come back. Don't worry about the others. No harm will come to them. You two are the ones in danger.'

'We're all getting out of here together,' said Will, rising to his feet. 'I'm not leaving anyone behind.' After slipping on his coat, he glanced up at Isobel who was removing the throw she'd placed over James. 'Help me lift him.'

James moved his head uneasily on the cushions.

'No,' he said weakly, 'you must leave me here. You can't take me with you …'

Will took his arm and pulled it round his neck. Lifting him, he could feel his ribs under his shirt and noticed his friend wince as he led him across the library.

'You think moving him is a good idea?' asked Isobel.

'No,' said Will, 'but it's better than leaving him here.'

Before leaving, Isobel noticed the sun had set, the terrace fading from view in the dusky twilight. They crossed the great hall, moving slowly, the shadows gathering round them. A tapestry hanging on the wall beside them moved, stirred by a draught.

Isobel glanced across the room at the staircase and shivered as the memory of the black dog charging up the stairs came to her.

Seeing James appeared to be losing consciousness again, she said, 'You didn't break the vase by accident, did you? What happened? Did you smash it over one of their heads?'

James nodded, pausing before continuing. 'I want you to know, I wasn't aware you'd been invited to the house and did not write the letters inviting you here … not consciously anyway.'

'It's okay,' said Isobel, her voice calm. 'We understand.'

'No, I don't think you do …'

Ahead the front door stood wide open, and they could see through the entrance hall to the courtyard beyond. They'd be out of the house and away before they knew it. Isobel was about to let out a sigh of relief when the door swung shut, plunging them into darkness. Both she and Will stood frozen to the spot, too terrified to move, neither daring to look behind them for fear of what they might see.

Will recovered his wits first. 'It was just the wind,' he said.

With his free hand, he reached for the handle, the door creaking as it swung open, the sound echoing throughout the great hall. He held the door open for Isobel who passed into the entrance porch before following after her, closing the door behind him. Once outside, they saw Miriam, Jemima and Alexander standing waiting for them by the fountain, their suitcases at their feet.

James's eyes flicked open, and he stared round in horror.

'Will,' he said, clutching his friend's jacket. 'You have to listen to me … I managed to escape once. I made my way through the wood and headed to the river …' Once again, he paused before continuing, his eyes glancing down the drive. 'But I soon realised I was being followed.'

'By the men holding you here?'

James shook his head violently. 'No,' he cried. 'It wasn't a person that was following me. It was a creature … It was a griffin! Will, the statues that stand over the gates had come alive!'

Will glanced at Isobel and saw there were tears streaming down her cheeks. She turned away, hiding her face from view.

'Man's lost his mind,' said Alexander.

Will promptly told him to shut up, before helping James through the entrance gateway.

When they reached the car, Jemima said, 'Aren't we going to

wait for Hodgson?'

'If an ambulance was coming,' said Will, opening a rear passenger door, 'it would have been here by now.'

'You think something's happened to him?' asked Isobel.

Alexander opened the boot of the car and shoved his suitcase inside. 'Maybe the statues got him,' he said, laughing.

Isobel glared at him, silencing his laughter.

Miriam pointed out that they were not all going to fit in one car. 'There wasn't enough room for four of us,' she said, 'let alone six.'

Will lowered James onto the backseat. 'We'll take James's car,' he said, strapping his friend in. 'It's parked down in the stables.'

'But we haven't got the keys,' said Isobel.

'Then I'll just have to hotwire it.'

'You know how to do that?'

'Of course.'

Miriam looked at Will despairingly. 'Oh God,' she muttered under her breath, 'I am never going to live this weekend down.'

'I used to fix ignitions, Miriam. Now will you please get in the car?' he asked, before turning to Alexander. He was about to tell him to accompany him down to the stables when he noticed he was staggering as he made his way round the car. 'How many glasses of whisky have you had?'

'Apparently, not enough.'

'You're in no fit state to drive.' He asked Jemima if she could drive.

She shook her head. 'I've always lived in London,' she said apologetically. 'I've never needed to learn.'

Will knew Miriam didn't drive for the same reason. Which meant only one thing …

Isobel placed her hand gently on his arm. 'I'll drive James's car,' she said.

Will felt his stomach tighten at the thought. 'Are you sure?' he said.

Isobel nodded and Will reluctantly agreed. He hadn't wanted her to leave his side but now it seemed he had no choice. Leaving James in his car, they set off down to the stables together.

*

In the stable block they found James's Triumph Stag parked

next to the Daimler that was still covered by a tarpaulin. Hodgson had taken the Land Rover. The roof of the sports car was off, and the tires sank low. They'd need some air once they reached Selkirk. Scattered about the stables were discarded overalls, tins of paint, old brushes, sawn-off bits of wood and other debris left by James's builders. In one corner Will noticed some oil cans and dirty rags that gave familiar, comforting smells that took him back to his childhood. He almost expected his father to slide out from under the Triumph as he'd seen him do on many occasions. He'd been the one who'd restored the sports car to its former glory for James and was there when it had been presented to him on his eighteenth birthday.

Isobel asked him if he'd seen any of the men guarding the house that day.

'Not so far,' he said.

'Who are they, Will?'

'I wish I knew.'

He climbed over the driver's door and slid down onto the leather seat. The keys weren't in the ignition. He tried the glove box. Except for a road map, it was empty.

'Whoever they are,' he said, 'they seem determined to drive James out of his mind.'

'I just wish we knew what they wanted with him,' said Isobel.

Will removed the ignition cover. 'If they intended to hold him for ransom,' he said, 'they'd have done it by now.' Pulling out his car keys from his pocket, he stripped the insulation off the ends of the wires.

'I keep wondering why they invited us to the house,' said Isobel, 'why they decided to involve us. We may have been close once, but I haven't seen James in years.'

'Maybe we're the only people they thought could be convinced into coming here. I doubt any of his other friends would have.'

'But why bring us in?'

'To force James into cooperating with them. They probably threatened our lives if he didn't.'

'Co-operate how? What could they possibly want with him?'

'Maybe it's not James they want. Maybe they're after something in the house.'

'Wychwood House has stood empty for over seventy years. If they wanted something from the house, they'd have had ample time to look before James moved in.'

Will noticed his hands were shaking as he fumbled with the wires. 'You know,' he said thoughtfully, 'if they hadn't gone after Jemima, we probably wouldn't have known they were guarding the house. She hadn't been able to see the man clearly in the corridor. If he'd just slipped into one of the rooms, or turned on his heels and simply walked away, she'd have simply assumed he was either James or Hodgson. Instead, he charged at her and tried to grab her in an attempt to silence her. He probably planned to threaten her into keeping quiet as they have Hodgson and James.'

'Considering how terrified she appeared afterwards, and her reluctance to discuss the incident, he may well have.'

'And in trying to silence her,' continued Will, 'he'd given the game away. That was a rash, ill-judged move, which means they're fallible. There may be hope for us yet.' He carefully touched the wires together. There was a spark and the engine fired up. 'Can you see any electrician's tape anywhere?'

Isobel glanced round the stables. 'There's some masking tape. Will that do?'

Will revved the engine. 'It'll have to.'

Isobel handed him the tape. 'What are we going to do if the gates are locked?'

'Force them into opening them for us.' Will covered the ends of the wires. When he was finished, he glanced at Isobel. 'You'd better take the gun -' He finished his sentence abruptly, his heart sinking as he realised his coat felt lighter than it should. He checked the inside pocket but found it empty. 'It's gone …'

Isobel glanced back up the hill to the house. 'It must have fallen out.'

'We'd have heard it if it had.'

'Then someone must have snuck into the library and taken it when I was in the study.'

'How would they know where to find it?'

'I guess they were watching us when we were examining it.' The thought made her shiver.

'There's not much petrol in either car,' said Will, promptly changing the subject, 'but we should be able to get to Selkirk.' He looked quickly at his watch but didn't register the time. 'We'll get directions to the nearest hospital from there. Once James is taken care of, I'll take the others to his apartment in Edinburgh. We're going to need Hodgson to get into the apartment. He has the keys. I'll call him when we get to Selkirk. They're probably jamming the signal here.'

'Can they do that?'

Will nodded. 'They use them in prisons.'

'How on earth do you know that?'

'I accompanied Bill once when he went to visit a client in Belmarsh and tried to use my phone.' After a pause, he said, 'I'll have to drive Alexander and Miriam back to London tomorrow.'

'Couldn't you just put them on a train?'

'I'm due at work on Tuesday,' said Will. 'The sooner I face Bill the better.'

'What do you think he'll do?'

'Tell me to clear my desk and kick me out on the street.'

'Over a silly misunderstanding?'

'I'm afraid Miriam will insist on it.'

'Will you look to finish your training at another firm?'

'Sure,' said Will, though he thought it unlikely he'd get a second contract after being dismissed from the first.

'I'll stay with James for as long as he needs me,' said Isobel.

'I'll try and come back. In the meantime, let me know how he's doing.'

Before heading up to the house they exchanged numbers.

At the top of the hill, Will brought the car to a stop. He couldn't see the gates through the trees and bushes that crowded the drive. He wouldn't know if they were open until he drew nearer. Miriam, Alexander and Jemima were standing outside his car, all three giving James a wide berth. He realised then his friend was going to have to travel with Isobel, her being more sympathetic to his plight.

'I'll bring James to you,' he said.

Isobel nodded agreeing that was best. Will stepped out of the Triumph Stag and approached his Mini. Through the window he saw James was barely conscious, his head drooping forward. He pulled open the car door and after gently rousing his friend, helped him to his sports car, lifting him over the door and lowering him down gently into the passenger seat. After strapping him in he glanced at Isobel who was now sitting in the driver's seat. He noticed she was playing idly with the necklace hanging round her neck and saw it was the triskele pendant he'd given her.

So, she did still have it …

He caught her eye.

'Stay close,' he said.

'I will.'

He gave her a reassuring smile and returned to his car, herding his passengers inside the vehicle before slipping into the driver's seat. Pausing momentarily before turning the ignition, he glanced up one last time at Wychwood House, glad to see the back of the place. The car started and he pressed his foot down on the accelerator, pulling away from the house.

No one spoke as they made their way down the drive. Will passed Isobel and she followed after him. The sun had sunk low below the horizon and twilight was rapidly fading into dusk. He flicked on his headlights and followed the curve of the drive, the gates coming into view before him. Seeing they stood open, he breathed a sigh of relief. They'd be in Selkirk soon and on their way to the nearest hospital. James's nightmare would soon be over.

He drove through the open gates and entered the Witches' Wood. They'd made it. They were clear. Before descending the hill, he glanced up at his rear-view mirror to check James and Isobel were safely out too, only to find the gates had swung shut on them, cutting them off.

His foot shifted to the brake, bringing the car to a violent, sudden stop.

Alexander jolted forward in his seat. 'Do you think you could warn me before doing that again?'

Twisting in his seat, Will looked out of his car's rear window. Two men were making their way down the drive towards Isobel and James who were still seated in the Triumph. A third man stood at the gates, a set of keys in his hand.

Turning back round, Will opened his door. 'Stay here,' he said, ducking out of the Mini.

The man, seeing him approach, quickly locked the gates and stepped back. Will, noticing he was the man with the scar he'd found unconscious in the attic, demanded he open them, but the man shook his head defiantly.

Seeing the other men were almost upon the Triumph, Will lunged forward, reached through the railings, and pulled the man towards him. 'Give me the keys!' he cried.

The man with the scar cried out for help, keeping the keys out of reach with one hand, his other hand struggling to free himself from Will's grip. Seeing them struggle, the larger of the two men, a bullish man with a shaved head, ran towards them, passing James and Isobel.

'Will, look out,' cried Isobel, 'he's got a knife!'

She glanced round to see the other man continuing towards the Triumph. When he was almost upon them, she reversed suddenly, slamming into the man, knocking him to the ground, before continuing back down the drive towards the house.

The man with the scar dropped the keys and kicked them away, out of reach, his now free hand reaching for Will's throat. Feeling his fingers tightening round his throat, Will pulled him repeatedly into the iron gates until his legs gave way and he fell to the ground.

Kneeling down, Will reached for the keys, the tips of his fingers touching them, but before he could pull them closer, he saw the shaven-headed man was almost upon him. When he saw the flick-knife in his hand, he immediately ducked back away from the gates, leaving the keys on the ground. Rising to his feet, he became aware that someone was behind him and spun round to see Alexander approaching him from his Mini.

'Come on, Hannibal,' he said, 'time to get back in the car.'

'I'm not leaving without them.' Will glanced down the drive and saw the Triumph Stag had disappeared from view.

'I don't think you have much of a choice, old man,' said Alexander. 'Looks like things are about to take a decidedly nasty turn.' Grabbing Will's arm, he steered him back to the car. 'We'll call the police from the village.'

The man with the scar, still lying on the ground, said, 'You won't get that far.' He glanced up at the stone posts and Will followed his gaze.

The statues that once adorned the gates were gone.

*

Isobel reversed past where the track branched off from the drive, before slamming on the brakes, bringing the car to a stop. Before proceeding, she glanced down the drive and saw the man she'd run down hobbling towards her. As he drew nearer, she saw, to her horror, he was the well-dressed man in the Italian shoes who'd sat opposite her on the train from King's Cross. Fortunately, he didn't seem to be moving very quickly. However, the shaven-headed man who appeared from behind him was, and he still had the flick-knife in his hand. At the speed he was running it wouldn't be long before he caught up with them.

Isobel shifted the gear stick into first and pressed down on the accelerator, the engine roaring, the tyres gouging the gravel. Turning the steering wheel, the wind caught her hair, blowing in her face as she headed down the winding track into the wood.

*

When Will and Alexander returned to the Mini Austin, Miriam asked them what was going on.

'Who are those men?' she asked.

Alexander gave a slight shrug of his shoulders. 'Whoever they are,' he said, 'they don't seem to want James to leave.'

Will nudged the car into gear and the Mini rumbled down the dirt track.

'They can't hold him there against his will,' said Miriam.

'They can't,' replied Alexander, 'but it appears they are.'

The car gathered momentum as they descended the steep slope, the wood growing thicker and darker.

'William, will you please slow down!' cried Miriam.

'We have to get to the village,' said Will. 'There's a phone in the pub.' He just hoped the police arrived before anything happened to Isobel and James.

Overhanging boughs knocked against the side of the Mini as though trying to force them off the road. Moments later they heard a loud thud as something hit the roof.

'What the hell was that?' asked Jemima.

'Must have been a branch blown from a tree,' said Will. Out of the corner of his eye, he caught a glimpse of what looked like a large bird disappearing into the trees.

'That wasn't a branch!'

'Looks like a large bird of prey,' said Miriam.

Alexander ducked down to see out of Will's window. 'Too big even for a golden eagle …'

'Whatever it is,' cried Jemima, 'it's circling us!'

The creature came into Will's line of sight, and he caught a glimpse of its flapping wings. It was heading straight towards them, its talons outstretched.

'What the blazes is that?' cried Alexander.

Will knew exactly what it was. He put his foot down on the accelerator and steered the car towards the creature.

Alexander gripped the sides of his seat. 'What are you doing?'

'I'm going to run it down.'

The creature beat its wings and rose up, clipping the side of the Mini before it disappeared over the top of the car. They heard another thud as the griffin landed on the roof, its razor-sharp claws gripping the side of the car.

'William, look out!' cried Miriam.

They were heading towards a steep embankment. Releasing its hold on the Mini, the griffin flew off sending the car sliding down the track, hurtling towards the steep bank. Will slammed on the brakes. The tyres, now caked in mud, lost traction. Realising he'd lost control of the car, he spun the wheel frantically.

'Hang on to something!' he cried.

His passengers braced themselves.

The car slid into the mud, shuddering to a stop, stalling just inches from the edge of the embankment. Will let out a sigh of relief and noticed his hands were shaking as he relaxed back into his seat.

'Where's it gone?' asked Jemima.

The four of them stared anxiously out of the windows. The creature was nowhere to be seen. Had it flown away?

'It's there in the trees!' cried Jemima. 'It's heading straight towards us!'

Will turned the keys in the ignition but the car failed to start.

'Now would be a good time to move, old man,' said Alexander anxiously, turning in his seat.

Will turned the key a second time but still the car wouldn't start. He tried to glimpse the griffin for himself but couldn't see past Alexander's wide shoulders.

'It's going to hit us!' cried Jemima. 'Move!'

'I'm trying!' replied Will, turning the key in the ignition for a third time. The engine started and he slammed his foot down on the accelerator.

The tyres spun in the mud. The Mini was stuck. Behind him, Jemima let out an ear-piercing scream.

The griffin swooped down towards them, striking the car with such force it toppled over the edge of the embankment, sending it hurtling towards the ditch below.

*

'Wake up, James,' said Isobel, unbuckling his seat belt.

Through the trees, she glimpsed the garden's high stone wall. If they skirted along the wall and followed it past the wooden door they could head down to the village through the Witches' Wood.

She opened the passenger door. 'Talk to me,' she said. 'Tell me about Henry.'

Taking his arm, pulling it round her shoulders, she lifted him onto his feet. She placed her other arm round his waist and leaving the car outside the dilapidated outbuilding, hauled him along beside her.

'Was Easton found guilty of Appleby's murder?'

James forced his sunken eyes open. 'He was,' he said, his voice weak, 'but was exonerated - eventually.'

They kept to the grass, avoiding the gravel to silence their footsteps and followed the crumbling stone wall, beating a path through the weeds and bracken, making their way towards the Witches' Wood.

'Henry had something to do with him being framed, didn't he?'

'I believe so.'

'Why,' asked Isobel, 'because Emily was in love with him?'

James nodded. 'Once Eaton was arrested and his name disgraced, Emily would have had no choice but to accept Henry's proposal of marriage. Her family probably forced her into accepting - it's unlikely they approved of her infatuation with Easton anyway.'

'Because he wasn't from the right family?'

'His family wouldn't have been poor - he was at Oxford with Henry, after all. They probably didn't want her giving up her life of privilege by marrying outside the nobility. You see, her father was a viscount.'

'And Henry was an earl,' said Isobel. 'Will and I paid a visit to your family's burial vault in the village,' she added by way of explanation.

'You have been busy.'

They continued on, their progress slow, making their way round the house until they came to the wooden gate. The gate still lay on the ground from when Will had kicked it open. Isobel glanced up at Wychwood House. They'd soon be discovered in the wood, but in the house, where there were plenty of places to hide, it would take their pursuers longer to find them - long enough for the police to arrive. Will and the others would be in the village by now and would have contacted the police. They wouldn't have to stay hidden for long …

Although it seemed hopeless - James could hardly walk - they had to try. If they skirted round the garden, instead of heading straight up the sloping lawn, the dark shadows of the trees would keep them hidden from view.

With James at her side, Isobel stepped through the open doorway and hurried under the cover of the trees, glancing up at the house as she went. Although dark, there were no lights on inside the rooms. Their two pursuers were most probably still searching for them at the stable block. The other man would have remained standing guard at the lodge.

Scattered across the lawn were several large black birds. When they caught sight of James and Isobel, they became agitated and began cawing at them. Isobel quickened her pace until she practically had to drag James along beside her. Seeing them approach, the birds took flight. Rooks, jackdaws, crows and ravens flew towards them. Isobel tried to wave them away, but they began jabbing at them with their beaks, stabbing at both her and James's legs and arms, their wings fluttering in their faces. When a large crow caught in her hair, she reached for it, losing her hold on James who fell to the ground. She removed the crow and flung it away before glancing down to find a large raven stabbing at James with its beak.

'Leave him alone!' she cried, kicking the large bird away.

Her sudden cry, and the violence of her actions, sent the birds scattering in all directions. Kneeling, she lifted James. Not much further now - they had almost reached the terrace. Soon they would be safe inside the house. She kept low as she approached the terrace steps, pulling James tightly towards her, so they wouldn't be seen from the house. Behind them, the birds began cawing. If there was someone in the house their attention would soon be drawn outside. She hesitated before proceeding, unsure whether to continue, but seeing the birds had taken flight and were heading in their direction, she continued, making her way up the steps to the terrace.

*

The faint sound of rain pattering on glass brought Will slowly back to consciousness. Opening his eyes, he looked about him, trying to get his bearings. The Mini Cooper had come to rest on its side in a ditch at the bottom of the embankment. He was held into his seat by his seatbelt, his head throbbing, his whole body aching. Turning, he saw Alexander slumped forward in his seat, resting against the passenger door. He felt for a pulse in his neck. To his relief, he quickly found one.

Twisting round, he glanced at his other passengers. Jemima was lying curled in a ball against her door and appeared to be slowly regaining consciousness. Miriam was out cold, though Will could see her chest gently rising as she breathed, her seatbelt holding her in place.

'Jemima, are you hurt?' he asked.

She shook her head.

Pressing down on the handle, Will tried to shoulder his door open but it wouldn't budge. He wound down the window, undid his seatbelt and hauled himself out of the car. The rain had begun to fall heavily, dripping down onto him from the branches and leaves of the surrounding trees. Without pausing for breath, he slid off the Mini, landing in a puddle of muddy water, crouching low to avoid being seen. There were scratches and deep grooves etched into the roof of his car. If that creature could do that to a car, he shuddered at the thought of what it could do to him.

Steadying himself against the vehicle, he looked up the steep embankment to the trees beyond. Was it up there somewhere, perched in one of the trees, watching him? The falling rain and the wind blowing through the trees were the only sounds he could hear. The griffin appeared to have gone.

Turning, he tried Miriam's door. To his surprise, it opened. Reaching into the car, he took hold of her.

'Jemima, can you undo Miriam's seatbelt, please?'

'Is it still out there?' she asked, her eyes wide with terror.

'No, it's gone,' Will assured her. 'Can you undo Miriam's seatbelt?' He heard Miriam groan. She was regaining consciousness.

Will heard a click as the seat belt loosened and Miriam's legs swung round.

'Help me lift her out,' said Will, pulling Miriam from the car.

Once clear, he laid her down on the embankment. Rising to his feet, he helped Jemima down from the car.

'What about Alexander?' she asked.

'We'll have to leave him where he is for now.'

Will knew they'd struggle to get Alexander out of the car. He weighed at least fourteen stone and he didn't want to chance moving him for fear he had other injuries.

'I'm going down to the village to get help,' he said. 'I'll be straight back.'

Jemima nodded in response before turning her attention to Miriam who, she noticed, had a cut on her forehead.

Will began to climb the steep embankment, pulling himself up on wet shrubs and roots. When he was almost at the top, he heard a crack as a branch broke and immediately fell against the bank, seeking shelter in the shrubbery. Tentatively, he lifted his head and glanced up at the trees but couldn't see anything. He continued pulling himself up, his feet sliding with the shifting mud. Suddenly, he lost his footing and instinctively reached out for something to grab onto, his hand finding a patch of stinging nettles. Crying out in pain, he began to slide down the embankment, tumbling over roots, scraping his arms and face as he plunged through bushes, before finally coming to rest in the wet ditch.

Wincing with pain, he rose to his feet. His head hurt and he felt something running down the side of his face. Touching his forehead with his hand, his fingers came away sticky with blood. After wiping his forehead clean, he started back up the embankment.

*

Isobel paused momentarily behind the balustrade and peered into the drawing room. Although shrouded in darkness the room appeared to be empty, so she hauled James up the terrace steps. Finding the doors to the French window unlocked, she pulled them open and, with a shudder, stepped back inside the house. After laying James down on the sofa, she returned to the French window to find the birds had congregated on the terrace, so quickly turned the key in the lock to keep them out.

Once locked, she glanced up to find the birds had vanished and a hooded figure in a black cloak now stood in their place, the sudden appearance of the figure making her jump.

Stepping back away from the French window, she hurried to James.

'Stay with me,' she said, dragging him to his feet.

She glanced over her shoulder to find the figure had gone.

Together, Isobel and James made their way across the drawing room. When they reached the doorway Isobel hesitated, ensuring the way was clear before proceeding. There were no lights on anywhere in the house. No candles burnt in the great hall. Parts of the room now lay in total darkness.

She knew she had to get James upstairs. Many of the bedrooms could be locked and the doors were sturdy. It would take their pursuers a long time and considerable effort to break one down. Enough time for the police to get there …

Whoever it was that had appeared on the terrace would now be making their way round the house in search of another entrance to the building, which meant they didn't have much time. To avoid being seen making their way upstairs, she decided to use the hidden staircase that linked the study to Henry's bedroom, rather than go up the main staircase. They started across the great hall, Isobel straining her ears and eyes for every sound and movement from the darkness that surrounded them.

Glancing at James, she saw he was flagging. 'When did you discover the room above the study, James?'

His eyes shut momentarily, and he muttered something, but she couldn't make out what it was.

'Was Henry's body in there?'

James nodded wearily.

'Did Emily leaving him drive Henry to take his own life?'

'Henry didn't take his own life,' said James, his words barely audible. 'He was shot while sitting at the desk and the gun was left on the floor about six feet in front of him.'

'You think Easton shot him?'

James nodded.

'But how could Emily marry someone who'd killed her husband in cold blood?' asked Isobel.

'Because Henry begged Easton to kill him. He knew Emily

would only be safe once he was dead.'

James's legs failed him, and he collapsed onto the stone floor. 'Please,' he said, his eyes weary as Isobel helped him to his feet, 'I have to rest.'

'Just a few more steps and we'll be in the library. You can rest there.'

The door remained open, just as she'd left it, the dusky room lit only by the faint glow that came from the dying embers of the fire, but it was enough for her to reach the sofa without bumping into anything on the way. She laid James back down on the Chesterfield.

To her dismay, she realised they'd come full circle.

Leaving James, she returned to the door. Seeing there was no key in the lock, she grabbed a chair and held it under the handle. As she fixed it in place, she heard what she thought sounded like the front door creaking open. They were in the house … She stood stock-still, not daring to move for fear the floorboards would creak under her feet and give them away. They had to get upstairs. They couldn't stay where they were, it would be one of the first places they'd look.

Behind her, she heard James say, 'Isobel, you have to end my suffering, just as Easton ended Henry's.'

Isobel turned to see him holding the Webley by its barrel, the handle towards her.

'Where did you get that?' she asked.

'I removed it from Will's coat and hid it under a cushion,' he said. 'I didn't want you using it. Isobel, there's only one way out of this,' he added gravely.

Isobel shook her head. 'No!' she cried. 'I could never do such a thing!'

*

At the top of the embankment, Will collapsed onto his side exhausted, his cheek pressed into the muddy ground. He'd made it - just. Feeling blood gushing out of the wound on his forehead, he groaned and rolled onto his back. Faintly, over the rain, he heard footsteps, and tilting his head back, saw a man trudge into his line of sight, the trees overhead spinning.

Was it the shaven-headed man with the knife coming to finish him off?

He had to get to his feet and make his way down to the village, but he found himself unable to move. As the figure loomed over him, his eyes lost focus and darkness engulfed him.

*

Out in the great hall, the grandfather clock began to chime.

Isobel grabbed the Webley from James. There were five bullets in the chamber. Not many - but enough. There were only two of them, three if she counted the robed figure - assuming, of course, the man with the scar remained at the lodge and hadn't joined them. The only weapon they had appeared to be a flick-knife. The Webley gave her an advantage over them.

From the sofa, James said, 'Isobel, did you ever wonder how your father found out you were seeing Will?'

Isobel shook her head. She didn't want to know …

'I was the one who told him,' he said, his eyes riveted on her. 'I discovered you together. If it wasn't for me, you'd be together now.'

Isobel avoided his eyes, glancing down at the floor. 'It doesn't matter,' she said. 'We will be together again.' She felt her hand tightening round the handle of the gun.

'No, you won't,' said James. 'Emily knew she would never be safe unless Henry was dead.'

'Why?' asked Isobel, fixing her eyes on James. 'This has something to do with the manuscript you and Henry were deciphering, doesn't it?'

'It belonged to Lord Roxburgh,' said James. 'It's a textbook of magic. Through studying ancient texts and grimoires - books of magic - he discovered a way to transcend our world and travel into the astral realm.'

'What's the astral realm?'

'The astral realm is an alternate plane of existence. It's the world of the celestial spheres - a spirit world between the earth and the heavens. There is an ancient Hindu scripture that claims that in addition to the two states for men - one in this world and one in the next - there is also a third intermediary state, similar to a dream state where the transcendent self resides. The Egyptians called this self the ka. For Theosophists, it was known as the astral body. No longer bound by space or time, Lord Roxburgh's transcendent self - his astral body - resides in the astral plane, and is neither dead nor alive, but waiting.'

'Waiting for what?'

'To return.' He paused before continuing, then added, 'Isobel, if you don't pull that trigger now, he will return at midnight tonight.'

Isobel shook her head and hot stinging tears filled her eyes. With an ache in her throat, she said, 'There has to be another way …'

'Please, there are fates worse than death …'

Hearing a floorboard creak, Isobel jerked her head round to find the shaven-headed man had entered the library through the study.

She held up the revolver, pointing it at him. 'Get out of here,' she cried, 'or I'll shoot.'

Undeterred, he drew closer, his small, shrewd eyes staring into hers. Although he wasn't very tall, he was solidly built with wide shoulders and a thick neck.

'I mean it,' she said, her voice trembling. 'I'll shoot you …'

He lunged forward, his actions so sudden and violent she was caught off guard, his large fist wrenching the revolver from her hand, sending it flying across the room. With his other hand, he grabbed her arm and flung her down on the sofa next to James.

Crossing the room, he removed the chair wedged under the handle and opened the door allowing the man in the Italian shoes into the room. A woman stepped into the room behind him. Although she'd removed her cloak, Isobel assumed she was the hooded figure she'd seen on the terrace.

'James needs a doctor,' she said. 'I demand you let us go!'

The woman didn't answer. Instead, she wandered over to one of the oil lamps, raised the glass chimney, struck a match and lit the wick. Replacing the chimney, she turned to face Isobel, who noticed she had fascinating, almost hypnotic eyes and a flawless, bronzed complexion. Her long, shiny, raven black hair flowed over her shoulders, and she was wearing a black dress and long black gloves.

'The police will be here soon.'

'No, they won't,' said the dark-haired woman. She spoke with an accent Isobel couldn't quite place. 'Your friends never made it to the village. He saw to that.'

'Who saw to that -' The answer came to her before the words had left her mouth. 'Lord Roxburgh …'

A vague smile appeared on the dark-haired woman's crimson lips.

'Who are you?' asked Isobel. 'What are you doing here? What do you want with James?'

'It's not James we want.'

Isobel sprang to her feet. Without turning round, the shaven-headed man said, 'Sit down.' His voice was deep and threatening.

'I will not sit down!' she cried.

The man's heavy hand swung round, catching her jaw, sending her crashing to the floor. She tried to stand but her knees gave way and she fell to the ground unconscious.

CHAPTER TWENTY-ONE

One Month Earlier

The search for the Sacred Seal of King Solomon continued in the weeks that followed. Cordelia searched all the rooms, working methodically through the house, but without success. She even asked James if he'd checked the pockets of the suit Henry was wearing when he died, clothes he'd subsequently been buried in. When he told her he wasn't in the habit of rifling through the pockets of dead men, she and the man with the scar headed down to the vault in the village, only to return an hour later empty-handed.

During the day, James was allowed into the library and the study. The doors leading to the great hall were locked and one of the men was always stationed in the room to keep a close eye on him. Sometimes, during particularly warm days, he was let out into the flower garden and onto the terrace for closely supervised walks and soon learnt all the gates remained locked, barring his exit. He couldn't help but laugh at the irony that the gates Hodgson had locked to keep the men out were now being used to keep him prisoner.

In the evenings Cordelia would insist he join her for dinner. When he asked her why she said she didn't like dining alone and hoped his level of conversation would be better than the other men in the house. They dressed for the occasion because she told him,

'I may be holding you prisoner in your own home, but there is no reason why we can't be civil about it.'

James did not know where the other men ate their meals. He presumed they dined in the kitchen or servants' hall, Cordelia appearing keen to keep them in their place. They slept in the attic in rooms adjacent to his, while Cordelia remained in Emily's room. He did not know where old Lionel slept, assuming he'd been given one of the more comfortable guest bedrooms. A grey-haired man joined the other two men keeping guard over him. He also glimpsed a younger, well-dressed man with them - though he didn't remain at the house for as long as the others. All wore the signet ring on the third finger of their left hands.

One evening, out of curiosity, he asked Cordelia why she didn't wear the ring like the others.

'Because it's ugly,' she said.

'Or is it because you're not actually a member of the Brotherhood?'

'Not as such.'

'Why, because they don't allow women in their organisation?'

'They have many women amongst their members.'

'Really?' said James. 'Anyone I might have heard of?'

Cordelia smiled. 'That would be telling.'

'If you're not a member, why are you working with them?'

'Because we're both after the same thing.'

'Wrayburn didn't appear to be after the Seal.'

'No, but others are.'

'You're working for someone else in the organisation?'

Cordelia shook her head. 'I answer to no one,' she said.

'Are you planning on selling the Seal once you've found it?'

'No,' she replied.

'Then why do you want it?'

'That's no one's business but mine.'

After that she insisted he stop asking her questions about the Brotherhood of Amun-Ra and the Seal of Solomon, telling him if he didn't, he'd be eating his meals in the servants' hall with the others.

'That really would be the final insult,' said James.

Cordelia grew increasingly frustrated as the days passed, and he could tell she was beginning to wonder if the Seal was in the house after all. Personally, he didn't think it was, leading him to believe

Wrayburn was right about it being nothing more than a myth. Henry had summoned the hellhound using Lord Roxburgh's manuscript, the conjuration being powerful enough on its own. There was no need for a magical ring or amulet to aid him in the ritual. If the Seal was in his possession, he would have kept it locked away in the desk in the hidden room and they'd have found it by now.

But just when he thought Cordelia was about to give up on the whole endeavour and leave, she invited him into the study to watch the film that had been in the Paillard-Bolex cine camera. The screen had already been set up when they entered the room and the projector stood on the desk. Neither spoke as they watched the film together, Cordelia on the chair, James perched on the desk. A robed figure they both assumed to be Henry stood within the magic circle, the same circle James had discovered painted on the floor of the great hall. Cordelia paid particular attention to Henry, her eyes lighting up when she saw an amulet hanging round his neck. Although they couldn't make out the design in any detail, she was confident it was the Seal.

'There,' she cried, her spirits lifting. 'That old fool Wrayburn was wrong. It does exist.'

James wasn't so sure it was the Seal of Solomon, but then he had no idea what it was supposed to look like. He'd found references to the ring before but had never seen an illustration of it - if he had he'd paid it little attention, not realising its importance at the time. Cordelia watched the film repeatedly to see if Henry had dropped the Seal as he fled the hall, but it appeared to remain hanging round his neck right up to the moment he entered the study.

James asked her why she thought Henry had summoned the hellhound.

'How should I know?' she replied curtly, her eyes fixed on the screen.

'Maybe his guests were holding him prisoner,' he said, 'just as you are holding me prisoner now.'

Cordelia glanced at him, her eyes meeting his, but she didn't say anything. Instead, she switched off the projector and called for one of her thugs to escort him to his room in the attic.

Before one had a chance to appear James continued.

'I wonder why they were holding him,' he said. 'It couldn't have been because they were after the Seal. If they were, they'd have just taken it from him. After all, Henry wasn't a big man, and there's more than enough of them in the room to overpower him. No, there has to be another reason.'

Just as there was another reason he was being held at the house, though Cordelia didn't appear to know what this reason was any more than he did. She wouldn't have made the mistake of showing him the film if she had.

The following day she left the house taking old Lionel with her. She didn't tell him where she was going or when she'd be back. He assumed she'd gone to see Wrayburn or whoever it was in the Brotherhood she was working with. She didn't take the film with her; it was returned to a drawer of the desk in the hidden room where no one would find it.

With Cordelia gone the other men in the house now ate their meals in the dining room with James. Without Lionel to cook for them, their meals were simple stews made from God knows what. James thought it best he didn't know.

Having seen the Seal and what it was capable of, he knew he couldn't let it fall into the hands of either Cordelia or the Brotherhood. If it was in the house, he had to find it before they did. And if he did find it, what then? Would he use it on his captors just as Henry had used it on his? No, he decided, he wouldn't. That was a path he didn't want to go down for fear of where it may lead. Summoning the hound would end badly for all involved, including him. He wasn't sure how he'd managed to exorcise the creature in the first place and thought it unlikely he'd be able to do it again. No, he thought, there had to be another way.

He soon came to realise it would be easier to escape from the house without Cordelia in the house. The men weren't as well-disciplined, often leaving him alone in the study or library. There were only three, sometimes four men in the house at a time, and only two of them watched over him at one given time while the others rested. He couldn't help but wonder where the gun was. He hadn't seen any of the men with it, which led him to believe they kept it in one of the bedrooms they were sleeping in. Rooms not far from his …

If only he could get into the rooms and search them, preferably in the dead of night, he might be able to lay his hands on the weapon. However, before he had a chance to formulate a plan, one evening, instead of being locked in his room in the attic, he found himself being taken to the hidden room above the study instead. He pleaded with them to reconsider but they ignored him and continued to lock him in the room on subsequent nights, evidently fearful of the repercussions that would ensue if he escaped during Cordelia's absence.

Upon releasing him, they would always lead him up to his bathroom to wash and dress for the day. His straight razor, bottle of cologne, shower gels and shaving creams had all been removed. Only the essentials - a comb, a deodorant, a toothbrush, a small tube of toothpaste and a bar of soap - remained. He wasn't even given a belt to wear. He wondered if that was because they were worried he'd either try to hang himself or strangle one of them with it.

Sometimes when being in the room became too much for him, he began hammering on the door, pleading with them to let him out. Sometimes they would, but more often than not they left him where he was. Cooped up amongst the dust-covered, worm-ridden books, he decided to study his great-uncle's journal in the hope it would – as Wrayburn had suggested - provide him with a way out of his predicament. Apart from a spell to turn himself invisible, which he instantly dismissed as being far too ridiculous, he concluded that Henry, finding himself in the same situation, had realised summoning the hellhound was the best option available to him.

However, to summon the hound, he'd need a magic circle and triangle of conjuration but didn't have enough space, or the materials required, to draw the circle in the room anyway. As he'd washed away both Henry's and his own magic circle from the great hall and library, summoning the creature was not an option available to him. He wouldn't be able to draw another, not with the men in the house anyway.

There is only one way for you to escape your imprisonment now.

He hadn't heard the voice since he'd been confined to the room. Instinctively he glanced round but saw no one.

'Who are you?'

You know who I am.

The voice was fainter than before, more distant, though just as terrifying.

James shook his head. 'Lord Roxburgh has been dead for over

four hundred years. He was killed in the fire that destroyed the Tower of Calidon.'

A true magician is not bound by space or time. I dwell on a different plane of existence now.

James covered his ears with his hands. 'You're not real!' he cried. 'I'm imagining you!'

Open your mind to me and you too could become immortal, possess powers only dreamt of by mortal man, powers only the gods themselves possess …

Imagine it, James, imagine the possibilities …

Rising from his seat, James ran across the room and began hammering on the steel door, pleading to be let out, but no one came to release him, his cries drowning out the voice until he could no longer hear it. For what seemed like hours he continued hammering on the door, crying out until his voice became so hoarse, he could no longer speak. Eventually, he passed out in front of the door, only waking when the men came to release him from his confinement the following morning.

Once again, he pleaded with them not to return him to the room, but once again he was ignored. That day he thought about his previous night's experience. Either his ancestor really did exist on another plane of existence, or he was losing his mind - he didn't know which option was worse. He soon came to the realisation he couldn't have been imagining it all. The last chapter of the manuscript that dealt with transcendental magic had been deciphered on the pages Henry had torn out of his journal, which could only mean one thing …

His great-uncle had heard the voice too.

Hearing the voice alone would not have caused him to rip out the pages, he must have uncovered something else too. Maybe he'd discovered how Lord Roxburgh had accomplished his incredible feat, escaping death in the process. Determined to find out, he decided to complete his translation of the final part of the manuscript. Beginning that night, he moved methodically through the manuscript, turning the folios of the tome carefully so as not to damage them. Unable to focus, his nerves on edge, his progress was slow, and he often grew tired and weary, falling asleep at the desk - though he never slept for long before waking.

The following week he noticed the food he was given to eat tasted even more awful than it had before - if such a thing were possible. Even the wine smelt bad. The others didn't appear to notice. When he asked them if they thought the food tasted a little off and the wine spoiled, not one of them answered him, though he noticed a quick cursory look of concern pass between two of the men. Only later would he learn they were drugging both his food and wine with laudanum. They'd also added it to the brandy and whisky kept in decanters on a side table that he regularly drank from. At the time he didn't know of the drug or its effects and didn't realise the tincture was the reason he began sleeping considerably better than he had before.

No longer tired, he set about completing his translation of the manuscript, and after a couple of nights found he could decipher the text without having to consult Trithemius' *Polygraphia.* He worked quickly through the text, sometimes feeling as though someone had taken control of his hand and was writing the words for him. He became so consumed by the task he completely lost all track of time, only knowing it was morning when one of the men came to fetch him from the room.

When he did sleep, usually during the day, he slept deeply. Memories from his childhood came to him in his laudanum-induced dreams, offering him a brief respite from his imprisonment, memories so vivid he felt a loss upon waking, memories that made him long to return to the Manor, to a time he and his friends thought would last forever, but now seemed so fleeting, a time he'd give anything to return to again, however briefly.

But other memories came to him. Ones he did not care to remember …

Music being played by a string quartet drifted across the garden, drawing him to the Manor. A small group of guests had gathered on the main lawn to play croquet, but he couldn't tell who they were, they all had their backs to him. He made his way through the garden to the terrace lawn where his mother stood waiting for him. Hearing the music fade he realised the party was coming to an end.

Seeing him approach, his mother said, 'Where have you been? Your friends are leaving. They've been asking after you.'

James didn't recognise the faces of any of the guests, and none of them acknowledged him.

'Where are Isobel and Will?' he asked.

'I saw Isobel with her mother. I think they were heading up to bed.'

'And Will?'

'I saw him wandering down the garden. He's probably home by now.'

But Isobel hadn't gone to bed. He remembered seeing her sneak out of the house and run down the garden to meet Will.

He didn't want to remember anymore but couldn't wake himself from his deep sleep.

You must remember.

James found himself shocked to hear the voice in his dream. Through focusing his mind on deciphering the manuscript he hadn't heard him when he was awake, and never thought for one moment he'd be able to reach him whilst he slept.

'I don't want to!' he cried.

Almost as if in defiance of his words the scene faded, and he found himself in the moonlit wood. Through the trees he glimpsed Will and Isobel lying together on the banks of the stream, Isobel wrapped in Will's jacket as he held her close, the sight of them together filling him with anger and rage. At the time he'd vowed revenge on them and had headed back to the house to tell Isobel's father he'd seen them together. Finding he'd retired for the evening, he decided to wait until the following morning before speaking to him, and he did, ensuring they would never be together again.

He'd regretted his actions ever since that day, his combined feelings of guilt and betrayal driving a wedge between him and Will that effectively brought an end to their friendship.

She should have been yours. You *should have been the one that confronted them …* You *should have been the one to punish them …*

'I did.'

You should have done it yourself, not let someone else do it for you. They betrayed you!

James knew he had to get him out of his head for fear of what else he might discover, vowing to remain awake for as long as possible, only sleeping in short bursts to avoid falling into a deep sleep to prevent his ancestor from gaining possession of his thoughts. But the laudanum he was being given prevented that and further dreams followed, though this time they were not from his childhood. What followed seemed to consist of seemingly unconnected memories with no chronology or order, excerpts and fragments from a life, incomplete and disjointed.

In one a young boy being held in his mother's arms was wrenched from her grip. The woman pleaded to be given her boy back but was ignored and dragged from the room, her cries resounding in his head long after she could no longer be heard. James found himself consumed by an overwhelming sense of loss as he witnessed the child calling for his mother, an awful, piteous scene he knew would take him a long time to forget.

It didn't take him long to figure out whose life he was witnessing. Most of the memories seemed to be from his time as March Warden, the setting a barren windswept land, bleak and desolate, with dull grey skies, the veiled horizons shrouded in mist. The memories revealed his ancestor to be a ruthless, vindictive man feared by all who encountered him as he mercilessly hunted down his victims.

Scenes of the witch trials at North Berwick followed, scenes Patrick Roxburgh seemed to have witnessed personally. He watched as the suspects knelt before their king, their heads shaved, begging for their lives as they were sentenced to death. He was amongst the crowd watching them being led up a scaffolding. James recognised the spot - they were at the top of Castlehill. Edinburgh Castle loomed in the distance behind them. Hideous scenes of the prisoners being strangled before being burnt at the stake followed, scenes all the more horrible because they were not nightmares or the imaginings of a horror writer but had actually happened.

Further trials followed, but this time it was Lord Roxburgh who the accused were brought before to be interrogated. Amongst the poor unfortunate souls who appeared before him was a face he recognised, a face older and more haggard than he remembered - it was the face of his mother. Even though he recognised her he showed her no mercy, sentencing her to death alongside the others.

'You could have saved her!' cried James.

She was beyond redemption. She had conspired with the Devil to bring about man's downfall, opening the gateway to sin, just as Eve did when she desecrated the tree of knowledge!

'She was your mother!'

She was a witch!

James woke up terrified, his body soaked in sweat, convinced, after witnessing the unutterable horror of his actions, more than ever of the awfulness of this man who'd caused immense suffering to all who'd encountered him, a horrific cruel man from a horrific cruel time. A man who now had an army of followers stretching across Britain and Europe, their anger, hatred, bigotry and prejudice keeping him alive after all these years.

The thought of the havoc he and his devotees could wreak terrified him.

*

Over the days that followed, he became increasingly nauseous and started vomiting, a side effect of the laudanum, and it didn't take him long to realise he was being drugged. He refused to eat the food he was given and only drank water from the tap in his bathroom, believing it better to starve than experience any more of Lord Roxburgh's memories. As a result, his health soon deteriorated, and it wasn't long before he overheard two of the men discussing his condition. Two days later a man they referred to as a doctor appeared, though whether he really was a doctor remained to be seen.

He saw James in the drawing room where he'd been laid out on the sofa, his greatcoat covering him to keep him warm. To his despair, he saw he was wearing the same signet ring on his left hand as the other men were. He examined him professionally, leading him to believe he really was a doctor, and gave him some pills - tranquilisers - to make him feel better, telling the men he needed rest - proper rest.

When the doctor had gone, one of the men said, 'Return him to the room.'

James, who was still lying on the sofa, could hear their voices but could not tell who was speaking.

'You heard what the doctor said. He needs rest. He can't rest in there.'

'You want to stay awake all night to keep watch over him?'

'He's not going anywhere.'

'Do you really want to take that chance?'

'All right. But we'd better keep an eye on him.'

They left him resting on the sofa until evening, then took him up to the room.

Once there James tried to focus his mind on deciphering the manuscript, eager to finish the text, but the symbols on the page blurred and his eyes lost focus.

You may be close to finishing my manuscript, but you are no closer to understanding it than you were when you began.

'I'm not looking to understand it. I'm looking for answers. I want to know why I'm being held prisoner in my own home. I want to know what the Brotherhood really wants with me.'

If you'd studied the manuscript, you'd have escaped your imprisonment by now.

'I have studied it. All I found were rituals to summon the dead, turn myself invisible, and imbue talismans and amulets with magical powers - none of which is much use to me in here.'

Had you studied it properly you'd have learnt how to harness the power of the elemental spheres in the celestial world through their corresponding element in the material world. For that, you don't need a magic circle, and neither talismans nor amulets are required. Simply focus on the element you wish to control, then picture it in your mind and draw its influence from the heavens.

'How?'

By speaking aloud the incantation that references the divine names of God and invoked the elemental ethers that live in the four elements - as described by Paracelsus - the Nymphæ in the element of water, the Sylphes in that of the air, the Pigmies in the earth, and the Salamanders in fire.

Turning the pages of Henry's journal, James found the incantation in the section that dealt with elemental magic. However absurd the idea seemed he knew he had to give it a try - he had no other option. If he could learn how to manipulate fire, he might be able to use it to defeat his captors. Although he only had the flickering candles set in the candelabra on the table in front of him to focus his mind on, it was a start.

He focused his mind on the flame and began reading from the journal.

'Per Adonaï Eloïm,' he began, 'Adonaï Jehova, Adonai Sabaoth, Metraton On Agla Adonaï Mathon, mysterium salamandrae, veni, veni, veni …'

But try as he might, he couldn't control the flames. He couldn't even make them flare up.

Despondent, he came to the conclusion that rather than by any inherent powers he may have possessed, his banishment of the hellhound had either been a fluke or had been achieved through the power of the magic circle or the words written within it.

You fail because you don't believe. You feel foolish even attempting such things.

'I fail because there are no elemental spheres to draw power from - they don't exist. The Earth doesn't lay at the centre of the universe. The Sun, the Moon and the planets do not orbit our planet. There is no spiritus mundi flowing through the universe; no heavenly spheres presided over by God and his angels -'

Agrippa wrote that it is in the power of the mind itself that magical works are done. Unlock your mind, James. Do not be afraid. There is nothing for you to fear. Although bound to earth by their physical bodies, through the purification of the soul, a man adept in magic - a magus - can shed his body and ascend through the spheres of the universe to the heavens.

'That is not possible.'

Look to the heavens, James. Ascend with me through the celestial spheres and I'll show you regions only dreamt of by mortal men.

'I'm not going anywhere with you …'

Only then did he realise he was no longer sitting in his chair, but floating above the desk, drifting towards the ceiling, or rather where the ceiling had once been, rising into the night until moments later he saw he was above the house. A gentle breeze stirred the trees, but he could feel neither the wind nor the cold night air upon him. His thoughts clearing, he realised he'd separated from his physical body and now existed as a disembodied presence, his spirit rising into the night. He became aware of something, he wasn't sure what, connecting his body, through which he could return, though how he did not know, and at present, he did not want to, keen to see what lay ahead of him, the night growing darker the higher he climbed.

That which is above is like that which is below, and that which is below is like that which is above. All that exists in the universe originated from the One. The Sun is its father, the Moon its mother. The Wind has borne it in her belly. The Earth has nourished it …

Moving beyond the clouds, James entered the stratosphere and soon found himself leaving the earth's atmosphere. He could not see his guide ahead of him - but didn't expect to, not yet anyway. Only when he entered the vacuum of space was he able to relax. Turning his head, he glanced back towards the Earth to find it shrouded in darkness. Only a very slender crescent remained illuminated, the blue oceans patterned with spiralling white clouds. As he drew further away, he glimpsed the Sun behind his home planet, before turning and looking ahead.

And from the Earth it ascends to the heavens, receiving the strength of things above and of things below, uniting the upper and lower realms.

James began wondering where his destination lay - how far into this universe he was being taken. In the distance to his right, he saw the Moon, its grey pockmarked surface instantly recognisable. Only when he drew closer did he see a transparent crystal sphere beyond the Moon, slowly turning and rotating the satellite round the Earth.

See, everything that exists in the material world is ruled by the celestial world, the spheres turned by the Hand of God.

He could just make out an almost imperceptible shadowy figure ahead of him. Its appearance was so slight he couldn't make it out in any detail and it remained always out of reach as he journeyed on. He passed into the sphere of Mercury and glimpsed the ivory planet Venus ahead of him, driven on by its sphere, a journey that should have taken months to make passing in moments. He felt as though he was travelling through a colossal armillary sphere. The Sun, the Moon and the planets all appeared to be of an equal distance apart, which he knew wasn't the case. In reality, they lay millions of miles apart - but then what he was seeing wasn't real.

And just as you must learn to control the elements in the natural world, so too must you learn to master and manipulate the energies in the celestial realms.

Only then will you become a true adept ...

James saw he was now approaching the red planet Mars and realised he could no longer see the figure ahead of him. He thought he'd gone, vanished, until he heard him speak again.

The Renaissance magi sung hymns to the planets, the strings of their lyres resonating with the music of the spheres. Listen, James. Listen to the music of the spheres.

He listened. Although the sound was faint at first, soon the celestial symphony began filling his ears as he passed from one sphere to the next, the light becoming brighter the higher they climbed.

He could see the appeal viewing the cosmos in this way held for his ancestors. In a changing world where their beliefs were being challenged, they sought comfort in the thought of an ordered universe made up of a series of vast crystal heavens full of meaning and significance, created by a sublime being far beyond imagination.

'But this realm does not exist. This is not how the universe really is. It's nothing more than a fantasy - a dream - none of this is real. How can I master a world that does not exist?'

But it does exist. I am proof of that. Hermes Trismegistus taught that unless you make yourself equal to God, you cannot understand Him. Only when you believe nothing is impossible, when you can know all, understand all - art, science and the nature of all things - will you be able to soar from the lowest depths up to the highest peaks. Breathe in the air, feel the heat of the sun, emerge yourself in water. Be everywhere at once, on the land, at sea, in the sky.

Imagine yourself before you existed, then as a child, growing stronger, exploring the world, becoming an adult, growing old until you are lying on your deathbed. Imagine that you are immortal and have existed since the beginning of time. Only then will you understand God and only then can you become equal to Him.

Jupiter and Saturn followed and then came the eighth sphere of fixed stars. Only when he began approaching the ninth sphere, the Primum Mobile, the abode of angels, did he realise he was alone now. Lord Roxburgh had gone.

Beyond lay the Empyrean, the dwelling place of God.

But where had he gone? And why was he being taken on this journey? He realised then he had to go back. Go back before it was too late …

Gripped by the fear that if he entered the final sphere he would not be able to return, he attempted to stop his flight but found himself being pulled onwards, drawn across an immense gulf of space by the music of the spheres. It was only when he drew nearer to the outer sphere that he realised the music was an echo of the voices of the seraphim, a heavenly choir of angels, and only then did he realise he could not, for the moment at least, stop his accent towards them.

But then why stop? Why not just accept his fate and keep going? In the past, the thought of an easeful death - to cease upon the midnight with no pain - had appealed to him. So why now when it was within his grasp did he hesitate? Was it because he was not ready to leave his life on earth, his friends and family? Or was it because he knew it would not be that simple – he knew he would not be able to cross this vast gulf of space that separated the fixed stars from the Primum Mobile.

Not yet anyway.

So why had he been brought there?

This question was answered when suddenly and seeming out of

nowhere, a long skeletal figure with sinewed arms and legs appeared before him. It had horns on its head and expansive bat-like wings, its presence terrifying him in this remote region of space, bringing him to a sudden stop.

He could go no further.

The demon then advanced upon him, and James, remembering the invisible force connecting him to his body, closed his eyes, relaxed and attempted to wake himself up. Unable to focus his mind - he could hear the demon approaching - he blocked out the sound and began listening to the music of the angels instead that echoed through the cosmos.

Moments later he felt himself falling back into the void of space, and woke with a sudden jerk, his heart beating rapidly, his body soaked in sweat.

Rising suddenly from his seat, he ran across the room and began hammering on the door to be let out, never expecting for one moment he would be answered. To his great surprise, he heard the key being inserted into the lock. This was his chance to escape, to flee the house once and for all. Returning to the desk, he grabbed the candelabra and quickly extinguished the flames before positioning himself beside the door so he wouldn't be seen when it opened.

Moments later the door swung open and he heard someone speak to him from outside the room.

'What is it?' asked one of the men, their voice groggy. Clearly, he'd just woken from a deep sleep. 'What do you want?'

The man stepped forward, his eyes struggling to penetrate the gloom. James saw he was the man with the shaven-head and found himself glad it was him. Out of all the men holding him in the house, he was the one he despised the most. Seizing his chance, he struck him from behind with all his strength, sending the candelabra crashing down on the back of his head. The shaven-headed man fell to the floor and James continued to strike him repeatedly to make sure he was unconscious, only stopping when he saw a pool of blood forming on the floor.

His eyes wide with fury, his whole body trembling, he ran from the room, closing the door behind him, swinging the bookcase back against the wall, before heading along the gallery and climbing down the wooden steps. Only then did he realise he hadn't taken the man's keys, though he soon discovered the fool hadn't locked the door leading from the library to the great hall, which meant he could get out. He had no idea where his car keys were, but that didn't matter, he'd be safer on foot.

According to the grandfather clock, it was only a few minutes after four, which gave him plenty of time to reach Selkirk before morning. It wouldn't begin to get light until well after six at that time of year - the sun didn't rise until half-past seven. Hopefully, the unconscious body of the shaven-headed man wouldn't be found until morning. It was unlikely he'd wake before then - if he ever woke at all.

The blood pulsing through his veins, James tore through the house, determined to attack anyone who stood in his way, ready to fight them to the death if necessary. He would be their prisoner no more. He made his way through the servants' quarters and came to the door leading to the courtyard. Finding it locked, he forced open the shutters covering a window. They were old, the wood rotten, and it didn't take much effort to prise them open. Through the window, he saw the sky was overcast - perfect conditions for him to make his escape. Once outside he ran across the courtyard and followed the track down to the wood, wrapping his overcoat tightly round him as he went.

He decided his best course of action was to use the river to guide his way to Selkirk, rather than follow the valley road. Once there he'd head straight to the police station - there had to be one there. Only then did he realise he didn't know what day it was. If it was Sunday it was bound to be shut. It would probably be shut if it was Saturday too. Even if it was closed, he could still call the police. He didn't have his phone but that didn't matter - there had to be a telephone box in the town. As well as the police, he'd call his father too - he could reverse the charges. He'd call Hodgson but didn't know his number. He didn't know any telephone numbers, the Manor's being the only one he knew from memory. But that didn't matter, his father would help him, he'd know what to do. But what if he wasn't home? What would he do then? He wondered if the police would believe his story considering the state he was in. He thought it unlikely.

Passing the stable block, he reached the end of the track and pausing momentarily he half leant against a tree to catch his breath. Although he felt faint and exhausted, he remained determined to continue. He'd make it. He had to.

Slowly he became aware Lord Roxburgh was still with him.

James, you have come far, but there is still a long way for you to go.

'But I don't want to go any further. I've seen what lies ahead. What was that creature you left me to face alone?'

That creature, as you call him, was the demon Choronzon, the Dweller in the Abyss.

'The Abyss?'

The ultimate test for the Adept. Only by crossing the Abyss will you attain true enlightenment.

'You expect me to defeat a demon?'

Only by submitting Choronzon to their will can the Adept proceed.

'And if they fail, what happens then?'

They become enslaved to him for all eternity.

'Is that the fate you hoped I'd suffer?'

No, that is the fate I want to help you avoid. Only by joining me can you hope to defeat Chronozon and reach true enlightenment.

'Even with your help, I wouldn't face such a creature.'

You cannot escape your destiny, James.

'I wouldn't be so sure about that,' he replied, his ancestor's words spurring him on.

An early morning mist hung thick and heavy in the air, rising from the banks of the river, nestling in the clefts of the hillside, settling amongst the hedgerows and gorse bushes. James emerged from the wood. Soon he'd reach Selkirk, leaving Wychwood House, the Witches' Wood and Lord Roxburgh far behind him …

He'd almost reached the banks of the river when he heard an almighty shriek echo throughout the valley. Turning suddenly, he caught sight of what looked like a large bird of prey emerging from the wood. Seeing it beat its wings before soaring towards him, he stumbled but stayed on his feet and hurried on to the riverbank.

Feeling the hairs rise on the back of his neck, he realised the creature was gaining on him and he decided to plunge himself into the river to escape the creature in the hope the fast-flowing current would carry him downstream to safety. But before he could even reach the bank the creature was upon him, clipping him with its talons, knocking him forward onto the ground.

His vision blurred, he glanced ahead and saw the bird had barred his way. When his eyes regained focus he saw it wasn't a bird. Although it had the head and wings of an eagle it had the body and back legs of a lion. Hardly able to believe what he was seeing he tried to stand only to find the whole landscape spinning round him.

He staggered to the ground, his eyes closing as he fell into unconsciousness.

*

He didn't fully regain consciousness that night, only becoming vaguely aware he was back in the house and lying in a bed. How he came to be there he didn't know but assumed his captors must have discovered him the following morning. Over the days that followed, he became consumed by a fever.

When the fever finally broke, he woke to find Hodgson sitting at the side of his bed. Unsure whether his eyes were deceiving him, he asked if it was really him.

His old friend nodded and offered him a glass of water. 'Here,' he said, 'drink this.'

James held the glass to his parched lips and sipped the water.

'When did you get back?'

'A few days ago now.'

'I've been like this for a few days?'

'For even longer than that, I'm afraid.'

'But where are the men?' asked James. 'Are they still here?'

Craning his neck, he glanced past Hodgson to the door. The man with the scar and the shaven-headed man loomed in the doorway.

'They've explained everything to me,' said Hodgson. 'Everything is going to be all right from now on.'

James stared disbelieving at Hodgson and shook his head. 'No!' he cried, 'everything is not going to be all right!'

He tried to get up, but Hodgson held him down.

'Help me with him,' he said, glancing over his shoulder to the men standing in the doorway.

They hurried into the room and helped him restrain James as he pleaded with them to let him go, his cries echoing throughout the house.

Glancing towards the door, James saw the doctor step into the room, a syringe and needle in his hand.

'No!' he cried. 'Not again! I beg of you!'

CHAPTER TWENTY-TWO

Will woke to find himself lying in a bed. His body felt dry and warm, and he could feel cotton sheets underneath him. Gradually, vague memories came to him, and he remembered Isobel and James being cut off as they left Wychwood House; the creature swooping down on them from the trees, its talons outstretched; the car plunging down the embankment …

He sat up suddenly and looked about him, eager to know where he was, his body aching as he moved, his head throbbing. Reaching up to his forehead, he felt a plaster now covered his wound. Seeing the thick curtains hanging at the windows let in very little light, he reached over to the bedside table and switched on a lamp, the light revealing an expensively furnished room, leading him to assume he was in James's apartment in Edinburgh. The faint muffled sound of traffic came up from the city streets below. Confused, he wondered how he'd come to be there. Where were the others, and, more importantly, what had happened to Isobel and James?

The door opened and Hodgson stepped into the room. He asked Will how he was feeling before closing the door gently behind him.

'How did I get here?' he asked, ignoring the question.

'I found you lying unconscious at the top of the embankment when I returned with the ambulance.'

'How are the others?'

Hodgson pulled a chair up to the side of the bed. 'They're fine, sir,' he said. 'They're here in the apartment. Miss Jemima is asleep in one of the guest bedrooms, and Miriam and Alexander are downstairs.' Sitting down, he filled a glass with water from a jug on the bedside table and offered it to Will. 'Please, have something to drink.'

Will took the glass. 'And Isobel and James?'

'The ambulance took them to the hospital.'

'Which hospital?'

'The Borders General Hospital in Melrose.'

'I don't understand,' said Will. 'The men at the house tried to stop James from leaving.'

'They were just acting under orders.'

Will stared into Hodgson's grey eyes. 'Whose orders?'

'Mr Roxburgh's orders.' Hodgson dropped his gaze, took the empty glass from Will and placed it back on the bedside table. 'As you know only too well, he's been worried about James for a long time now. He employed those men to keep a close eye on him.'

'To keep an eye on him?' said Will incredulously.

The thought that they could have been hired by James's father had briefly crossed his mind while they were at the house - a thought he'd quickly dismissed. Robert would have told him he'd employed men to keep an eye on his son. Even if he hadn't told him, worried he would mention it to James, it didn't explain the man Jemima had encountered in the corridor, or what happened when they tried to leave.

'One of them pulled a knife on me.'

'I'm afraid they have been a bit heavy-handed in their approach,' said Hodgson calmly. 'I have raised my concerns about their suitability in the past, but Mr Roxburgh feels they are necessary. I'm afraid Master James has become quite delusional recently.'

'Has he really?' said Will suspiciously. 'Or is Master James being driven to thinking he's having psychotic delusions by the men holding him prisoner at Wychwood House?' Seeing Hodgson look at him sceptically, he continued. 'I saw one of those delusions for myself when I was driving down to the village.'

'What was it you saw?'

'I don't know.' Seeing Hodgson look at him sceptically, Will continued. 'It looked like a large bird of prey - a golden eagle - though we were meant to think it was something else, just as I'm sure James was.'

'Something else?'

'A griffin. They'd even gone so far as to remove the statues from the gates. It worked too. If we'd thought it was just an eagle, we wouldn't have ended up in the ditch.'

'How did you end up in the ditch?'

'We were knocked into it.'

'By a bird of prey?' asked Hodgson. 'That doesn't sound very likely.'

No, thought Will, it didn't. So, what had hit them?

'I'm guessing they played the same trick on James when he tried to escape.'

'I wasn't aware Master James ever attempted such a thing.'

'Well, he did,' said Will. 'And they brought him back. It must have happened before you returned.' He rubbed his temples, his head still throbbing.

'Let me give you something for your head,' said Hodgson. Reaching into the pocket of his jacket, he pulled out an unlabelled bottle of pills. He refilled the empty glass from the jug. 'Now, you need to rest, you have a nasty cut on your head.' Unscrewing the bottle, he tipped two pills into the palm of his hand and offered them to Will with the glass of water. 'You'll feel better in the morning. Here take these, they'll help you sleep.'

Will refused them. 'No, I don't want to sleep,' he said impatiently. 'I need to get to the hospital.'

'You're in no fit state to go anywhere.'

Will studied Hodgson's face. 'Isobel and James aren't at the hospital …'

'Of course they are. Where else would they be? I'll take you to see them in the morning if you like.'

'No,' said Will, 'it'll be too late in the morning.' After a pause, he added, 'I want to talk to James's father. If you're telling the truth he'll confirm it.'

'You can ask him in person. When I told him what happened, he jumped on the first available train. He should be here in a few hours.'

'Well, I don't have a few hours to wait. I'll call him now.'

'As you wish, sir. You can call him on my phone.'

'That's okay, I'll use mine.'

'I'm afraid yours was lost in the ditch.'

'How convenient.'

'Here, let me bring up the number for you.'

Hodgson handed him his phone and Will called the number. There was no reply.

'You'll just have to try him again later,' said Hodgson, retrieving the phone from Will.

'I don't believe for one minute the men holding James are employed by his father.'

'Why else would they be there?'

'I haven't worked that out yet, but I'm sure I will once I get back to Wychwood House.'

'Why would you want to go back to Wychwood House? Miss Isobel and Master James are at the hospital.'

'I'd call them to confirm that, but I doubt either would answer.'

'Please, I insist, sir. Take the pills.'

'Stop calling me sir! Who are they really? And why aren't you telling me the truth? Who are you trying to protect, us or them?' After a pause, he said, 'Of course … your sister. That car crash she had was no accident. What happened? Did you notice the men watching the house and confront one of them, only to be told there'd be consequences if you tried to interfere? Naturally, you didn't believe them, and tried to find out who they were and what they wanted with James, only to learn your sister had been involved in an accident.'

'My sister's car crash was just an accident, nothing more. No one's life's been threatened.'

'Mine was.' Will glanced at the pills Hodgson still held in the palm of his hand. 'Are those even headache pills?'

'Of course.'

'Then you take them. How can you just sit there and not do anything? How could you let this happen? You're betraying both Isobel and James by letting those men hold them at Wychwood House. For God's sake, man, their lives are in danger!'

Hodgson sighed. 'No harm will come to Isobel if we don't interfere.'

'What about James?'

'Neither you nor I, or anyone else for that matter, can save him now. His fate is in his own hands.'

'Why, what are they going to do to him?'

'I don't know, and I don't want to know - and neither do you. All I can tell you is this … If you return to Wychwood House, you will surely die.'

Slowly and with extreme care, the bedroom door was pushed open, and Alexander crept quietly into the room.

Seeing him edge towards Hodgson, Will swung his legs over the bed and said, 'I have to go back. I have to save them.'

Hodgson leapt up suddenly, grabbed Will's face and tried to force the pills down his throat. 'I'm sorry, Will,' he said, 'I can't let you do that.'

Alexander picked an empty vase off a chest of drawers and brought it crashing down over Hodgson's head. He slumped to the floor, the vase shattering into pieces about him.

'Sorry, eavesdropping again,' said Alexander, casually brushing debris from the vase off his trousers. 'Terrible habit of mine.'

Will removed the pills from his mouth, placing them on the bedside table. 'Was that really necessary?'

'Under the circumstances, I thought it the best thing to do.'

When Will stood up he realised he was only wearing his black trunks. 'Where are my clothes?' he asked.

'In the wash.'

He crossed to the fitted wardrobe and pulled open the doors. Hanging on a rail were trousers and shirts. 'Is everyone all right?' he asked, pulling on a pair of dark chinos.

'A few cuts and bruises, but we'll live.'

He slipped on one of James's bespoke Turnbull & Asser shirts. Although a little tight on him, it still fit. He gestured to Hodgson lying on the floor and said, 'Help me lift him off the floor.'

Alexander lifted Hodgson's legs and together they laid him down on the bed.

'I always did have my suspicions about him,' said Alexander. 'He always seemed too good to be true - good staff being so hard to find these days.'

'What time is it?'

'Almost ten. You've been asleep for hours.'

'What the hell was that thing that attacked us?'

'It was just an eagle,' said Alexander.

'It was too big to be an eagle.'

'You may have thought that, but I doubt it really was. By removing the statues from the gates, you were led to believe they'd come alive. The power of suggestion is a powerful thing.'

Will had to agree, it was the only plausible explanation after all.

'How did we get here?' he asked.

'It's all a bit of a blur, I'm afraid. When I came to Hodgson was trying to lift me out of the car. You'd been knocked for six and were laid out in the Land Rover.'

'Where's my car now?'

'Still in the ditch.'

'Then I'll take the Land Rover.'

Crossing to the window, pulling back the curtains, he peered down at the street below and noticed it had become a little foggy. Orange street lamps reflected off the wet pavement and cars that lined the street, his attention drawn to the Land Rover parked outside the townhouse. He had expected to see someone keeping guard over the apartment, but there didn't appear to be anyone out there.

Alexander produced a bundle of letters from his jacket pocket. 'I found these,' he said. 'Most of them are addressed to you. Looks like they've been intercepting his post ever since he moved to Wychwood House.'

'At least now we have some proof,' said Will. 'Call the police. Have them meet me in the village.'

Alexander nodded. 'Will, I'm afraid I've been a bit of an arse this weekend,' he said, teetering on his heels. 'I shouldn't have spoken to you the way I did. I should have shown you more respect …' He hesitated before proceeding. 'You are, and always will be, a *primus inter pares* - a first among equals.'

Not knowing what to say, Will patted Alexander on the shoulder. 'Stay here,' he said, after a pause. 'Don't leave the apartment.'

When he stepped out into the hall, he saw the door to the guest bedroom was ajar. Jemima lay asleep on the bed, curled up in the sheets. He found Miriam in the family room, sitting on a sofa flicking through the channels on the television. On the table in front of her were some bottles of red wine and a pizza box.

Seeing him appear, Miriam rose to her feet. 'There's some pizza left if you want some,' she said, glancing nervously up at him as he entered the room.

'Are you all right?' he asked her.

'Of course I am,' she snapped. 'Why wouldn't I be?'

'We've just been involved in an accident, Miriam.'

'Oh, yes,' she said, growing increasingly flustered. 'Of course, how silly of me … I'm fine … Thank you for asking.'

Although he wasn't hungry, Will thought it a good idea to eat something, so flipped open the pizza box and lifted out a slice. Leaving the family room, he began searching the apartment for the keys, eventually finding them on the console table by the front door.

Seeing him pocket the keys, Miriam asked him where he was going.

'Back to Wychwood House, of course.' Kneeling down, he picked up his boots and slipped them on his feet.

'William, wait …'

Will glanced up at her. 'I don't have time now, Miriam.' He noticed she was chewing her nails and glancing nervously down the hall to the staircase.

'Do you think he knows?'

Will frowned and said, 'Does who know what?'

'You know perfectly well who,' said Miriam curtly. 'Does Alexander know how I feel about him?'

Will straightened up. 'I really have to go …'

Miriam placed her hand on his arm. 'Please, Will.'

Only when he saw the concern in her eyes did the awfulness of what he'd done dawn on him. He shouldn't have told Alexander she had feelings for him.

Not knowing what to say, he offered the usual vacuous and lazy platitudes. 'Talk to him,' he said. 'Be honest with him … Tell him how you feel … I think you'll be surprised how he'll react.'

Miriam looked doubtful. 'You think so?'

Will nodded reassuringly, though deep down knew Alexander's reaction wouldn't be the one she sought. 'After I've gone,' he said, 'lock the door, and don't let anyone in until you've heard from me.'

Miriam nodded in agreement.

Will passed through the entrance hall, crossing the mosaic floor, and dressed in just a shirt and chinos, stepped out into the night. The gathering fog crept across the pavement from Moray Place Gardens, swirling in between the cars. Unable to shake the feeling he was being watched, he hurried down the short flight of stone steps to the Land Rover. After unlocking the vehicle, he climbed into the driver's seat, closing the door as quietly as possible so as not to draw attention to himself. Any hopes he had of slipping away discreetly were dashed when he turned the key in the ignition.

The engine choked and spluttered, making a noise loud enough to wake the dead.

Leaving the townhouse behind him, he drove down the street, glancing in the rear-view mirror now and again to check he wasn't being followed. But then it was unlikely he would be - they knew where he was headed.

Unsure which way to go, he turned left onto Darnaway Street, then made his way along Heriot Row, reading the names of the roads as he went. After passing Queen's Street Gardens, he came to the main road, the fog growing denser as he made his way through the city, making it difficult to read the road signs. He heard distant, muffled voices, and saw vague outlines of people as they headed to pubs and restaurants, as though it were just another Sunday evening.

Eventually, he reached Princess Street and drove through Edinburgh's New Town, its shops veiled by the mist. From there he followed the signs out of the city.

*

Miriam, her mind swimming, returned to the family room, the smell of the pizzas making her feel nauseous. Sipping from a glass of wine, she went over in her head the conversation she'd had with Will.

Maybe he was right, maybe it was time she told Alexander how she felt.

No, she told herself, you've just been involved in an accident. Your emotions are running high. Now is not the time to be impulsive. At least wait until you are back in London. After all, they still had to travel back home together. If she told him how she felt, and he didn't reciprocate, it would make their journey even more excruciating than it was already going to be. If only she knew how he felt about her before taking the plunge. If only he'd stop acting like a cad all the time and be honest with her. If only …

Why, oh why couldn't she have fallen for Will, or someone like him, someone honest and hardworking? But no, she had to fall in love with an oaf like Alexander.

At the same moment, these thoughts were running through her head, the man himself stepped into the room. Miriam felt herself tense up at the sight of him. After closing the door gently behind him, he sidled over to the sofa and sat himself down next to her.

After an awkward pause, he asked her how she was.

'I'm fine, thank you,' she assured him, shifting herself away from him slightly.

He took his hand in hers. 'You know, Miriam,' he said. 'When Will's car rolled down that embankment, my whole life flashed before my eyes.'

Miriam extracted her hand from his. 'How awful for you.'

'I realised afterwards I had but one regret.'

'Only one? Just off the top of my head, I can think of at least a dozen.'

'Will you please stop interrupting me? Don't you want to know what my one regret was?'

Miriam shifted herself further away from him. 'I think I can guess,' she said.

'It's that I never kissed you.'

Miriam sighed despondently. 'Is that really the best you can come up with?'

She looked him straight in the eye, waiting expectantly for him to say something else, hoping he would realise it was not the time for him to delve into his extensive repertoire of pick-up lines.

'When the car spun out of control,' he said, 'you reached for me. I felt your hand on my shoulder and I placed my hand on yours. Our first instinct was to seek each other out. At that moment I knew you cared for me, and I realised I cared for you.' Their eyes met and he continued. 'There's no point denying our feelings anymore.'

No, she thought, there wasn't. He pulled her close and she let herself be taken, falling back in his arms. He held her tight as he leant in to kiss her, their lips meeting momentarily before the door to the room swung open. They both sat bolt upright before glancing across the room to find Jemima standing in the doorway.

She glared furiously at them. 'Couldn't you have waited until you were back in London, and I was out of the picture?'

Both Miriam and Alexander muttered apologies under their breaths. Jemima grabbed the door handle, slamming it shut as she left the room. With their heads hanging in shame, they both sat awkwardly on the sofa together, neither saying a word until finally, Alexander rose to his feet.

'She's right, of course,' he said.

'She is,' agreed Miriam.

'We should wait until we are back in London before we … you know …'

'No, I don't know. Please go on.'

'Quite.' Alexander cleared his throat. 'Well,' he said, moving awkwardly towards the door. 'I have some phone calls to make.' He reached for the door's handles. 'Cuiusvis hominis est errare …' he began muttering under his breath.

'What did you say?'

'Any man can make a mistake, but only a fool keeps making the same one.'

After pulling open the door, he promptly left the room leaving Miriam sitting alone on the sofa. When he was gone, she internally reprimanded herself for letting him kiss her. All his talk of caring for her was nothing more than a line - and one she'd fallen for. He felt nothing for her, just as he felt nothing for all the women he pursued. Oh well, she told herself as she reached for her glass of wine on the table, she'd know better next time.

Next time! There wouldn't be a next time - she would make certain of that! After drinking down her wine, she proceeded to pour herself out another, fuller glass.

*

When Isobel regained consciousness, she opened her eyes to find herself surrounded by darkness. She was lying on her back on top of the padded eiderdown, not underneath it, her arms at her side, positioned in the middle of Emily's four-poster bed. Although dark, she could see the curtains had been drawn round the bed. She wondered how long she'd been out. Rubbing her aching jaw, she pulled back the curtains, reached across to the lamp on the bedside table, and pressed the switch. When the light didn't come on, she threw her legs over the edge of the bed.

Only when she stood up did she register that she was wearing the silk satin sheath dress she'd worn on the night of the party. On closer inspection, she found she had a chemise on underneath the dress and there were silk stockings on her legs. Even her pendant had been removed. The horrible thought struck her that someone had undressed her. She hoped it was the dark-haired woman and not the man in the Italian shoes. She shuddered at the thought of him undressing her.

Her eyes having adjusted to the darkness, she glanced round for her clothes, eager to change out of the dress, but couldn't see them anywhere. All she really needed was a coat and boots. Without them, she wouldn't get far. Maybe that was the point ...

Crossing the room, she made her way over to the bay window and pulled back the curtains. The windows had been shuttered but she could see thin strips of sunlight peeping in through the wooden slats. It was daytime - which meant she'd been asleep all night. Her thoughts immediately turned to Will and the others. They couldn't have made it to the village, or the police would be there. So, what had happened to them? Had they been brought back to the house? Were they being held prisoner in their rooms as she was?

She opened the shutters, filling the room with light, to find the house shrouded by a fog so thick she couldn't even see the terrace below. Turning to explore the room for her clothes, she noticed a thick layer of dust now covered the perfume bottles, jewellery and trinket boxes that stood on the dressing table. A sickly sentimental Victorian lithograph of two children cosying up to one another hung on the wall in place of the painting of Lady Roxburgh.

'I think I preferred the portrait,' she said.

Flinging open the wardrobe, she found Emily's gowns and dresses hanging on the rail, but her clothes were nowhere to be found. At the bottom of the wardrobe, she noticed a pair of T-strap evening shoes. She needed boots, not dancing shoes, but as they were better than nothing, she slipped them on her feet. Passing the carriage clock on the mantelpiece, she saw, to her dismay, it had stopped working. Like her clothes, her phone was nowhere to be found. She would have to wait until she was downstairs to learn the time, though she had a strong suspicion she'd find the door locked, confining her to the room until someone came to let her out.

She tried the door just to make sure it was locked, only to find, to her great surprise, it opened. Cautiously, she peered out into the corridor, expecting to find someone standing guard outside her door, but there was no one there. She glanced both ways down the corridor but couldn't see anything in the darkness. All the other doors were closed. Feeling her way along the corridor, treading carefully to avoid stepping on any loose floorboards, she headed to James's bedroom. His door was also unlocked, but when she looked inside the room, she found it empty. Closing the door, she vowed she wouldn't leave until she'd found him, and he was safely away from Wychwood House.

Retracing her steps, she made her way back down the corridor, passing the door to Emily's bedroom as she went. When she reached the gallery, she heard music drifting up through the house from downstairs. Someone was in the drawing room listening to records on the gramophone. She instantly recognised the song being played; it was the one Will had put on for them to dance to. Hearing the staircase creak and groan underneath her feet as she made her way downstairs, she glanced down and saw the stairs were warped. Several spindles had become dislodged from the banister and were now hanging loose.

The drawing room door was open casting a faint light into the great hall. Dust and rubble covered the hall's floor, and she noticed a sofa that hadn't been there before. Confused, she wondered what had been going on. Where had all the dust and rubble come from? Stepping off the staircase, she half-tiptoed across the great hall, her heart quickening as she edged closer to the drawing room.

Before reaching the doorway, she heard a young woman with a Scottish accent say, 'Turn that off, will you?'

Another girl with the same accent said, 'What's wrong with it?'

Isobel, stopping before the doorway, peered cautiously into the room, to find one of the girls standing by the gramophone. A pretty girl, she was wearing a sleeveless mini dress and go-go boots, her mass of red curls piled on top of her head. She looked about sixteen, seventeen at most. The other girl, the one Isobel assumed had asked for the record to be stopped, was slouching on the sofa, a cigarette in one hand, a cocktail in the other. From where she was standing, Isobel couldn't see either her face or what she was wearing but saw she had mousy blonde hair styled into a beehive.

There were two boys in the room with them. The first, who was standing by the drinks cabinet mixing cocktails, was a little older than the other. Dressed in drainpipe jeans and a button-down shirt, he had a mop-top haircut with a side-swept parting. Standing by the French window, looking out across the terrace to the lawns, the younger boy was also wearing a button-down shirt, but it didn't fit him and looked like it had been lent to him by the older boy, leading Isobel to assume they were brothers. The younger boy seemed familiar to her, and it took a moment for her to realise he bore a resemblance to Tom, the old man they'd met in the pub. Seeing he had the same blue eyes and facial expressions, she thought he must be a close relation to the older man - probably his grandson.

'Who are you?' she asked, stepping into the room. Dust sheets lay scattered across the floor, piled next to the furniture they had once covered. 'What are you doing here?'

No one in the room answered her. They didn't even appear to have heard her. Infuriated, Isobel repeated her question, but, once again, she was ignored.

'What happened to the people that lived here?' asked the girl with the beehive, before sipping her Manhattan.

'Who cares,' said the older boy.

'Ever since I can remember,' said the red-haired girl, 'my gran told me to stay away from Wychwood House. Whenever I ask her why she refuses to tell me.'

'No one in the village ever speaks about the house,' said the younger boy, 'or the people that lived here.'

Isobel wondered if they were ghosts. No, they were very real, solid figures. The floorboards creaked under their feet; their bodies cast shadows. She contemplated approaching one, grabbing them and shaking them violently, forcing them to acknowledge her, but stopped herself, afraid of what would happen if she did. Seeing the doors of the French window were open, she realised she could get out of the house ...

Crossing the room, she noticed the red-haired girl lift the sterling silver photograph frame standing on the walnut side table next to her.

'Is this them?' she asked, showing it to the younger boy.

Stepping in front of the boy, Isobel saw his eyes pass straight through her as he looked at the framed photograph of Emily and Henry.

'Must be,' he said. 'They had no children of their own; it was just the two of them living here - and their servants of course.'

Glancing over her shoulder, Isobel saw the red-haired girl's eyes did the same as she looked back at the younger boy. They weren't ignoring her - neither of them could see her. Continuing on, she saw heavy planks of wood had been nailed to the outside of the French window. Three of the planks had been prised loose and now lay on the terrace. Sunlight streamed in through the French window, but when Isobel glanced out, she saw the house remained shrouded by thick fog. She found she couldn't quite bring herself to step out onto the terrace. Anyway, she told herself, she couldn't leave without James. She had to find him. He had to be somewhere in the house.

She heard the older boy say, 'Why don't we talk about something else instead?'

Turning, she watched him pour out a generous measure of whisky into a crystal tumbler. When the song came to an end, the red-haired girl removed the needle from the record and replaced the stylus, leaving the lid up.

'Sounded like something my gran would listen to,' said the other girl. Isobel could see her more clearly now. She was wearing pink lipstick and had heavily made-up eyes with false eyelashes and painted bottom lashes.

'Well, I liked it,' said the red-haired girl.

'You would,' said the girl with the false eyelashes. 'Do they have anything by the Ronettes?'

The red-haired girl sighed and said, 'Ronnie, no one's lived here for almost thirty years. Of course they don't.'

Hearing this, Isobel felt her stomach tighten. Thirty years … Surely, she meant seventy, didn't she?

There was something strange, almost unreal about what she was seeing, and it slowly dawned on her that they weren't from her time. According to James, Henry and Emily left Wychwood House in the late 1930s. Thirty years on from then would make it the 1960s. Isobel glanced at the four people in the room. They certainly looked like they could have been from the sixties. Although the mop-top was still fashionable, hardly anyone had a beehive anymore - well not in that style anyway.

Which meant the boy standing by the French window wasn't a relative of Tom - he was a much younger version of the old man. Although it seemed incredible, after everything she'd seen that day, it no longer felt outside the realms of possibility. She moved round the room, transfixed by what she was seeing, though couldn't quite work out why she was seeing it. Was it a dream? It certainly didn't feel like one. She felt very much awake. So, what was it? How could she be seeing something that had taken place over forty years ago?

The older boy, an unlit cigarette held between his lips, filled another glass from the cocktail shaker, his gaze following the pretty red-haired girl as she made her way towards him.

'I made you a Manhattan,' he said, placing the long-stemmed cocktail glass into her hand.

After thanking him, the red-haired girl walked over to the sofa and sat next to the girl Isobel now knew was called Ronnie.

'Do you know what happened to the people that lived here, Tom?' she asked, before sipping her Manhattan and placing the cocktail glass down on the walnut coffee table.

The younger boy nodded. 'Yes, I do,' he said.

'Then tell us.'

'How about a drink, Tom?' said the older boy. 'It'll help you relax.'

Tom declined his brother's offer. Isobel thought the older boy coarse and unpleasant and watched him closely as he took a sip from his glass.

'It's good stuff,' he said. 'It tastes a hell of a lot better than the whisky Dad used to buy, that's for sure.'

'I'm fine, Andy,' insisted Tom.

Ignoring his brother, Andy poured a small measure into another glass. He seemed eager to stop his brother recounting the story that years later he would tell her. Isobel couldn't blame him; the tale would only have scared the girls off. It's unlikely either would have wanted to remain in the house after hearing it.

'Both Henry and his wife disappeared suddenly,' began Tom, 'leaving the house deserted.'

'What happened to their servants?' asked the red-haired girl.

'They vanished too.'

'No one saw them leaving?'

Tom shook his head. 'No.'

'Then they must have fled the house in the middle of the night,' said Ronnie.

'They couldn't have,' explained Tom. 'Their Daimler was still in the garage. When some of the villagers went up to the house to check on their laird, they found the doors locked and all the windows shuttered.'

'Was there an investigation?' asked the red-haired girl.

'No, their sudden disappearance was never reported to the police. The villagers preferred not to know what happened to their laird.'

'If no one ever speaks about the house,' asked Ronnie, 'how do you know all this?'

'Mr Ballantyne told us.'

The red-haired girl scoffed and said, 'The old drunk who's always being thrown out of the pub?'

'That's the one,' said Andy, finishing off his drink. He set his empty glass down on the mirrored sliding tray of the cocktail cabinet.

'And you believed him?'

Tom nodded, his gaze dropping to the floor.

'Well, I wouldn't believe a word of what *he* says,' said the red-haired girl, picking up a copy of *Tatler* that lay on the table. 'I doubt any of it's true,' she added, before flicking through the pages of the magazine.

'I hope it isn't,' muttered Tom under his breath.

So that's where he learnt about Henry Roxburgh and his fascination with his ancient ancestor, Lord Roxburgh, a devotee of the occult arts. A story he'd only half-believed. A story he'd soon learn was true … The realisation then hit her that somehow all this was all Lord Roxburgh's doing. How he was accomplishing this incredible feat, she did not know and was sure she never would but accomplishing it he was.

She decided to leave the drawing room and resume her search for James. He had to be somewhere in the house. She'd only taken a few steps across the great hall when she heard a muffled cry and caught a glimpse of Andy and the red-haired girl sitting together on the staircase, the transistor radio at their feet. Music playing from the radio echoed round the old medieval hall.

For a moment she thought her eyes were playing tricks on her. Moments before both had been in the drawing room. How did they get into the hall without passing her? Glancing back into the drawing room she saw Tom, who was sitting on the sofa next to Ronnie, spring to his feet, knocking Hazel's cocktail glass off the table as he hurried into the hall.

Seeing him approach, Andy rose to his feet.

'What do you want?' he asked.

'I heard a cry,' said Tom. 'I came to check you were okay.'

'We're fine.'

Tom glanced down at the red-haired girl. Her face looked ashen in the candlelight.

'Are you all right, Hazel?' he asked, noticing her smooth down her dress.

Andy stepped forward, squaring his shoulders. 'She's fine. Now get lost.'

Tom asked Hazel if she wanted to return to the drawing room with him. Hazel nodded and rose to her feet, but Andy held her back with his hand.

'She's all right out here,' he growled, the fist of his other hand clenched at his side. 'Now leave us be.' There was a savage, fierce look in his deep-set eyes.

Smelling whisky on his brother's breath, Tom said, 'You know, Andy.' He looked him straight in the eye. 'You're getting more like dad every day.'

From the drawing room, they heard Ronnie say, 'What is that?'

They all turned, Isobel included, to see her pointing across the room, her eyes searching the darkness.

'There's something there,' she said.

The music being played from the transistor radio was lost to crackling static, and moments later they all saw red eyes glowing in the darkness.

Hazel, standing up suddenly, knocked the transistor radio onto the stone floor. 'What the hell is it?' she asked.

Isobel knew exactly what it was. 'Get out of here,' she said, but again no one heard her. 'For God's sake, listen to me!'

'Looks like a dog to me,' said Andy. 'It must be the caretaker's dog. The old bastard must have left it guarding the house when he went into town.'

'That's not the caretaker's dog,' said Tom.

'I'm getting out of here,' whimpered Ronnie. She turned to leave at the same moment the hellhound appeared from the shadows. Seeing her run, it leapt at her suddenly.

Isobel turned away, hiding her eyes, unable to watch the ensuing scene. She ran across the great hall towards the front door, keeping her eyes low to avoid seeing what was happening. Only when she reached the door did she realise she hadn't heard any further screams or cries for help. Turning suddenly, she saw the room was empty. Tom, his brother, and Hazel were gone. Even the transistor radio was nowhere to be seen.

Glancing round, she noticed palm trees in brass pots, an oriental screen and a grand piano; objects she hadn't been able to see before in the gloom. An eerie, awful silence reigned throughout the house, the stillness growing more and more intense until it became so unbearable, she wanted to scream. Across the hall, the grandfather clock began to chime, breaking the silence. Then, in the distance, faint at first, she heard the hum of a car. Was it Will? Had he returned with the police?

She tried the front door but found it locked so ran down the passageway to the servants' quarters. Passing the office, she reached the entrance hall and tried the door there, only to find it too had been locked. Pulling back the heavy, hardwood shutters of one of the two windows beside the door, she peered out onto the drive just as a car pulled up outside the house, catching her in its headlights.

Shielding her eyes, she ducked back away from the window to avoid being seen and waited until the car's lights had been switched off before looking out again. When the headlights dimmed and went out, she heard muffled voices and shoes on gravel. The car was neither Will's Mini Austin nor a police car, but a vintage Ford Saloon. Four men had entered the porch. When they found the door locked, they made their way round the house, to, Isobel assumed, the side door.

Pulling off her shoes to avoid making a sound, she tiptoed across the sandstone floor, and retracing her steps, hurried back through the servants' quarters, stopping before she reached the end of the corridor. Her back to the wall, she edged her way along the corridor, keeping hidden in the dark shadows as she waited for the men to appear. She didn't have to wait long before she heard voices as the intruders made their way through the house, passing the kitchen before making their way through the servants' quarters.

Glancing over her shoulder, she saw the men appear. All were wearing double-breasted suits with broad shoulders and wide lapels. Two had Trilbies on their heads, the third a Fedora. Seeing the man in the Fedora approach her, Isobel ducked back to avoid being seen, and stood motionless, not daring even to breathe. When he stepped into her line of sight, she felt her heart skip a beat. A few more steps and he'd see her …

'It's this way,' said one of the other men.

The man in the Fedora turned and followed the other two down the passageway. When she'd had time to catch her breath, Isobel followed after them, keeping her distance, staying hidden in the shadows.

Cries of terror stopped her dead in her tracks. Gunshots rang throughout the great hall.

'Get out of here!' cried one of the men.

Moments later, the man in the Fedora appeared at the mouth of the passageway and ran towards her, a look of sheer terror on his face. He didn't get far before he was seized from behind and dragged back into the great hall.

Once again, Isobel turned her face away, unable to bear the sight of the hellhound attacking its prey. She had to get out of there in case it found her too. Turning, she ran back down the corridor, returning to the servants' quarters. Hearing hurried footsteps, she came face to face with a woman dressed as a maid scurrying past the butler's pantry. She was a shy, timid little thing with an anxious, apprehensive look on her face. Instinctively, Isobel stepped back, allowing her to pass. She opened the baized-back door and passed into the drawing room. Isobel followed her and heard *These Foolish Things* being played on the gramophone as she entered the room.

Sunlight streaming in through the windows hurt her eyes. Before they'd had time to adjust, she heard the maid say, 'Ma'am, there's someone here to see you.'

Isobel, her eyes focusing, looked at the woman the maid had addressed. She recognised her at once.

'Emily?' she said, hardly believing her eyes.

CHAPTER TWENTY-THREE

Emily, wearing a navy blue crepe dress, paced frantically about the room, nervously biting the nails of one hand, a cigarette in the other.

'I don't want to see anyone,' she said, glancing at the maid through heavy lashes.

Drawing closer, Isobel saw she was wearing thick red lipstick and rouge, the powder on her face unable to conceal the dark shadows under her eyes.

'The gentleman is very insistent.'

Emily stubbed out her cigarette in a glass ashtray on the coffee table. 'Can't Richard deal with him?'

'There's no one left but me, ma'am.'

'Emily …'

Spinning round, Isobel saw a young man with high cheekbones and piercing blue eyes had entered the room. He was wearing a double-breasted suit with broad lapels and square shoulders, an overcoat draped over his arm, a trilby in his hand. Isobel instantly recognised him as Guy Easton from the photograph she'd seen in Emily's locket.

'I'm sorry, ma'am,' said the maid. 'I told him to wait.'

'It's all right, Mabel,' said Emily. 'You may leave us.'

'Very good, ma'am.' The maid curtsied awkwardly and scurried out of the room as quickly as she'd entered.

'Guy, what are you doing here?' asked Emily, her eyes briefly meeting his before she turned away, hiding her face from him.

Easton lay his overcoat over the arm of the sofa. Only then did Isobel notice the dust sheets still covered the furniture. Only the gramophone and coffee table remained uncovered.

Easton gestured to the coffee table with his trilby. 'I see you received my letter,' he said.

Emily glanced over at the fireplace. 'I did - but I didn't believe a word of it.'

Isobel noticed an opened envelope lying on the table. Glancing across the room, following Emily's gaze, she saw the charred remains of a letter on the hearth.

'Didn't you?' asked Easton sceptically.

The record being played on the gramophone ended. Emily crossed the room and lifted the lid.

'How could I?' she said, before clumsily knocking the arm, sending the needle scratching across the record. Slamming the lid shut, she turned and glanced out of the French window at the low setting sun. 'Why would Henry do such a thing?'

Out in the hall, they heard a man say, 'To stop you from being together.'

Henry, his face drawn and haggard, stepped into the room.

'My God, man,' said Easton, 'what's happened to you?' He cast a quick glance at Emily whose face he could now see clearly, and added, 'What's happened to both of you?'

He looked shocked to see her in such a desperate state. She looked distraught and appeared close to having a nervous breakdown.

Turning away from him, Emily caught her breath and said, 'So it is true. Why Henry, why would you do such a thing?'

Henry took a hesitant step towards her, his dull grey eyes meeting hers.

'Because I thought I knew what was best for you.' He picked up a silver cigarette case off the coffee table. 'I realise now I was wrong.' Opening the case, he offered a cigarette to Easton. 'They're Turkish.'

'I prefer mine blended,' replied Easton, pulling out a packet of Camels from his jacket pocket.

Emily, wringing her hands, began pacing up and down the room. Isobel saw there were tears in her eyes. 'But I don't understand,' she said, her lips trembling, 'I was told you were sure to hang …'

'Fortunately, I was only sentenced to penal servitude for life,' said Easton. 'I'd still be in Dartmoor now if new evidence hadn't emerged, resulting in my acquittal.' He glanced at Henry. 'I presume I have you to thank for that …'

Nodding, Henry placed a cigarette between his thin, dry lips. 'I knew you'd come for Emily.' His hands trembled as he lit the cigarette. 'Easton, I need you to take her away from here.'

'I intend to.'

'But before you go, there's one thing I want you to do for me.'

'Why should I do anything for you?'

Henry crossed to the drinks cabinet and fixed himself a whisky and soda. 'Because both your lives depend on it.' He picked up his glass and slowly emptied its contents, savouring the taste, as though it was the last drink he would ever have …

Because, Isobel thought, it was the last drink he'd ever have. The realisation suddenly dawned on her that she was watching the last few hours, if not minutes, of Henry's life. She couldn't help but wonder how he persuaded Easton to end his life. He certainly didn't look like the sort of man who'd be capable of shooting someone in cold blood.

'You see, I only provided the evidence,' said Henry. 'Others are responsible for your release.'

'Others?' said Easton. 'You mean …?'

Henry nodded. 'You know the people I was involved with,' he said. 'You know what they're capable of.'

'I've spent the last two years in prison. I know exactly what they are capable of. Wait, you said the people you *were* involved with?'

'I brought an end to our association.'

'That couldn't have been easy. Once the Brotherhood of Amun-Ra gets their claws into you they're hard to shake off.'

'They've gone for now, but they'll be back before nightfall.'

Emily glanced up at Easton with frightened eyes.

Henry, after extinguishing his cigarette in the ashtray, picked up the keys to the house that lay on the coffee table. 'Have the windows been shuttered and all the doors locked as I instructed?' he asked Emily.

She nodded meekly in response to his question. Isobel glanced across the room. The doors of the French window were shut, but the key remained in the lock.

'Come with me' said Henry, his face damp with sweat as he

headed for the door. 'We're running out of time.' He led them out of the room.

Isobel hurried after them as they crossed the great hall. Emily stopped at the entrance to the library, refusing to go any further. It took Henry a minute or so to persuade her it was safe for her to enter the room. Once they were in the library, Easton asked Henry how he became involved with the Brotherhood in the first place.

'The way all who are ensnared by them do - through greed, vanity and pride. Being too easily goaded into taking risks, I gambled recklessly and lost a considerable amount of money in a very short space of time. Of course, that was when they stepped in, promising that if I became a member of their order, my debts would be settled. But that was not all they promised. They claimed to wield considerable influence within society and told me that upon joining the Brotherhood all that I desired would become mine. At first, I didn't believe them, but my scepticism ended once you were arrested for the murder of Appleby. At the time, the incident shocked me. I knew you weren't responsible for his murder and began to have concerns about my new friends. These fears were pushed to the back of my mind when, shortly afterwards, Emily consented to be my wife.

'Following my initiation into the order, to distance myself from the Brotherhood, I brought Emily up here to be married. For a while I was happy, I like to think we both were, but I soon came to realise the Brotherhood wanted, or rather expected, something from me, something I couldn't have imagined even in my wildest dreams.

'Not long after joining the order, I was presented with a cipher manuscript, a foundation text upon which the order's rituals were based. I was told the author of this manuscript was my sixteenth-century ancestor, Lord Roxburgh, who, in his time, had been one of the most powerful men in Scotland. His treatise on magic had been very popular throughout Britain and Europe, inspiring many to study the occult and practice magic.

'Until then, I'd known nothing about my esteemed ancestor, I wasn't even aware of his existence. No one in my family ever spoke about him. His son, the first Earl of Leithen, was often mentioned, as were the subsequent earls, but not Lord Roxburgh. I believed this was because of his reputation as a necromancer and sorcerer who, during his lifetime, had been accused of murder, consorting with witches, and even of making a pact with the Devil, accusations I believed at the time to be nonsense. When I learnt he wasn't laid to rest in the Roxburgh family vault, feeling he'd suffered an injustice, I set about trying to find where he had been buried, eventually learning he had been interred in an unmarked grave in Dryburgh Abbey. Realising finding his remains would be an almost impossible task, I was persuaded by a close friend of mine, a member of the Brotherhood, into performing a ritual to summon him, to invoke his spirit to learn where his body lay.

'At the time I was unfamiliar with magic and such things were beyond my comprehension and ability. I acted recklessly, foolishly, never for a moment considering the consequences of my actions and was unprepared for what happened next. In summoning him, I bound him to me, and over the weeks that followed his evil spirit began to possess me, filling my mind with thoughts that weren't my own, consuming me with feelings of fury and rage. Every day I could feel him growing stronger, and every day I conceded a little more of myself to him.

'After burying his bones in the family vault, I had a priest perform last rites in an attempt to lay his spirit to rest. When that did not work, the same priest performed an exorcism in the house to drive him away, but again his attempts failed. Regrettably, these ceremonies and rituals soon attracted the attention of the local police, and it wasn't long before word of my activities reached the Brotherhood. Soon afterwards, steps were taken to ensure I made no further attempts to rid myself of my ancestor's evil spirit.

'Members of the society arrived here under the pretence of beginning my studies into the occult. I was told that many amongst them hoped I would rise quickly through the grades and one day assume leadership of the order. They remained at the house, during which time lavish parties were arranged so Emily and I could get to know other members of the society better. To placate my uninvited guests, I threw myself into my studies, telling them I would decipher the manuscript myself in an attempt to understand the work. I had been told by other members of the order that previous translations of the text had been unsatisfactory. Many had been embellished with the translator's own studies and were not true to the original manuscript.

"In truth, I was hoping to find an exorcism ritual in the work to rid myself of my esteemed ancestor once and for all. To my horror, while deciphering the manuscript, I read sections that referred to the Egyptian belief in the transmigration of the soul and discovered rituals that once performed would enable the passing of the soul at death into another body, rituals I believed the Brotherhood intended to perform on me. You see, I wasn't the one they hoped would one day lead them. That position was to be held by Lord Roxburgh, heralding a new age for the society. However, unbeknownst to them, when I recovered my ancestors' remains, I also discovered this.'

Reaching into his pocket he pulled out an amulet and showed it to Easton.

'What is it?' he asked.

'The Sacred Seal of King Solomon,' said Henry, 'a powerful talisman. Although it may not seem like much, it can wield great power. I kept its existence a secret from my guests and used it to summon a hound from Hell, catching them unaware.' He paused briefly before continuing. 'I had only intended to scare them away, but lost control of the beast …'

'What happened?'

'Much to my regret, carnage ensued. Many lives were lost that day.'

'So that's how you ended your association with the Brotherhood.'

Henry nodded mournfully.

'May God have mercy on your soul,' said Easton.

'I pray He does too.'

Glancing up at the gallery, Isobel saw the bookcase stood away from the wall, and the door to the hidden room was open.

Henry glanced out of the window to see it was now dark outside. 'Darkness has fallen,' he said, lighting an oil lamp, 'and the midnight hour is fast approaching. I can already feel myself growing weak. Quickly, we don't have much time left.'

With the oil lamp in hand, he climbed the steps, leading the way along the gallery. He cut a mournful figure as he made his way to the room, like a prisoner on death row making his way to his place of execution. Isobel kept expecting members of the so-called Brotherhood of Amun-Ra to appear, believing they were the ones responsible for Henry's death, coming to avenge their fallen comrades. But she'd already witnessed that scene and dismissed the thought from her mind. They'd broken in after Henry had been killed and Easton and Emily had fled the house. Which meant either Easton or Emily was responsible for his death. Easton had just spent two years in Dartmoor for a murder he didn't commit. She thought it unlikely he'd want to risk being sent back to prison for the same crime. Which, by a very short process of elimination, left only Emily …

Once inside the room, Henry sat himself down at the desk, placing the oil lamp, the Seal of Solomon and the keys to the house down before him.

'Give this to my brother, along with the keys to the house,' he said, opening the top drawer of the desk. Pulling out a letter he sealed the document in an envelope. 'You'd better give him any keys you have too,' he added, addressing Emily, before handing the letter over to Easton. 'Where's your car?'

'In town,' said Easton, pocketing the letter. 'I travelled cross-country to avoid being seen. I assumed if I drove straight here, I'd be intercepted.'

'You would have been. Return the same way. Take whoever is left in the house with you. No one is to be left behind, and no one should be allowed to step foot inside Wychwood House ever again.'

'You're not coming with us?'

'I'm afraid it is too late for me.'

'But the Brotherhood must be brought to justice …'

'That's what Appleby thought,' said Henry. 'And look what happened to him.'

'He was one man acting alone,' said Easton. 'If we face them together, we could bring them down. They have to pay for their crimes.'

'Their time will come. Guy, you must promise me you'll keep Emily safe. You can't do that if you try to take on the Brotherhood of Amun-Ra.'

'But they'll come after us. Both Emily and I know about the society and its members. We're a threat to them.'

'Through the power of the Seal of King Solomon, I have commanded the hellhound to guard this room. No one will be able to enter here without facing the beast. They've lost too many members through this little endeavour; they won't want to lose anymore. Once I'm dead, and the Seal is locked in here, they will abandon their plans.'

'Once you are dead …?'

'Death is the only escape for me now,' said Henry. 'My body must remain here, locked in this room, alongside the Seal.' He lifted the Webley from the desk drawer.

'You want me to shoot you?' asked Easton incredulously.

'I want you to end my suffering. If I could do it myself, I would, but he prevents me from doing so. Please, I have made my peace with myself. I am ready.'

'No, I can't,' said Easton, aghast. 'It's too horrible.'

'Easton, your presence here today, of all days, is no coincidence. The Brotherhood took great pains to ensure you arrived when you did. While I am alive, you won't get far. Lord Roxburgh will see to that. Only when I am dead will you both be safe.'

Henry glanced up as though startled by something he'd heard out in the library.

'No,' he cried, covering his ears with his hands. 'Not yet!'

Isobel wondered what it was that had scared him.

'Take me,' he pleaded, 'but for pity's sake, let them go!'

Isobel glanced at the door, expecting to see someone standing in the doorway before it dawned on her that he was addressing Lord Roxburgh. Easton, his eyes fixed on Henry, edged back towards the door, reaching for Emily as he went.

Removing his hands, Henry glanced up to face them both.

'There is no escape for them now …' he said, but it wasn't Henry's voice they heard. It could have been a trick of the light, but his face looked slightly different too. Even his eyes, which Isobel had thought were grey, now looked bluer.

Easton stared at the man sitting across the desk, unsure what to do, or what to make of the situation, the slow realisation creeping over him that it wasn't Henry he was looking at anymore.

Beside him, Emily began shaking her head frantically. 'No … no!' she cried despairingly.

The door swung shut behind them, trapping them in the room. Startled, Easton ran to the door and tried in vain to open it. At the same moment, Emily reached forward for the revolver lying on the desk.

'Easton,' cried Isobel, 'she's got the gun!'

Almost as if he'd heard her, Easton spun round to see Emily raise the Webley and point it at her husband. Darting forward, he cried out to her, but she pulled the trigger before he reached her, the sound of the gunshot stopping him in his tracks. With tears streaming down her face, Emily then turned the gun on herself, placing the muzzle to her temple.

'Emily,' said Easton calmly. 'Put down the gun.'

Emily shook her head gently. 'No,' she said, 'it's still out there. It won't let us leave.'

'What's out there?'

'The screams,' she murmured, 'you should have heard the screams …'

Although Isobel knew Emily wouldn't fire the gun, she stood rooted to the spot, holding her breath in anticipation of what would happen next.

Seeing Emily's finger tighten round the revolver's trigger, Easton said, 'It's going to be all right. I'm going to get you out of here.' He glanced at the talisman lying on the desk. 'It won't attack us if we have this.' He reached for the Seal of Solomon. 'Here,' he said, offering it to her. 'Take it, it will keep you safe.'

Removing her finger from the trigger, Emily lowered the weapon, before dropping it onto the floor.

'But Henry wanted it locked in here,' she said, sobbing, taking the talisman from him. 'He doesn't want the Brotherhood getting their hands on it.'

'Once we're safely back in London,' said Easton, 'I'll hand it over to his brother. He'll know what to do with it.'

Isobel couldn't remember seeing such an object among James's grandfather's belongings. Had Easton gone back on his word and kept the talisman for himself?

'Everything is going to be all right from now on.' Easton took Emily's hand in his, his other hand reaching for the items on the desk. Lifting both the keys and the oil lamp, he crossed the room.

The door opened and together they slipped out into the library, Isobel following after them. Once on the gallery, Easton handed Emily the oil lamp, closed and locked the door before swinging the bookshelves back against the wall. With the keys to the house in one hand and Emily's hand in the other, he led the way along the gallery. Emily moved slowly and cautiously at his side, though now she had the talisman for protection she did not seem as nervous leaving the room as she had been entering it.

Isobel wondered why the hellhound hadn't attacked James when he arrived at the house. Had it simply returned from whence it came, or had something happened to the creature in the intervening years? Clearly, it was no longer in the house or they'd have noticed it. Its overpowering smell of sulphur was unmistakable, and they'd certainly have seen its red glowing eyes as it watched them from the shadows. And their captors, who she now believed were also members of the Brotherhood, certainly wouldn't have entered Wychwood House if they suspected the hellhound was still there, knowing what happened to their forebears.

She waited on the gallery, watching Easton and Emily make their way across the library, only following them once they had left the room.

And now, she told herself, it was time she and James left Wychwood House for good too.

*

By the time Will reached the village, he couldn't see more than a few feet ahead of him, his car's headlights struggling to penetrate the dense fog. The journey had taken longer than he'd anticipated, the fog slowing him down. There was no clock in the Land Rover, and without a watch, he didn't know how long the journey had taken. He estimated a couple of hours. He had no idea where his mobile phone was. Hodgson was probably telling the truth when he said it had slipped out of his pocket when he'd climbed the embankment and was now lost in the mud at the bottom of the ditch.

He just hoped the police had waited for him. They'd put a stop to whatever those men had planned for James. If any of them had laid a hand on Isobel, they'd regret it, he'd see to that. He felt the anger rise in him at the thought.

Street lights glimmered faintly along the street, the houses hidden in the gloom. He pulled up in front of the pub, the brakes squeaking as he came to a stop. Slipping out of the Land Rover, he ran forward in the headlights, crossed the pavement and came to the sturdy wooden door of the pub. Turning the handle he found it was locked.

'Open up!' he cried, hammering on the door with his fists.

'We're closed,' came the reply. He recognised the landlord's voice.

'Please, it's an emergency.'

When there was no reply, he pounded on the door again. Pausing for a moment, he heard lumbering footsteps, followed by the sound of the door being unbolted. Moments later, it swung open to reveal the landlord stood in the doorway.

Will stepped forward. 'Have the police been through here?' he asked.

The landlord stepped back allowing him to enter. 'We haven't seen anyone.' He closed the door behind him.

The smoke-filled room was as dark and gloomy as the foggy streets outside. The men he'd seen playing dominoes earlier that day were still there sitting on the stools at the bar. Only Tom was absent.

Will crossed to the fire and warmed himself. 'Have you seen Isobel?'

'Who?'

'The young woman I was in here with earlier.'

The landlord shook his head. 'No, we haven't seen anyone all night.'

He needed to call Alexander and find out what's going on. He prayed nothing had happened to them …

'Can I use your phone?'

The landlord stepped forward, blocking his way. 'The phone's out,' he said, crossing his heavy, thick arms.

'Is there another one I could use?'

'All the phones are out in the village. A tree must have blown over in the wind and taken the line down. It happens all the time up here.'

One of the old men suggested he try Selkirk.

Will shook his head. 'There's no time.'

'Looks like you're on your own,' said the other man.

The landlord glanced at the old men sitting at the bar. 'Come on you two, time to go.'

Will noticed the landlord no longer spoke with a Scottish brogue. Instead, he now had a coarse London accent. Was the phone really out? He considered checking just to make sure, but the landlord was a big man and looked like he could handle himself. If he was working with the men at the house, he didn't want to get into a fight with him. Instead, he turned to leave, following after the two old men. He didn't want to be left alone with the landlord, worried what would happen if he was.

*

When Isobel returned to the great hall, she found two men attired in long white robes with yellow sashes round their waists standing by the doorway, the sight of them stopping her dead in her tracks, though she did not bother to hide from them. Neither of the men noticed her enter the room. Both had their backs to her, their eyes fixed on something happening across the room. Following their gaze, she looked across the dimly lit room and glimpse another man, also clad in a long white robe, standing motionless in a magic circle painted onto the stone floor. He was the same figure she'd seen in the film she'd watched with Will.

Flaming torches flickered in brackets attached to the walls of the medieval hall. Drawing closer, breathing in the sweet smell of incense burning somewhere in the room as she went, Isobel noticed the Seal of Solomon attached to a chain hanging round his neck. The circle drawn on the floor of the hall looked larger than it had in the film. She estimated it measured at least ten feet across, the four candles burning brightly within the hexagrams revealing the design to her.

Set a couple of feet in front of the circle lay a triangle that she hadn't been able to see in the film very clearly. It was about three feet across and surrounded a further circle that, on closer inspection, she saw was a black concave mirror. She glimpsed Henry's face under the hood of his robe and saw drops of perspiration glistening on his pale face. A shiver ran down her spine in anticipation of what was to come …

Other robed figures, hidden in the shadows, lay scattered round the room. Many had pentacles sewn into their garments, others wore them as amulets that hung round their necks. Isobel felt helpless as she moved about the hall, passing unseen through the shadows amongst the robed men, unable to warn them of their impending fate. Glancing across the room to a far corner, she saw the cameraman filming the ceremony and noticed a chafing dish full of incense burning on hot coals, the dish the young man would trip over before …

From the middle of the circle, Henry spoke in a loud authoritative voice.

'Ecce Pentaculum Salomonis,' he cried, 'quod ante vestram adduxi præsentiam.' He held the talisman out before him. 'Ego vos invoco, et invocando vos conjure, potenter impero …' The other robed figures began repeating the invocation, their voice echoing round the hall. '… per Michael, Gabriel, Uriel et Raphael.'

Henry continued the invocation. 'I call on thee Lucifer. I conjure your hounds, your bearers of death, Cerberus, Barghest, Cŵn Annwn, Gytrash, from the gates of Hell, to stand here before me, brought to me through the power of the Sacred Seal of King Solomon.'

Thunder roared overhead and the wind began howling round the house with a terrifying ferocity. Isobel noticed the robed men and women were trembling as they watched the proceedings, a look of concern appearing on many of their faces, almost as if they had realised, only too late, their host's intentions.

Henry raised his hands and Isobel watched on in horror as a dark, indefinable shape rose from the floor and began materialising into the hellhound before her eyes. Screams and cries of terror echoed throughout the hall at the creature's appearance. Snarling, baring its fangs, the hellhound stepped forward, glancing at the robed figures as it began prowling towards Henry, its glowing eyes coming to rest on Isobel.

She shrank back in horror. Could it see her? Looking on with morbid curiosity at the ensuing scene, she watched Henry, his face deathly pale and stricken with fear, hold out the amulet before him.

'Behold the Sacred Seal of King Solomon!' he cried. 'Obey your master and come when you are called, and only when you are called!'

But the seal did not deter the creature, it continued to creep towards Henry.

Unable to bear the awful scene any longer, Isobel ran across the hall. Mounting the staircase, she heard Henry cry out: 'In nomine patris et filii et spiritus sancti - withdraw I say. Let there be peace between us …'

But Isobel knew there would never be peace between them.

Once on the landing, she glanced back to see Henry's guests running frantically about the room and saw the young man trip over the chafing dish, the burning coals scattering across the floor. The creature appeared suddenly and without warning, pouncing on him as he lay stunned on the floor.

Isobel closed her eyes.

'Why are you showing me this?' she cried out in desperation, her voice echoing throughout the great hall.

A voice spoke.

You wished to learn the mystery of Wychwood House.

Isobel spun round, expecting to find someone standing behind her, but there was no one there. But then she didn't need to see him, she knew who was speaking.

'And now I have,' she said. 'I demand you let me go!'

You have yet to serve your purpose.

'You let Emily go before she'd served hers.'

Henry lacked the strength of mind to control the Sacred Seal of King Solomon. I require someone stronger, someone with fire and passion coursing through their veins …

'Someone like James …'

Yes. Someone like James. Not that snivelling coward.

Isobel glimpsed the terrified Henry calling to the hellhound as his guests ran for their lives.

Look how he cowers in fear, powerless against the creature. Watch now as he runs for his life.

Seeing the creature approach, Henry turned and ran into the study, slamming the door behind him.

Once he had unleashed the hellhound, he had served his purpose. James faced the creature without the Seal of Solomon, taming the beast. It became subject to his will, it obeyed his voice, departing as ordered from this house. Henry could never have accomplished such a feat. No ordinary man could.

So that's what happened to the creature.

You see, defeating the hellhound was a test. One he passed, proving himself worthy.

'No, don't do this,' said Isobel. 'Leave him alone. You've had a life. His is just beginning.'

There you are wrong. It is my life that is just beginning.

Isobel told herself this was all a dream, an awful, horrible dream. If she just went back to bed, lay down and tried to wake herself, she would, and everything would go back to normal. Turning, she was about to continue up the stairs when she saw a woman dressed as a medieval damsel step off the gallery and make her way down the staircase, stopping a couple of steps before her.

Glancing over her shoulder, addressing someone behind her, she said, 'Come on. Your guests are waiting.'

Moments later Emily, wearing the long flowing blue dress with the lions embroidered on the hem, stepped off the gallery. Isobel was surprised at how colourful the dress was having only seen it in a black and white photograph. Together they passed Isobel and continued down the staircase, Emily moving ahead of the other woman. Before reaching the bottom of the stairs a court jester approached her, took her hand and led her across the great hall to where the young people dressed as fauns, satyrs and nymphs danced energetically round the room.

The great hall no longer seemed as oppressive as it once had. Tabletop and floor standing candelabras flooded the room with light, and there were several vases overflowing with flowers. Many of the women in the room, including Emily, were wearing flowers in their hair. A jazz band with a female vocalist had assembled round the piano at the far end of the room. Laughter, conversation and music filled the great hall, a stark contrast to the scene she'd witnessed only moments before. Isobel moved unnoticed amongst the guests, passing the butler and footmen as they handed out canapés and glasses of champagne. She saw Emily dancing with the court jester, her eyes scanning the room for Henry.

When the music stopped momentarily, Emily reached for a glass of champagne from a passing waiter.

'Has anyone seen my husband?' she asked breathlessly, before sipping the champagne.

The woman dressed as a medieval damsel took the flute from her. 'He's in the study,' she replied.

'Still?' said Emily, swept away in her partner's arms. 'Could you go and fetch him for me please?'

Isobel pictured Henry sitting at his desk deciphering the ancient manuscript, looking for a way out of his nightmare, just as she was looking for a way out of hers, both trapped in the house, both imprisoned by forces beyond their control. Maybe there was an answer amongst the notes he'd made, a way for her to end her imprisonment at least. Passing the Russian Countess and the red-faced man, dressed as the goddess Diana and Emperor Nero respectively, their eyes fixed on the dancers, she hurried into the study, only to find the room empty.

Henry was nowhere to be found. She wondered if he'd locked himself in the room above, and was just about to go and take a look when she realised she could no longer hear the music being played out in the great hall. Glancing over her shoulder, she saw the room was now empty. All the guests had vanished. Once again, she found herself alone.

From somewhere in the house, a voice said, 'Can anyone hear me?'

Although the voice was faint, the sound of someone calling out to her made her jump.

'I can hear you,' she said, thinking it unlikely she'd be heard.

'Come closer, child. Your voice is faint.'

There was somebody else in the house, somebody who could hear her. Perhaps they could help her find a way out …

The oil lamps in the library were turned down low. Five people had gathered round a circular table position before the window. The curtains were open and their pale, sallow faces were just visible under the light of a pale moon. Isobel instantly realised she was speaking to a spirit medium conducting a séance. She recognised James's great-grandfather George Roxburgh sitting at the table, clutching his wife's hand.

'Come closer,' said the medium, her eyes remaining closed. 'Do not be afraid. We are all friends here.'

'You can hear me?' asked Isobel.

Before the woman could answer, George Roxburgh said, 'Is it Edward?'

'No,' replied the medium. 'It is a young woman. Tell us your name, dear.'

They were attempting to contact the spirit of George's dead son Edward.

Glancing up, Isobel noticed a figure wearing an infantry uniform caked in blood and mud standing on the terrace outside the window, staring into the room with cold, dead eyes, his expressionless face a deathly white. When he noticed her, he glanced up, his eyes meeting hers, and he beckoned her to join him as he moved away from the window. Seeing him disappear into the fog, Isobel ran from the room in terror.

Once in the great hall, she heard someone cry out in anger and glimpsed a young man hurl an oil lamp at a portrait hanging above the fireplace. Isobel caught a brief glimpse of the painting before it was consumed by flames and saw it showed an army officer in his dress uniform. It was the missing portrait of William Roxburgh.

A woman screaming out in terror caught her attention. 'You'll burn down the house!' she cried.

Isobel then saw the young man, who she now realised was William Roxburgh's wayward son, fall to his knees, sobbing. Hurrying on, leaving the scene behind her, she stepped into the drawing room to find hunting trophies mounted on plaques on walls, the sight of the stuffed heads of lions, leopards and gazelles giving her a shock, their glass eyes staring down at her. A tiger skin rug with head, its mouth open and roaring, lay before the fireplace. Momentarily confused, she soon realised this was how the room would have looked in the nineteenth-century. Sombre, austere armchairs and a sofa stood in place of the art deco furniture.

Across the room, moonlight streamed in through the French window. Seeing the doors were open, she ran out onto the terrace. An elderly man appeared ahead of her, emerging through the fog as he began climbing the steps from the garden up to the terrace. Isobel instantly recognised him as William Roxburgh whose portrait she'd just seen destroyed. Drawing closer, she saw he was staggering, his face drained of blood. Moments later, he clutched at his chest and fell onto the stone steps, his hand reaching out to her for assistance, his eyes meeting hers.

'I'll go and get help,' she said instinctively, running back into the house. Of course, she knew she couldn't help him, but felt impelled to try.

When she emerged in the great hall, she became overcome by a stench of mould and decay that almost made her wretch. No pictures hung on the walls. The piano had gone and even the tapestries had been removed. There was not a piece of furniture in the room. Most surprising of all was the grand staircase had been replaced by a smaller staircase that was set against a wall.

Isobel swayed uncertainly for a second and thought she was going to pass out. Stumbling a little, she made her way back to the drawing room, her breath coming in low rasping gasps. No light came from within the drawing room. The doors of the French window were hidden by shadows - if they were there at all. The hunting trophies and lion skin rug had gone. Wallpaper now peeled from the walls and the carpet was rotting underneath her feet.

Behind her, something scurried across the floor. Turning, she caught a fleeting glimpse of a large rat disappearing into a dark corner. Feeling faint once again, she steadied herself against the wall before proceeding.

Across the darkened room, she heard the stairs creak and glimpsed shadows cast by a flickering candle move across the walls as someone made their way downstairs. A woman, carrying a single candle, dressed in a nightdress with a blanket draped over her shoulders, stepped off the staircase. As she drew nearer, Isobel saw her face more clearly. She had pale drawn features and sunken cheeks and was instantly recognisable from the painting that had hung in Emily's bedroom.

'Who's there?' said Lady Roxburgh. 'Who is it?'

As she spoke, Isobel saw she had no teeth.

'Get out of my house!' she cried.

But Isobel could not get out. Feeling dizzy, she gasped for breath in the suffocating atmosphere, the room spinning round. Screaming, she collapsed onto the cold stone floor.

*

Will sat in the Land Rover contemplating what to do next. Although it was still only eleven-thirty, it would take him at least ten minutes to reach Selkirk, which didn't leave him much time to get there and back before midnight. No, he thought, he had to call from the village. There must be someone there whose phone he could use.

Switching off the engine, he pocketed the keys and stepped out of the Land Rover. Behind him, footsteps echoed down the street, and he turned suddenly to see Tom emerge from the gloom.

'Have you seen the police pass through here this evening?'

'No one has passed through the village all night,' replied Tom. 'That young lady you were with - she's still up there, isn't she?'

Will nodded. 'Both she and James are being held in the house,' he said. 'I don't know why, or what the men holding them there are planning, but James is very ill and if he doesn't get medical help soon, he's going to die. Can I use your phone to call the police?'

'All the phones in the village are out.'

'Then drive to Selkirk for me and call them from there.' He pushed the keys into Tom's hand. 'Tell them what's happening and have them meet me at the house. You'd better get them to send an ambulance too.'

'The police won't be able to help you. They won't be able to follow where you are going.'

'Please, do as I ask -'

'If you want help,' said Tom, handing him back the keys, 'come with me.'

Turning, he made his way back down the street.

Will followed the old man through the kirkyard gate. 'Where are we going?' he asked.

Mist drifting between the gravestones encircled their feet as they made their way up the path to the parish kirk. The warped iron door creaked as it swung open, and upon entering Will saw the pews had gone. Blown by the wind, dead leaves scuttled and swirled across the dusty, rubble covered floor. Glancing up, he saw mist creeping in through the broken lancet windows.

'How long has the church been like this?' asked Will.

'Since Revered Curran was killed following his visit to Wychwood House,' said Tom. 'Understandably, no replacement could be found after that.'

Tom led him down the nave towards the altar. A pine pulpit stood at the far end of the nave. Nearby a stack of mildewed, disintegrating Bibles lay strewn across the floor. Will asked him why he'd brought him there, and the old man gestured to a rapier that had been attached to the wall.

'It's the weapon used by Eleanor Lowther's fiancé, the young sergeant who slew the demonic creature that stood guard over the Black Tower of Calidon. Over the years that followed, it became an emblem in the village for the power of good over evil.'

'I don't have time for this,' said Will, turning to leave. 'I have to get back to the house.'

'Take the sword,' said Tom. 'Do not return the Witches' Wood unarmed. You were lucky to get out of there alive, you won't be so lucky a second time.'

Will's eyes narrowed. 'How do you know what happened to us?' he asked.

'I saw your car in the ditch for myself and noticed the scratches on the roof. I know what caused them too, and so do you.'

An image of the griffin swooping down at his car flashed through Will's mind.

'Such things aren't possible,' he said, dismissing the memory.

'I wish they weren't. The creature that attacked you is real. It wasn't a dream or a hallucination, and it won't go away if you close your eyes. The griffins that guard the house are living, breathing creatures that won't hesitate to kill you. I know it sounds incredible, but if I'd believed the stories about Wychwood House my brother, Ronnie and Hazel would still be alive today.'

After a pause, Will said, 'All right, help me take it down.'

Crouching down, Tom interlaced his fingers. Will stepped onto his hands, and steadying himself against the wall, reached up for the sword. Grasping the hilt, he pulled it down off the wall.

'It's in remarkably good condition considering it's over four hundred years old,' he said. The weapon looked like it had been recently sharpened.

'Find your young lass and get her out of there,' said Tom. 'Under no circumstances should you go looking for your friend.'

'Why not?'

Tom glanced at his watch. 'You've only about twenty minutes to reach the house before midnight,' he said impatiently. 'There's no time for any more questions. Just go!'

Turning, Will hurried across the empty kirk. Stepping out into the night, he heard Tom say, 'Don't let Wychwood House claim another victim.'

Will ran quickly through the kirkyard and headed down the street towards the inn. If he followed the track up the hill, he'd be there in less than five minutes. However, after some consideration, he decided against it. The shaven-headed man and the other goons would be guarding the gates. Which meant he'd have to go round the back. It wouldn't be easy reaching the house before midnight, especially with the sword weighing him down, but he had no choice. At the end of the street, he found the path and followed it past the abandoned house, the thick fog curling and looping round him as he continued across the open fields towards the dark wood beyond.

*

Feeling herself being lifted off the floor, Isobel opened her eyes to see a pair of Italian shoes and glanced up to see their owner hauling her to her feet.

'Let me go,' she said, struggling to free herself from his grip.

The dark-haired woman appeared from across the great hall and made her way towards them. She was wearing a blue kalasiris - a long linen dress - held up by two straps that attached behind her neck, bangles on her wrists, and a headdress. Isobel noticed there was a representation of a blue lotus flower crowning the headdress, and round her neck hung a beaded necklace, the whole ensemble making her look like an Egyptian priestess.

Glancing round, Isobel noticed there were several Egyptian lamps dotted round the room. Some were made of clay, some terracotta, other ceramic; all were of different shapes and sizes. To her horror she saw Lord Roxburgh's sarcophagus, also decorated with lotus blossoms, standing in the centre of the room, next to a sturdy oak table where she assumed James was to be placed. Before both was an altar where the dark-haired woman would - she assumed - perform the ritual.

'Where's James?' she asked. 'What have you done with him?'

'He is being prepared,' said the dark-haired woman enigmatically. 'Don't worry, you'll be seeing him again soon enough.'

'But it won't be him, will it? Why are you aiding a man like Lord Roxburgh? Don't you know what he is capable of?'

'I know only too well what he is capable of.' Glancing at the man in the Italian shoes, she gestured towards the cellar.

'Then you know what will happen if he's allowed to return.'

Turning, the dark-haired woman walked back across the great hall towards the sarcophagus.

'He's a murderer,' cried Isobel, protesting and stumbling as she was hauled across the hall. 'He's killed many, including the woman he forced into marrying him.'

The man in the Italian shoes produced a key from his pocket. As he pulled open the cellar door, Isobel noticed he was trembling slightly.

Turning her gaze on him, she caught his eye and noticed a look of trepidation, fear even, cross his face. 'Don't do this,' she implored him. 'I beg of you.'

'You know,' he whispered, ignoring her, 'if you'd just given me your number things might have been different.'

Swinging her free hand round, Isobel slapped him hard across the face before he had a chance to react. Momentarily dazed, the man rubbed his face. Then grinning, he pulled open the cellar door and pushed her into the vaulted room, closing and locking the door after her.

CHAPTER TWENTY-FOUR

Cordelia moved round the great hall, lighting the Egyptian lamps. When all were lit, she extinguished the candles in the room and waited for James to be brought to her. A few minutes later he was carried into the room, her men laying his weak, lifeless body down on the table next to the sarcophagus.

When they stepped away from the table, she noticed her assistants cast uncomfortable looks at each other, all apparently feeling apprehensive of what lay ahead. Cordelia, however, betrayed no such remorse or pity for the fate of the unfortunate man lying before her, remaining resolute in her determination to perform the ritual. Once they had covered James with a white sheet, she promptly ordered them to change into their robes.

Eager to start the ceremony, she knelt before the altar and began unrolling a scroll of papyrus from which she was to recite her incantation. Beside her lay a bowl of burning incense that she was to offer to the god Nefertum.

When the men returned dressed in their long white robes, Cordelia handed the grey-haired man the scroll. He held it before her to read whilst the others took their places round the sarcophagus. All stood listening to the clock tick away the seconds, waiting for the moment the chimes would ring out the midnight hour and they could proceed with the ceremony.

*

Will fumbled uncertainly up the hill, the fog thickening, the silence of the wood unnerving him, making him aware of even the slightest sound he made as he progressed through the woodland. Dog-like barking and yelping, followed by a shrill, whooping screech broke the silence – hideous, unearthly sounds he knew were just animal cries. Nevertheless, he still found them terrifying, the hairs rising on the back of his neck at the sound of them.

Staying alert and vigilant, keeping a watchful eye on what lay ahead, his thoughts turned to the creatures Tom claimed were awaiting him further up the hill. Even armed with a sword he wondered how the old man thought he could defeat mythological creatures as ferocious as lions and as fast as eagles with just a sword. Their strength was far greater than his own. Their talons alone could rip him to shreds. Deep down he knew he didn't stand a chance against such beasts. Had he really believed they existed he wouldn't have proceeded, but thankfully he didn't. He did not know what had attacked his car as they drove through the wood, but he was certain it was not a griffin.

Despite himself, he began seeing indistinct shapes in the patterns of light and shadow that loomed before him. Horrifying forms with hideous faces began taking shape in the swirling, twisting fog, conjuring up visions of the monsters that lurked in the nightmares he had as a child. Swiping at them with his rapier, dispersing the fog, he ran on, his resolve strengthening. Eventually, he came to a path and followed its steep incline up the hill.

Only when he reached the top of the hill did the fog begin to thin out, dispersed by the wind blowing through the valley. Stepping out from under the cover of the trees, the moon, though not yet visible through the swirling mist, shone down upon him, illuminating him for all to see. Immediately, to avoid being seen, he returned to the cover of the trees, the dense shadows swallowing him up, continuing through ferns so tall they almost reached his waist.

Ahead he saw the ridge, which meant there wasn't much further to go. When the trees thinned out, he had no choice but to leave the cover of their branches. Stepping onto the path, he'd only taken a few steps when he caught a glimpse of what looked like a large bird perched high up in a tree ahead of him.

Petrified, he instinctively dropped to the ground. Overhead the moon, blurred by the drifting fog, shone down on him once again.

If there was something ahead, it wouldn't be long before it spotted him. He remained motionless until the moon disappeared behind a cloud and the night darkened. Only then did he raise his head and glance up the hill to the ridge. Through the fog and gloom, he could just make out the vague outline of the trunk of a large tree, its branches stirred by the wind. There was, of course, nothing there. There never had been.

He realised then he shouldn't have listened to the old man. With his talk of griffins and demonic creatures, he'd filled his head with nonsense, the result being he'd been fooled into seeing things that weren't there by a simple trick of the light.

Scrambling to his feet, he continued along the path, only pausing for breath when he reached the ridge, coming to rest with his back against a large rock. He then came to the decision he would scale the house's perimeter wall, rather than enter the grounds through the doorway where the wooden door he'd kicked down earlier that day once hung. Either someone would be waiting on the other side of the wall, or - more likely - keeping a lookout for him from the house.

Drawing a deep breath, he pushed himself off the rock and continued along the ridge. He hadn't progressed very far when, feeling he was being watched, he stopped dead in his tracks and glanced cautiously over his shoulder. Once again, he glimpsed what looked like a large bird perched on a tree, except it looked too big to be a bird. He could almost picture its pale-yellow eyes focusing on him as it turned its monstrous head and caught him in its sights.

Had this creature, or whatever it was, circled round behind him? Of course it hadn't. There was nothing there …

Turning, he glanced ahead and saw there were no trees for at least fifty, sixty metres. If there was something there, would he be able to reach the trees before it reached him?

There's nothing there …

But if there was? Well, there was only one way to find out …

Panic coursing through him, he sprinted along the ridge. Then hearing the flutter of wings, he jerked his head back and saw a blur of movement. Something, he couldn't quite make out what, was descending upon him. He ran for his life, the hairs rising on the back of his neck, his heart pounding in his chest, the sound of beating wings growing louder with every stride he made. He felt like a rabbit being hunted by a bird of prey, instinct driving him on.

The creature was almost upon him - he wasn't going to make it to the trees. Altering his direction suddenly, he hurled himself to the ground, then hearing the flapping of wings as the creature descended upon him, he rolled over the edge of the ridge, plummeting down the sharp embankment towards the river below. He landed heavily, hitting the ground with a thud that winded him, knocking the rapier from his hand. Regaining his composure, he glanced round to find the sword teetering precariously on the edge of the riverbank. Without the weapon, he was defenceless.

Hearing another flutter of wings, he glanced up expecting to see the griffin, but there was nothing there. Keeping still, he listened intently, not even daring to breathe, but heard nothing more. If there had been something there, it had gone now. For all he knew, it could just have been a large crow, or the raven he'd seen the other day. Whatever it was, it hadn't been a griffin or some demonic creature. Of that he was certain.

Embarrassed and feeling more than a little ridiculous with himself, he retrieved the sword and rose to his feet before climbing back up the ridge and continuing along the path.

*

Isobel remained at the top of the steps, standing just behind the door listening for any sounds coming from the great hall, but heard nothing. They didn't appear to have begun the ceremony, but then it wasn't quite midnight. The man in the Italian shoes appeared to have left the room after locking her in the cellar. He'd probably gone to fetch James. She wondered what they planned to do with her next. Was she to remain locked in there, or was she to participate in the ritual? If so, what could they possibly need her for?

Kneeling, she tried to look through the keyhole, only to find the key had been left in the lock. The cellar, however, was not in complete darkness. A faint light came in from under the door. She could see the steep stone steps, though the light did not penetrate far enough for her to see the vaulted chamber below in any detail.

The previous night she'd spotted rows of dusty, cobweb-covered wine racks in the cellar, and contemplated retrieving a bottle from one of the shelves to use as a weapon if the man in the Italian shoes came back for her. Nothing would have given her greater pleasure than smashing a bottle of wine, or better still a magnum of champagne, over his head.

Although she couldn't see the racks, she was sure she could feel her way round the walls until she found them. She could even stay hidden down there until they came for her, giving her the element of surprise over her captors. One thing was for certain, she wasn't going to die down there, vowing to fight on until the bitter end.

Only when she stepped onto the first of the stone steps and felt they were damp and slippery to the touch, did she realise her feet were bare - she'd left her shoes in the great hall. Steadying herself against the wall, she began her descent into the darkness, feeling her way with her hands and bare feet. She'd only descended a few steps when she heard what sounded like a young woman weeping.

Although she still couldn't see anything in the dark depths of the room, she was sure there was someone in the cellar with her. It sounded as though they were dragging themselves across the floor towards the steps. She knew at once it was the same woman she'd glimpsed hauling herself up the steps the previous day. Which meant it wouldn't be long before she reached her ...

Still struggling to see anything through the pervading darkness, Isobel stood trembling as she waited to learn, once and for all, who was haunting the house. Was it the ghost of Eleanor Lowther as she suspected, or was it someone else?

She edged her way up the steps to the door, her eyes remaining fixed on the darkness below. When she reached the top step, she stood with her back to the door, her whole body shaking as she waited for the ghostly, corpse-like figure to appear.

She didn't have long to wait ...

A thin, decaying hand reached up the steps towards her. Seeing the spectral figure emerge from the darkness, Isobel screamed out in terror. Her hair, though brittle and lifeless, was the same colour as hers. Her attention shifted to the woman's face. Although her cheeks were sunken and her face contorted with fear, she saw that the face that met hers was her own.

She was the woman in the cellar!

To her horror, she saw she was wearing the same dress she had on. Which meant -

She didn't want to think about what it meant. She just had to focus on getting out of there. Feeling faint, she thought she was going to be sick, but instead, summoning the last of her energy, she began hammering on the door with all her strength.

'Somebody, please help me!' she cried out, realising only too late what she'd said.

Gasping and shivering, she fell to her knees and slid down the wall. Drawing up her knees, curling into a ball, she shut her eyes, unable to bear the sight of the approaching figure, only opening her eyes when she felt it was almost upon her.

Her ghostly self reached out a hand and cried out:

Somebody, please help me!

Then, when all seemed lost, she heard footsteps that seemed to be growing louder with every step. Hearing the key turn in the lock, she scrambled to her feet, crouching low, ready to pounce. The door was thrown open, but it wasn't the man in the Italian shoes who appeared in the doorway.

'Will?' she said uncertainly, unable to believe her eyes.

Will pulled her to him, embracing her. 'Thank God you're safe,' he whispered.

He held her so close she could feel his heart pounding in his chest.

He led her out of the cellar, closing the door behind them. 'They left the key in the lock,' he said.

Isobel then gestured to the rapier he held in his hand. 'Where did you get that from?' she asked him.

'From the church in the village,' he said. He explained Tom had led him to it, telling him it had once belonged to the young sergeant who'd been killed trying to rescue Eleanor Lowther from the Black Tower of Calidon.

'It's been hanging on a wall in the church for over four hundred years?'

'I didn't believe him either, but he insisted I take it. Apparently, for the villagers, it became a symbol for the power of good over evil.'

We're going to need more than a symbol to beat this evil, thought Isobel.

The only light in the great hall came from the fireplace. The candles had either been blown out or had burnt out. The Egyptian lamps were gone, as was the sarcophagus, table and altar. Holding the sword before him, Will led the way across the hall, keeping a tight hold on Isobel's hand as he went.

'Do you know where they are holding James?' he asked,

glancing furtively round the hall. He couldn't see anything in the darkness.

'No, I don't,' replied Isobel despondently.

'We have to find him.'

Tightening her grip on his hand, Isobel drew him across the stone floor, pulling him into the deep shadows. 'No,' she said, 'we have to get out of here.'

Will held back and turned his eyes on her. 'I'm not leaving without him.'

Turning, Isobel saw the front door was open. They could get out. 'Please, Will. We have to go … now!'

Only then did Will notice what she had on. She explained she'd woken up wearing it and hadn't been able to find her own clothes.

Glancing down, Will noticed her feet were bare. 'You'll need shoes.'

Isobel couldn't see her shoes lying on the floor of the great hall. 'I'll be fine,' she assured him.

Keeping their backs to the wall, they edged closer to the entrance porch. Swirling mist drifted in through the open doorway.

Will paused momentarily before proceeding. 'They could be guarding the entrance,' he whispered.

'No, they won't,' said Isobel. 'They want us to get away.'

'Why?'

'So they can come after us.'

Together they ducked through the open doorway and hurried through the entrance porch, stepping out into the night. When she saw they were descending a flight of radial steps, Isobel glanced back at the house and saw a gun-loop in the shape of an inverted-keyhole above the doorway, her eyes drifting up the course rubble walls, past medieval arrow slits, to the high parapet barely visible through the fog and darkness.

Momentarily disorientated, they both looked in disbelief at what they were seeing, their eyes struggling to penetrate the thick fog. They could just about make out the barmkin that ran round the courtyard and several outbuildings in the gloom. The sound of voices drifted across the cobbled courtyard. Inside the nearest building, through a half-opened door, they saw a blacksmith remove a sword from a forge and place the glowing blade on an anvil.

Seeing the gate was open, they ran across the courtyard, moving quickly to avoid being seen. When they passed through the gateway, Will headed in the direction of the village, but Isobel stopped him, leading him towards the Witches' Wood.

'We have to get down to the village,' he said.

'We'll never make it. They can't follow us through here - not on horseback anyway.'

'Who can't?' asked Will. The words had barely left his mouth when he heard horses' hooves clattering on the courtyard stones.

Glancing back through the gateway, he glimpsed men mounting horses. They were wearing long riding boots, steel helmets and breastplates, and held long, heavy swords in their hands. Will stood open-mouthed, unable to believe what he was seeing. Behind the men, illuminated by moonlight, encircled by the drifting fog, stood the Black Tower of Calidon.

Down in the village, they heard the church clock chiming the midnight hour.

Isobel pulled Will on, dragging him into the dense thicket of trees. Together they scrambled blindly through the bushes and ferns, thorns tearing at their face and hands. They continued moving through the wood in silence, their feet making no sound upon the thick blanket of leaves. They hadn't gone far when Will tripped over a tree root protruding above the ground. He staggered and fell, pulling Isobel down with him, his sword slipping from his hand.

Hearing the rumble of hooves growing louder, they kept low so as not to be seen, staring anxiously into one another's eyes, listening to the riders calling out as they searched the wood. They remained rooted to the spot, both keeping still, neither daring to move or even breathe for fear they would draw attention to themselves. There was not a breath of wind. Only the voices of the riders broke the silence, their calls growing faint as they headed to the village.

Only when they could no longer be heard did they dare speak. Will asked Isobel what was going on, but she didn't answer his question.

Instead, she said, 'Will, I want you to know no matter how hard I tried to forget you, I couldn't. I never stopped loving you …' She paused briefly before proceeding, the tears welling up in her eyes. 'I will never stop loving you.'

Will wondered why she was telling him this now. Sensing the

fear in her voice, the realisation hit him that it was the last chance she'd get.

Neither of them was likely to survive the night.

'It's going to be okay,' he assured her. 'We're going to get through this.'

Before she had a chance to reply, he pulled her close, kissing her, the touch of her lips soft on his. She murmured something under her breath, but her words were too faint to hear.

Hearing a horse neigh, they both opened their eyes to see one of the riders making their way down the track, not far from where they were.

'They're over there!' he cried, his voice muffled by the trees.

They had to go - but Isobel could not tear herself from Will's embrace. She kissed him once more before he reached for the rapier and rose to his feet, lifting her up with him. They moved deeper into the silent wood, the air becoming stagnant, the darkness growing more intense the further they ventured from the track. Everything in the wood seemed menacing and larger than life. Nettles barred their way, and the ferns and bushes seemed higher, crowding round them much closer than before.

Brambles caught on Isobel's dress and her feet became entangled in ferns. As she struggled to free herself, she glanced up at a tree looming before her and saw a silhouetted figure of a woman hanging from a branch, a rope tied round her neck. Other bodies hung from the trees surrounding them. Isobel had to stop herself from screaming out at the sight of them.

Once she'd freed herself, they continued on, neither saying a word, their one impulse to get out of the wood. Through the trees ahead of them, they saw the crumbling barmkin. Somehow, they'd come full circle and were heading back to the tower.

Seeing her dress was torn, her legs covered in scratches and her feet were bleeding, Will led her out of the wood. They dragged and hauled themselves through the bushes until finally, they emerged dishevelled onto the track. Without pausing for breath, they continued down the hill towards the old stable block. They hadn't gone far when they saw a horse tethered to a tree further down the track. Drawing closer, they saw the rider had dismounted and was searching the wood for them on foot.

Seeing he was quite some way from the track - far enough for them to be able to take his horse before he reached them - Isobel approached the animal, calling to it in a low gentle voice so as not to startle it, stroking its mane as she unhitched the reins from the branch. Will helped her onto the saddle, then vaulted up onto the horse behind her.

The horses' rider appeared suddenly from the wood, running at them, his backsword raised. Will, seeing him approach, kicked their assailant, striking him across his breastplate, knocking him against a tree. Isobel spurred the startled horse on, and they set off at a gallop through the wood, Will glancing sporadically over his shoulder to check they weren't being followed, whilst Isobel kept her eyes fixed on the way ahead.

Leaving the Witches' Wood, they emerged onto a rocky, heather covered slope.

'Oh, God no …' muttered Isobel, choking back a scream.

Will turned, following her gaze.

They were heading towards the circle of standing stones that crowned the hill ahead.

*

'Wake up, James.'

James opened his eyes to find a young girl standing beside his bed. Sunlight streaming in through the window haloed her unkempt chestnut brown hair.

'Isobel?' he asked.

'Of course. Who else would I be?'

Sitting up, James saw he was in his bedroom at the Manor. The curtains were open, and birdsong drifted in from the garden through an open window.

'Come on. Will's waiting for us.'

Before he could say anything, the young girl had dragged him from his bed and began leading him from the room before he'd even had a chance to dress.

'Wait. I have to put some clothes on.'

'You already have them on, stupid.'

Glancing down, James saw he was wearing a t-shirt and shorts, clothes he must have slept in, which was often the case, especially during the summer. To his surprise, he also found he had a pair of trainers on too - which he thought odd. He could have sworn his feet were bare when he stepped onto the floor.

The door to his parents' bedroom stood ajar, but his mother wasn't sitting at her dressing table. He'd often find her there in the morning, running a brush through her long dark hair. Continuing on, they made their way down the staircase, James leaping down the first flight of steps before bounding down the rest.

With the young girl at his side, he crept past the parlour. The Cranford armchair - his grandmother's chair - stood empty before the fire. The smell of cooking drifted through the air, but Hodgson didn't appear to be in the kitchen. As far as he could tell there didn't appear to be anyone in the house except for the two of them.

Passing the kitchen, they continued down the dim passageway towards the back door that had been left open. A gentle breeze blew in from the garden filling the passageway with the smell of lavender. Leaving the house, stepping into the warm sunshine, James breathed in the scents of the flowers in the borders and watched butterflies flit from one bud to the next.

The gardens were even more beautiful than he remembered.

Than he remembered …

'How did I come to be here?'

'How do you think? You live here.'

'No, I don't. Not anymore.'

'Well,' said the young girl, humouring him, 'where do you live now?'

'I'm not sure.'

All he could remember was a large, uninhabited house with empty, shuttered rooms. Someone had been living there with him. A grey-haired man.

'I live with Hodgson now. In a house in Scotland … Wychwood House.'

'How could you? Hodgson lives here.'

'Not anymore.'

'So you keep saying.' Turning, she set off through the garden. 'Come on, Will is waiting for us.' She ran down the long curving path to the orchard, the lichen-encrusted wall at her side.

'So you keep saying,' muttered James, setting off after her.

Once in the arboretum, they ran past the summerhouse, and made their way round the red horse chestnut tree and weeping silver lime.

Ahead, waiting for them on the edge of the wood, stood Will.

'Come on,' he cried, beckoning them on.

Another memory came to James, stopping him dead in his tracks.

Isobel - she'd been at his side, half-dragging, half-carrying him up through the gardens and into the house. Why? Who had they been running away from? Of course - the dark-haired woman. Isobel had been with him when she'd appeared …

'James needs a doctor. I demand you let us go!'

She'd even threatened a man with a gun before he'd taken the weapon from her. He remembered her being struck violently by the man - he had a shaven head - and he'd knocked her unconscious.

And Will and the others? What became of them? Of course, they'd been driving down to the village through the wood ...

But what had happened to him? Although he'd only been vaguely aware of his surroundings, like a sleeping child being carried to their bed by a parent, he remembered being taken to the great hall and laid down on a table before an altar. Cordelia had been kneeling before the altar reading words from a scroll held up before her.

So why was he here now? Why was he seeing the house and its gardens, and more importantly, why was he a young boy again?

The young girl, who had come to an abrupt stop beside him, turned to face him.

'Did you hear that?' she said.

'Hear what?'

'There are men in the garden. They're heading this way.'

Instinctively, James spun round, expecting to find them approaching, but there was no one there. Then he too heard the sounds, faint at first, then growing in volume until he could hear them more clearly.

'It's nothing,' he said. 'Come on, Will is waiting for us.'

Further sound followed, the whinny of a horse, hooves clattering over what sounded like cobblestones. He pictured the men on horseback passing through a gateway before heading towards the Witches' Wood.

Closing his eyes, he covered his ears in an attempt to drown out the sounds and the images they were conjuring in his mind. He could feel them drawing him away from the Manor, back to the Witches' Wood.

But he didn't want to go back. He wanted to stay there, to forget all that was happening. There he was safe. If he went back then …

But you can't stay there. This world no longer exists, and you don't belong there anymore. They saw to that when they betrayed you.

'They didn't betray me. They were scared, that's all.'

They should have trusted you. Instead, they deceived you, lied to you.

'They made a mistake.'

For which they should be punished.

'No -'

Look at them James - see how they run from you.

But James didn't want to see. He tried to keep his eyes shut but found he couldn't. When they opened, he saw he was riding through the Witches' Wood, a horse beneath him. There were other riders at his side. They were chasing someone. He could see the bloodlust in their eyes.

Ahead he glimpsed Isobel and Will both mounted on the same horse, though he couldn't see their faces. Only when they emerged from the wood into a clearing and turned their heads to glance back at their pursuers, did he see their frightened faces caught in the moonlight.

Terror gripped his heart. He had to do something. He had to stop Lord Roxburgh's men from catching up with his friends. Soon they would reach the circle of standing stones …

When Will came to the tower, he did not try to find you. He only sought out Isobel.

'I told him to get her out of the house. He was simply following my instructions.'

No, James. He left you to your fate - they both did. Neither of them cares about you, they never have. Oh, they pitied you, felt sorry for you, but they never really understood you.

'You're wrong!' James could feel the anger rising in him, consuming him, overpowering him, and he found himself leaning forward, urging his horse on, the reins tightening in his hands.

Lord Roxburgh was right. It had been their fault, all of it. They'd betrayed him, just as they were betraying him now, lying to him, sneaking round the house - his house - in the middle of the night just to be together. And now, reunited, once again they were running off to be together, leaving him to his fate. Why hadn't they come to find him, to help him? Why hadn't they tried to get him out of there?

Hunt them down, James. Show no mercy.

'Show no mercy ...'

*

The dull thunder of hooves echoed through the valley. The riders had emerged from the wood. Pulling the reins, Isobel slowed the horse before wheeling the animal about and heading down to the Yarrow. They had almost reached the river when, out of the corner of his eye, Will caught a glimpse of something flying through the air beside them, and turned to see one of the griffins was circling them. Although some distance away, he knew the creature would soon reach them.

'Head for those trees,' he cried, pointing to a copse ahead.

'Why?' asked Isobel, glancing over her shoulder, glimpsing the creature as it began its descent. 'What is that?'

'Head to the trees,' repeated Will, urging her on.

But it was too late.

Seeing the creature swoop down upon them, their horse reared back on its hind legs, sending Will crashing to the ground. Isobel remained in the saddle but couldn't control the animal. It shied and bolted, carrying her away with it. No matter how hard she pulled the reins, the horse, fleeing in terror from the creature, would not stop. Even at a gallop, it could not outrun the griffin and nearly reared over backwards as once more it bore down upon them.

In fear of her life, Isobel jumped from the saddle onto the ground, keeping low as the horse kicked and reared, its hooves landing just inches from her head. She rolled clear of the horse and watched as it galloped away to the small cluster of trees further along the track, pursued by the winged creature.

Will appeared at her side, and helping her to her feet, glanced towards the approaching riders. When the lead rider spotted them, he fired a pistol into the air and called to his companions. Isobel and Will stood together, their bodies trembling. There was nowhere for them to go now. Seeing the reivers raise their backswords, Will dragged Isobel towards the stone circle, knowing the mercenaries would run them down without a moment's hesitation given the chance.

When they drew closer to the ancient circle, they saw there were six stones, not three, and all stood upright, but before they could reach the monoliths the lead rider bore down upon them. Raising his sword, Will turned to face the man, moving Isobel behind him. The rider's horse, seeing the rapier glimmering in the moonlight, reared up, almost throwing its rider. Will and Isobel ran on, reaching the circle of stones before the other riders reached them. Together they stood side by side waiting to engage their pursuers.

Four of the men dismounted, two others remained on their horses, and closing rank, marched on them in tight formation, their backswords drawn. One lunged clumsily at Will, sparks flying as his sword clashed against an ancient monolith. Will darted forward, grabbing the man's arm, swinging him round, slamming him into one of the stones. Winded, his sword fell from his hand and the reiver dropped to the ground. Will then stuck his steel bonnet with the hilt of his sword, the mercenary collapsing onto the ground in a heap.

When he engaged another of the men, Isobel reached for the unconscious man's sword lying on the ground beside him, picking it up by its basket hilt. When she stood upright, she felt herself being wrenched backwards and turned to find one of the riders had crept up behind her. He pulled her towards him, and she jerked sideways, twisting herself free from his grip, swinging her sword with all her might, striking him in his side, just below his breastplate.

Clutching his wound, the reiver stumbled back in pain, his armour heavy and clumsy. Isobel could smell alcohol on his breath and realised he was drunk. When he saw his wound was slight, he regained his composure, stepping towards her, his rapier raised. Instinctively, Isobel's grasp tightened on the handle of her own sword. She knew she had to strike first - but hesitated, unable to inflict the fatal blow. Instead, she swung the backsword blindly at him, sending it crashing down on the mercenary, striking his armour. The reiver cried out in pain and fell to the ground.

The breath searing in her lungs, Isobel spun round. Three of the soldiers lay on the ground, two wounded, the third regaining consciousness. The other two had dismounted their horses and were now advancing remorselessly upon them. One engaged Will, the other charging at Isobel, his sword still in his scabbard. Her heart pounding, she swung her backsword blindly at him, her long hair falling wildly about her face, her legs buckling with exhaustion and fear as the man engaged her. Restraining himself, he hesitated before striking her. Clearly, he was acting on orders that she shouldn't be harmed. Instead, holding the tip of his rapier before her, he ordered her to drop her weapon and she conceded defeat, dropping her backsword onto the ground before raising her hands in surrender.

Glancing over her shoulder, she saw Will block a thrust, the tip of his opponent's rapier no more than an inch from his face. With gritted teeth, Will lunged back, his thrust parried with the reiver's main-gauche dagger, trapping his blade in the fork of his hilt. Immediately, his opponent thrust forward with his rapier that ripped through the front of Will's shirt, grazing his chest. Will, disengaging his sword from the parrying dagger, swung back, their swords clashing, steel striking steel, the reiver stumbling back. Although a less experienced swordsman, Will was stronger, faster and more agile than the man he faced, and before his opponent could regain his balance, Will sprang at him and they crashed to the ground together, the reiver's steel helmet falling off.

Springing to his feet, wiping blood from his eyes with the back of his hand, Will looked down to see the man lying on the ground was James. Confused, he turned to look at Isobel, momentarily turning his back on his opponent.

'It isn't James!' she cried, half choking on the words.

Behind him, James rose to his feet, his face contorted into a mask of hate and fury, barely recognisable. Isobel cried out in horror when she saw him drive his rapier through Will, its bloodied tip protruding through his ribs. Wincing in pain, Will staggered forward, his frightened eyes staring into Isobel's as he fell to his knees.

Seeing him fall, Isobel hurried over to him, falling to her knees before him. She took his face in her hands.

'It's going to be all right,' she said, struggling to keep the fear out of her voice. She looked up at James, her eyes full of anger and hatred. 'Do something!' she cried. 'Don't just stand there!'

But she knew it wasn't James she was looking at.

'No one can save him now, young lady.'

Seeing a smile cross his face, she grabbed Will's rapier and ran at him with the last of her energy, but he effortlessly parried her thrust with his dagger and she fell to the ground sobbing. Turning back to Will, she heard his breaths were growing steadily weaker and more irregular as blood pumped from his wound. She scrambled over to him, her hand finding his.

'Stay with me,' she sobbed, tears spilling down her cheeks.

Glancing down, she saw, to her horror, a large dark pool of blood spreading underneath him. Consciousness slipped away from him. His eyes glazed over, and Isobel heard him exhale his final breath.

Seeing him lying dead on the ground before her, Isobel felt an almost physical pain surge through her body. Fighting her first instinct to grab the rapier and charge at Lord Roxburgh once again, knowing it would be no use, all her fear and anger exploded within her and she collapsed onto the ground, sobbing uncontrollably.

Closing her eyes, she prayed she would wake up from this nightmare to find none of it had been real. But then none of it was real. She didn't know where they were but knew it was all Lord Roxburgh's creation. He'd driven James on, drawing on his feelings of betrayal. If any part of James had survived, it had been lost the moment he struck the fatal blow that killed Will.

*

'Why didn't you do more to stop him?'

James turned to find the young girl standing at his side.

'What chance do I have against such a man?'

'You have to face him.'

'I can't.'

'You have to end this once and for all. '

He knew she was right. Others' lives depended on him. Lives only he could save now.

You really think you can defeat me?

'I have to …'

I know your fears, your failures, your weaknesses, just as you know what kind of man I am and what I'm capable of. And whereas you are alone, I - as you so distinctly put it - have an army of followers. Out of the two of us, who do you think is going to succeed?

'But I'm not alone. My friends are still fighting for me.'

One of your friends is dead. The other will soon follow him.

'What purpose did killing Will serve?'

We both know I wasn't the one who killed him. It was you who struck the fatal blow. It was your anger driving me on - not the other way round.

James glanced at the bloodied tip of the rapier he still held in his hand.

The young girl looked at him incredulously. 'You killed him, didn't you? You killed Will.'

James threw the weapon onto the ground. 'No,' he cried. 'I'm no killer!'

Yes, my boy, you are.

When James looked for the young girl, he found he was back in the gardens at the Manor. Instead of the t-shirt and shorts he'd been wearing, he now had on boots, woollen breeches and a doublet with slashed sleeves worn under plate armour that covered his chest and back. The cotton shirt he had on underneath the doublet had lace cuffs. These were the clothes of a nobleman.

They were the clothes of Lord Roxburgh.

Through the trees ahead, he glimpsed the young girl running through the wood towards a distant figure. It was Will. When the young girl reached him, she took his hand and they continued on, disappearing from sight.

James called out to them to wait for him and set off in pursuit, entering the wood. He hadn't gone far when the light began to fade, and the wood grew darker. All round him the trees began twisting into warped, gnarled, deformed shapes that crowded together, blocking his way. Finding he could go no further, he came to a stop.

The stale air wreaked of death. Overhead, bodies hung limply from the branches of the trees. He was back in the Witches' Wood. Turning, he saw the Manor and gardens had vanished. In their place, at the top of the hill, looming ominously before him, stood the Black Tower of Calidon.

There, one way or another, his journey would finally come to an end.

*

The last vestiges of emotion torn from her, Isobel stared at Lord Roxburgh with vacant eyes, her face blank. What would he do to her now? What could he do to her now?

'You've taken everything from me. I had him back for a brief time, only to lose him again. Why do such a thing?'

Would he take her back to the tower as he had Eleanor

Lowther? But then he hadn't taken her back, she knew that now. She hadn't been the one haunting Wychwood House. So, what did he do to her?

'Wasn't it enough that you murdered the man she loved? Why punish her further? What kind of person are you? What kind of monster are you? Why be so cruel to someone you loved, if such a feeling is possible in you.'

But there was something worse he could do.

'You could keep them apart forever. Not just in this life, but in the next as well. That's why her body was never discovered. You had her dragged down to Hell, didn't you?'

Lord Roxburgh's eyes met hers, and she noticed him flinch as a memory came to him.

'I cast her back from whence she came,' he said.

'You were keen to show me the mysteries of Wychwood House,' said Isobel, 'well the fate of Eleanor Lowther is the biggest mystery of them all. Show me her fate …'

She wanted him to see it, to relive the moment once more, a moment that had haunted him ever since.

'Show me!' she cried.

Glancing down, she saw the young sergeant lying on the ground beside her in place of Will and turned to see a young woman being held by Lord Roxburgh's men, screaming at the sight of her fiancé lying dead before her.

'Let her go,' said Lord Roxburgh. 'I'll leave her to the hounds to dispose of.'

'No!' cried Eleanor. 'I beg of you, don't do this!'

Seeing two hounds materialise in the darkness, their red eyes fixed on her, Eleanor ran in fear of her life as the demonic creatures set off in pursuit of her. Isobel turned away, not wishing to witness the ensuing scene, her eyes falling on Lord Roxburgh's men who recoiled in horror at the sight of the hellhounds pursuing their prey.

She then glanced at Lord Roxburgh and saw him shut his eyes as his young bride's screams echoed through the valley.

'Closing your eyes won't make this nightmare go away,' she said.

*

Ripped from its hinges, the entrance gate lay on the ground. Several men, and a few women, had gathered in the courtyard and were setting fire to the outbuildings. None of the intruders appeared to have approached the tower, all seemingly wary of its diabolical resident.

Although he was dressed as a reiver, no one noticed James as he ran past them. Upon reaching the tower, he climbed a short flight of radial steps and pushed against a sturdy wooden door. To his surprise, it yielded to his touch, and he stepped inside the tower. When he closed the door behind him, he noticed one of several keys attached to a brass ring was still in the lock. Not wishing others to gain access to the building - not yet anyway - he locked the door before proceeding.

The ground floor, which was being used as a storage area, appeared to be empty. There was no sign of any of Lord Roxburgh's men, or of Isobel for that matter. She had to be somewhere in the tower - but where? Was his ancestor keeping her close to lure him further into the tower?

An iron yett, which had been left unlocked, covered the entrance to a spiral stone staircase. James pulled the grille of lattice wrought iron bars open and began climbing the steps. Upon reaching the first floor he entered a chamber where he found his ancestor sitting at a table, his manuscript lying open before him. James couldn't see his face; it was hidden by the hood of the black ceremonial robe he was wearing. Other than the table there was very little furniture in the chamber. Tapestries hung on the walls and there was a single window protected by an iron grill.

Sensing James was in the room, Lord Roxburgh rose to his feet and turned to face him. A ram's head skull covered his face and attached to a chain that hung round his neck was the Sacred Seal of King Solomon.

Clearly, he was expecting him.

James asked him where Isobel was.

'There is no need for you to concern yourself with her.'

James called out to her but received no reply.

'Where is she?'

'My men will be taking good care of her.'

'Your men have deserted you.'

Once more James called out to Isobel but once more his cry was met with silence. He was about to try again when he heard a loud crash as the intruders began battering the tower's wooden door with something heavy. Hurrying over to the window, he glanced down into the courtyard and saw the mob were crowded round the tower, though he couldn't see what they were striking the door with from the window.

'They'll break it down soon.'

'The tower is impenetrable,' said Lord Roxburgh, dismissively. 'They'll never get in.'

'I imagine you would have said the same of the barmkin, but somehow they've managed to break down the gates.'

'They won't be able to gain access to the tower so easily.'

As he stepped back away from the window, James glanced up and saw the land round the tower looked desolate and barren. The dark skies were overcast, the horizon veiled in mist, just as it had been in his dreams - or rather in his nightmares.

He turned to face his ancestor. 'Tell me where Isobel is,' he said, the anger rising in his voice, 'I demand you let her go.'

'You are in no position to make demands. You are here at my bidding.'

James wondered why that was. What did his ancestor want with him, and why bring him to this particular moment in time? It had been here, trapped in the tower as it burnt down, that he had escaped death. A moment that must have taken place days, if not weeks, after he murdered his young bride and her fiancé.

Feelings of dread crept over him, and he grew nervous in anticipation of what was to come.

'Only by joining me will this nightmare end,' said Lord Roxburgh. 'Only then will you have the power to return your friends and yourself to your own world.'

And if he did he would be consumed by anger and rage, just as he had been when pursuing Will and Isobel through the Witches' Wood, until nothing of himself remained. No, he couldn't let that happen. There had to be another way …

'And if I refuse, what then?'

Flames suddenly appeared at his ancestor's feet. 'Ecce Pentaculum Salomonis,' he cried, 'quod ante vestram adduxi præsentiam.' Drawing nearer, James saw he was standing within a flaming pentacle. 'Ignei, aerii, aquatani spiritus, salvete! Orientis princeps Belzebub, inferni ardentis monarcha, et Demogorgon, propitiatus vos, ut appareat et surgat Mephistophilis!'

A feeling they were no longer alone in the room came to James. Someone, or rather something, was in the chamber with them. Although hidden in the darkness, he could just make out its long feathered wings, taloned feet and a barbed tail. Only when it drew nearer did he see its goat-like face, horns and small beard. He knew at once what it was, who it was …

'All those innocent people you had executed,' said James, stepping towards Lord Roxburgh, 'when all along you were the one conspiring with demons. Instead of fighting for what you believed, you let your world, a world of superstition and fear corrupt you. You, not those you murdered, were the disciple of Satan.' He began circling his ancestor. 'You spoke of understanding God and becoming his equal when all along, believing you'd never be forgiven for your sins, you turned your back on Him, pledging your soul in exchange for your diabolic powers - the result being you were doomed to wander through time in search of another's soul to offer in place of yours - my soul.'

From somewhere in the tower, James heard Isobel calling out for help, and noticed the tapestry that hung on the wall behind his ancestor was on fire.

'She's calling to you, James, begging for your help. Help her, James.'

'I refuse you because of her. Because I know she - and Will - would rather die than let a man like you live.'

'Then she will die, and you will spend eternity in Hell.'

'And then you too will die.'

'No, James. Then, within you, I shall be reborn!'

That was something he could not let happen. He had to find a way to stop him, to defeat him, to end his reign of terror once and for all. He could feel the anger, the rage, rising in him, just as it had when he'd pursued his friends through the Witches' Wood. He had been the one who killed Will. It had been his anger driving him on – not his ancestor's. He realised that now. For too long he'd tried to repress these feelings deep down inside of him, feelings that had always threatened to reappear, as they had when he'd seen Will and Isobel together, leading to him to betray his friends, feelings he could now harness and use to save Isobel and maybe even Will too.

He came to a stop before the fireplace. Feeling the heat of the flames against his back, he closed his eyes and began picturing the fire in his mind.

'Per Adonaï Eloïm, Adonaï Jehova, Adonai Sabaoth …'

As he spoke, he drew the flames from the fire, swirling them round the room, sending a ball of flames flying through the air towards his ancestor. Lord Roxburgh raised his hands to his face as the fire engulfed him, sending him crashing to the ground, knocking his mask from his face. It smashed into pieces on the hard, stone floor.

He turned to face James, his cold, lifeless, light blue, almost grey eyes, meeting his. His face was badly scarred from wounds inflicted in combat, his cheeks gaunt, his thinning hair grey and matted. Was this really the face of the man whose voice had so terrified him? Now he could see him for what he really was, he looked old and weak, a pitiable individual, not at all like the strong, powerful man he'd imagined who'd haunted his dreams.

'You're no magician. In life you were nothing more than a sorcerer dabbling in black magic. In death you're nothing more than a shadow, a shadow without form, existing now only in the darkness.'

'That's as maybe,' said Lord Roxburgh, rising to his feet, 'but whilst I hold the Sacred Seal of King Solomon, you're no match for me.' He held up the amulet, incapacitating James, who fell to his knees, crippled by an immense pain, as if he'd been struck by lightning. 'This is your last chance, James. Refuse me and I will have to fulfil my side of the bargain. Join me and you and your friends will leave this place -'

Overhead the wooden beams cracked loudly in the heat as the fire began spreading through the room, filling the chamber with smoke. Once again, he heard Isobel crying out for help. He knew he had to get her out of there before the whole tower was consumed by flames. But how? While his ancestor held the Seal before him there was no way he could get to her.

'Join me, James. If not to save yourself, to save her.'

Drained of all the energy in his being, James collapsed onto the cold, stone floor. Behind him, the fireplace began growing in size, the lintel rising like a mouth opening wide. Beads of perspiration appeared on his forehead, when, through the thickening smoke, he saw the demon step towards him.

Believing the end had finally come, he awaited his fate, only to see the creature come to a sudden stop.

Of course - it couldn't proceed while Lord Roxburgh was

channelling the power of the Seal.

At that moment he recalled the words his ancestor had once said to him. "… become a magus capable not only of creating storms and raging tempests … but of tearing asunder the earth, causing earthquakes of staggering destructive power!"

Make the ground tremble beneath your feet ...

Feeling the anger burning through his soul, he summoned the last of energy, focusing his mind on the ground beneath him, on the earth and the rocks upon which the tower stood.

Tear asunder the earth!

Slowly at first, he felt the floor vibrating beneath him. Then out of nowhere, a storm began raging overhead, the tower trembling in its wake. Cracks appeared on the walls, stones became dislodged, rubble fell from the ceiling reigning down on Lord Roxburgh, unbalancing him.

'Take him,' he cried, addressing the demon. 'Take him now!' He had no choice but to lower the amulet. If he didn't the whole tower would come crashing down upon them.

The creature stepped towards James.

Now was his chance. The only one he'd get.

Springing to his feet, he charged at his ancestor, pushing him back across the room, slamming him against a wall. Pinning his left arm against his neck, he grabbed the amulet with his right hand, the chain of which his ancestor still held in his hand. He wanted to hit him, to beat him mercilessly, to rip him apart limb by limb, to destroy him until nothing of him remained, but knew he didn't need to.

His fate was already sealed.

'"What art thou, Faustus,"' said James through gritted teeth, yanking the amulet from his grip, breaking the chain, '"but a man condemn'd to die? Thy fatal time doth draw to final end."'

When he stepped back, Lord Roxburgh, gasping for breath, reached for him, but it was too late. James was now standing inside the pentacle. His attention then shifted to the approaching demon. Without the Seal, he was defenceless against the creature.

'I summoned you!' he cried. 'You must obey me!'

'There is still time for you to repent and save your soul,' said James.

'Never!' his ancestor cried defiantly.

Seizing Lord Roxburgh, the demon dragged him towards the

fireplace that now resembled the mouth of a monstrous creature, his protesting cries ignored as he was pulled towards the fires of Hell, the mouth swallowing him up as his soul was dragged away, his lifeless body falling to the floor.

James, leaving his ancestor to his eternal damnation, turned away expecting everything to return to normal, for him to find himself back in Wychwood House, but he remained where he was. How were they going to get back now?

Of course - the Seal. He could use its power to return them. But if he did would the amulet return with him? Having witnessed its incredible power, he did not want it falling into the hands of the Brotherhood, so decided, reluctantly, to leave it where it was, throwing it onto the body of his ancestor that was now entirely consumed by flames.

He would have to find another way.

The smoke swirling round him, he scrambled blindly across the room and came to the spiral staircase. He hurried down the stone steps until he reached the ground floor. Two further steps led to a wooden door, behind which he assumed was the cellar. Once more, he called out to Isobel and heard her voice, faint at first, then growing louder. Without further delay, he retrieved the ring of keys from the front door and unlocked the cellar. Pushing the door open, he stared down into the vaulted chamber. Emerging from the darkness, Isobel began dragging herself up the stairs, her hand reaching out to him. She looked frail and weak, as though she hadn't eaten in days.

James hurried down the steps and took her hand in his, but when she glanced up and saw it was him, she shrank back in horror, her eyes wide with fear.

'It's okay,' said James. 'You're safe now.'

Tentatively she allowed him to lead her out of the cellar. When they emerged into the light, James noticed her hair was a tangled mess, her cheeks stained with tears and her dress was torn.

He asked her if she was okay, and she told him she was.

'Where's Will?' he said, glancing past her into the cellar.

'They left him where he fell,' she murmured, her voice hoarse.

Together, they stepped out into the night, running across the courtyard past the burning outbuildings. The villagers were gone, having fled in terror. Once away from the tower they began their descent of the hill before entering the Witches' Wood.

They found Will's body lying before the stone circle. Seeing his body lying on the cold, hard ground, Isobel burst into tears.

She glanced at James, the tears rolling down her cheeks. 'You can still save him,' she said.

'How?

'By taking us back to our world.'

But how could he without the Seal of Solomon? He regretted not bringing it with him, but it was too late to go back for it now. His ancestor would have been able to take them back – after all, he'd been the one who'd brought them there, but how could he return them without him?

James's head dropped forward, his shoulders slouching. 'I don't know how,' he muttered, the awfulness of their situation dawning on him.

'Yes, you do, James,' said Isobel, wiping away her tears. 'Lord Roxburgh chose you because of your strength, because you tamed the hellhound, something he told me no ordinary man could accomplish.'

James realised then his ancestor had been harnessing the power within him. A power he didn't possess. If he did, he'd never had made a pact with that demon. He wouldn't have to.

He didn't need Lord Roxburgh – or the Seal for that matter – to get back to his world. His ancestor had needed him. Which meant …

Overhead a faint star broke through the darkness. Others followed, then the moon appeared until the whole night sky revealed itself to him.

Moonlight shone down upon the stone circle, illuminating the ancient monoliths.

Sensing an energy emanating from the stones, James said, 'Help me carry him into the circle.'

Together they lifted Will's body, carrying it to the monoliths, laying it down gently on the ground.

Isobel then watched as James placed his hands on one of the ancient stones as though drawing on its power. Focusing his mind, he closed his eyes and began muttering an incantation under his breath.

'Per Adonaï Eloïm, Adonaï Jehova, Adonai Sabaoth, Metraton On Agla Adonaï Mathon, verbum pythonicum, mysterium salamandrae, conventus, antra gnomorum, daemonia coeli gad,

Almousin, Gibor, Jehosua, Evam, Zariatnatmik …'

Overhead the stars shone in the night sky with a brilliance Isobel had never witnessed before, her view suddenly obscured by storm clouds sweeping across the valley. Thunder sounded from the far horizon …

Soon the thunderclouds were upon them, driven by what looked like faint, almost invisible, ethereal figures. Before Isobel could see them in any detail, lightning flashed across the sky, striking the ground not far from where they stood. Isobel then watched James as he raised his hands to the heavens and began channelling the full fury of the storm that raged above them, to - Isobel knew - wrench them back through space and time to their world.

Howling winds sent dirt and earth swirling round the ancient stone circle, creating a vortex. The ground beneath their feet trembled, the storm uprooting trees leaving devastation in its wake. Even the monoliths shook as though they were going to be uprooted and ripped from the ground. Isobel felt as though they were standing in the eye of a hurricane, and once again glimpsed the translucent, ethereal forms that were driving on the winds. As the immense power of the vortex increased, the sound became deafening, terrifying Isobel and she screamed out in terror.

Then, just as she felt she was going to be drawn into the vortex herself, there was silence.

CHAPTER TWENTY-FIVE

From somewhere in the darkness a clock chimed the hour.

Opening her eyes, Isobel saw they were standing in the library. Clutched in her right hand was the revolver. She had on her boots, jeans and flannel shirt, the clothes she was wearing before -

Before what? She felt as though she had woken from a long sleep, and all that had happened had been nothing more than a dream that was already beginning to fade from her memory. Dazed and disorientated, she steadied herself on the back of a chair and looked across the room to see James standing by the fireplace, staring into the embers of the dying fire.

'James?' she asked cautiously, her finger tightening on the gun's trigger.

Turning, he looked at her as if he too had just woken from a dream, his dark eyes meeting hers. Smiling, he nodded at her and Isobel, letting out a sigh of relief, dropped the Webley and ran to him.

'It's all right,' he said, pulling her close. 'You're safe now.'

Isobel glanced round the darkened room, her heart sinking when she saw Will wasn't in the room with them.

'Where could he be?' she asked.

'He and the others must have reached the village by now.'

'No, they didn't.'

'How do you know?'

'The dark-haired woman told me.'

'When?'

'When she came into the library …'

But how did she get in? There was a chair wedged under the door. Of course, the shaven-headed man had entered from the study …

At the same moment, this memory came to her, the man with the shaved head entered the room, the floorboards creaking underneath him. When he saw James was on his feet, he stopped dead in his tracks.

'James,' cried Isobel, 'the gun!'

James glanced down at the revolver lying on the carpet where Isobel had dropped it. He made a dash for the weapon, but the shaven-headed man reached it first.

Raising the revolver, he pointed it at James who shielded Isobel behind him. Keeping both James and Isobel in his sights, he crossed the room and removed the door wedged under the handle. The door swung open and the man in the Italian shoes entered the room, closely followed by the dark-haired woman.

'You've failed, Cordelia,' said James. 'Lord Roxburgh has been defeated.'

Isobel glanced at James, surprised he knew her.

Cordelia's face turned crimson. 'You fool!' she cried, unable to contain her anger. 'You don't realise what you've done!'

'Come on,' said the man in the Italian shoes, glancing at the shaven-headed man, 'let's get out of here.' He made for the door.

Cordelia stepped forward. 'No,' she said, blocking his way. 'Stay where you are.'

'It's over.'

Cordelia faltered, but only for a moment. She looked at the shaven-headed man first, then the man in the Italian shoes. 'You know what to do,' she said.

The man in the Italian shoes stared blankly back at her.

'Burn it down!'

Isobel stepped out from behind James. 'No, you can't!' she cried.

The man in the Italian shoes moved about the room, lighting the oil lamps.

'What are we going to do about them?' said the shaven-headed man, gesturing to Isobel and James. 'They've seen our faces.'

'So shoot them.'

The shaven-headed man swallowed nervously. Clearly, he

hadn't anticipated being called upon to kill them in cold blood.

'You don't have to do this,' said Isobel, keeping her voice calm. 'You can still walk away.'

'Shut up!' Cordelia swung her arm round to strike Isobel, but James caught it mid-flight.

'Don't you dare touch her!' he said, his voice commanding, threatening.

Cordelia's eyes fixed on his and she smiled. 'Maybe not all is lost after all.' The tip of her tongue passed slowly over her red lips.

She was testing James. She wanted to know what he was capable of.

Isobel placed her hand gently on James's arm. 'Let her go,' she said.

James released his grip on the woman, and she stepped away.

*

When Will regained consciousness he found himself lying on the back seat of the Land Rover, his jacket laid over him. A tumbling torrent of images filled his mind and he struggled to piece together what had happened. He remembered waking up in James's apartment in Edinburgh. Hodgson had been there. He told him James and Isobel were at the hospital, though he couldn't remember which one. The rest was, for the moment at least, a blur.

Opening a door, he stepped out onto the embankment to find Alexander leaning against the vehicle. Jemima stood a few paces away, her back to him as she consoled Miriam who had tears rolling down her face. Seeing Will approach, Alexander turned a deathly pale as though he'd seen a ghost. He reached for Jemima. When she turned round, Will saw there were tears in her eyes too. She ran towards him, flinging her arms round him.

'What's going on?' he asked.

'We thought you were -' She left her sentence unfinished. 'It doesn't matter now.'

'Where's Hodgson?'

Alexander ran a hand through his thick mane of red hair. 'He's gone up to the house.' His hands were visibly shaking.

'Why didn't you go with him? He might need help.'

'We didn't want to leave you here alone,' said Jemima.

'Why not? What's going on? How did you get here? Did

Hodgson bring you back?'

Miriam wiped the tears from her face. 'Back from where?' she asked.

'From Edinburgh.'

'What on earth are you talking about?' said Alexander. 'We haven't been to Edinburgh.'

'We were in James's apartment. You smashed a vase over Hodgson's head, knocking him out cold.'

'I did no such thing.'

'Jemima was asleep in one of the spare bedrooms. Miriam was downstairs drinking red wine and eating pizza -'

'Does that sound like something I would do?' snapped Miriam.

She glanced furtively at Alexander and he at her. When their eyes met, they quickly looked away, both turning their backs on the other.

'Jemima, surely you remember …'

'How could I? Apparently, I was asleep.'

Will glanced back at Alexander. 'What happened to you?' he asked. 'Why didn't you call the police? They weren't there to meet me when I returned to the village.' Further memories came to him. 'I had to make my way through the wood alone …' He recalled the griffin swooping down on him. 'I found Isobel locked in the cellar. The key was in the lock. They came after us …'

'Who?'

'The men on horseback. They chased us through the wood to the stone circle …' He stopped himself.

Alexander patted Will on the shoulder. 'Sounds like quite a dream you've had there, old man.'

Had all that had happened been nothing more than a bad dream? But then it was too vivid to be a nightmare and too extraordinary to be anything else.

'No,' he insisted, 'it wasn't a dream.' He remembered the reivers charging at them, their backswords drawn, their swords clashing as he fought the men. Then James had appeared and he'd been struck down, a rapier driven through his back. The last thing he remembered was falling to the ground and being swallowed up by darkness.

He suddenly became aware of his heart pounding in his chest. He was alive. But how?

He glanced at Alexander. 'You really don't remember?'

Alexander said nothing. He simply stared at Will, his eyes widening.

'Don't look at me like I'm crazy!' he cried. 'What about the creature that attacked us, you must remember that.'

'It was just an eagle,' said Alexander.

'It was too big to be an eagle.'

'You may have thought that, but I doubt it really was. By removing the statues from the gates, you were led to believe they'd come alive. The power of suggestion is -'

'A powerful thing. I know. You already told me that once before.' If they really didn't remember, why was he the only one that did? 'Where are Isobel and James? Are they back at the house?'

Alexander shrugged his wide shoulders. 'I've no idea where they are.'

*

When the man in the Italian shoes had lit the last of the oil lamps, he threw one against a bookcase. The lamp smashed and flames leapt up in a hot flash, igniting the old books on the shelves. He threw another of the lamps out into the great hall, and the last at the Chesterfield.

Seeing black smoke spreading through the room, the shaven-headed man retreated a few steps, the revolver still in his hand. Isobel glanced at James. His eyes were fixed on the man. She could see the anger rising in his face and wondered what he'd do next. But then, what could he do? Their situation seemed hopeless.

'What are you waiting for?' cried Cordelia. 'Shoot them!'

The words had barely left her mouth when there was an almighty crash and all in the room turned to see one of the griffins smash through the tall, mullioned windows. The shave-headed man spun round and cried out in terror as the monstrous creature descended upon him, crushing him underneath its weight, gripping him with its sharp talons. As he struggled to free himself the griffin jabbed at him with its beak, silencing his screams.

Isobel looked away in disgust and felt herself being pulled across the room by James, the griffin leaping forward as all in the room ran for the door, setting his sights on Cordelia, catching her before she reached the doorway, enfolding her in its wings.

The great hall was alive with fire. Flames licked at the banisters, reaching up to the gallery, consuming the portraits and hunting trophies on the walls, leaving nothing but blackened and charred remains in their wake. Ahead of them, a smouldering tapestry fell onto the stone floor, falling just inches from the man in the Italian shoes as he ran towards the entrance hall. Through the open doorway, Isobel watched in horror as another griffin swooped upon him as he charged down the stone steps. He cried out in terror, his arms flailing wildly about him as the creature hauled him off the ground and carried him up into the air.

Swathes of black smoke billowed across the room, engulfing them, filling their lungs, leaving them gasping for breath. From above they heard a crack as beams from the gallery split and fell towards them. Isobel felt herself being flung forward as James pushed her clear, the beams crashing down upon him, pinning him to the floor.

Coughing and spluttering, Isobel scrambled to her feet and tried to drag James free, only to find his legs were trapped under one of the beams. She glanced anxiously round for something to release him with, her gaze coming to rest on one on the floor standing candelabras. Crossing the hall, she watched in horror as black smoke curled up the walls.

At the rate the fire was spreading, it wouldn't be long before the whole roof came crashing down upon them.

*

Thick reams of black smoke drifted up into the night sky.

Jemima pointed up the hill towards the house. 'Look!' she cried.

Seeing the smoke drifting overhead, Will ordered the others into the Land Rover. Once all were inside, he slid behind the wheel, turned the keys in the ignition and slammed his foot down hard on the accelerator. The gates at the top of the hill stood open, and they drove on, the drive straightening. Hodgson, his frightened face caught in the headlights, came into view. He was speaking into a mobile phone held to his ear. Seeing them approach, he stepped aside, allowing them to pass.

The Land Rover skidded to a stop in front of the house. Isobel and James were nowhere to be seen.

'Stay here,' said Will, addressing his passengers. He opened his door to leave.

'You're not going in there, are you?' asked Alexander.

Will nodded. 'I'll be fine.'

'You'll be killed.'

'Well,' he muttered under his breath, 'it wouldn't be the first time tonight …'

Leaving the Land Rover, he headed for the gateway and heard Hodgson calling to him as he ran through the entrance porch. Ignoring him, he ran on, fighting his way blindly through the thick smoke, unable to see more than a few feet ahead of him. He called out to Isobel and James, the smoke suffocating him, burning his lungs.

Immediately he heard Isobel calling back to him from across the hall. He ran on, following the sound of her voice, the heat becoming unbearable. His eyes stinging, he peered through the smoke and glimpsed Isobel kneeling before James. Both were covered in ash and soot, and hurrying closer, he saw James's legs were trapped under a charred, fallen beam. Isobel appeared to be levering a candelabra under the beam in an attempt to free him.

'Help me!' she cried, her breathing laboured.

Will darted forward, scorching and blistering his hands as he helped Isobel lift the beam off their friend. When he was free, Will helped Isobel to her feet.

'Get out of here,' he said.

Isobel, gasping for air, nodded and ran for the door, encountering Hodgson on the way. He led her through the noxious black smoke to safety.

Will knelt before James. 'Can you walk?' he asked.

'I think so,' replied James, his voice hoarse.

Will helped him to his feet, gently pulling his arm round his shoulder for support. He led him across the great hall, James limping heavily on his right leg, both keeping low, their progress slow. As they drew closer to the front door, finding James could no longer walk, his right leg proving too painful to put any weight on, Will hoisted him up over his shoulder and carried him through the entrance porch just as the ceiling gave way and came crashing down behind them.

Once clear of the house they both breathed in the cool night air and Will lay James down onto the soft grass beside the fountain.

'Are you all right here?' he said. 'I'm going to check on Isobel.'

James assured him he was fine, and Will left his friend.

Crossing the courtyard, he glimpsed Miriam and Alexander through the gateway standing together by the Land Rover. He found Isobel with Jemima and Hodgson. Seeing him approach, tears welled up in her eyes and she ran to him, flinging her arms round him.

'You're alive,' she sobbed, the tears rolling down her cheeks.

She remembered. So, it had all happened - all of it.

'How did we get back here?' he asked, wiping her hair out of her face.

'James …' she murmured; her words too faint to hear. 'James brought us back.'

'It's all right,' said Will soothingly, pulling her close. 'It's over.'

Glancing over her shoulder, Isobel watched James stagger to his feet as he attempted to stand, his body silhouetted against the searing tongues of fire pouring out of every window of Wychwood House.

Was it? she thought. Or was it just the beginning?

*

Four fire engines arrived at the scene to tackle the blaze. Although unable to enter the house for fear the walls might collapse, the firefighters eventually extinguished the flames in the early hours of the morning. The damage to Wychwood House caused by the fire was significant and the officer present thought it unlikely the place would ever be habitable again. Considering what had happened there, no one thought it likely James, or anyone else for that matter, would ever wish to return to the house, let alone live there.

When the police arrived, statements of all present were taken, and they were told they would all be interviewed the following day. An ambulance then took James and Isobel to the Borders General Hospital in Melrose where they stayed overnight. Before parting, Isobel had exchanged numbers with Jemima, though deep down they both knew it was just a formality, it being unlikely they'd see the other again. Hodgson then drove Miriam, Alexander and Jemima to Edinburgh in the Land Rover, with Will following behind in James's car.

Whilst waiting for the ambulance to arrive, Will had sensed a certain animosity between Hodgson and James. They didn't speak once, both doing their best to avoid the other. Although Will didn't know what had happened at the house before their arrival, he knew Hodgson had done what he could to help them since. The fact that none of them had come to any harm was, in part at least, due to him.

During the drive up to Edinburgh, Will considered what he would tell the police when they came to interview him. When he tried to piece together what had happened, he found his mind a blur, the events of the night a jumbled mess in his head. He didn't even know the reason why James had been held at the house, let alone who was responsible for his imprisonment. Of course, his friend would know who they were and what they wanted with him, but whether he'd be willing to impart that information remained to be seen. Deep down, Will knew it was unlikely.

When they arrived at Moray Place Will instantly recognised James's apartment. Despite Alexander's assurance that they'd never been to Edinburgh, he was more certain than ever that they had – though the others genuinely didn't seem to recognise the place. The rooms, however, seemed familiar to him and he distinctly remembered waking up in James's bed.

But then he couldn't have. He'd woken on the back seat of the Land Rover, his jacket laid over him. Another realisation then came to him. They hadn't just covered his body with the jacket, they'd laid it over his head too. You only did that to a person who was … He dismissed the thought from his mind.

He determined to speak to Isobel when he saw her next. She'd be able to tell him what happened. But he didn't speak to her about it. By the time he saw her again he'd forgotten all that had happened, the events of the night having passed from his memory, like a dream upon waking.

No one slept that night, all remaining awake until the morning. Shortly before lunch a fire investigating officer and two police officers arrived to speak to each of them to hear their version of events. Isobel and James had, they were told, already been interviewed at the hospital. Will was disappointed he hadn't been present when they'd spoken to James. He'd like to have heard what his friend had to say.

After lunch, Hodgson drove Miriam, Alexander and Jemima to Berwick station, where they caught a train back to London. Hodgson didn't say what he planned to do after that, and when he didn't return, Will assumed he'd driven down south to the Manor. Later that day, following their release from the hospital, Isobel and James joined Will in Edinburgh where they were to remain until James was strong enough to face the journey back home.

The doctors at the hospital had told him he'd only sustained a minor fracture that wouldn't take long to heal. Although he did not need a cast, he did require a cane to help him walk. Whilst there, he'd contacted his parents who wanted to travel up to see him, but he'd told them he was fine, assuring them he'd be with them soon, preferring to spend time alone with his friends before returning home.

When they arrived at the apartment James greeted Will warmly. Isobel then embraced him and whispered into his ear, 'I've missed you,' before asking after the others. Will told her they'd returned to London.

'Then it's just the three of us?'

Will nodded. 'Just like old times,' he said. He then told them he'd made dinner and it was in the oven, ready to dish up.

James told Isobel he wanted to have a quick word with Will. Leaving them, Isobel disappeared into the kitchen and James drew Will into the study, closing the door behind him.

'Have the police been to see you?' he asked.

'Yes. They interviewed us all this morning.'

'What did you tell them?'

'Only what I know, which isn't much. I couldn't even give them details of the men holding you at the house. I only saw a couple up close and all I could tell them about one was he had a shaved head and was stocky with a thick neck, a description that could apply to thousands of men. Who were they James and what did they want with you?'

'The less you and Isobel know the better.'

'They have to be brought to justice for what they've done.'

'They will be,' said James. 'The police will find them.' He didn't sound entirely convinced by this.

'There must be something we can do to help.'

'There's nothing we can do. Our involvement ends here.'

'Why?'

James sighed then said, 'When Hodgson tried to find out who they were they went after his sister to silence him. If you or I go after them, who do you think they'll go after to silence us?'

At that moment the door opened, and Isobel stepped into the room. 'There you are,' she said. 'Dinner's on the table.'

Will glanced at James and his friend met his eye. He knew he was right and after that decide to let the matter drop.

They spent the subsequent days together in the apartment, getting to know one another again, finding they still enjoyed each other's company, often talking late into the night, just as they had done when they were younger. However, it soon became clear James was not well. At first, he struggled to eat and appeared to be in considerable pain. Both Isobel and Will had put this down to his injury, but when they noticed him visible sweating and shaking, they soon came to realise there was more to it than that. He slept only fitfully, and regularly became anxious, and there was a noticeable drop in his mood as the day progressed.

Eventually he had to tell them how his captors had drugged him, and he was simply experiencing withdrawal symptoms now he was no longer receiving the laudanum and morphine they'd given him, assuring them he would speak to his family doctor when he was back home if the symptoms persisted.

He then told them, now that they were no longer making a secret of the fact they were together, he didn't mind if they wanted to share a room, but both declined the offer, neither thinking it appropriate.

Will couldn't help but worry about his future with Isobel, but these fears were laid to rest when later in the week he received a call from Bill. Apparently, Miriam had told him he'd been the one who'd insisted they leave Wychwood House when he realised they were in danger. She'd also mentioned how he'd run into a burning building to save Isobel and James from certain death.

Will told Bill he couldn't claim all the credit for getting them safely out of there. Both Isobel and Hodgson, not to mention James, had all played their part. Nevertheless, he had earned Bill's eternal gratitude, leading him to assure Will his future at the firm was secured, which came as a relief, for it meant he could remain in London close to Isobel for the foreseeable future. He couldn't help but feel Miriam had told her father this as a way of apologising for the way she'd spoken to him shortly before they'd left the house.

On their last day together, whilst Will went to collect his car from the garage where it had been repaired, Isobel and James were once again visited by the police who asked them to provide descriptions of their captors to a sketch artist. By the time Will returned to the apartment, the police had gone, and they spent the rest of the afternoon in the family room together.

Outside the rain fell heavily adding a melancholic feel to the scene. Will and James played chess together, neither saying very much, while Isobel sat on a window seat watching the gathering beads of water join and part as they rolled down the glass, the clock hanging on the wall ticking away the minutes and hours of the day. Even at dinner, their conversations hadn't flowed as easily as they had on previous evenings. All were subdued; each knowing life was never going to be the same again once they returned home.

The following day they set off early, arriving at the Manor just before lunch, turning off the main road before they reached the village. Isobel glimpsed one of the many standing stones that formed part of the outer circle that surrounded Abury, the sight of the ancient megaliths sending a shiver down her spine.

James's parents were there to welcome him home, his mother embracing him before his father led them inside the house. Although eager to return to London, Will and Isobel agreed to stay for lunch. Hodgson did not appear to be at the Manor and as James did not ask after him neither did Will.

Before leaving James's father thanked Will for what he had done. Will could tell he had questions he wanted answers to but knew they would have to wait for another time. Will and Isobel then resumed their journey home, though it took them longer to reach Grosvenor Square than they would have wished.

When they finally arrived at their destination, Will parked on the cobbled courtyard outside the house Isobel lived in and, carrying her suitcase, followed her up two flights of stairs to the top floor. Once inside her flat, he put her suitcase down in the hall, neither speaking as she led him through to the living room. There she turned to face him, her eyes meeting his.

Finally, they were alone.

EPILOGUE

In the afternoon after his return to the Manor, shortly after Will and Isobel left him, James wandered into the churchyard to take a look at the inscription on his great-grandfather's grave. When he reached the chest tomb, he saw the inscription had been worn down by time and the elements and was only partly legible and did not reveal his title as the twelfth Earl of Leithen. Finding that the truth about his family hadn't been right under his nose all the time made him feel a little better about himself.

His great-grandfather had been buried alongside his first wife and their son, Edward, both of whom were taken from him at a tragically young age. His wife, whose name was lost, had only been twenty at the time of her death, and their son had been killed when he was only eighteen. James hadn't realised until then quite how young he'd been, how young both of them had been. George Roxburgh had died in 1935 at the age of sixty. He couldn't find his older brother Albert's grave. The eleventh earl hadn't been interned in the burial vault in Scotland. He'd probably been buried in Edinburgh somewhere.

George's second wife, James's great-grandmother, who had only been in her forties when her husband died, had remarried, and in doing so she had forfeited her title, which was why she was not referred to as the Countess of Leithen on her gravestone. She'd continued living at the Manor with her second husband and had died peacefully in her sleep, tucked up in her bed at the ripe old age of eighty-three. Her husband, a local doctor with a practice in

Marlborough, had preceded her, and they now lay buried alongside each other not far from George's tomb.

James had always believed the Manor had been his great-grandmother's ancestral home, but unlike Wychwood House, which had been owned exclusively by his family, the Manor had never been owned by one particular family, having changed hands many times over the years.

Before returning to the Manor, he paused momentarily at his grandfather's grave. He'd thought about him a lot over the past week and had often wondered if he knew what went on at Wychwood House. While he knew he wasn't particularly close to Henry they were brothers, which counted for something. Did he know of his involvement with the Brotherhood of Amun-Ra? Had he been the one who'd concocted the story of him dying in North Africa, a story undoubtedly told to prevent people learning his true fate, or had someone else been responsible for that? Joseph Wrayburn immediately sprang to mind. He wondered if he knew his brother's body had been left to rot in that hidden room, or of the presence of the hellhound and the Sacred Seal of King Solomon.

James couldn't help but wonder what had become of that ancient talisman. It certainly wasn't in the house, if it was Cordelia would have found it. Fortunately, she seemed to be the only one who'd been after it, which hopefully meant it would be forgotten. Wrayburn certainly didn't seem to want it – he didn't even believe it really existed. Having been on the receiving end of its immense power, James knew differently and prayed it would stay lost.

He couldn't help but feel a pang of regret at the death of Cordelia. While admittedly she had tried to kill both himself and Isobel, he didn't think she'd deserved to die like she had. Under different circumstances he imagined they could have gone on to become, if not quite friends, not quite enemies either.

His thoughts then turned to Emily and Easton. While he knew his great-uncle's wife had remarried, he did not know if it was to Easton. Had they got married and lived happily ever, or had they suffered one final cruel twist of fate that had prevented them from being together?

These questions, like so many others he wanted answers to, would, he knew, never be answered, most having gone to the grave with his grandfather. Anyway, there was no time to dwell on the past when he still had the future to worry about. The thought of the Brotherhood of Amun-Ra plotting against him as they prepared to strike back preyed heavily on his mind. The loss of Cordelia would have been a blow that would have been hard to take, but one they would undoubtably recover from. The question now was, would they leave things as they were, or would there be retaliations?

And if there were, what then? He knew he had to be ready for them. He had, after all, defeated Lord Roxburgh, hadn't he? Unlike his friends, he'd retained memories of that fateful night. But then he'd been on a different plane of existence, another dimension. Here, in the real world, were such things possible?

He had many sleepless nights in the weeks that followed, his experiences continuing to haunt him long after he'd returned from Wychwood House. Unsure where his dreams ended and reality began, he eventually convinced himself that much of what he'd experienced had been nothing more than hallucinations, dreams and nightmares, brought about by the laudanum he'd been given.

At night, unable to sleep, he would lie in bed listening to the pipes groaning and the floorboards creaking as the Manor settled. More than once he became convinced men had broken into the house and were coming for him, though his fears soon proved unfounded. When he did sleep, he was plagued by nightmares in which he'd woken to find dark, shadowy figures looming over him. When they'd seen he was awake, they'd grabbed him and he'd looked across his room to see the doctor standing in the doorway, a syringe in his hand.

During the day, on more than one occasion he'd glimpsed figures in the churchyard, who he was convinced were covertly watching the house. They were, in all probability, just tourists. Even in November the village attracted visitors, though not in quite the same numbers as it did in the summer.

One morning he woke to find he hadn't drawn the curtains the night before. Dawn's faint light had crept into his bedroom, falling on him as he slept. When he went to close the curtains, he'd glanced out across the garden to the churchyard and the high street beyond. A tingling sensation ran down his spine. Goosebumps appeared on his arms, and he felt the hairs stand up on the back of his neck. Something was out there, calling to him, drawing him out.

He knew at once what it was …

He dressed quickly, leaving the house before anyone else woke. Wrapped in his greatcoat and walking with his cane for support, he made his way through the churchyard to the high street. When he reached the pub, he crossed the road, entering a field where many of the ancient monoliths of the stone circle that surrounded the village stood, a walk he'd often made when he'd been younger.

He wondered if those responsible for putting the stones there had aligned them with the Sun and the Moon in an attempt to harness the power of the heavens, just as he'd learnt the Renaissance magus had done with talismans, amulets and Orphic songs.

He thought back to when he'd harnessed the powers of the monoliths of the stone circle in the Witches' Wood, channelling the energies of the universe to wrench Isobel, Will and himself back to their world. He could feel the same power emanating from the stones in the field and wondered what he could accomplish given their increased strength here.

Feeling a gentle breeze blow upon him, once again he closed his eyes and began uttering the incantation. Drawing on the influence of the stones, he began channelling the energies of the elemental ethers. Slowly, but surely, the wind began picking up speed, sweeping across the countryside and through the village until he could hear the air roar past him. Overhead, in the darkening sky, thunderclouds had gathered, the falling rain drenching him. Thunder crashed and lightning flashed across the sky, the raging tempest encircling him until even the earth trembled beneath his feet.

Once again channelling these energies made him feel immortal, eternal, infinite, making him realise once and for all that the powers he was drawing on were not just in the ancient monoliths but were inherent within him too - powers he possessed and had always possessed.

Powers only dreamt of by mortal man.

Powers that made him feel like a god.

ABOUT THE AUTHOR

Born in East London but currently living in County Durham, Myles has been writing from an early age. Although a reader of many different writers and genres he was particularly drawn to the supernatural horror stories of Algernon Blackwood, William Hope Hodgson, M.R. James and H.P. Lovecraft, amongst others, that inspired *The House in the Witches' Wood*, his first novel. He is currently working on *The Brotherhood of Amun-Ra*, the next book in the series.

Printed in Great Britain
by Amazon